CHAPTER ONE
THE BOOK IS FINALLY COMPLETED

"You want me to what?" I asked, looking up from my cubicle. It contained a messy collection of papers, Post-it notes, and a pewter dragon that was the only sign of my humanity permitted by employers. Such was the soul crushing nature of my job as an Epic Dungeoneering™ programmer.

Be a video game designer!

Write amazing stories!

Program new worlds!

It was difficult to imagine I'd been so naive in college but, somehow, I'd convinced myself that this was the career I'd wanted. I'd ended up signing a lifetime contract, which seems like I'm exaggerating but doesn't feel like it, with a company that had a non-compete clause for about a million years in every similar field. That was something that also should be illegal, but the company was fully willing to drag out in court as poor Sue Wilson had found out. Given the company was based in Ledziania (wasn't that where Doctor Doom lived?) but I operated from their office in Michigan, I suspected there may also be some international laws at play as well.

The thing was that I'd been working at programming and pitching game material at Epic Dungeoneering™ for about ten years now. So far, despite claiming we were a family, I was the deformed relative they kept tied up in the attic and every single idea I'd proposed had been shot down. It had been endless parades of crunch, bug fixing, and working on live service monetization that made me feel like I was preying on my fellow gamers.

"Meet with Larry C.C. Weis," Barbara Wojciechowski said. No, I had no idea how to pronounce that and my family was Polish. My mother would be so ashamed. I only knew how it was spelled from the name plate on her desk. I don't think she'd ever said her last name in person, or I might have been able to fake it.

Barbara was one of the Epic Dungoneering™ staff had transferred over from Eastern Europe oversee the American part of the company and was an extremely pleasant fifty-something brown haired woman who I suspected had been a kindergarten teacher before communism fell. At least she treated her staff like children and sometimes pulled out a hand puppet to explain difficult concepts to us like, "You're going to be doing a lot of overtime and not getting paid any extra for it. Oh, and try to find a job in this economy. Bark-bark." The hand-puppet was a dog, you see. She dressed in a long cotton dress and tweed sweater that still had big mom energy, albeit the mom who locked her children in the aforementioned attic.

"You're kidding, right?" I asked, looking up.

Barbara scrunched her nose. "Why would I be kidding?"

I blinked, wondering if this was a prank before realizing I didn't want to know if it was. Larry C.C. Weis was the patron saint of Epic Dungeoneering™ and the reason it had gone from an obscure Eastern European gaming studio to an international phenomenon with multiple streaming shows and one other semi-successful franchise.

Sort of a Ledzianian George R.R. Martin or Iron Curtain Tolkien, Larry C.C. Weis had written the Dark Undermaster series and Epic Dungeoneering™ had bought the rights back when it had probably cost sixty rupees and a goat. Okay, seriously, I'm not trying to be stereotypical here, but I just worked forty hours straight trying to get the Witch Queen of Angho'horak from clipping through her armor. Something I was pretty sure the base game programmers had done deliberately.

LORDS OF DRAGON KEEP

BOOK ONE, DARK UNDERMASTER SAGA

C.T. PHIPPS

"You want me to what?" I asked, looking up from my cubicle. It contained a messy collection of papers, Post-it notes, and a pewter dragon that was the only sign of my humanity permitted by employers. Such was the soul crushing nature of my job as an Epic Dungeoneering™ programmer.

Be a video game designer!

Write amazing stories!

Program new worlds!

It was difficult to imagine I'd been so naive in college but, somehow, I'd convinced myself that this was the career I'd wanted. I'd ended up signing a lifetime contract, which seems like I'm exaggerating but doesn't feel like it, with a company that had a non-compete clause for about a million years in every similar field. That was something that also should be illegal, but the company was fully willing to drag out in court as poor Sue Wilson had found out. Given the company was based in Ledziania (wasn't that where Doctor Doom lived?) but I operated from their office in Michigan, I suspected there may also be some international laws at play as well.

The thing was that I'd been working at programming and pitching game material at Epic Dungeoneering™ for about ten years now. So far, despite claiming we were a family, I was the deformed relative they kept tied up in the attic and every single idea I'd proposed had been shot down. It had been endless parades of crunch, bug fixing, and working on live service monetization that made me feel like I was preying on my fellow gamers.

"Meet with Larry C.C. Weis," Barbara Wojciechowski said. No, I had no idea how to pronounce that and my family was Polish. My mother would be so ashamed. I only knew how it was spelled from the name plate on her desk. I don't think she'd ever said her last name in person, or I might have been able to fake it.

Well, in the wake of *Game of Thrones*, the Dark Undermaster series had ended up being an international success and the third one topped twenty-million sales. That was in addition to all the spin-offs and merchandizing that had ticked off Larry C.C. Weis something fierce. He hadn't gotten a big enough of a cut of the pie due to not negotiating better with Epic Dungoneering™.

If you believed the online rumors, Larry had been so pissed off that he'd stopped writing the Dark Undermaster series right before the epic climax and was no longer interested in finishing it. This despite millions of fans anxiously waiting for the next installment and all the adaptations running out of material. Err, bring to life. It was particularly problematic for Epic Dungeoneering™ because they depended on their reputation as a scrappy underdog developer that honored the fandom despite keeping people like me chained up to our computers.

"*The* Larry C.C. Weis?" I asked, blinking. I briefly wondered if there was another Larry C.C. Weis in accounting or something. It wasn't entirely impossible since one of my fellow programmers was named Jon Snowman. I bet his parents were regretting that bit of naming convention. Then again, I couldn't really complain myself given my name.

Barbara sniffed the air as if there was something foul in it. Her accent became sharper and went into full Natasha Fatale territory. "Yes, *the writer*."

The executives at Epic Dungeoneering™ had developed a love-hate-hate relationship with Larry as I'd understood it and it had trickled down to the middle managers like Barbara. Some of my fellow programmers had even developed the hissing and spitting at his name that seemed in vogue but most of us kept a wry respect for the old dude. After all, we all had developed a burning hatred for the guys at the top. They may have started as fellow geeks, but they'd all ended up as Sauron rather than Frodo.

"Why the hell does Larry C.C. Weis want to speak with me?" I asked, wishing I had some coffee right now, but I'd have to fight six other guys at the break room who had been working even longer than

I had. "How the hell does Larry C.C. Weis even know who the hell I am?"

"Listen, Aragorn," Barbara started to speak.

"Aaron," I said, softly correcting her for the fifteenth time.

"It says Aragorn on your employment sheet," Barbara said, as if I didn't know my own name.

"Yes, but I go by Aaron," I said, annoyed.

"Why?" Barbara asked.

"So, I could survive high school," I replied, sighing. "As Aaron Bartkowski is more likely to make it past their freshmen year."

"Mr. Aragorn Bartkowski," Barbara said, reaching into her dress pockets (which was a good thing to see they had) and removed the hand puppet. She then started speaking in a little children's dog voice. "Grr, you need to go meet with Mr. Weis and get some contracts signed. He requested you personally. Bark-bark."

I stared at her. "Is the hand puppet strictly necessary?"

I bet you thought I'd been kidding about the hand puppet? Welcome to my life.

"Ruff! Yes," Barbara said, not displaying any self-awareness. "Otherwise, it's your job. Bark."

I took a deep breath. "So, is he in Latveria? Do I have to get a plane ticket? Please tell me you're springing for it."

"Ledziania," Barbara corrected. "It's on the border between Poland and Romania."

"They don't share a border," I said, wondering if Barbara was aware of where the company's home country was. I mean, I wasn't, but I had an excuse. I didn't care. "It's supposed to be between Poland and Belarus, though I'm not sure where in the big national forest there that it's supposed to be."

"Whatever," Barbara said, wiggling her hand puppet's nose in the air. "Either way, he lives in America now and has since the first *Dark Undermaster* game. Louis."

A well-dressed bespectacled man with smoothed over red hair in a suit that he wore constantly came over. Louis Tolliver was Barbara's majordomo and reminded me suspiciously of Wayland Smithers from

The Simpsons. The fact he was sucking up to Barbara made me wonder if he shouldn't have been slightly more ambitious as a yes man. In his hands was a black briefcase that he handed over to me like we were in *Pulp Fiction*.

"The code is 1-2-3-4-5," Louis said, nodding.

I stared at him. "Big *Spaceballs* fan, huh?"

Louis looked confused.

I shook my head and opened the briefcase, revealing a bunch of white sheets of paper as well as a gold bracelet that looked like an oversized ring of power. It even had the elvish looking writing on the side. My eyes watered a bit, and I swear, I heard a little bit of whispering coming from it. I shook my head and the sound dissipated.

"This is the contract for *Lords of Dragon Keep*," Barbara said, looking from side to side as if she was spreading secret information.

Which it was. "What? Really? It's done?"

Lords of Dragon Keep was the mythical fourth and final volume of the Dark Undermaster saga. The one that he had been working on for the better part of eleven years and everyone had long since given up on him completing. I was surprisingly excited, and it reminded me of the fact that I used to be a fan of the series as well. Well, at least until Season Five of Dark Undermaster when they'd tried to wrap up the story and ruined everything.

Hell, there had been a time when I'd been a "Undermasterling" every bit as fanatical as any other in the fandom. I'd loved how dark and gritty Westeros had been but had done the teenage boy thing of thinking, "but what if they added more sex and violence." The kind of kid who didn't understand grimdark was meant to be a pejorative. Knowing that the story was going to be finished was something that caused a little chill to run down my spine. Even if it was nonsensical for me to be involved.

"Yes, the book is done. This contract provides us the rights to adapt the book to the game series as well as gives us all future rights to the franchise in exchange for a generous lump sum as well as a portion of all future merchandising rights," Barbara said, her tone suggesting the terms were excessive in the author's favor.

"Good," I said, before realizing what I was saying. "Err—"

"Yes, well, he was very specific," Barbara said, annoyed. "You're also supposed to wear the bracelet."

"Wear the bracelet," I said, looking at the gold band. "Am I being punked?"

"I don't know what that means," Barbara said. "However, I expect your instructions to be followed to the letter. Be sure to make sure he signs the contract, though."

"Isn't this the kind of thing that should be done by a lawyer?" I asked, getting the increasing sense something very weird was going on.

"The contract has been approved by both parties, Mr. Bartkowski," Louis said, his voice cold and flat like a robot's. "Mr. Weis just enjoys meeting with the people he thinks are the important parts of game development."

"Uh huh," I said, wondering where he'd been for the entirety of the previous three Dark Undermaster game developments. The guy had been born in 1948 and probably hadn't seen a computer until he was my dad's age. Then again, I was used to the suits lying their asses off. On the other hand, if the guy had picked my name out of a hat or off an employee registry, I wasn't about to complain. I could become the king of the internet by being the guy to leak this.

"You will, of course, be bound by all confidentiality agreements," Barbara said, immediately crushing my dream of internet fame.

"Of course," I said, sighing. I noted they still hadn't said if they were covering my plane ticket. "So where does the guy live in America? Los Angeles? Chicago."

"1313 Mockingbird Avenue," Louis said. "It's about a twenty-minute drive."

I blinked. "He *lives* in Livonia, Michigan?"

I suddenly felt like an idiot, wondering how I didn't know one of my favorite authors lived where I worked. Then again, he was supposed to be a recluse. Still, I would have thought that would have been the kind of thing I'd have found out.

"You are very easily surprised, Mr. Bartkowski," Barbara said, maneuvering her little toy dog puppet to look disapproving somehow.

"Please don't do that," I muttered, creeped out. "Okay, I'll go tomorrow morning."

I'd finally managed to fix the Witch Queen of Angho'horak's clipping nudity problem that would have been a selling point before they'd dramatically dialed back the Mature-rated content for DU3 so they could sell console versions. Now I was running on fumes and needed to collapse on my bed for at least four hours. I was going to be working through the weekend regardless, but I needed to make sure my brain didn't leak out the side of my ear. You wouldn't think it would be possible to become desensitized to boobs, digital or otherwise, but somehow it had happened.

"You'll go now," Barbara said, her voice sounding almost threatening. "Clock out of your workstation and head there immediately. Be sure to wear the bracelet and make sure he signs the contracts before you sign anything."

Why was I even surprised. "Sure, I guess. Fine. Wait, why would I sign anything?"

"Don't fail us like, Mr. Snowman did," Barbara said.

I blinked rapidly and looked around for him. I hadn't seen him in a few days but hadn't paid much attention in the fury of debugging. I wondered if they'd been fired. Honestly, non-compete clause or not, we had a high turnover rate. "Is he okay?"

"You have a bright future ahead of you in Epic Dungeoneering™, Mr. Bartkowski," Louis said. "If you pull this off, you might be looking at a promotion. Imagine yourself as the Team Head for Pwiffle the Mobile Game."

Pwiffle was the card game that came with *Dark Undermaster III* and had managed to get a bunch of free publicity from the Far Right when they released a topless card set during a particularly slow news day. They'd recalled that, as they'd always planned to do so, and the current version was designed to be sold to eight-year-olds who had access to their parents' credit cards. The current Team Head, Becky, described it as being worse than an elementary school drug dealer. I had my own issues with Pwiffle that would make me joining the team a problem.

"Super!" I said, faking as much as enthusiasm as I was humanly capable of, which wasn't much. It wasn't so much that I was opposed to selling out, but corporate life didn't even pay you very much for your soul. I think Becky made like two dollars extra an hour.

"Be sure to wear the bracelet," Barbara said before waving her hand puppet in the air and speaking in the dog voice. "Bark-bye!"

I watched them leave. "So, this is what the tenth circle of Hell is like."

As usual, there was no one there to appreciate my scintillating wit. Sighing, I reached into the briefcase and picked up the bracelet, which was a lot heavier than I expected. It almost felt like real gold.

"Huh," I said, sliding it on my wrist where it was far too big. Almost immediately, it shrunk down tightly, and the elvish runes glowed bright as I felt an intense stinging sensation like a bee jamming itself into my skin. "Muther—"

I was caught off-guard by the pain vanishing as a little holographic display of the kind you'd normally see in movies appeared above the bracelet, which was obviously some kind of badly designed theme telephone.

The display was a little white and black box that showed a bunch of information spread across several menu screens. It was clearly an RPG character sheet, and I could hear the Dark Undermaster theme [violin version] playing in the background.

ARAGORN "AARON" BARTKOWSKI
LVL: 1
CLASS: N/A (see Menu Options)
ALIGNMENT: GRAY
AGE: 34
SEX: MALE
RACE: HUMAN
STR: 10

AGI: 10
CON: 9
INT: 16
WIS: 7
COM: 15
CHA: 13

ARMOR CLASS: 0
ATTACK: 0
HEALTH: 5

FEAT: Taunt

SPECIAL ABILITIES: NA (see Menu Options)

Okay. that was weird and slightly insulting about my wisdom. A lot of the menu options were blacked out but there was a typical collection of maps (this one showed Livonia, Michigan as well as the office) as well as items, spell lists, and so on. I played with it for a bit but couldn't get the class options, so I just gave up. Also, for a cell phone, it didn't seem to be able to call anybody or play any games. Typical.

Anyway, I decided to do the job. It wasn't every day that one got the chance to meet one's favorite author.

CHAPTER TWO
NEVER MEET YOUR HEROES

"You've got to be kidding me," I muttered, staring at the sight of the house that greeted me as I parked my car at the foot of the crumbling sidewalk in front of it.

1313 Mockingbird Lane proved to be harder to find than I'd initially suspected. Not the least of which being because it was the address of a TV show family from the Sixties called *The Munsters*.

However, with a great deal of perseverance and after falling asleep at a gas station for four hours, I finally managed to find the place. At least, the numbers on the mailbox said 1313 and it was the kind of place you expected an author of grimdark epic fantasy to live in.

Basically, it looked like a haunted house.

Not just the, "it looked kind of run down and in need of condemning" but "Scooby Doo and his friends should be checking this place for real estate fraudsters dressed as ghosts." The place was a Victorian looking place with castle-like towers on each side of the building, an overgrown yard, dead trees, and iron bars on the windows. The house had an extra-large front porch with a swinging bench that was covered in, I kid you not, ravens. The dead trees also sported branches full of crows, all of them looming like they'd stepped out of a Hitchcock movie.

The rest of the houses in the neighborhood were comparatively normal looking and I had to wonder if they had any opinions on the guy choosing to live like Norman Bates. Still, there was a clean concrete walkway up from the sidewalk to the door and it was only about eight thirty. I wish I could have called ahead but my employers hadn't given me Weis' number and I wasn't about to mention that my 'immediately' had utterly failed to be anything approaching such. I just hoped the old guy hadn't gone to bed.

Dude was almost eighty after all.

The bracelet on my wrist, which I hadn't figured out a way to remove yet, burned as I picked up the briefcase to my side and stepped out of my used Kia. The car had been a gift from my sister when she'd married her boss and let me know, in no uncertain terms, that she was really hoping I could get a real job at some point. I'd managed to hold down my response that my job was more real than her breaking up a guy's marriage after a boob job.

Yeah. I was the younger sibling, could you tell?

Arwen "Wendy" Bartkowski, yes, our parents had named their kids after fictional lovers, had been yet another product of our fantasy loving household. Mama and Papa Bartkowski had both been Polish immigrants that had fallen in love with the world of J.R.R Tolkien and indoctrinated us in an everlasting love of fictional worlds.

Or at least that had been the plan.

The simple fact was that it had partially worked with me, but I primarily enjoyed fiction where the princes and princesses died horribly of dysentery. Arwen, by contrast, had formally rejected all things fantastic and the most fictional thing she enjoyed these days were episodes of *The Bachelor* and *Masked Singer*.

Heading up to the front door, I took a deep breath and proceeded to push the doorbell. That was when I noticed the crows all looking at me. They hadn't flown away at my presence but were just gazing at me like I was the new meat in the prison yard.

I gave them the peace sign. "Nevermore."

One of them, I swear, lifted its wing up as if it was flipping me off.

Before I could react to that strange turn of events, the door opened, and I found myself looking down at the five-foot three form of Larry C.C. Weis. He was a man with a long white beard, deep black eyes, and dirty ink-stained fingernails. He was dressed in a black Michigan Wolverines sweatsuit with its hoodie up that strangely reminded me of a wizard. He was wearing green Cthulhu house slippers, and I was briefly rendered senseless by the incongruity of the guy's appearance. I saw the exact same sort of bracelet I was wearing on his wrist as well. Its runes started to glow alongside mine.

"Uh, hey," I said, looking at my wrist.

"Welcome!" The man spoke in a voice that was higher pitched than I expected and threw his hands up in the air. "You're just in time!"

"Just in time for what?" I asked.

Larry responded by grabbing me by the arm and pulling me into his house before slamming the door behind me. All the crows jumped from their position on the front porch and lawn before filling the air with hundreds of flapping wings. I was briefly thrown by the experience and needed a second to reorientate myself.

The interior of Larry C.C. Weis' home was enough to cause me to pause even more than any of the other weird things around me had before. It was, in simple terms, the ultimate fantasy man cave. On YouTube, I'd watched a video of Joe Manganiello's basement that he'd turned into a gigantic *Dungeons & Dragons* palace with a mounted dragon head, throne, and massive gaming table.

Dude had nothing on Weis.

The place's living room was full of bookshelves full of paperback fantasy of all sorts, a stuffed dragon about the size of a car standing up, a dining room table with a gigantic map of the Southern Kingdoms under glass, framed paintings of his characters along the wall (particularly the women), walls full of replica weapons, an antique looking globe, an owlbear rug (a replica surely), and a burning fireplace that had the heraldry of House Rose over it. The fireplace contained a bubbling cauldron on it as the place smelled of what I was pretty sure was a mixture of weed, incense, and verbena. I recognized all three from my last girlfriend, Nightchilde, who was a great believer in the paganism she'd learned from Amazon's recommended New Age reading list. Light orchestra music was playing from no discernible source.

"Wow," I said, staring. "Nice place."

No man who owned this place would ever get laid, but it was a nice place.

"Oh, I have hookers for that," Larry said, responding as if he could read my mind.

"Oh wow," I said, realizing I must have spoken that aloud. "Sorry."

"No need, no need," Larry said. "The world's oldest profession for a reason! So, you're Aragorn Bartkowski."

"So, they tell me," I said, overwhelmed. Much to my surprise, I noticed one of the ravens had gotten into the house and was sitting on the globe. That was when I noticed the globe was of the world of Mokosh, the setting for the Dark Undermaster saga. Seriously, this guy had clearly been given a lot of merch as part of whatever new deal he'd arranged with the Epic Dungeoneering™ folk.

"And you're of pure Slavic descent?" Larry asked.

I frowned. "I'm not sure you're legally allowed to ask that, sir."

"Eh, it's not a racism thing," Larry said, dismissively. "No one's blood is better or worse, but the magic is tied to the Earth and is tied to the blood. The Old Gods are hungry and spread their seed among certain lines. If you're going to invoke them, then you need to make sure that you have their lineage within the tithe. Otherwise, it doesn't work."

"Uh huh," I said, wondering if he was talking about his books. "The Old Gods."

"Perun, Svarog, Baba Yaga, Chernobog, and Veles. You know them, right?" Larry asked.

"I've read your books," I said. "So, I know the names and that Baba Yaga isn't a god but the mother of all wicked witches. Otherwise, I only know Chernobog from *Fantasia*."

Larry smiled. "The kingdom of Ledziania existed once in the place where the Białowieża Forest stands today. It was the last place where the Old Gods were able to make their stand against the Christian knights and their Roman trained wizards. A dark pact was struck with Veles the God of Death, and he pulled the kingdom between this world as well as the next. The people of Ledziania were cheated, though, and the dead would harass them continuously."

"Yeah, I've played the games too," I replied. "That's the premise for *Eldritch Ring*, right? You wrote the script for the third game?"

Larry frowned. "It is unfortunate that Ledziania keeps trying to come back to this world. It is now a place of black and foul magics that can only bring ruin as well as horror to this world. Sacrifices can keep it bound in its place between worlds but only a champion can lay to rest the spirits of the Old Gods long enough to preserve the world for another generation. Tell me, have you chosen a class yet?"

Larry C.C. Weis was simultaneously everything I could have hoped and clearly a complete nutjob. It was nice to know there were some genuine eccentrics out there and I wouldn't have been surprised if his creativity was, shall we say, "chemically enhanced."

"Not yet," I said, keeping my thoughts to myself. "I take it the bracelet is some sort of tie-in merchandise?"

"It is the Mark of the Champion," Larry said. "I have sent others into the living story but all of them have either failed to complete the main quest or simply died. The Old Gods are feasting upon these fallen heroes and growing stronger than they've ever before. I believe some of the heroes have even chosen to side with them in hopes of riches and power."

"Yeah, the option to go Black Alignment was something that was really popular in *Dark Undermaster* 1 and 2," I said. "It was a big mistake removing the chance to go evil in the third game. Majorly reduces replay value. After all, why save the world when you can rule it?"

Larry glared at me.

"Right, yeah," I muttered. "Heroism is good. Evil bad."

Larry shook his head. "I wrote the stories of the Dark Undermaster saga as a warning against fantasy losing its understanding of the costs of good versus evil. That the triumph of virtue was not always guaranteed and that it often had horrific costs."

"Yeah, when Lord Rose got his head cut off, I was hooked," I explained. "Not to mention the Dread Dinner."

Larry narrowed his eyes. "Tell me, do you have the heart of a hero?"

I paused. "No."

Larry smirked. "At least you are honest. What about the heart of a mercenary? Gold, women, and blood in exchange for deadly adventure?"

"Uh, two of those sound good," I said, shrugging. "Honestly, I haven't had much time for relationships since taking this job. Nightchilde ended up dumping me for the guy who runs the vape shop. I was never much of a player but let's just say I was never too tired for her."

Okay, way too much information being shared here. Something about Larry made me want to open up to the guy, though. He was like a living Gandalf or, at least, Radagast the Brown.

Larry shrugged. "It will have to do, I suppose. My compact with the video game makers was that they would be rewarded so long as they could provide the chosen ones. The bracelet accepts you and we do not have many left."

As much as I was enjoying being with the cloud cuckoo lander, I unfortunately was coming here to protect my job. "Mr. Weis, I think you need to fill out these forms. We're all excited at Epic Dungeoneering—"

"Don't forget the trademark," Larry said.

"I'm glad you've completed the book," I said, taking a deep breath. "I'm sure that they'll make a fantastic game out of it."

Larry's expression became unreadable. "Would you like to take a look?"

I absolutely wanted to. "Would I? Absolutely."

The contract was forgotten, and I put the briefcase on the ground when Larry went over to a nearby bookshelf and removed a stack of several hundred pages with a contract on top of it. "Obviously, you'll have to sign the non-disclosure agreement on the top," Larry said, his voice taking the slightest bit of an edge.

I remembered Barbara had warned me about signing anything but, honestly, I hated my employers so why the hell not? Larry handed me a pen and I took the contract from the top of the manuscript.

I didn't immediately sign, though, for one obvious reason. "This is in Polish."

"Shame you can't read the mother tongue," Larry said.

"Yeah, well the Soviet Union dissolved when I was a newborn," I said, staring at the contract then the manuscript. "Liberty, Fraternity, and Equality."

"That's the French Revolution," Larry said. "In any case, I suppose you don't want to know what happened to Ser Garland after his death at the hands of his fellow Undermasters or whether I ever resolved the Dragon Queen's rule over the Slave Pits of Jorgoth—"

I signed the contract immediately. "Show me the new novel."

"I'll do you one better," Larry said. "You can live it."

Larry's smile became frightening as his black eyes turned red. That was when the glow on my bracelet became blinding.

I found myself on the ground, briefly blinded by the flash, and I wondered if I was losing my mind. I was sick of the bracelet and promotional item or not, it was something I didn't want on anymore. Reaching down to try and rip it off, I found my hand felt *different*. There was also smoke in the air, and I found myself coughing while a rank smell filled my nostrils akin to rotting meat. The heat from the fireplace now felt like it was all around me.

"Very funny, Larry," I replied, blinking rapidly. "But I think this needs a few more months in R&D before you release it. No one wants a flashbang around their wrist."

That was when I heard the screams.

My vision cleared to the sight of hell on Earth. I was in some kind of Medieval village with most of the place on fire and bodies surrounding me. The sky was black with a blood red moon hanging in the air crisscrossed with the smoke from the inferno around me. Looming above the village was a dark and foreboding castle made of black stone that seemed like something out of a heavy metal album cover, particularly with the dragons flying around in the air.

I was *different* too. I was bulkier and wearing a suit of damaged armor that felt like it was weighing me down like an anchor. I had a sword at my side as well, not a fake one either but a heavy one. Oh, and a cloak. It didn't take much to figure out where I was or, even, who I was. I was in the Southern Kingdoms of Mokosh. I was also dressed as one of the Dark Undermasters, demon hunters who had been largely wiped out before the events of the series by the Mad Queen of the Empire.

"Oh god," I said, taking a step back. "I am tripping balls."

Larry C.C. Weis must have slipped me something, except I hadn't drank or eaten anything in his presence. I might have been inhaling something but unless he'd been putting PCP mixed with fairy dust in the air, I doubted that would have the effect I was currently experiencing. No, I had to be dreaming still in the car and I was going to wake up any second now.

My denial lasted only about as long as it did to accidentally walk back into a burning house and feel a brief intense rush of heat that hurt like hell. As Eddie Murphy said in the 1980s classic, *The Golden Child*, you couldn't feel pain in a dream. No, as insane as it was, I'd somehow found myself transported into the fiction of my third favorite fantasy author.

"I wonder if I look like Henry Cavill now," I muttered, trying to get ahold of myself.

"You wish," a voice spoke from one of the nearby hut's roofs. "Personally, I think he was smart to do *The Witcher* instead of the *other* famous Eastern European high fantasy video game series."

I looked up to see a raven sitting where the voice was coming from.

"So, you're a talking raven," I said, pausing. "I'm entirely fine with that given the circumstances."

"Yes and no," the raven responded. "It's me, Jon."

I stared at him. "Snowman?"

"Snowan," Jon said, sounding very much like my coworker despite having a beak instead of a mouth. "Jesus, have you been getting my name wrong this entire time? We've been friends for like two years."

I got defensive. "We've been coworkers for like two years and I remind you that you thought my first name was Bart for half of them. Why are you a raven or is this going to be a place where the answers will just lead to more questions."

"I died," Jon said. "So, yes, they will do that. If you're a Champion in this world and die, you reincarnate into a raven,"

I stared at him. "Give me the incredibly short summary of what the hell is going on, please. The kind you could fit into a movie trailer."

"You're trapped in a dark fantasy video game world based on a hack author's rip off of better books."

"Uh huh. Maybe you could be a *bit* more detailed."

Things were too insane to disbelieve, ironically enough, or maybe I was just too stunned to retreat into denial.

"You're in Ledziania, the magical kingdom that inspired the Dark Undermaster books," Jon said. "Larry C.C. Weis is a wizard or druid or something and manufactured the bracelets with the power of the Earthmother to fight the Old Gods here. They're all batshit crazy now. The bracelet, or Mark of Champions as they call it here, gives you the power of a video game character. Epic Dungeoneering™ has been sending their programmers as human sacrifices in exchange for wealth as well as success. Mostly by adapting his books that he'd otherwise not license."

I stared at me. "You've got to be kidding me. I'm trapped in an isekai?"

"More like a LitRPG novel," Jon said. "But I know you weren't a fan of those. Think of it like a tabletop RPG only the violence is very real but so are the perks. You're now totally ripped, and every lady looks like they were made by horny nerd programmers. You know, people like us. Plus, magic is real."

"Uh huh," I said, not too concerned with that right now. "How the hell do I get out?"

"Why would you want that?" Jon asked. "This place is awesome."

I stared at the raven. "Until you die and develop a taste of carrion."

"There is that," Jon said. "I dunno, I guess you might be able to get out if you defeat the Old Gods."

"Defeat gods, is that all?" I asked, sarcastically.

"Hey man, just level up and do it," Jon said. "I was to level eighteen when I finally got capped and that was just because I thought I could ignore the recommended levels for the quest to bang the Dragon Queen. Turns out that's not a quest reward and her dragon had an autokill. Speaking of levels, have you chosen a class yet?"

"No," I muttered. "They were blacked out as an option."

"You should take care of that, like now," Jon said, his voice now sounding concerned.

"Why?" I asked.

That was when my bracelet glowed again with the words, BEGIN TUTORIAL. I heard the bracelet start playing the combat music theme from the games.

"That's why," Jon said. "You don't have any fighting skills yet."

"Ah crap," I muttered.

That was when the skeletons attacked.

CHAPTER THREE
FIRST LEVEL IS NO FUN AT ALL

Skeletons.

Yeah, the thing about skeletons is that Gary Gygax and countless childhood Halloween decorations have made them something that doesn't strike fear into the heart of the average adventurer. After all, they're just a bunch of easily smashable bones, right? Well, there's a difference between the things mom and dad put up on the house when you're five and the real animated deal.

Particularly when you're a 1st level and trapped in a video game world adapted from books described as, "the goriest most nightmarish world ever put from pen to paper." Which was starting to make me wish I'd gotten trapped in Narnia instead. Getting preached at by Lion Jesus was looking real good right now by comparison.

The real deal in this case was a bunch of glowing eyed upright collections of bones wearing the clothes and armor that they'd presumably been buried in. There was a thin layer of skin covering some of them that added to the horror and reminded me that as realistic as we'd managed to make the DU games, they had nothing on the surreal universe I'd managed to find myself in. They had swords, spears, and spiked clubs. There were five of them in total, but I could see other skeletons spread throughout the village, carrying out a massacre of the people within. I, of course, managed to keep my dignity when I made a strategic retreat.

"Run-run-run!" I shouted, jogging away from the creatures and feeling weighed down by the armor I was wearing.

"These things don't tire, Aaron!" Jon said, flying beside me. "You need to choose a class!"

"Kind of busy now!" I said, running through the burning remains of the village as I saw the holographic light above my bracelet flicker.

Remembering, of all things, *Resident Evil 4* and having the insane idea that if Epic Dungeoneering™ ripped it off in previous games then they might do it in future ones, I proceeded to look for a hut that had an open door. It was larger than the other huts in the village and two stories tall. Heading into it, I proceeded to slam the door behind me. Just like in the village from RE4, I also saw there was a brace to lock the door as well as a shelf to move in front of the hut's window. Why a house mostly made of straw had a window was a design flaw I'd question later.

The interior of the building had a kitchen, table, staircase leading up to the second floor. It was dirty and looked like someone's popular conception of what a Medieval house might have looked like. It made me wonder if this world was one created by the video game, Weis' stories, or existed independently while just looking like a fantasy world.

Jon took rest on my shoulder as I finally got a chance to check my bracelet. The map had changed to something called DRAGON KEEP AND CROSSROAD VILLAGE. Also, thankfully, the class options were no longer blacked out. There was an inventory menu, spell list, and other things I couldn't really deal with right now.

CLASS CHOICES

UNDERMASTER WARRIOR
UNDERMASTER ROGUE
UNDERMASTER SORCERER

I stared and shook my head. "Really? Three classes? What the hell happened to the variety of DU2? Barbarian, bare-fisted monk, and bard. Okay, not bard, but you know what I mean."

The situation was so ridiculous I might as well make fun of it.

"They're all specializations now," Jon said. "Ooo, you should choose sorcerer. You're not optimized for anything else. Also, why the hell did you take Comeliness of 15? All the good romance paths are Comeliness independent. You can look like Freddy Krueger's uglier gnome brother and women will still bang you. Or dudes, I don't judge."

I choose Sorcerer and immediately was presented with a vast list of spells that wouldn't help me in my situation because they were all one use: LIGHT, FOG, JUMP, ARMOR, CURE (I), PUSH, MAGIC ARROW, and CHILL TOUCH were the only ones I remembered the actual use for. The rest were mostly transfers from the pen and paper Dark Undermaster RPG that had been a third-party licensing deal that Epic Dungeoneering™ had later ripped off.

"Take PUSH," Jon said, looking down at me.

"What, not CURE?" I asked. "Because I'm pretty sure I'm going to need that. Hell, MAGIC ARROW at least is an attack."

"Trust me," Jon said. "Save that one. Just hit accept and go to Special Abilities."

I did and was immediately deluged with a bunch of abilities ranging from SPEAK (ANIMAL) to PLAY (MUSICAL INSTRUMENT). There had to be at least forty choices of questionable abilities, and it seemed like they were playing into those idiotic specializations when my eyes went to one at the top that I'd almost skipped over: ARCANE FIRE.

"Hell yes," I said, remembering that every developer had argued this was overpowered from DU 1 onward, but the players had absolutely revolted at any attempt to remove or nerf it. I hit on it and the bracelet asked, ACCEPT CHARACTER CHANGES? Y/N?

Before I could hit the Y button, axes started smashing against the door as the skeletons began pushing over the dresser that blocked the window. They were ready to tear me apart and we were in a full-on homage to *Night of the Living Dead*. Shaking my head, I pushed the Y button and felt something strange pass through me. It was as if I instantly knew how to conjure magical fire from my hands and it was there waiting to be called.

"Burn baby burn!" I shouted, lifting my hands and shooting out a blast of blue-white fire that struck the first of the skeletons. It proceeded to explode into a pile of bones across the floor as I walked backwards, conjuring another and blasting a second. It was a basic strategy but seemed to be working.

Unfortunately, I had forgotten that developers absolutely love to put little traps in for players. No sooner did I start going up the staircase to be able to continue blasting the remaining three skeletons then I heard another moaning monster above me. I'd blasted the third of the skeletons when I found a zombified villager, looking considerably *fresher* than the others, biting into my leg.

Mothersucker!

The pain was agonizing, like, well, a frigging zombie biting into the side of my leg. I had no idea if that was going to turn me into one of them. Then again, this was a video game brought to life so maybe I was worrying about nothing. That thought dissipated with the sight of the skeleton swinging an ax at my head before I barely got out of the way in time. Pulling myself free and feeling the blood trickle down from my leg, I managed to jump off the side of the staircase and land with a painful thud on the ground.

From there, I proceeded to lift my hand up and continued to use my Arcane Fire to destroy the remaining skeletons as well as the zombie on the stairs. As soon as I did, the battle music ended, and I managed to take a few much-needed breaths. My bracelet proceeded to list +70 EXP and +5 GP on its screen with a little coin jingle noise, which seemed like an awfully small amount. I also saw, +1 LEATHER BELT.

I didn't see an actual leather belt appear anywhere but felt like I was weighed slightly more down. Checking the leather bag on my side, I saw a plain strip of leather with a buckle was now inside it alongside five gold coins emblazoned with the image of Perun's hammer. This was so goddamn weird.

"Go team, go!" Jon said, flapping uselessly in the air.

"Fat lot of good you were!" I snapped at the raven.

"Hey, you wouldn't even know what the hell was happening if I wasn't here," Jon explained. "Besides, what the hell am I going to do? I'm a bird."

"You have a point," I muttered, deciding to check my stats.

ARAGORN "AARON" BARTKOWSKI
LVL: 1
CLASS: UNDERMASTER SORCERER
ALIGNMENT: GRAY
AGE: 34
SEX: MALE
RACE: HUMAN
STR: 10
AGI: 10
CON: 9
INT: 16
WIS: 7
COM: 15
CHA: 13

ARMOR CLASS: 0
ATTACK: +1
HEALTH: 3/5 (*Minor Injury*)

FEAT: Taunt

SPECIAL ABILITIES: ARCANE FIRE (1d6+3 INT bonus, Eldritch Damage)
SPELL LIST (1): PUSH

"Like I said, good call on picking Sorcerer," Jon said, perching on my shoulder. "You would have been screwed choosing Warrior or Rogue with that build. Mind you, most of us programmers went with it. Very few of us were jacked before our transformation. A couple went Rogue."

I looked at him. "Just how many people have been dumped in this place, anyway?"

"I dunno, fifteen or twenty?" Jon shrugged his wings. "It's hard to keep track of every other Undermaster here. There's story confusion too. Every one of us starts as Garland, even the women, and yet we all share the same game world."

Ser Garland of Nowhere was the protagonist, as much as the books had one, of the Dark Undermaster books. He was the adopted son of Lord Beorn Rose and, unbeknownst to him, the son of the god Perun. Basically, he was a kind of Clint Eastwood in Fantasyland sort of character who snarked his way through a bunch of fractured fairy tales while angsting about how meaningless the world was. Oh, and having ridiculous numbers of affairs with beautiful women while caught between Ania the Assassin and the Dragon Queen. His adventures were like crack to my fourteen-year-old self.

Ser Garland had also been the protagonist of the past three DU games, which had never really made much sense as each game had to find increasingly contrived ways of restarting him from level 1 at the start of each game. Each game was a loose adaptation of the plots of the book but could often go in wildly different directions. Supposedly, one of the reasons that Weis had been upset with them was that you could have Ser Garland be a complete bastard and sack whole towns or side with the Old Gods. His distaste suddenly made a lot more sense now that I was realizing it seemingly effected real people.

Actually, now I was wondering if my own programming had been altering things inside this world like I was a secret architect of the Matrix or a user from *Tron*. Okay, I needed to stop thinking about that since in that way lied madness.

"That makes no sense," I said, just shaking my head. "How the hell does a world operate on video game logic?"

"It's magic," Jon said. "The author doesn't have to explain shit. Who do you think Weis is, Brandon Sanderson?"

I pulled out the belt and tied it around my waist. My stats immediately went from Armor Class 0 to Armor Class 1. It didn't seem like a great improvement, but I wasn't exactly going to complain about following the rules when the other option was ending up transformed into a raven. "Anything else I need to know?"

"This world is a very R-rated dark fantasy RPG," Jon explained. "You and I both know how that goes since we programmed the previous game."

"I actually mostly worked on *Cyber Dragons 2080*," I muttered.

"For which you should be horribly ashamed," Jon said, shaking his head.

"I didn't decide to launch it like that!" I said. "Besides, it ended up awesome."

"Keep telling yourself that, chief," Jon said. "Just fight, loot, and side quest until you feel you can do the main quests. This isn't a turn-based RPG, so tactics and skill do play a factor."

"Yeah, I noticed when I almost got eaten," I muttered, sarcastically. "What about food, sleep, and so on?"

"All necessary," Jon said. "We're in a worst of both worlds sort of situation. Get used to using a privy and this kind of lamb skin covered rod instead of toilet—"

"Too much info, Jon," I muttered. "What about the people. Are they like…real?"

"That's a bit philosophical for my tastes," Jon explained. "The short version is that I think they're a lot more real than you or I would probably be comfortable with killing them. They don't respawn, they sometimes seem to have knowledge of other loops, other times they don't, and they have their own lives beyond the pretty awful set of circumstances they've found themselves in."

"Great, I'm trapped in Westworld," I muttered. "Except instead of androids, they're video game characters."

"Pretty much," Jon said. "They definitely do work in all the ways that matter, though, if you know what I mean."

The raven winked. I didn't even know they could do that.

"No, I don't I do," I said.

"They brought back brothels for this game!" Jon said. "50 GP a night at the Black Cat. Plus, you can sleep with Farmer Grub's wife when he's away from his house. It's a side quest,"

I stared at him. "Did you spend the entire time you were in here getting laid?"

"Hey, you get a bonus card for each time you get laid," Jon said, defensively. "I'm also just being true to Garland's character."

I stared at him. "I thought the game got rid of the sex cards for being a sexist promotional gimmick."

"They were the best part of Pwiffle," Jon said, annoyed. "I got to level 16 chasing the cards without ever touching any of the main quest."

I shook my head, hearing the screams and battle outside. "Well, I'm not much of a hero but if I'm going to get the hell out of here then I guess I better start the main quest. What do I do now?"

"We're still in the tutorial," Jon said. "Every Garland starts in the sacking of Dragon Keep. There are some story reasons that I honestly didn't pay attention to, but you're supposed to rescue as many villagers as possible before converging on the keep to face the Skull King."

"Skull King?" I asked, not remembering him from the books. Then again, it had been almost ten years ago since I'd last read them and this was clearly incorporating stuff from the games as well as licensed media. God, I was really taking to this too well. I wished I could have healed my injury, but the wound didn't feel like it was getting worse and I could still walk as well as hopefully fight. I also didn't know anything about first aid. I just hoped that picking PUSH turned out to be as good a choice as Jon seemed to think.

"Yeah, the Skull King's a bad guy," Jon explained. "Just head to the keep and kill everything on your way. Hopefully, you'll get a companion along the way."

"Hopefully?" I asked, wondering what he meant.

"She's a bit...temperamental."

CHAPTER FOUR
DEVELOPING MY PARTY

"The Sacking of Dragon Keep" was listed in my bracelet interface as the Main Quest with objectives like Rescue Villagers 0/10, Slay Undead 6/20 listed underneath. I mostly didn't pay attention to them because I was less following their instructions than basic human decency. I saw villagers getting murdered by skeletons or zombies, I blasted the skeletons and zombies. I saw skeletons and zombies just shambling around, I still blasted them since I was pretty sure there weren't examples of the undead just minding their own business in the world of Mokosh. It was more *Dawn of the Dead* than *Twilight*.

One thing I didn't bother with was using my sword during any of these encounters. I had a level 1 "Basic Sword" in my inventory, and I took it out to give some practice swings, but it didn't do anything other than make me feel like I was going to fall over. I didn't even know why I had a sword as a Sorcerer, but I supposed it was because Garland was a master swordsman as well as a wizard in the books. He was also a master thief. Literary accuracy had to take a backseat to game balance, I guess.

Thankfully, I wasn't running into any issues so far despite my lost hit points. Arcane Fire was my go-to, one might say only move, and working fine if I stayed out of the clutches of the supernatural beasties rampaging through the town. It helped to think of all of this as a video game because I didn't want to think of these being real people having their home attacked and being slaughtered. The bodies on the ground certainly looked real enough.

"Do you ever feel guilty using Arcane Fire so extensively?" Jon asked, flying beside me.

"No," I said.

"I mean, it's a bit like Indiana Jones and the Swordsman," Jon said, referencing *Raiders of the Lost Ark*. "It's basically like owning a gun in a world full of swords and spears."

"There's also like a hundred of them and one of me," I said, really hoping none of the dragons in the sky flew down to kill me. I was depending on the fact they were probably just background material for the opening level. Mind you, at any point, this entire "video game" could go off the rails too because I was pretty sure that Weis' writing absolutely loved unexpected turnabouts. There were no less than five chapters in the first book where prospective characters were set up only to end up dying horribly without fanfare.

"Fine-fine," Jon said. "Anyway, you're doing fine. Albeit, your timing on this level sucks. I was able to speedrun it in like five minutes and that was my first and only try."

I was about to ask Jon how the hell he could speedrun his way through a nightmare like this when I heard battle from nearby. That was when my attention was drawn down an alleyway where a woman was fighting off no less than three undead warriors at once. These ones looking a lot tougher and better armored than the typical members of the horde I'd been fighting.

The woman was dressed in a set of red leather armor that was form-fitting but not quite as ridiculous as you'd see in Hollywood, covered in metal scales with a kerchief around her lower face. Bright red hair was hanging out down around her shoulders that was a different shade than just about everyone else I'd seen so far in this place of predominately blonde and brunette peasantry. She also had a bow on her back that was smaller than any normal example of the weapon I'd seen in real life. I recognized it as Lightbringer, her rune weapon from the novels that never ran out of mystical arrows.

The warrior woman moved with a kind of inhuman grace that you only saw in martial arts movies, slashing the creatures she was facing with a curved katana-like blade in one hand and a shorter Western sword in her other hand. The strange mixture of weapons didn't inhibit her from parrying, stabbing, slashing, and even somersaulting over one of the creatures before decapitating it from behind. It was a display of fighting prowess that was beyond anything I would have imagined myself capable of at any level. I instantly knew who she was.

Jon, by contrast, was decidedly less than impressed. "I hate these opening cutscenes. They always make the companions look incredibly badass but then they nerf them to be the exact same level as you."

"Ania Rose," I said, with the kind of fanboyish awe you might hear other geeks refer to Mary Jane Watson Parker or Lady Lara Croft.

Yes, those fictional crushes that boys develop at a certain age on women in media that signal that girls were no longer icky but were still entirely in the realm of fantasy. My mentor in coding had a poster of Slave Bikini Leia in his office, before HR had made him take it down, and the rather uncomfortable moment of oversharing where he said that *Return of the Jedi* had ushered him into puberty.

"Seriously?" Jon said, looking at me. "Tell me, you're not a fanboy."

I grimaced. "Err, of course not."

But that was a bold-faced lie and we both knew it. In the case of Ania Rose, I'd been about the same age as the actress they'd cast for Garland's foster sister in the original live action show for the FANT channel (before it became FYN for copyright reasons). I'd developed more than a little crush on her during my socially awkward years and bonded with the character both onscreen as well as her book counterpart. So much so that I, and a legion of other young men, had ignored how weird it was that one of Garland's two primary love interests was the girl he was raised with. Something that, as an adopted son of my family, I could absolutely confirm was not a thing that happened in real life.

It shouldn't have surprised me to find out she was the first companion in the game since she was a wildly popular character with the fanbase. Both male and female. Indeed, apparently Weis had received death threats for some of the horror show he'd put her through in Book 3 where she'd ended up losing her father, tortured, her female elvish lover executed, and her head shaved. Something that had caused her actress to almost quit the show over since she'd been trying to get into romantic comedies. The fact she'd ended up some kind of weird Slavic ninja and the only female Dark Undermaster didn't really improve things in fan's eyes.

"Yeah, well wanting is better than having," Jon said, sounding surprisingly salty. "She may look good but she's a real bitch. Her writers must have watched way too much anime growing up. Verbal abuse is not sexy."

I wanted to punch my raven companion in the beak. Admittedly, not every writer had been able to capture Weis' character voices in the licensed material. There was a reason a lot of fans preferred the Dragon Queen or even secondary characters like Lady Agata Rose.

No, I wasn't counting slash writers either.

Before I had a chance of saying something, I saw Ania finish off the remaining skeleton warrior and pulled out her bow before aiming at me. A glowing arrow appeared and flew out, zipping over my shoulder and striking a skeleton warrior silently coming up behind me.

"That is such a cheap movie trick," Jon said, resettling on my shoulder and raising a wing. "Undead don't sneak! We totally would have heard him coming."

"Oh, shut up, bird brain," Ania said, surprising me by responding to Jon. I hadn't known that other people could hear and understand him. "Go peck out someone's eyes."

That made me assume the 'cut scene' or whatever was going on was over and I could respond. Knowing I was Garland in this universe put me on the spot and I tried to figure out what to say or do. The Mark of the Champion wasn't giving me any dialogue options, which I supposed was a blessing. I tried to adopt Garland's trademark growl and remember how he talked. "Err, hello, sister. It is good to see you again. I am, uh, here."

Ania narrowed her eyes. "You're another off-worlder from Earth. Sent here by Larry C.C. Weis to try to save the world. Except, he's probably sent you here with absolutely no skill in combat or equipment that would let you do it. Oh, and everyone is going to react to you like you're my dead brother."

I blinked. "Huh. I did not see that coming."

"Me neither," Jon said, looking at me then her. "Was this in the script? I really should have been paying more attention to what all the NPCs were saying."

I wanted to bring up that he'd mentioned that other people here were aware but was too busy focusing on Ania. "Oh, well, hi."

Ania looked away annoyed and lifted her right arm, revealing another Mark of the Champion. "I managed to recover one of these from a dead Garland copy. Since then, I know when the world repeats its loops. This is like the seventh or eighth time I've seen Dragon Keep and Crossroad sacked."

"You've escaped *The Matrix*!" I blurted out.

Jon, of course, was more focused on other things. "That better not be my bracelet! I had like fifty Pwiffle cards accumulated, including the dirty ones!"

Ania rolled her eyes. "Such a wonderful set of champions that Weis has sent us."

"By the way, is that like an Anglicization?" Jon asked. "Like, shouldn't his name be Laurencjusz or something? Also, Weis is German. Also, is he from our world or yours? I probably should have been investigating this in-between getting laid."

"I see your Spirit Guide is a wonderful source of information," Ania said. "Come on, we need to get to the castle. To answer your unspoken question, no, when the world resets, people don't come back from the dead. New people wander in to resettle as if in a trance. The world has been getting more vacant and empty each failure of previous champions. The Dark Undermasters are almost extinct, and the Old Gods are on the brink of escaping. Then our world will die and yours will soon follow."

"Hey, no pressure," I nodded. "Lead the way."

"Hey! Don't follow the NPCs! The NPCs follow you," Jon said.

I shook my head at Jon's behavior. Then again, I couldn't really blame him. This was an insane situation and if his way of coping was dismissing everyone around him as 'just' video game characters then I couldn't hardly blame him. Except, I very much could. Everyone here seemed real and without any proof that I'd gone insane (which probably was more likely), it was best to treat everyone as real.

Mind you, it helped I was following a pretty girl and someone who seemed like they knew what the hell they were doing. If that sounded like a less than heroic attitude, well, it was about my last three relationships. Working for Epic Dungoneering™ hadn't left much time for dating, and I admitted, it had also beaten a lot of my sense of initiative out of me. If that insultingly low WIS score was accurate, and I feared it was, I suspected it was because I'd become "conflict adverse" out of a desire to go along to get along. A trait that had led me to signing a contract with a shady as shit dark fantasy author who was apparently accepting human sacrifices from my employers.

I had no idea what I would do should I actually get back to the "real" world because I wasn't sure what even could be done. Report them to the police? FBI? Men in Black? I'm sorry, officer, but I was tricked into putting on the One Bracelet of Sauron by my hand puppet obsessed boss and her chief minion as part of an evil ritual. That was even assuming I was able to get back to my old life.

Unless I managed to figure out a way to escape soon, I'd probably end up being reported as a missing person and eventually considered dead. I hadn't noticed Jon Snowan disappearing and apparently plenty of other coworkers over the past few years had been disappeared. Who would even miss me back in my "old" life? My parents? Yeah. My sister? We'd spoken maybe once in the past three months. Friends? Girlfriends? I'd sacrificed all of them on the altar of being the absolute best corporate drone I could be.

Crap.

Maybe I deserved to be here.

"Follow my lead and try not to get killed," Ania said, lifting her bow and firing down at another group of skeleton warriors. "We need to get to the Skull King before he kills Lord Emberly."

Piotr Emberly was one of the main supporting characters of the series, being Garland's mentor and one of the few remaining veteran Undermasters. "Wait, Lord Emberly dies in the new book?"

One of the skeleton warriors charged at us, only for me to hit it with arcane fire. Unlike the earlier skeletons, though, it didn't immediately die and started charging again. I managed to blast it apart with a second blast, though. Yeah, that was how it was going to be it seemed. There were going to be increasingly tougher enemies as we moved along.

Ania shot me a glare that told me that my reference wasn't appreciated. "Not if we can help it. I've managed to prevent him from getting killed each time but it's always close."

"It's a scripted event," Jon said. "I wouldn't worry about it."

"The script is not set," Ania said, shaking her head. "I've lived through multiple loops, you haven't. Whatever the way things were supposed to be, they get worse each time. I don't know what my world is to yours, some kind of play or fiction, but it's becoming influenced by the Old Gods. Whatever was meant to happen isn't happening"

"Great, so it's not just *Eldritch Ring*," Jon said, citing one of my favorite video games that Larry C.C. Weis had written for. "We're now incorporating *Alan Wake* nonsense."

"What kind of changes are we talking about?" I asked.

Ania finished off the last of the skeleton warriors. "Garland being dead for example."

She'd mentioned that earlier and I thought back to *The Princes of Sorrow*, the previous book. Garland had been killed by a group of traitorous Undermasters and everyone had assumed he was going to get himself resurrected because, well, there was no book series without him. Everyone had assumed he'd get resurrected by blood sorcery or some other contrived method. Certainly, that was what the show had gone with, and most people assumed the video games would too.

But what if it hadn't been Larry's intent? What if he had decided to stick to his guns and keep Garland dead? He'd made his bones as a writer with shocking deaths of other main characters after all. No, that didn't make any sense. Or did it? Also, if this wasn't the world he created by writing but an actual place, did his writer intent make any difference whatsoever? Or was the fact that Weis was sending "heroes" into this world to make up for the fact that its actual champion was dead. Dammit, I needed something to distract me from this metaphysical nonsense.

"I'm sorry," I said, surprising myself. "I know he was important to you, Ania."

"You have no idea, imposter," Ania said.

Yeah, we weren't going to be friends any time soon.

That was when we came to the town square of Crossroad at the foot of the entrance to Dragon Keep. Dragon Keep was an immense castle, even more so now that we'd traveled closer to it. It was a lot larger and more grandiose than the ones in the show or even the previous games where engine limitations had prevented it from being realized like it had been in the text.

Supposedly, it had been constructed by giants during the ancient days when the gods had walked among men. It had been used by Perun to breed dragons and house them for war against Veles' armies of the dead. That was before they'd all been corrupted into the *zmei*. In the first book, after Lord Rose had been executed, the surviving Rose family had vowed to retake it only for the Undermasters to end up making it their new headquarters. Thus, they could never return home.

The former family holding of the Rose family had been gutted by dragon fire, though, and the armies involved. The ancient statues of the guardian wyrms around it were now cracked and broken with its defenders slaughtered to the man. Its drawbridge had been forcibly pulled down by the sight of the broken chains and shattered door.

The moat that had previously surrounded the castle had been boiled away, leaving just a massive pit that was surrounded by horrifically burned defenders that were scattered round like broken toys. Some of them were moaning and I couldn't imagine what kind of pain they were in, still alive after being essentially boiled to death.

Jesus, Superman, and Crom.

That was messed up.

"Time to face the Skull King," Jon muttered. "Oh, I should probably mention that he's invincible."

"Wait, what?" I asked, doing a double take.

CHAPTER FIVE
WELL, THAT WAS UNEXPECTED

"What? He's *invincible*?" I asked, stunned. "What the hell kind of tutorial is this?"

Jon looked at me as if I was being an idiot. "Skull King isn't actually meant to die in this battle. It's one of those early boss fights where no matter how well you do, they kick your ass. Don't worry about it. You're supposed to fight him later at like level 20. Like I said, I never followed the main quest. I am my own man."

"Silence," Ania said, making a slicing gesture across her neck. Which didn't strike me as the way you should tell someone to shut up unless you were a psychopath. "This is a graveyard for heroes, Imposter."

"He said it," I said, pointing to Jon. "Also, I really wish you wouldn't call me that."

Ania shook her head and turned back to the castle, her gaze showing a haunted look that I'd only seen on my cousin, Alek. He'd been a part of the NATO forces in Afghanistan and had seen some shit. It was weird to compare a character I'd previously only known from fiction dealing with such raw emotions, but I sympathized. Or tried to. I couldn't imagine what Ania was thinking since this was her home. One that she'd apparently seen attacked multiple times and getting worse each time.

I only knew the Dragon Keep media but seeing it like this was still a punch in the gut. It was like seeing someone go through the New Zealand *Lord of the Rings* sets and burning them before taking a giant dump on Bag End. Except with more corpses.

"It's the smell that gets me every time. Why can birds even smell? We don't have noses. I mean, we have nostrils but it's just not the same," Jon said, pointing out an element of my surroundings I'd been judiciously ignoring. It was like steamed pork mixed with a lot of other nastier smells ranging from rotting meat to excrement. Seriously, battlefields stunk. Especially ones full of undead.

Ania put away her bow and pulled out her katana to wave. "Valentin Velesson, Skull King, I call upon you! Dark Demigod and Pillager of the Vistula, Enemy of Man, and Paladin of Death! We have danced this dance before, and you have escaped each time! Bring me Lord Emberly and let us fight once more! You may yet scurry off to fight again!"

"See?" Jon said, nodding. "She knows the drill. This is not meant to be where you die. Like only two other players never made it past the tutorial. Don't worry."

I very much was worried because an enormous knight wearing black armor decorated in bones came out on a gigantic demon steed with glowing red eyes as well as black bat-like wings. If I wasn't dating myself too much, he reminded me most of General Kael from 1988's *Willow*. Basically, Darth Vader with a skull mask. Except this guy was about eight feet tall on a horse that was proportionately larger. Strapped on the back of Skull King's monster steed was a crumpled over black cloaked figure that I assumed to be Lord Emberly.

The Skull King pulled out his sword from behind his back, which I'd been told dozens of times was a stupid place to store your weapon, and watched it light up with blue-white fire. Some stupid media obsessed portion of my brain started playing John Parr's "Saint Elmo's Fire" in the back of my head and I was just glad the bracelet wasn't following suit. Both my bracelet and Ania's *were* playing ominous music, though, like something from Basil Poledouris' *Conan the Barbarian* score. It made me assume that we would never ever be able to sneak up on anyone. Which was a shame since I'd heard they'd been planning to introduce stealth mechanics to DU 4.

"*Yet another child is sent by Perun's voice to die,*" The Skull King said in a voice that sounded like he'd stuffed his mouth full of gravel before putting it on a speaker. Seriously, the guy sounded like Ron Pearlman with a voice modulator. "*You have crossed worlds and time to meet your death, boy. Your blood will nourish the hungry spirits and bring my father one step closer to unleashing the Unmaking.*"

"Is he talking to me?" I asked Jon.

"Yes, dumbass," Jon said. "You're the main character."

"You speak to me, Skull King!" Ania said, seriously insulted by his presence. "Not the man wearing my brother's visage."

Okay, that was a creepy way of phrasing that. "Yeah, you're speaking to her!"

Jon covered his beak with both wings, clearly ashamed of being in my company.

"*A stolen Rheingold bracelet does not a hero make, Daughter of House Rose!*" The Skull King said. "*Dress as a man and kill as an assassin you may but your destiny has always been to take more lives than you save. You are a bent, broken, and sullied wretch of a woman that no man would have even as a slave. Go back to the hole you had been hiding in or die among those your brother failed to protect.*"

Okay, wow, that guy was an ass.

Ania, at least, wasn't intimidated by his trash talk. "Have at you, fiend!"

The Skull King reared his horse back up and drew back his sword to charge at us both.

"Screw it," I said, conjuring the one magic spell I knew. "PUSH!"

I didn't know if I was just supposed to say the name of the spell or if it was meant to have some kind of incantation or not, but this was all instinctual anyway. The power of the only magic I knew aside from Arcane Fire (which was a special ability I could use every round anyway) flew out of my fingertips. It was less like a gust of wind and more a telekinetic battering ram that proceeded to slam right into Skull King's chest.

Much to my surprise, Skull King was knocked off his demon steed and fell back into the moat pit behind him with a startled scream. The moat pit was something like seventy or eighty feet deep and he'd gone down headfirst, meaning he'd probably been cracked like an egg when he'd hit the ground. I didn't know if that was lethal for undead as everything became unearthly silent for a second. Then a rapid series of pinging noises came from my bracelet.

ACHIEVEMENT UNLOCKED: The Bigger They Are
(A) 25 - Defeat The Skull King in Tutorial (Secret)

ACHIEVEMENT UNLOCKED: Wilhelm Scream
(A) 25 - Defeat The Skull King by pushing him into the Moat (Secret)

ACHIEVEMENT UNLOCKED: Castle Reclaimed
(A) 25 - Become the Lord of Dragon Keep (Finish Tutorial)

I stared at my bracelet. "This thing comes with actual achievements? You've got to be kidding me."

Jon was too busy staring at the now rider-less demon steed, though. Well, riderless except for the fallen Lord Emberly on his back. "What the actual…"

Ania looked every bit as shocked as Jon, staring at the sight of the fallen Skull King with an expression between disbelief and horror. It was not the kind of expression I expected for a sudden but unexpected victory.

YOU HAVE REACHED LEVEL 2!
+3000 EXP BONUS FOR SECRET ACHIEVEMENT

+ YOU HAVE RECEIVED *GHOST SWORD* [Witchfire]
+ YOU HAVE RECEIVED DEMON STEED [Mount]
+ YOU HAVE RECEIVED *GHOST ARMOR* [Heavy]

+ YOU HAVE RECEIVED *GHOST HELMET* [Heavy]
+ YOU HAVE RECEIVED 365 GP
+ YOU HAVE RECEIVED *ALCHEMICAL STONE* [RED]

What followed was feeling like I was suddenly carrying about fifty or sixty extra pounds of weight that caused me to fall over due to my bad, still bleeding, leg. If this was what being over encumbered was like in a video game, I had to make a serious effort to have my characters carry less.

"How the hell did you pull that off?" Jon asked, flying up in front of my face.

I stared at him. "You told me to get PUSH! So, I used PUSH!"

"That's just because it's awesome and looks like you're a Jedi!" Jon said, pausing. "I mean, the Prequel Jedi suck but they have pretty awesome moves."

I almost throttled him but was stopped by Ania coming to my side and pulling out a bandage. "You're injured."

"Yes," I said. "I got bitten by a zombie. It's fine, though. Only two hit points damage."

Ania stared at me like I was insane. "Injuries get worse, you idiot."

She proceeded to pull out a jar full of some kind of gray goo from one of her side pouches before slathering it over my injury. The sting was worse than the bite before she pulled out another bandage and wrapped it around the now goo-covered spot. Much to my surprise, she then placed her hand over both and a little green glow passed between her fingers as well as the bandage.

CURE (1) – 2 HP RECOVERED; MINOR INJURY HEALED.

"You have magic?" Jon asked. "But you're a Rogue! You don't get that until 9th level!"

Feeling slightly better after the initial pain had passed, I took up my bracelet and checked it. There was now a menu for PARTY MEMBERS, and it contained both an entry for Ania as well as Jon. Jon was listed as FAMILIAR level 1 with his alignment listed as Gray. Ania was DARK

UNDERMASTER ROGUE 9, SPECIALIZATION: MOON ASSASSIN 1 with a Black Alignment. Probably because of all the murders she'd committed in her quest for revenge against the Mad Queen and her conspirators.

"I qualify as a *familiar*?" Jon asked. "Weis, you rotten bastard."

"Huh," I said, staring at the statistic. "Ania, you are *way* higher level than me."

"Still not enough to beat the Skull King, though," Jon said. "No offense. I'm sure you would have done fine. For a girl."

Ania swatted him, sending him tumbling to the ground. "I still maintain some of this experience nonsense from the previous two loops I've had this thing. Unfortunately, every time I tried to work with the Imposters, they blew me off to do their own nonsense."

Jon struggled to get up. "Not me! I totally ignored you and the other Companion NPCs! More experience for me that way!"

I struggled to get up and managed to heft the armor now in a backpack on my back that previously hadn't existed. "Well, I'm glad for you. I guess we managed to make one real achievement here today."

"Perhaps," Ania muttered. "The Skull King was on my list."

"Your murder list?" I asked.

Ania looked up. "You know about that too, huh?"

"Sorry," I replied, not wanting to get into it by pointing out she was my favorite character. "At least you can mark off one."

"I'm not so sure about that," Ania said, helping me steady myself. "Veles is the God of Death. While our side stays dead with each loop, he can bring back his people each time. Kind of why we're losing this war."

The Dark Undermaster books had been heavily divided into their political and supernatural elements. Veles the God of the Underworld was as close to a Sauron or Morgoth figure as existed in the books, but all the Old Gods had gone mad except for the Earthmother and maybe Perun, depending on which book you were reading. The thing was I'd never been interested in the zombie apocalypse sections and had been far more interested in the politicking—even if it was the undead sections that made the video games. Again, I really wish I'd brought my Epic Reader with me or copies of the books.

Great, not only was I trapped in a dark fantasy world where every other hero had been killed then reincarnated into a raven, but it was a dark fantasy world where the forces of evil could respawn. "Well, that's not very fair."

Ania snorted. "Fairness doesn't enter the equation."

I looked at the beautiful but hardened woman beside me, noticing the scar on her lip from where she'd been tortured by the Blood Reaver and other signs of what had previously only been stories for me. "Listen, I don't know anything about this world and didn't agree to come here. I've been kidnapped and thrown here. I know you must absolutely hate the fact people are wandering around with your brother's identity. I know I would hate myself for it. I also don't have any real combat ability—"

"You're really selling yourself up here, friend," Jon said, looking up.

"You don't need to explain, Imposter," Ania said, her face briefly cracking with concern. It was an unexpected look to see given her initial hostility.

I grimaced at her use of the word. "But I'm here now and I'm willing to help, as much as I'm humanly able to."

It was a stupid and silly promise to make. I should have been focused entirely on figuring out a way to get out of here. If I was going to survive this, I needed to figure out how the magic worked and whatever the "rules" were of this situation. Instead, though, I was invested on some level. I wanted to help her and be part of a story.

There was a moment of empathy I could see in her eyes that swiftly passed. "I'll win this war with or without you, Imposter. You got lucky. Weis has sent you here to die and I have not enough sympathy to spare to both you as well as the hundreds of people who I grew up around that are now strewn like fish across the surface of a poisoned lake. Take care of yourself because no one else will."

Ania stood up and headed over to the demon steed where I could see Lord Emberly was getting up off the back of the monster horse, unsteadily. The dragons had left, and the blood moon had transformed back into a white-gray one. It seemed we'd won, or whatever passed for such a thing, and the dead were retreating.

Jon looked up, walking on the ground rather than flying. "See, what did I tell you? Complete bitch."

My leg felt fully healed but still burned with the bandage and ointment on it. I decided not to disturb it. "Jon, did it occur to you that maybe you should be treating these people like, you know, actual people?"

Jon seemed to ponder that then shook his head. "Nope!"

I checked my character sheet and noted that it now said:

ARAGORN "AARON" BARTKOWSKI
LVL: 2
CLASS: UNDERMASTER SORCERER
ALIGNMENT: GRAY
AGE: 34
SEX: MALE
RACE: HUMAN
STR: 10
AGI: 10
CON: 9
INT: 16
WIS: 8
COM: 15
CHA: 13

ARMOR CLASS: 1
ATTACK: +1
HEALTH: 10

FEAT: Taunt

SPECIAL ABILITIES: ARCANE FIRE (1d6+3 INT bonus,

Eldritch Damage)
SPELL LIST (2): PUSH

Beneath my stats, it said that I had Attribute (1) and Spell (1) to choose. Getting an attribute point every level seemed excessive but I suppose it was a compromise for the fact that they reset Garland's levels every game. It was strange to imagine him as a real person and that I was occupying his place in Mokosh history.

"Can I wear the armor of the Skull King?" I asked.

"Nope," Jon said. "Heavy armor is solely for Undermaster Warriors. I mean, you could, but you won't be able to cast spells and that would screw you over something fierce."

"Do I even want to know why armor interferes with magic?" I asked.

"Because that's the way the world works," Jon said. "I don't question it and neither should you. So just sell the armor when you get a chance or wait for a warrior to join the party."

"Is that likely?" I asked.

"No idea," Jon said. "I do know that I'll level up with you, though. Get myself some pecking powers."

I didn't even look at him, studying the rules as best I could. They were pretty like standard tabletop roleplaying game ones and the previous games in particular but not identical. "Uh huh."

"You should keep the sword, though," Jon said. "As an emergency weapon if nothing else. You never know when you'll hit a magic dead zone or against something immune to sorcery. Think of it like Leon Kennedy's knife."

"What about the Alchemist Stone?" I asked, checking my pockets for it. It was like a piece of red quartz and looked like a piece of candy. "What's it do?"

"You swallow it," Jon said, surprising me. "Each one grants a specific ability, but you have to either throw it up or expel it another way in order to change them out. Red ones are the most common. They add about fifty pounds to your carrying capacity."

I immediately swallowed it. Huh, cherry taste. Much to my surprise, I felt significantly better in the amount I could carry.

"Try not to think about the fact that was probably in Skull King's zombified stomach until recently," Jon replied.

I almost threw it up then and there.

"Mmm hmm," I muttered, pushing away that thought. "I need you to be honest with me. There's been like fifteen champions sent by Weis, right?"

"So, they tell me," Jon said. "I've even met a few of my fellow ravens. Never one in the field, though."

"How far did any of them get?" I asked. "In defeating this big, huge epic threat, I mean."

Jon paused. "You're here, aren't you? Some have gotten close to Veles' sanctum, but no one has ever defeated any of his lieutenant gods. All of them are just sitting on their grand temples' thrones, chilling and spreading evil while the land tears itself up in civil war. With that kind of environment, why not just collect cards and chill?"

"You didn't want to fight."

"I didn't want to die. We saw how that worked out. I think that kind of summarizes everything, doesn't it?"

Yeah, it did.

I ended up choosing WIS to enhance to 8 and the spell CURE (I). I couldn't always rely on Ania, it seemed.

"You should be focused on increasing your Intelligence, chief," Jon said, looking up at me. "Wisdom is a dump stat in this game. Same as Comeliness."

"If I'd had more of it in real life, I wouldn't be in this world," I said, looking down at the crow.

Jon had no response for that.

CHAPTER SIX
THE NEW LORD OF DRAGON KEEP

Finishing up my updating of my character sheet, I found a button that allowed me to close it out as well as mute the music being provided by the bracelet. The orchestra music playing was soothing but added to the unreality of everything in a way I didn't want to deal with. I wanted my brain to catch up with the fact that this was really happening. I'd been grabbed by the proverbial tornado and dumped in the land of Oz. Unfortunately, there was no yellow brick road to follow and no ruby slippers to click three times to take me home.

I briefly explored the other options with the bracelet's menu. It really did function like a video game interface but was lacking any way to log out, save game, or pause. I couldn't adjust the difficulty either. That made sense with the idea this world was "real" but I wasn't taking anything for granted right now. Another thing I noticed was that the bracelet came with a glossary and codex.

Huh, that would be useful.

One thing was glaringly absent, though. "No actual instructions on how to use any of this."

Jon took rest on a nearby signpost. "You expected it to teach you how to shoot WEB and equip your clothing?"

"Kind of, yeah," I replied.

"Well, that's why I'm here," Jon replied. "Weis reincarnated us with the purpose of passing on our advice to future champions in hopes we could advise you to not get yourself killed in the same stupid ways we did."

Looking around the village, I noticed people were already pouring out from where they were hiding to gather around at the keep. Some of them were putting the destroyed undead into piles or gathering bodies. Others were gathering buckets to put out fires. A lot more people seemed to have survived the battle than I expected. Which, to my surprise, I felt no small amount of pride in. I may have been kidnapped to come here but I'd done real good in my short time here.

Probably something more important than anything else I'd done in my life so far. After all, I didn't have a wife or kids or career where I saved lives. I hadn't even created anything of note as a software programmer. The most important thing I'd done was updating *Cyber Dragons 2080,* so it didn't crash every time you passed 75 mph while driving downtown on a motorcycle. Players really hated that.

"Well don't expect me to repeat it but I owe you, Jon," I replied. "I probably wouldn't have managed to survive the tutorial without your guidance."

"Oh, you absolutely wouldn't have," Jon said. "Also, I'm a way better mentor than the raven that was assigned to me. She was like, 'save innocents this', 'fight evil that', and even suggested I *roleplay.* God."

"Don't ever change, Jon," I said, before a sad thought crossed my mind. "Is there any way to get you back to, uh, normal?"

"I'm dead, Aragorn, not cursed," Jon said. "No cure for that."

I wasn't so sure about that. "You said the bad guys can bring back their minions, Jon. Also, you're alive. Just different."

"Resurrection is strictly a better living through evil sort of thing," Jon said. "Besides, you've seen how people typically come back. Skeletons and zombies for the lower-level goons, strigoi and death lords for the higher levels. Reincarnation seems to be how the good guys do it. Which sucks because I have to live vicariously through you now."

"Ah," I said, trying to articulate my thought. "But—"

"Ravens can't exactly wag the dog if you catch my meaning," Jon said. "At least, I haven't figured out a way to."

I didn't. "What?"

"Choke the chicken, spank the monkey, stroke the—" Jon started to explain.

"Ah," I said, interrupting. "Gotcha."

"I still am attracted to humans and humanoids," Jon said. "It's hellish, really. But if you let me watch while you—"

"No," I interrupted again. "Never bring that up again."

"Spoilsport."

"But we're not in our bodies when we moved to this world," I said, looking at myself. "At least I wasn't this ripped when I was a geek from Michigan. Maybe they're waiting for us back on Earth. Maybe if I do manage to beat Veles and the other Old Gods, we'll like, I dunno, wake up back on our world with everyone restored."

"Like *Jumanji*?" Jon asked, confused.

"I never saw those movies," I muttered. "A shame because I'm a huge Robin Williams and Karen Gillan fan."

"For different reasons I assume," Jon said before sighing. "But no, I don't think it's that kind of story, Arago—"

"Aaron, please," I corrected.

"It fits better here," Jon said. "No one has read the books or even watched the movies here but us."

"Please," I added.

Jon shrugged. "Fine. I don't think it's that kind of story. Weis may be the resident Gandalf or Merlin of this world but he's not exactly Lawful Good if you catch my meaning. Or White Alignment as this rip off world calls it. He's called the Wise Man here and what little I bothered to learn about the local lore says he's very much an 'ends justify the means' sort of guy. He doesn't care how his champions beat the Old Gods as long as they do. Also, how many innocents get caught in the crossfire."

That tracked with my impression of him. "Yeah, Wise Man is literally what wizard translates to."

"Don't tell me how making a multimedia fantasy franchise plays into that," Jon said. "I hope it was for more reasons than just believing software jockeys were the best people to fight evil because, wow, that was not a smart play."

"Right," I muttered.

Jon surprised me with his next words. "You can actually go out to where I died and find my body. It's probably been picked over by scavengers, but it might be worth it to check it out. For my cards if nothing else."

My bracelet pinged:

SIDE QUEST(S) ADDED:

RECOVER JON SNOWAN'S REMAINS
Recommended Level: 18
Reward: Jon Snowan's possessions

"Oh, you've got to be kidding me," I muttered, looking at the sight.

"Yeah, don't try and go for it before then," Jon said. "The beef gate is punishing for going outside of the right areas you're leveled for."

"Jon, is it possible that, maybe, you're just viewing this world the wrong way?" I asked.

"Says the guy who just got three achievements," Jon said.

That was when I noticed many townsfolk were gathered outside of the town square before Dragon Keep's entrance. There was a lot of whispering, pointing, and discussion that made me uncomfortable. Ania and Ser Emberly were also finishing up their conversation in front of the late Skull king's mount. The demon steed hadn't moved at all since the death of its master, and I was still confused at how I now "owned" it.

That was when Ser Emberly turned around and waved to me. "Garland, my boy!"

Piotr Emberly had been a character since the first book, *A Court of Devils,* and had taken on Garland as an apprentice after he'd been kicked out of the Rose House for some reason. Literally, I was just hitting puberty when I last read it. He'd once been one of the greatest demon hunters in the world but had lost himself to food, drink, womanizing, and corruption. He still fought the Old Gods and their minions but regularly accepted bribes from the Empire and other shady parties while overcharging villagers for monster slaying. Despite this, the books had always treated him as a good man who'd lost his way rather than a genuinely evil one.

Piotr certainly looked like the image I'd had in my head with a salt and pepper beard, round belly, plus armor that didn't quite look right. I could see the many glowing runes woven into his black coat, weapons, and jewelry too. He might not have had much in the way of fighting prowess in his body, but magic was a hell of a compensator. Probably the equivalent of a performance enhancing drug regime for guys who should have retired by now.

"I'm not Garland," I replied, looking at him. "I just look like him but I'm really from—"

I noticed Ania shaking her head.

Piotr came up to me and slapped me on the back. "Oh, you lovable rogue, you! Always with the pranks. What a jest! What a jest!"

I blinked. "Right, yes, I'm joking."

"Brilliant work with the Skull King," Piotr said. "I understand you carved a nice slice from his forces on your way to relieve me too."

Piotr seemed to be over-selling my efforts in the tutorial, unexpected ending as it may have been. "Ania did a lot of the work herself."

"It was a miserable defeat," Ania said, not mincing words. "There's almost no remnants of the Undermaster order left. Not to mention the civilian casualties."

"Shame, shame," Piotr said as if he wasn't really listening. "The fact remains we do have a headquarters without an order, though. I know you wish to take the fight to the Old Gods in their grand temples—"

"I do?" I asked, skeptically.

"But we need an army to distract Veles forces for you to get close to him," Piotr said. "Only by banishing him to the Underworld again can we bring an end to this curse. That means getting allies."

I found myself annoyed with the lack of originality on display here. Was this final book really going to be a rehash of assembling allies to fight the Dark Lord ala *The Lord of the Rings*? Hell, *Dragon Age* and *Mass Effect 3*. What was next? Go gather the four orbs of light by slaying the Elemental Fiends?

"You'll also have to destroy each of the lieutenant gods' avatars in their grand temples before relighting the sacred fires. Each corresponds to one of the alchemical elements that empower the world's magic," Piotr said.

Mothersucker. That *was* the plot to the original *Final Fantasy*. Maybe I'd overestimated Weis' writing ability. "That sounds like a tall order."

"You'll have to assemble your old companions if you want to have a chance," Piotr said, seemingly not missing an opportunity to revisit every cliche in the book. "I won't lie to you, this is probably a suicide mission but if there's anyone in the world, I trust to defeat this threat then it is you, Garland."

Ania narrowed her eyes at me, silently saying, *This is all your fault.*

I glared back at her, replying with my stare, *I didn't do this!*

Ania turned to Piotr. "We should contact the Dragon Queen. Her forces would be essential to fighting this threat."

Piotr got a sour expression on his face. "Celestyne von Piast-Jagiellon is a poor choice in allies despite Garland's, ahem, close ties with her."

Ania's expression soured.

"Yeah, those ties," I muttered.

"Her excessive affection for peasants and army of nonhuman vagrants has not won her the love of the nobility," Piotr said. "Instead, she has been driven back to the city of Kalizov and is presently under siege by her sister, Queen Apollonia. I believe it will not be long until Celestyne is slain and labeled a usurper."

"So, what, you suggest we ally with the Mad Queen?" Ania asked.

"I wouldn't call her that and yes," Piotr replied, resolutely. "After all, she can't conquer the Southern Kingdoms if everyone is undead."

The primary political conflict of the books had always been between the identical twin sisters of the Kingdom's (never named

Ledziania in the books) royal family. The short version being Celestyne was the good one and Apollonia was the bad one. Apollonia used magic to turn her sister into a dragon, hence Celestyne's nickname, and ruled in her sister's place with great cruelty as a catspaw of the Empire. Garland broke the spell in the first book and Celestyne became a kind of weredragon that occasionally showed up to blast his enemies. She also tried to assemble an army to help her overthrow her sister. I mostly remembered the plots for the long and involved sex scenes and excessive amounts of fan art done about her.

"I assume the other two groups we should recruit are the Northmen Rus and Great Forest elves," Ania said, as if she'd had this conversation before and resented having to repeat it. Which she probably had multiple times.

"If the Great Forest elves don't help, choose to contact the Vukodlaks," Piotr said. "The wolfmen are no friends of Veles."

Yeah, this was all typical good but less effective versus evil and more powerful choices. Very lazy storytelling and I had to wonder if this was what we'd really waited almost eleven years to read. "What will you be doing?"

"Contacting the Empire," Piotr said as if this was the hardest job of them all. Which it possibly was. Being a guy who had grown up in Poland in the aftermath of WW2, or so he'd claimed, Weis wrote the German-coded Empire as complete bastards. A pretty easy way to make sure your books got past the Soviet-era censors. Then again, I was once more confronted with the fact this wasn't a product of Larry C.C. Weis' imagination but history he'd been recording. Maybe? I mean, Ania didn't look like she'd aged eleven years since the last book. Dammit, I kept falling down the hole of trying to think this through.

"Yeah, well, good luck with that," I said, wondering what the likelihood of him succeeding would be according to the laws of narrative.

Dammit, there I went again.

Piotr looked back to the gutted ruins of Dragon Keep. "Which brings me to my next point. The Dark Undermaster order has been savaged. There may be less than a hundred of us left in the world."

"More like three," Ania muttered under her breath. "This was the last bunch."

"Nonsense," Piotr said. "We'd have to have lost Dragon Keep a dozen times to be completely wiped out."

Somehow even Jon looked pained at that statement.

Piotr didn't seem to notice. "We will need a place to rally our forces once we've assembled them all and Dragon Keep is in no shape to handle them now. So I am, as the highest-ranking Dark Undermaster left, appointing you as Brother Lord of Dragon Keep."

"What," I said simultaneously with Ania.

Clearly, this part hadn't occurred in previous loops.

"Wow, congratulations," Jon said, hopping up and down. "The game changed its storyline. If you're defeated by Skull King, you just get named castellan. You don't get named Lord until you actually beat-beat Skull King, or so the quest journal indicated."

"Aw, isn't it cute how your little pet bird squawks," Piotr said, reaching over to pet it. Apparently, only bearers of the mark could understand him. Maybe druids or rangers too if they existed in this world. Again, it had been a long time since I'd read them.

Jon snapped at him and flipped him off with one wing.

"I'm not worthy," I said, absolutely meaning it.

"Nonsense, Garland!" Piotr said, slapping me on the back. "If we had a quorum, I might elect you as the new Overmaster of our order. You are a legendary hero in the making and Dragon Keep was as much your home as any other member of the Rose family."

"It really wasn't," Ania interjected.

"It is only right that you serve as its lord and master for the rest of your natural life," Piotr said. "Obviously, you'll have to rebuild it for the coming battle, though. I'm sure an enterprising young man as yourself will be able to find the masons, carpenters, iron, and gold to pay for it, though."

Oh great, another obvious quest and it was a construction one. "Ania would be much better—"

"Our first and only sister will be welcome, of course," Piotr said. "Perhaps she will even have her lineage take over as the next Brother

Lord. Our order may be forbidden from taking wives, but bastards have long been a source of new recruits and I'm sure you'll provide us with dozens."

Ania's hand moved down to her short sword and her eyes told me she was considering murdering us all.

I couldn't blame her as I was stealing her family's ancestral home. "I'm really not Garland."

"Farewell, Garland!" Piotr said, walking over to a fully saddled war horse one of the villagers brought to him. "Remember, you're our last hope!"

He proceeded to trot off without saying another word.

MAIN QUEST(S) ADDED:

ASSEMBLE ARMIES TO FIGHT VELES' HORDE 0/3
Recommended Level: Explore further to find out
Reward: Unknown

ASSEMBLE COMPANIONS (1/6)
Recommended Level: Explore further to find out
Reward: Recruitable Companion

DEFEAT THE OLD GODS SERVING VELES (0/4)
Recommended Level: Explore further to find out
Reward: Unknown

REBUILD DRAGON KEEP (0/12)
Recommended Level: Any
Reward: Upgraded Dragon Keep

SIDE QUEST(S) ADDED:

EXPLORE DRAGON KEEP WITH ANIA (0/1)
Recommended Level: 2
Reward: 200 EXP

Ania stared at me then turned around and walked over to Dragon Keep's entrance where some elderly villagers stood. I couldn't help but feel terrible about all this. I also felt terrible about the fact I checked out how tight armor fitted her.

Oof.

Not the time, Aaron.

"Well, that went well," Jon said, looking between us.

CHAPTER SEVEN
HOME SWEET HOME

I stood there for an uncomfortably long time, not sure what to do when the demon steed wandered over to me and started snorting in my face. It had hellish red eyes and seemed to crackle with a mystical energy that seemed to ionize the air around it.

"Uh, hey," I said, staring uncomfortably. "So, is this like a Nightmare?"

"I think that's a pun that only works in English," Jon said, taking roost on the top of my head.

"What are we speaking?" I asked, confused.

"Like Fantasy Polish?" Jon suggested, clearly not sure how to explain. "I'm actually speaking crow, and no one can understand me but you or other people wearing the Mark. Well, you, fellow champions, and people who can talk to animals. There's like a dozen languages in the Southern Kingdoms but the mark translates those too."

"Convenient," I said, still thinking about Ania and how ticked off she was.

"Yeah, well Garland spoke a dozen languages and we're Garland of Nowhere or you are," Jon said, looking up at the sky.

I followed his gaze. The constellations were completely different from the ones on Earth. The night sky was also clearer than I'd ever seen it. The moon was slightly 'off', too, with its craters in different places. Frowning, I lightly petting the snout of the demon steed. It shook affectionately like a normal animal. "Yeah, that's another thing I noticed. Piotr reacted strangely every time I tried to say I wasn't Garland."

"Yeah, that's generally how people react to people saying they're not who they say they are," Jon said. "Everyone will react to you as if you're Garland and ignore any claims or evidence to the contrary. Even if, again, you're a lady like my raven was."

"Which I'm not," I said, staring at my hands. "I'm just like a bigger, bulkier version of me."

"It was the same with me," Jon said. "Like I said, it's magic."

"Weird, I'm not stronger despite my new appearance."

"Attributes don't change from your body on Earth even if you look different. Don't ask me why. You've got to just accept a lot of stuff on faith here."

I frowned, uncomfortable with this turn in the conversation. "I'm not a big fan of faith. My parents weren't exactly followers of any traditional religion. My grandparents had been die-hard communists, and my parents wanted nothing to do with any of that. Mikhail and Sasha Bartkowski wanted my sister and me to worship, I dunno, Eru or nature or whatever. Which both me and my sister found silly. Religion has never really been part of our lives."

"Yeah, well, it's less a matter of faith around here," Jon said. "If it helps, just think of them as big aliens like Thor or Q."

"I'm not militant," I said, annoyed. "I just don't practice. I'm pretty sure magic, gods, and undeath are real now. Seeing is believing or spelling in this case."

I had magic now and that was something I was going to have to get used to. I could feel it boiling within me and wondered if it would come with me back to the "Real" World if I managed to escape it. Magic had to exist in my world as well since, well, I'd been sent here.

Thinking about magic, the demon steed began to glow and slowly disintegrated into shadows before swirling into a glowing blue rune on the back of my hand. I realized, then, I could conjure or dismiss it at will. Yet another ability I just sort of understood instinctively. "Is that normal?"

"Yeah, demons can be claimed like Pokémon on this world," Jon explained. "Especially mounts. Obviously, most people make do with horses, but the Undermasters have a lot of them in their service."

I'd forgotten that from the books, probably because the show had just had them riding horses. "And because I killed Skull King, I get his stuff."

"The Necromonger way!" Jon said.

I stared at him. "Does anyone get any of the references you're making?"

"Only you," Jon said. "I kind of admit that being a bird may have driven me insane."

"Are you coming?" Ania asked, surprising me.

I looked up. "Oh hey, sorry, I thought you walked off in a huff."

"A huff?" Ania asked.

I was an idiot. "Err, it's just a thing I have a history of. Women walking away from me, I mean."

Oh God, did I say that too?

Ania raised an eyebrow.

"Are you sure you have a high Charisma score?" Jon asked. "Because even I would be doing better."

"Just come here," Ania said. "Dragon Keep is still smoldering but the village elders are willing to help clear out the bodies and do some basic maintenance. Anything more, though, and we're going to have to shell out of our pockets. Unfortunately, Valentin's people looted the treasury, presumably to pay the dragons."

"Dragons work for gold?" I asked.

"Most people do," Ania replied. "Veles is the god of death, ground, and wealth. He has access to vast amounts of gold, silver, and gemstones to pay his armies. You know, plus the legions of the dead. He's also a giant worm with the head of a bear and the horns of a bull."

I tried picturing that. "So, a dragon."

"When he's not taking other forms, yeah," Ania said.

"The father of all dragons," Jon corrected. "At least since he killed all the good ones. Celestyne is the last one who isn't on his side."

Ania nodded. "He's the opposite of Perun the Sky God. Supposedly, they created the world together before turning against one another."

"Supposedly?" I asked.

"Gods lie," Ania said, sounding like she had personal experience. Which surprised me since I hadn't read any encounters between her and the deities of the books. Maybe it was just a general distaste for the fact they all seemed to be on the bad guys' side.

"Right," I said. "He sounds like Hades from Greek Mythology but much-much worse."

"I haven't been beyond the Empire to the Far Lands. I understand they used to worship Veles as Pluto, though, before switching to venerating Mythras," Ania said.

That was another weird little detail, Ledziania didn't seem to be the only place here despite Weis claiming it had originally been part of our world. Mokosh seemed to be an entire other planet that was like my world but different in smaller or greater ways. I hadn't questioned it when it was just Weis being a 'hack' writer inserting fantasy counterpart cultures but now I had to wonder how the hell that had come to pass. Had history just unfolded remarkably similarly or had this world been populated by refugees or colonists from my world? It was the kind of thing I'd love to ask about when I wasn't surrounded by boiled bodies.

Ania changed subjects by turning to survey 'my' keep. "Sweet Perun, how are we going to pay for this?"

"Kill monsters and take their stuff?" I suggested.

Ania glanced at me.

"What?" I asked.

"Sure," Ania said, shaking her head. "I guess that is the traditional way to raise funds around here."

"I'm sorry about your home," I said, unsure what else to say here.

"It's not been my home for a long time," Ania said, biting her lip in a surprisingly childish gesture. "Home is family and mine are scattered to the winds or dead. You really want to help me try to rebuild this place?"

"Yeah," I said, stretching out my hands. "Even if it wasn't my only way home, which it might not be, I don't feel like just leaving you out to dry. I mean, what if this world does get conquered and it's mine next? You'd have to be a real asshole to just come to this new world and goof off."

Jon was conspicuously silent.

"You wouldn't have been the first," Ania said. "Like I said, I've dealt with other Garland Imposters before. Some of them have been my friends, one was something more. However, most of them treat this world, my world, as just their own personal playground. If you are willing to help, truly want to help, I appreciate it, but I don't intend to wait for another tourist to save us."

"You have *tourists*?" I asked, envisioning people going up to Gondor to gaze at the dead tree and statues of Isildur.

Ania blinked. "That's what you took from that?"

"I dunno, I just never thought about it," I said, pausing. "I mean I suppose you could go to fairs, tournaments, and on pilgrimages or whatnot."

"You are easily distracted," Ania replied.

"So, I've been told," I replied, huffing. "I might be on the spectrum, but I never got myself tested."

"The spectrum of what?" Ania asked, blinking.

"I'm just letting you know I'm one of the good ones," I said, pausing. "And I know how that sounds, but I'm not one of the bad ones who says they're one of the good ones; I'm actually one of the good ones who says they're one of the good ones. And I know how that sounds—"

"That's literally from *Brooklyn 99*," Jon said. "God, I miss television. It's like the only thing I don't have here that I want. You'd think I'd miss the internet, but the lack of social media almost makes up for the horrifying monsters."

"Come on," Ania gestured. "We'll get you set up in the tower. If you're serious about this, we can start going through the town to see if there's any help we can lend to the villagers. From there, we can start figuring out where to raise the necessary gold to fix Dragon Keep. I know Piotr wants us to raise an army against Veles, but we need supplies and a place to start before we even think about this."

"It'll be a long road," I said, pausing before reciting the lyrics from the *Enterprise* theme. "Getting from there to here. But I've got faith. Faith of the heart."

Ania just stared blankly.

"Song lyrics," I replied.

"Then shouldn't you be singing them?" Ania asked.

"Please don't," Jon said.

"Yeah, I'm just nervous," I muttered. "I recite pop culture when I get that way. Fighting monsters? That's easy. Social situations? Not so much. I either respond with immense sarcasm and pop culture references or no, that's pretty much it. This is the first time in a long time when I haven't tried to be an asshole as a response."

"I can't imagine why most women walk out on you then," Ania said, walking across the damaged drawbridge.

I grimaced. "Smooth, Aragorn. Smooth."

"Please tell me you don't intend to court Cattie Brie here," Jon said.

I didn't get it. "Sorry."

"The Legend of Drizzt? Forgotten Realms? D&D?" Jon asked. "I thought all of us spoke the same language of dice rolling."

"I was more a *Warhammer Fantasy* guy," I replied, somewhat exaggerating. I played D&D, just wasn't a huge fan of the novels. Even then, they'd just been too PG for me. "That is until I found something *darker. The Black Company* by Glen Cook. Erikson's Malazan. Oo, baby."

"I'm just saying, she'll break your heart," Jon said. "Also, cut your dick off. Which is worse. Find someone less high maintenance. There are easier ways to get laid in Fantasy Land. It's a regular World of Whorecraft in some places. They have temple prostitutes in some places—"

"You've never had a steady girlfriend, have you?" I asked. "Someone you were actually friends with, I mean?"

Jon looked away but I saw real emotion in his eyes. Impressive given he was a frigging bird. "I've been in love, Aaron. It's not something that I recommend around here."

I wondered what he meant by that, but I'd somehow shut him up somehow since he didn't say anything more.

I reluctantly headed across the broken drawbridge of Dragon Keep. Ania had walked further in, and I found myself in an immense main hall that had been formed for dragons to be mounted then released through a tremendous skylight. Unfortunately, that had provided a way for the dragons to get inside.

It seemed like the entire place had been an abandoned ruin for years rather than a place that had been newly sacked by the undead and mercenaries. The furniture had been tossed in piles before being set alight. The tapestries had been ripped off the walls and defecated on. The Dark Undermasters had been in decline for centuries according to the books, but this was an explicit sign of just how hard they'd fallen.

Still, I was impressed at how well the artists for the books and on fan sites had successfully captured the interior of Dragon Keep. Even in its diminished state, it was an incredible sight to behold.

"Wow, what a shit show," Jon said.

"Well, it's been sacked a dozen times," Ania said, looking around. "Frankly, I'm surprised anything is still left standing. The only thing left intact, though, is the library. That's protected by the blessings of the twin Zoryas, so it's fine. Otherwise, we'll have to start from scratch."

I checked my bracelet and the quest journal for repairing Dragon Keep.

REBUILD DRAGON KEEP REQUIREMENTS (0/12):

* Rebuild Ania's Room (cost: 100 GP)
* Rebuild Garland's Room (cost: 200 GP)
* Restore Drawbridge (300 GP)
* Restore Tapestries (500 GP)
* Restore Alchemical Lab (1000 GP)
* Restore Moat (2000 GP)

* **Restore Armory (2000 GP)**
* **Restore Blacksmith (2000 GP)**
* **Restore Stables (5000 GP)**
* **Restore Chapel (5000 GP)**
* **Restore Battlements (10,000 GP)**
* **Restore Dragon Pit (50,000 GP)**

"Wow," I said, whistling. "That is going to be *expensive*."

Jon said, once more hoping on my shoulder. "This is clearly an endgame sort of accomplishment."

"Gold must be worthless," I said, staring.

"Actually, gold piece is an extrapolation," Jon explained. "Almost every coin in the realm just has a tiny bit of gold enamel on top of a lead coin. Its why prostitutes cost me fifty gold piece."

"No, Maelor the Black was just way overcharging you," Ania said, walking up to me. "None of the champions I remember were able to rebuild the keep but some were able to get some work done before things 'reset.' I'm biased here since I grew up running across the battlements and trained to be a Dark Undermaster here. If we are to rebuild it completely, we'll probably have to find the surviving champions as well as carefully manage our—"

PURCHASE ANIA'S ROOM UPGRADE Y/N?

"Yes," I said, tapping Y.

"Wait, what are you doing?" Ania asked.

PURCHASE GARLAND'S ROOM UPGRADE Y/N?

I tapped Y again.

REBUILD DRAGON KEEP QUEST UPDATED (2/12)
MAIN QUEST UPDATE: QUEST COMPLETED: EXPLORE DRAGON KEEP WITH ANIA (1/1)

+200 EXP

The bracelet projected an image of the top rooms on both the Southeastern and Southwestern towers. Both suddenly filled with beds, decorations, and artifacts from the books. Both went from empty dungeon-like cells to comfy Medieval-themed hotel rooms with burning hearths. I also felt like my purse had become a little lighter. It seemed that the bracelet was able to make instant changes in exchange for cash.

"House flipping, Medieval style," Jon said. "Vanilla Ice couldn't have done it any better."

Ania grimaced. "You had three hundred gold pieces lying around and you used to give us comfortable rooms versus saving it or, I dunno, *repair the front doors*?"

I looked at her, confused. "You're welcome?"

Ania threw her hands up in the air and walked off.

"You're right, you do encourage women to do that a lot," Jon said.

CHAPTER EIGHT
FIGURING OUT HOW THE TOILETS WORK

The upgraded room for Garland of Nowhere was rather nice. Like if you were staying at a Renaissance Fair-themed hotel room or something. It was warm, inviting, and came equipped with furniture. Basically, it was the exact opposite of the rest of the castle. It even had a perch for Jon, which made me wonder if it was meant for the "Garlands" who replaced the real McCoy. The fire in the hearth was magical and could be conjured or dismissed at will, just by concentrating on it.

Neat, a Medieval heat pump.

Plates of fresh fruit were laid out with pitchers of surprisingly clean water as well as bottles of wine. I hadn't had lunch that evening, so I ended up gorging myself on the spread before flopping myself on the bed. It was different feeling from your typical mattress but not necessarily worse. I was also exhausted from trying to be a hero and about ready to collapse either way. I barely managed to get my armor off before nodding off.

The last thing I saw before sleep was the portrait of the Rose family hanging over the hearth. A red bearded man in a lordly attire that I couldn't really identify the time of but vaguely a suit with a high collar. That, I presumed was Lord Tomas Rose. At his feet were the seventeen- and sixteen-year-old daughters, Ania and Agata. Ania was the younger one with red hair like her father and Agata had raven tresses like her mother.

Both daughters were wearing blue dresses that seemed more *Bridgerton* or *Anastasia* than Middle Ages. They both looked happy, so this was presumably before the traumatizing horrors of the first book. Finally, their mother was present with the brunette woman wearing a black Gothic-looking dress. Maria Rose had a severe expression that seemed almost accusatory toward the bed where I lay. Maria had been a minor daughter of the royal family that had hated Garland from the day he'd arrived. She believed he was her husband's bastard and that the idea he was Perun's son was ridiculous. Things had gotten worse once the attraction between her daughters and the seventeen-year-old Garland had become noticeable.

What had happened in the ensuing fifteen or so years of book time? Lord Rose ended up killed by the Mad Queen's brother, Lady Maria had been turned into a vampire by Veles, and both daughters had suffered terribly in the interim. All the secondary supporting characters had ended up killed, tortured, or corrupted as well until the castle's original inhabitants had all been wiped out. As a teenager, I'd thought this was the coolest thing in the world but as an adult I'd just wanted the remaining Rose family members to reunite. Now it was never going to happen.

Garland was dead, I *was* an imposter.

"Don't think about this as stealing a dead man's life," Jon said, sitting on his perch. "Instead, think of this as taking all of his stuff after he doesn't have any use for it anymore."

I threw a pillow at the raven before entering a strangely dreamless sleep. The next morning, I awoke to deal with pressing concerns.

"Seriously, man, I can't believe you're struggling with how to use the bathroom," Jon muttered as I left the private bathroom that the quarters came with. I'd managed to get "close enough" to figuring how it worked but the specifics were still eluding me. However, the next time I needed to use the bathroom, I suspected I might be in trouble.

"Listen, the other option is the bidet," Jon said, looking genuinely pained at my ignorance. "It's a washing bin you use after you use the hole in the tower bathrooms. They work just like outhouses and drop it all into the pits below."

"Uh huh," I said, looking at the sun streaming in through the windows of my room. It was a new day in this place. I could still smell the smoke from yesterday's attack, though. "Isn't that a security concern? I mean, if you're undead and don't care about wading through crap?"

Jon paused at that. "That might explain a few of the castles falling in the region. But let's put a pin in that until later."

"So, the bidet—" I asked.

"You use your hands and oil," Jon said. "It's how the Tarks do it in the Eastern Lands past the Great Forest and Mountains of Death."

"You've got to be kidding me," I said, disgusted. "My hands? Is there not a cantrip or something we can use instead?"

"Yes, use phenomenal cosmic power to clean yourself," Jon said, sarcastically.

"Like you wouldn't," I snapped, putting my hardened leather armor back on. It was a poor substitute for chain mail, but I had to make do with what I had. The real Garland had sacred metal forged from a star and enchanted by elves but, like with his levels, he had to start over each game with basic equipment.

"Just follow the instructions I gave you," Jon said. "A bunch of disposable paper isn't going to get you any cleaner really than the way they use what they use around here. There's also not exactly a supply of Charmin around these parts if you catch my drift. I got used to it and you'll eventually get used to it too."

I paused before shaking my head. "Screw it, I'm just going to get a bunch of leaves."

Jon covered his face with his wing. "Wait til we talk about bathing. You're going to have to start learning to wash your face and hands regularly but not take actual showers or baths save when you come across a waterfall or pond. Plus, sharing water is a thing."

"Ugh."

"On the plus side, communal bathing is totally a thing. They have bath houses for it and everything." Jon's voice took on a suggestive tone, implying that whatever the villagers got up to in the bathhouses wasn't just cleaning themselves.

I stared at Jon. "Just how horny are you at all times, raven?"

"On a scale of 1-10? 12."

I almost made a joke whether that was an actual stat, but I didn't want to know the answer. Instead, I decided to check my stats to see how far I was from leveling up again. Every new level, the counter for EXP reset and you had to grind an increasingly higher number of points. At least if it was like the game.

Level 2 to 3
3200/5000 EXP

"That's actually really good," Jon said, looking at my bracelet feed. "I was only at 200 points when I finished the tutorial. You're going to start wanting to level grind as soon as you're in the village, but you have a pretty good head start. You should be at least 4th level before you leave Crossroad. This is a basic starting area."

"Isn't that a rather dismissive way of referring to a town that just got sacked by Harryhausen skeletons?" I asked.

"I'm pretty sure that it's exactly as dismissive as that statement," Jon said. "But the fact is that, at least as I did it, the village of Crossroad is a place full of procedurally generated quests and content that will allow you to figure out how to use your powers. Also, get a few more Companions. As useless as I've always found them to be."

I felt a headache coming on. "I don't suppose it's the fact you treat them like NPCs that may be the reason they aren't your friends?"

"They are NPCs," Jon said, frowning. "They live in a video game world. They only exist now to help the main character."

"So do you," I point out.

Jon paused, not responding for a moment. "Crap."

"Yeah," I pointed out. "Also, procedurally generated? What do you mean?"

"As I understand, all the quests are different from Garland to Garland," Jon said, glad to change topics. "Sometimes the village is suffering from people needing to be rescued from lingering monsters. Sometimes they need you to do personal shit. It's all randomized."

I bit my lip. "I'm going to take a wild stab in the dark, Jon, and suggest that may actually not be procedurally generated content."

"Oh, then why is it different each time?" Jon asked.

"Because each of the sequences is with different people and every single one of these events *matters*," I said, wondering what I'd done in life to be cursed with such a self-absorbed familiar.

Jon seemed, again, to be affected by this. I was reaching him. I just wasn't sure that it was worth the effort. "Yeah, well, I bet Farmer Grub's wife is still fu—"

Whatever he was going to say was cut off by a knocking on the wooden door of Garland's quarters.

"Who is it?" I asked.

"There's literally only one other person in the castle," Ania said.

"Oh right," I said, heading to the door and opening it up.

Ania was on the other side of the door, once more dressed in her armor and prepared for battle. She had her hair up, though, and it kind of reminded me of Princess Leia on Endor. "Did you figure out the privy?"

I blinked. "Is that a common problem for the Garlands?"

"The two I met before you, yeah," Ania replied. "Honestly, I'm not sure how you keep yourselves clean."

"I plead the fifth," I said.

"The fifth of what?" Ania asked, confused.

"Nevermind," I muttered, looking around. "I was just about to go out and, uh, level grind."

Ania blinked. "Right. Well, how about we go together? The village is in dire need of help, and you are someone with at least some ability to fight."

"Some," Jon muttered.

"I have a pretty good idea at least some of Garland and my old companions are also at the local tavern," Ania said.

"We're heading to a bar? It's like nine the morning," I asked, confused. "What kind of drunken losers would be getting wasted at this hour of the day."

"The kind who may or may not have seen their wives, sons, daughters, or brothers dragged off to the Underworld by the living dead yesterday," Ania replied.

I paused. "Right. I suppose I'd be having a whiskey, neat after that myself."

"Well on the rocks isn't really an option around here," Jon replied. "Not unless you have ice magic."

"Fair point," I admitted.

Jon jumped from his perch and landed on my shoulder in one easy motion. "Wait, is it the Black Cat? The city's brothel? Because I'm in."

"Yes, it's the Black Cat," Ania said. "It always survives the siege intact. It's also, technically, a tavern."

I scrunched my brow. "The city's brothel is called the Black Cat? Why?"

Ania stared at me and raised one eyebrow. "Think on it."

The meaning clicked for me. "Ah, I get it now."

"It's not an exact translation, I think," Jon replied. "Anyway, it's also the base for a lot of the Dark Undermasters seeking extra work. Dragon Keep accepted petitions from all over the Southern Kingdoms but if you wanted actual action then you'd just put it up on the wall of the brothel."

"Yeah, I've read the short stories."

The Dark Undermaster collections had the typical premise of Garland in an unnamed brothel finding out about some local monster haunting the region or a twisted fairy tale story happening nearby. He'd try to intervene, everything would go horribly wrong, and there would be some valuable lesson at the end about how heroism sucked. In retrospect, they were kind of repetitive as well as needlessly nihilistic, but they were my jam growing up.

"Anyway, if it's like before then other friends and family will be drawn back here," Ania said, turning around and walking away.

I ended up following her. The halls of Dragon Keep looked slightly better in the morning with the extinguished fire no longer smoldering, sunlight streaming in from the various broken windows, and the overall effect more like immense emptiness than being the sight of a massacre. Still, I wasn't going to forget what I'd seen the night before. Maybe Jon had been trying to cope with his situation by thinking of it in purely video game terms, but I was very much aware that this was real. No continues, no save scumming, and real consequences for people other than myself.

"Anyone I know?" I asked.

"I dunno," Ania replied. "I don't know who you know."

Fair enough.

"So, what were the other Garlands like? I mean, the ones you remembered because of the bracelet," I said, interested if there was anything I could learn from them. It was a long shot, but I wasn't about to take on the Dark Lord and all his minions by myself. The bracelet was leading me to try to recruit more companions, but they'd all think I was Garland, and I didn't want to deal with pretending to be someone I wasn't, especially around Ania.

"They weren't Garlands," Ania said, sharply. "They were Imposters, just like you."

"Sorry," I said, grimacing. Clearly, I'd just erased whatever goodwill I'd managed to accumulate yesterday.

Ania sighed. "You already met the first one."

"What?" I asked.

"Skull King," Ania said, not bothering to look back. "He started as one of you people."

You people, I assume, meaning champions from Earth. This was a bombshell she'd rather casually dropped and changed the entire nature of my encounter with the dead man. I'd killed a "real" person, which made me feel like a hypocrite for feeling like since I'd already just reassured myself that I wasn't like Jon. Then again, I'd previously thought Skull King was undead and I was entirely okay with divorcing living people from undead monsters.

"What?" I asked. "He was from my world?"

"Yes, what?" Jon asked.

"Not everyone who dies becomes a crow," Ania explained, shrugging. "It's possible to make a pact with Veles and switch sides. The God of the Dead proceeds to make you a permanent part of this world and one of his minions. Valentin loved the fact he was trapped in a world where he was the strongest person around and he abused his powers every chance he could. I was too weak to stop him. I was confused, horrified, and angry at 'Garland' for most of our time together."

"You didn't know he was a champion at first?" I asked, avoiding the word imposter.

"I couldn't," Ania said. "The damn spell that Weis wove over us all made me crazy. I kept trying to justify his actions until I finally snapped."

"What caused that?" I asked, wondering if it would be possible to break other locals out of their confusion.

"He killed another Imposter," Ania asked, her expression haunted. "Another champion of Weis who was actually trying to make a difference here. I never knew their name but the incongruity of seeing two of them fight finally snapped me out of it. After Valentin won, I took the bracelet off their opponent's dead body, and everything changed. I started to see the walls of the prison I was in."

She lifted her bracelet. That was when I noticed it had suffered some damage and had scratches all over its runes.

"Did the other Garland have an Ania?" I asked, letting my mind wander.

"Huh?" Ania asked, doing a double take.

"I mean, if there's multiple Garlands running around, do they come with their own Anias?" I asked, speculating aloud. "It says I should recruit six companions. Is it possible that they're all the same you've been magically cloned or something.

Ania stopped cold and turned to look at me.

"Oh, right, yeah," I muttered. "That problem would be disturbing to think about."

"No, she came back here," Jon said. "So, there's got to be recycling of characters. I guess that means we're all competing to see who gets a full group."

"You Imposters are so damn weird."

"Gotta catch 'em all!" I said, cheerfully.

CHAPTER NINE
EXPLORING THE STARTING AREA

"So, who was the second champion you met?" I asked, remembering that she'd claimed to have met two.

"Her name was Francine," Ania said, a wistful tone to her voice. "Francine DuBois."

"Ah, French chicks," Jon said, nodding. "Say no more."

"French Canadian, actually," I replied. "She was before your time."

I knew Francine Dubois in a, 'we shared coffee a few times in the break room' sort of way. She was an actual writer on the Dark Undermaster games. Francine had played Women's College Basketball, was a bit on the butch side, and was one of the nicest people I'd ever met. Francine had her desk cleaned out a few years ago and everyone assumed she'd been fired. The popular theory was she'd attempted to argue microtransactions and live service were terrible ideas, so they should focus on story instead. Try and get a positive single player experience going. You know, career suicide.

"Needless to say, given she was a woman, it was ridiculous that people treated her as Garland," Ania said. "But I came to believe she was a hero in her own right."

It was the first sign that Ania didn't hold all the champions in contempt. "I take it the romance path wasn't involved."

Okay, that was more a hope on my part.

"You'd be surprised," Ania said.

"Yeah, all companions are player sexual," Jon said. "Which is totally against the books. On the other hand, it's good marketing. Fenris is the best *Dragon Age 2* companion. I was always disappointed they didn't let you romance Kate Mulgrew's Flemeth. Ooo, Captain Janeway, you naughty-naughty swamp witch GILF."

I needed to clean my brain out with arcane fire.

Ania's stance hardened. "In the end, Francine proved to be just as rotten as the rest of them."

"Really," I said.

We reached the main hall and the broken door to Crossroad. "Yeah, she ended up choosing to support the Dragon Queen's attempt to conquer the Southern Kingdoms and reunite the Old Kingdom of Ledziania. Basically, she got so obsessed with the political bullshit and intrigue that she forgot we were trying to prevent the *end of the world*."

I managed to keep myself from pointing out that was one of the biggest divides in the fandom. There were people vastly more interested in the Mad Queen vs. Dragon Queen plot as well as all the feuding houses over the giant zombie hordes. Same in reverse. Personally, I thought the two plots interwove well and were why the Dark Undermaster books had such a wide fanbase. But just try to share that kind of opinion on DarkUndermaster.Org.

"A reunited Ledziania would be pretty good for fighting hordes of the undead," Jon said, surprising me by showing actual interest in the world's story. "Whether it had a weredragon and her army of peasants on it or the Mad Queen and her Imperial lightning knights. Which, *oh my god*, I just now got were a reference to stormtroopers."

"Uh huh," I said. "Also, the blitzkrieg, yes."

"I mean, just because I ignored most of the plot of the games doesn't mean I was completely ignorant," Jon said, a little too defensively. "I was doing the Dragon Queen plot when I was killed! God, the animations on her outfit with all the jiggle physics…"

"The Mad Queen slaughtered my family," Ania said, shaking her head. "My father believed that Princess Celestyne was the true heir even though Apollonia was born like a minute after her. His honor and integrity brought nothing but misery to our house. The Dragon Queen has been waging war on the rest of the Southern Kingdoms ever since, fighting for her rights while the rest of the world burns."

"Plus, Garland was porking her," Jon said, nodding.

"He was porking half of the women in the Southern Kingdoms," Ania muttered, *not at all* bitter. "But I loved him despite his flaws. It's going to break Agata's heart when she finds out he's truly dead."

"How's she going to do that?" I asked, wondering just how far off script we were potentially going.

Hopefully a lot.

Agata Rose had almost as tragic a backstory as Ania but had been hated by much of the fandom for her behavior in the first book. She'd constantly bullied and insulted Garland growing up due to the latter's bastardry. She'd also been the Mad Queen's handmaiden, albeit under duress. A series of terrible marriages, abuse, and almost comical tragedy had softened the fandom's opinion toward Agata, but a lot of readers would still have been happy to see her dead. The ones who didn't confuse insults with sexual tension, at least. The last Agata had been seen was before the five-year time skip when she'd been spirited away to a Sisters of Mokosh abbey. Everyone was expecting she'd return as a religious fanatic or something worse.

"With this," Ania said, producing another bracelet. This one was red hued but recognizably a Mark of the Champion.

"Where did you that get that?" I asked, stunned.

"Valentin's body," Ania said. "Veles may resurrect him or not, but he won't have the Rheingold. He won't be able to gain any more power through this 'leveling' system."

"That cheating bastard!" Jon said, disgusted. "No wonder he was unbeatable! He was team killing the whole time."

I wasn't so sure since Jon clearly had survived an encounter with Valentin during his run. If Valentin had 'free will' for lack of a better term and was from our world, he should have just been able to kill every champion at the starting level. It would have been pragmatic behavior for a player character gone evil (Christ, I was falling into the same habit of referring to everything in RPG terms as Jon). Instead, he'd apparently just beaten them up and gone off to do whatever. It didn't make sense and implied something more was going on here than met the eye. You know, beyond being transported to a magical fairy land that ran on discount D&D rules.

"How do you think she'll react?" I asked.

"To the idea we're playthings for the gods and our brother is dead but you're walking around with his identity? Probably badly," Ania said.

Great.

"Do you know where your sister is?" I asked, uncertainly.

"Yep," Ania said, not elaborating. "At least if events hold to how they usually go down."

That wasn't reassuring.

Crossroad was a place that didn't look much better in the daytime than it did at night but at least the fires had been put out and the bodies had been collected. There were several pyres in the distance, and I had the strong suspicion that the locals had taken to cremation with the advent of the rising dead.

Still, despite all the damage, the place was quite nice to look upon from a purely aesthetic point of view. Its stone and thatched buildings spread out in a way that invoked the kind of idealized Medieval ambiance that had inspired so many RPGs over the decades. About the only thing that wasn't picturesque, aside from the burned or collapsed parts, was the smell. There was no sewer system in the town, and I was now aware as to why everyone I saw wore boots. People just threw their crap out the window.

Literally.

Crossroad wasn't a small village either and probably was bordering on the size of a town, even with the deaths from the night before as well as previous cycles. There were vast golden fields stretched out around the village as well as a small river that served as a barrier between them. Crossroad was a farming community, alright, and I could see multiple roads leading out of its corners in every point of the compass. This was probably where the place had gotten its name. There were a few more permanent looking buildings than the straw roofed houses of the locals and I noted them as we walked. There was the blacksmith, the stables, the church (or temple since Christianity didn't exist in this world), and one two story mansion that pretty much dominated the North side of the community.

"Is that the Black Cat?" I asked, staring at it.

"Yep," Ania said.

"Sex and booze seem to be very profitable around these parts," I said, blinking. It would have been considered an extremely nice home in my world.

"It usually is," Ania said. "But the Black Cat was built to cater to the Dark Undermasters after my family was driven out. It was also constructed by a retired adventurer with his fortune. Some people have interesting ways of spending their retirement."

Strangely, Jon didn't have any comment on that one.

"Maelor the Black," I said, remembering a name she said earlier.

"Got it in one," Ania said.

Maelor the Black was a character in the books but for the life of me I couldn't remember what his deal was. He only showed up in the third book in the Ania parts of the series I'd kind of skimmed past. He had some sort of secret that fans had speculated on and seemed to be set up for a larger role down the line. One thing I did note was that female readers really loved him, and he was the primary source of slash fiction as well as fan art. His being left out of the television show had caused a near-boycott of the FANT network among certain groups, at least according to Nightchilde.

"Maybe he's the companion we're supposed to find," I replied.

"Not from what I recall," Jon said. "He's a vendor and quest giver instead. Be glad, if you recruited him, you'd never get laid again. Unless you're more open minded about these things than you come off. No offense but you have serious vanilla energy."

I sighed. "Why did I have to get Charlie Sheen as my spirit animal?"

"*Eurasian* Charlie Sheen, which is like 2% cooler due to having a Japanese granddad," Jon said. "Just because I'm all black and feathery now doesn't mean I've forgotten where I come from! Modesto, California! Home of George Lucas and absolutely jack shit else."

"I remember what you look like, Jon," I said, thinking back to the handsome but awkward man who'd worked two cubicles down. The guy who absolutely insisted that he looked like a young Keanu Reeves but didn't in the slightest.

"Good," Jon muttered before lowering his voice, "One of us has to. It gets harder and harder to remember the longer I spend like this."

I made a mental vow to find a way to help Jon. Much to my surprise, that resulted in another ping from my bracelet.

HELP JON SNOWAN
Recommended Level: Any
Reward: Familiar Upgrade

"Huh," Jon said, surprised.

"Neat," I said, staring at it. "I guess there's hope after all."

We passed through the town square on our way to the Black Cat and I saw there was a crowd gathered around a man in stocks. He was huge, at least seven feet tall, with skin the shade of tanned leather and a pair of horns sticking out of his head like he was a bull. His body was decorated in thick furs, and he looked like some fantasy artist's conception of a barbarian. The crowd was throwing vegetables, cow pies, and worse at him while a crier spoke an almost indescribably foul litany of insults toward him.

The peasants of Crossroad didn't dress like I'd think Medieval people would but more like Puritans or maybe Puritans dressed like Medieval Fantasy Polish people. Either way, there was a lot of bonnets, blacks, browns, and heavy clothing that lacked anything resembling style. One thing they all seemed to share was a look of shared outrage and joy at humiliating their prisoner. There were even children among them.

"Who the hell is that?" I asked, uncomfortable with such public mob violence.

"Kragen Bloodstorm," Ania said, shaking her head. "He's a Rus berserker and a mercenary for hire. The townsfolk hired him to defend the village only for him to end up looting a merchant's home after slaughtering both him as well as his children."

"Ah," I said, losing most of my sympathy. I didn't remember such a character from the books and wondered if he was an invention for *Lords of Dragon Keep* or just one of the people that lived in this world. Then I decided it didn't matter.

"I actually recruited him as a companion," Jon said, surprising me. "He's a Warrior and good at tanking damage. His DPS isn't bad either. I mean, yeah, he suffers violent psychotic murder episodes but that's just part of his story. Plus, he's a demigod like you."

Ania looked over my shoulder. "Who is his godly parent?"

"The Crone," Jon said, as if afraid to say Baba Yaga. "Apparently, the old witch gets horny every few decades and takes a comely—"

"She's not a goddess," Ania said. "She's the mother of all hags, ogres, and other monsters, though."

I waited for the bracelet to ping and say to recruit him as a companion, but it didn't. Apparently, I'd have to make the effort to get him and wasn't sure I wanted to. I already had a Black alignment companion and one who might as well have been. I was pretty sure I wanted to do a White alignment run here, well, as much as I could if it managed to get me out of this place.

"Maybe we should ask if we could take him into our custody," I said, uncomfortable with the prospect but knowing we weren't exactly high on resources at this moment. Indeed, as Jon had pointed out, we were a Rogue and a Sorcerer (and a familiar). We were a Warrior short. You needed all three for a well-balanced party and probably a healing focused sorcerer too.

"Do what you want," Ania said. "I'm planning to make as many arrangements as we can to travel to Kalizov next."

"Kalizov?" I asked, wondering when that was decided.

"We need to complete these missions if we're going to stop Veles so we might as well try to recruit the Dragon Queen or Queen Apollonia first," Ania said. "If they can't tell you're Garland, then that might be something we can leverage. I don't know what we could offer the Jarls of the Rus or the Elves. You may have to sleep with one or both of them, though."

I stopped in mid-step. "What?"

"Clearly, I underestimated you as a companion, Ania," Jon said, sounding impressed. "I am so sorry that I drove you off by not paying attention to your approval score."

"I'm glad I don't remember you, Jon," Ania said, not bothering to stop as we passed out of the town square.

"No offense intended?" Jon asked.

"I didn't say that," Ania said, smirking.

"I'm not comfortable with that," I replied, thinking I would never want to be with someone who thought I was someone else.

I wouldn't do it.

"Yes, because your comfort is what matters," Ania muttered. "We're all going to have to make sacrifices, Imposter, if we're to save the world."

"He won't be able to pull it off," Jon said. "Believe me."

"Thank you, I think."

"I mean, *I* wasn't able to seduce the queen. What chance do you have?"

I shook my head.

CHAPTER TEN
YOU ALL MEET IN AN INN (OKAY, A BROTHEL)

We arrived at the Black Cat, and it was a place that looked out of place in the quaint little nowhere town of Crossroad, almost as much as Dragon Keep. It had frosted windows with iron bars and was made of high-quality wood. Really, the architecture looked more Renaissance than Middle Ages and there was a smell of incense about the place rather than the ever-present excrement smell.

A sign with a lounging black cat on it hung beside an awning overlooking the door. I could hear a little music coming from inside the place as well that could best be described as "generic lute music from a fantasy game."

Not really interested in delaying any further, I opened the door and headed inside. I was immediately assaulted by scents of incense, flowers, and perfumes that I suspected existed to keep as much of the outside odor out as possible. There was also a pair of doormats that were filthy but showed someone was taking hygiene seriously. The floor was also made of flagstones, and I couldn't help but think that would make it easier to clean.

Was I overthinking the Medieval fantasy world? Or was it just that my mind was way too focused on toilet matters after Jon's failed attempt to educate me on how things worked in my upgraded tower room? Seriously, if I hadn't upgraded it, I would have been using a chamber pot and I didn't even want to think about that.

The interior of the Black Cat was exceptionally large and already packed to the gills with probably a dozen tables on the first floor, a staircase leading up the second floor where there were numerous doors to what I presumed to be rooms for "business", a wooden bar that wouldn't have been out of place in my time, and the stereotypical casks of ale that dotted your typical tavern or inn. It reminded me that the laziest way of starting any tabletop RPG was to say you all met in an inn.

This was the R-rated version of such a place, though, and the lower level was full of attractive cleavage-showing waitresses and shirtless men (yay for equality, I guess) serving a mixed crowd of patrons. They were extremely well-dressed in a variety of strange clothing that I assumed were from the other five realms of the Southern Kingdoms or maybe even the Empire. There were lots of people who came to petition the Dark Undermasters for their help in solving monster problems, but they weren't going to find any of that here anymore.

I noticed the ratio of male travelers to female was also about 1:1, which surprised me but probably shouldn't have. The Dark Undermaster series hadn't skewed so heavily male as others. Indeed, it seemed to also fit the harlots I spotted above, who were basically the same as the servers but wearing much-much less.

"Fifty gold pieces a pop, huh," I muttered, not at all tempted. I figured if I was going to have sex, I'd probably want to do it with someone who wanted to be with me and probably who hadn't been with three other persons that day.

"The usual charge is five," Ania said, shaking her head. "That's not even including the Undermaster discount that Maelor usually gives. He must have really hated you, Jon."

"Guys, you're killing me," Jon said, shaking his little head.

"Only if I miss," Ania replied, absently. "My sister should be here somewhere so look at the ladies wearing hoods or veils. If you're serious about helping me, Imposter—"

"You can call me Aaron," I said, absently.

Ania paused. "*Aaron*, then you check the news board. Maelor the Black owns a printing press that he acquired from the Empire and uses it to provide the Dark Undermasters with work. We'll need to raise as much coin as possible for our trip and acquire for you better equipment. I won't have you slowing me down. You also need some experience in monster hunting."

Given she was 9th level, and I was 2nd, there was something to that logic, but I couldn't help but feel insulted. Jon may have been an ass by insisting that we were the main characters in a world with real people and real consequences but that didn't mean I wanted to be a sidekick either. I wanted to help these people and being a complete amateur wasn't going to help matters. So, against my better judgment, I was going to have to follow Jon's advice and level up fast. Otherwise, I would just be a burden, Arcane Fire and PUSH aside.

"Where do I find these Medieval Craigslist notes?" I asked, not bothering to worry about the translation.

Ania pointed literally a foot to my left where there was a bunch of notices hammered up against the wall.

"Oh," I said, blinking. "I suppose that would be it, yes."

It seemed I also needed to level up my WIS score some more.

"You can also find Pwiffle matches here or bare fisted boxing," Jon said. "You know, the usual stuff you find here."

"I have very little interest in either," I replied. "I hate Pwiffle."

Jon stared in horror. "Blasphemy."

Ania smiled. "You may have to overcome that aversion. My brother was an addict at Pwiffle, and wrestling is a good source of income."

"My stats aren't exactly optimized for that," I replied. I may look a great deal buffer in this world but that didn't translate to STR or CON bonuses.

"You should also try and sell the Skull King's armor and helmet," Ania added. "Most of the locals wouldn't touch it but Maelor will give you a thoroughly underwhelming price for it and might sell you some decent equipment in turn."

I never liked buying equipment versus acquiring it in the field when I played RPGs. I always felt like I was being cheated because the game developers knew most people would go with what they got from quests over hanging around vendors. Now that it was my life that I was playing with, I was much more comfortable buying if it meant raising my chances of survival from zero to slim. Too bad that I'd already spent most of the coin that I'd acquired from killing the Skull King. I briefly glanced at my bracelet menu to see how much I had in the way of money.

73 GP

Great.

According to Jon, that wouldn't buy me much more than a roll in the hay I didn't want.

"Right," I said, nodding. "You go look for your sister and I'll check for new quests. I'll check the broadsheets."

Ania nodded then turned to walk among the crowds, seemingly slipping among them despite the fact she should have been one of the most famous people in the region due to her historical connection with the Rose family as well as Undermasters both.

"Come on, man," Jon said. "Pwiffle, Pwiffle, Pwiffle. It's fun to say Pwiffle."

I ignored him and looked over the news board and found myself finding a few messages about missing people, food shortages, and more that I couldn't help with. It was only the papers that were marked with the Dark Undermaster's seal, a sword crossed with a staff over a skull, that I paid attention to. I made a mental note to look into the others as well, though. The "game" might not want me to do so but I was determined to do whatever I could. Each time I examined one of the notes, my bracelet updated. Apparently, it had a sense of humor by the descriptions that were greatly at odds with its previous professional tone.

SIDE QUEST(S) ADDED:

WET AND WILD GIRLS
Recommended Level: 2
Reward: 1000 EXP, *ring of protection* +1, 50 GP

Description: A mother and father want you to rescue their son from the lusty caresses of a Rusalka, a sort of *Little Mermaid* for adults.

"I felt *The Little Mermaid* was plenty adult," Jon replied. "Mind you, I didn't know Ariel was supposed to be fifteen."

"Never say that again," I replied.

"Seriously, Esmerelda is the only legal one," Jon said. "Unless you have a thing for Maleficent, which I did."

"*Everyone* had a thing for Maleficent," I replied. "There's a reason they had Angelina Jolie play her in the live action movie."

LOOK AT THE BONES
Recommended Level: 2
Reward: 1000 EXP, *boots of speed*, 50 GP
Description: A horrifying monster has taken root in the fields and slain a dozen men. Save the village from this evil!

"It's going to be a rabbit or something adorable, isn't it?" I asked Jon.

"Probably," Jon said. "We were overdue for a Monty Python reference."

RATS IN THE CELLAR
Recommended Level: 2
Reward: 1000 EXP, *cloak of protection* +1, 100 GP

"Ah, killing rats," Jon said, sighing. "The most basic of all adventurer quests."

"Is it just me or are they offering a lot of magical items at a very low level?" I asked, confused.

"There's a lot of dead Undermasters," Jon explained. "Let's just say that they probably didn't get buried with their boots on."

I'd have complained but I'd been robbing the corpses of everyone I'd slain too. "Watch there be some kind of horrifying twist on this."

"Probably," Jon admitted. "That's kind of how this world rolls."

MY KIDS LOOK LIKE THE MILKMAN
Recommended Level: 4
Reward: 5000 EXP, Pwiffle Card (Hag), 500 GP
Description: Farmer Grub thinks an incubus is visiting his wife in the afternoon. Drive it off to preserve the sanctity of their loveless, sexless marriage.

"Did the writer change for the descriptions in these bracelets or did Weis develop a sense of whimsy?" I asked, tapping it on the side.

"Trust me, this is the easiest quest in the game," Jon said, referring to his earlier recommendations for sex tourist-ing across Ledziania. "You just go to Farmer Grubs, accept the quest, and then slip Mrs. Grub the Polish sausage. She gives you the card and you lie about driving her incubus lover off. Everyone is happy and gets laid, except Farmer Grub but screw that guy. Or not in this case as he's a weird religious nut who hates fun."

"This quest seems overly generous if all you have to do is have sex with a bored housewife," I replied, not having any intention of going that route. For the noble reason of not wanting to be party to adultery and fraud as well as the less noble but no less present motivation of not wanting to be party to Jon's sloppy seconds.

"It's one of those quests that they make to trick players into thinking the game rewards creative thinking over pure combat," Jon replied. "They always throw a few quests in here that can be resolved by talking rather than murder in order to pretend it's deep or make some sort of point about multiple choice. Or a secret way to resolve the quest with unusual uses of strategic thinking."

"You mean like using PUSH to kill the boss attacking the town," I said, dryly.

"Showoff," Jon muttered. "You got lucky. I remind you that you have a WIS score of 8."

"Yeah, and I'm starting to think the average score around here is around 3-4."

Jon paused for a second. "Okay, that was actually pretty funny so I'm going to let it slide."

"What was your WIS score?" I asked.

"I'm not telling," Jon said.

There were no other notices of importance, and I was about to turn back to join with Ania when I heard a shout as well as a chair sliding off the stone cobblestones.

"Heretic! Blasphemer! Traitor! You are the one we seek!" A man spoke with a heavy German accent.

I turned around to see a table full of men in chain mail with red tabards bearing the symbol of the Empire's Golden Bull. They also had a red robed man with a shaved head and long red beard who looked less like a wizard and more like Max Von Sydow's Ming the Merciless from *Flash Gordon* (Ah-AAAHHH!! Savior of the Universe!). He was a wizard, though, because he started chanting in an alien language that wasn't quite Latin.

This would have been alarming enough if not for the fact they were clearly about to fight Ania and another woman that it took me a second to recognize as the one she'd sought. Whereas Ania was a short, tomboyish, and shapely redhead, Agata Rose was a tall and slender brunette with long dark tresses trailing down over her shoulders. She was wearing a flattering green gown with a blue hooded cloak that looked way too nice for this place (and this was the nicest place in Crossroad). She had a jeweled staff with a silver eagle on the top of it clutching a sapphire in its mouth. If she was trying to stay inconspicuous, she was failing miserably.

I wasn't sure what Larry C.C. Weis had been thinking planning to make Agata into one of Garland's companions because she'd never been an adventurer. Indeed, most of her scenes in the books had been about how stupidly romantic her worldview of heroic knights as well as handsome princes was. Weis had seemingly taken a perverse delight in torturing her and disabusing her of every romantic notion she'd held.

I prepared Arcane Fire to help when Agata slammed down the bottom of her staff against the floor, causing an explosion of blue, white energy that sent all six of the Imperials flying. She then covered herself in an ARMOR spell even as her sister moved to draw her bow, Lightbringer.

"Huh," I said, staring. "Agata Starek is a witch now."

I had not seen that coming.

"Don't just stand there, Imposter! Kill them!" Ania shouted.

"Right!" I said, firing Arcane Fire at the wizard on the ground because I assumed him to be the most dangerous. Unfortunately, this proved to be a stupid idea as the flame struck a glowing aura around him that absorbed it completely. Crap, I forgot Arcane Fire didn't work on wizards. It was one of those stupid rules made up for the books.

"Garland of Nowhere, I will have your heart and offer it up to the Emperor!" the red robed wizard said, shooting a bolt of glowing green energy that struck me in the chest. It felt like someone stuck my entire lower body in liquid nitrogen. I felt cold, sick, and worse than when I'd caught Covid-19 in 2020.

Another hit or two like that and I was dead.

PUSH wouldn't do much good here, so I decided to do something stupid and pulled out the Skull King's sword before wildly swinging it around. Much to my surprise, the blade cut through the wizard's throat, and he fell to the ground with copious amounts of black inhuman ichor flying out. His body turned gray and inhuman before disintegrating on the ground.

Damn.

Two of the Imperials had been struck down by Ania sticking two glowing arrows into the throats of the soldiers. A third had gone for Agata with his mace, only to have it bounce against her armor before she put her hand on his face and conjured Arcane Fire of her own. His death scream was horrifying but Agata didn't even flinch.

That left two Imperials, both exchanging a glance. Unfortunately, it wasn't to do the sane and rationale thing of retreating. No, surrounded by all the other brothel guests and workers watching this like a MMA fight, they turned toward me before charging. Apparently, they didn't mind if they died if they took down the great Garland of Nowhere.

This was going to suck.

CHAPTER ELEVEN
NO EASY WAY OUT IS NOT JUST A ROCKY IV SONG

The Imperial lightning knights were minor villains in the books. The comparison to stormtroopers was pretty apt. They were supposed to be some of the best trained warriors in the world and, compared to the typical levied peasant with a pitchfork, they probably were. However, the books also made them utterly useless against Garland and his companions. They tore through the lightning knights by the dozens and the supposed elite troopers were basically just excuses for action scenes. Two wouldn't have caused any of the books' heroes to sweat. Two bearing down on me with their swords was almost certain death.

It didn't help that whatever the wizard had done to me left me feeling like I was about to fall over and die. It should have been illegal to have red robed guys use ice magic, national color of the Empire or not. Still, I had the Skull King's sword in my hands and was ready to fight, even though I had almost zero ability to do so.

No saves, no continues.

I had to remember that.

"Roll!" Jon shouted, reminding me that the combat of the games was incredibly broken with its dodge mechanics.

I threw myself on the ground and rolled across the ground like Captain Kirk did fighting the Gorn. Much to my surprise, I moved with a swiftness and clarity I never possessed on Earth. The first sword attack slammed against the ground without striking me and I rolled again, dodging away from the attacking Imperial who looked at me like my actions were more silly than effective.

At least, he seemed to be looking that way before I plunged the sword into his chest. It was like sliding a knife through a slice of warm butter, his armor practically useless against the rune weapon's magic. The man's eyes sunk back into his face as his flesh became ashen then rotted away to a skeleton underneath his clothes.

It wasn't just limited to the flesh of the dead soldier, either. The chain mail rusted over and disintegrate while the red tabard rotted like it had been stunk in a flooded basement for a decade. Whatever "witchfire" was, it turned out it was damn terrifying in its effects. It reminded me of the death animation from the old, animated *Dragon's Lair* game. The effect was so shocking that I found myself frozen in place, needing a moment to breathe from my rolls.

Unfortunately, that left me wide open to the guy I'd dodged in the first place. "Die, Knight of Nowhere!"

I didn't get a chance to roll again before he came at me. He didn't get a chance to stab me, though, because a glowing arrow struck into the side of his head, sending him to the ground. Ania was standing across the room, holding it.

"You know your Arcane Fire works on regular soldiers, right?" Ania asked.

"Sorry!" I snapped. "I'm still new at this."

"Are you alright, Bastard Brother?" Agata asked, walking over to me. "You fought like a dairy farmer."

"Well, they fought like cows," I muttered, falling to one knee and feeling like I was about to vomit on the floor.

Around us, the various patrons of the brothel clapped like we'd provided a floor show. The Empire's soldiers were unpopular everywhere and a large reason why the Mad Queen was considered a monster. It had been her decree that gave them free reign of the kingdoms and the ability to enforce Imperial laws within its borders.

"They totally ripped off *Monkey Island* for *Pirates of the Caribbean*," Jon said, taking rest on the top of a wooden chair.

I checked my bracelet for just how badly I was off.

HEALTH: 3/10 (*Major Injury, Frost Sickness*)

I had no idea what Frost Sickness was but suspected it wasn't good. I ended up letting loose a horrible series of coughs and felt like throwing up.

HEALTH: 2/10 (*Major Injury, Frost Sickness*)

Crap.

I reached down and tried to cast a CURE spell. Instead, Agata lifted her staff and spoke a melodic series of words. It made me feel terrible for the fact my spells just involved saying the spell's name. It felt like I was cheating somehow.

I wasn't about to question her facility with sorcery, though, because Agata's magic moved through my body like a warm liquid. The pain in my chest subsided and I no longer felt like I was dying. Nevertheless, I checked my bracelet and saw the difference.

HEALTH: 6/10

Still, not great. So, I put my hand on my chest and spoke, "CURE."

Much to my surprise, it managed to fix everything else wrong with me. I felt better, stronger, and well rested.

Then I threw up.

HEALTH 10/10

"You should always apply a healing ointment before that," Ania said, shaking her head. "Magic may fix you up but it sure as shit hurts."

Agata sniffed the air. "You don't need to lecture our brother on such things, dear sister. He has more experience than any man alive in the combination of both swordsmanship and sorcery."

"Because all the other Dark Undermasters are dead," Jon said. "Well, except Piotr and that guy probably can only slay a leg of mutton these days. I've got to say I approve of the glow up they've given Agata, though. Her actress never got to slink around like the rest of the female cast. I think she married a One Direction member after the last season. They're probably divorced now."

Ania shot Jon a glare.

I stood up and shook my head. "Thank you for your help."

"I am here not to provide you help, Bastard Brother," Agata said, addressing me. "Instead, I come here representing the will of Mokosh. She came to me in a dream and said that it was my destiny to aid thee in driving away the Old Gods and bringing an end to the Rising Shadow. Do not think this means the things between us are settled, though. I blame thee for your role in the downfall of our house."

"Right, sure," I muttered.

"Hot," Jon said. "Clearly Weis had a thing for verbally abusive women. Him and Robert Jordan both."

AGATA ROSE HAS JOINED THE PARTY
Class: Priestess of Mokosh Sorceress
Level: 2
Alignment: White

ASSEMBLE COMPANIONS UPDATED (2/6)

+200 EXP [Ice Wizard]
+300 EXP [Storm Knights]
+500 EXP [Story Bonus]
+25 GP

Level 2 to 3
4200/5000 EXP

Ania walked over to her sister. "Hold on, Agata. Stand still."

"I do not need you arguing on his behalf as you have always—" Agata started to speak before Ania snapped the late Skull King's bracelet on her left arm.

"What is this?" Agata asked, looking like she was having a fog lifted from her eyes.

"It'll help," Ania said. "In any case, we need to talk. At length."

Before Agata had a chance to respond, she collapsed into Ania's arms and the shorter of the two sisters dragged her to a nearby wooden chair that she propped her up in.

"Is she going to be alright?" I asked.

"Yeah," Ania said. "But the memories of the past cycles are going to hit her and it's not going to be pleasant."

"She'll remember everything?" I asked, surprised.

"Not even close," Ania said. "However, there will be dreams, fragmentary visions, and hallucinations. I'll help her through it, though."

I looked around to the gathered people. "Should we really be talking about this in public?"

"We're speaking the Old Tongue," Ania replied.

"Oh," I said, shaking my head. "Of course."

This world made no sense.

"I can't believe Weis had Agata join the Sex Witches," Jon said.

"They're not sex witches," I muttered, going to check on her and wishing there was a place we could take her, but I wasn't sure I could fire man's carry her back to the keep. The upstairs was also probably occupied.

The Priestesses of Mokosh were the largest surviving organized religion in the Southern Kingdoms. All the others had fallen into disrepute. It helped the other Old Gods were jerks and the New Gods had been brought by foreign invaders. Mokosh was the goddess of the Earth, fertility, fate, harvest, and childbirth.

Also, yeah, sex.

Mokosh was kind of an Aphrodite and Gaia figure simultaneously. Weis took a *great deal* of time describing their temple prostitution and holy sexual rites. Obviously, that had been of great interest in teenage me but now seemed kind of embarrassing as me missing the subtleties of the faith. Nightchilde said they represented Pre-Christian female worship that was totally not just a horny old man writing about a bunch of sexy mages.

"Oh, they're *absolutely* sex witches," Ania said, checking her sister's eyes as if she was seeing if she had a concussion. "Mom would be scandalized by her joining. Good."

Ah, yes. Lady Maria Rose and Ania hadn't had a chance to reconnect before she'd become one of the living dead. I tried to remember if Ania knew about her mother's transformation or whether she just thought Maria was dead-dead. If so, that would be an awkward conversation.

"Do you need help getting her anywhere?" I asked.

"I'm good," Ania said. "You need to deal with the owner. See if you can smooth things over with him."

"What?" I asked.

Ania hoisted up Agata over her shoulder and carried her to the door. "Use that Charisma score of yours!"

I tried to parse the logic of a literary character, who was a real person, referring to game mechanics that only existed because of an author from her world licensing a video game from her non-fictional life. That wasn't down the rabbit hole or through the looking glass, that was straight up turtles all the way down.

The vast number of conversations occurring stopped at his presence, which surprised me since it implied that he was a lot more important than "local pimp and tavern keep" might imply.

In the simplest terms, Maelor the Black did not look like he belonged in a Medieval Fantasy World. Not even with the Renaissance Age architecture of his brothel. No, instead I'd say he looked more like he belonged in a Goth Rock band from the Nineties. The guy was wearing an open button silk shirt that showed his hairless chest, smoked black lensed glasses that weren't anachronistic but still looked damned strange for our surroundings, and had black pants that I was pretty sure were the scales of some kind of giant lizard.

The dude himself was not human and I mean that in the most literal sense. He was probably an elf by the pointed ears, ivory white skin, and slightly off proportions. Elves in the Dark Undermaster series were on the tall side rather than short with him about six or six five, towering over most of the people here. There were other tiny things that drew attention like the fact that he had tufts of hair behind his ears, two fingers on each hand that were identical in length, and arms that were unusually long.

Which told me he was a vampire.

Now you might be confused about how I came to this conclusion. I don't blame you. We were, in fact, in the middle of the daytime. However, vampires (or "strigoi" if you wanted to be traditional) in this universe were like Blade or the Cullen family in that they didn't die in the sun. The lesser versions had to sleep during the day, but it wasn't quite as dramatic as in movies. The more powerful, strigoi nobles, could go about in the day just fine.

I tried to remember if Maelor had been a vampire in his brief appearance or if this was a new development, but my mind was blanking. A lot of characters had been cut from the show after all. Anyway, my brilliant deductive powers knew a vampire when I saw one. That and he looked identical to the art for the Pwiffle (Vampire) collectible card. Yeah-yeah, I'm talking myself up. What can I say? I wasn't sure that my chief advantage here on this world was the fact I had a passing familiarity with its version of the *Monstrous Manual*. I probably should have realized they were the same character but blame the low WIS score.

"Garland, my boy," Maelor spoke in a smooth accent that invoked the kind of romance fiction that Nightchilde loved, "you have certainly made a mess here, haven't you?"

Maelor was handsome, I should point out. No matter how much he should have evoked the uncanny valley affect, he was close enough to a human in appearance that even I had slight movement on my personal Kinsey scale. Like 0 to .1. He was like Neil Gaiman's Dream crossed with Andrew Eldritch or Elliot Smith.

"Yeah," I said, uncomfortable. "Old friend. I certainly did make…a mess."

Yeah, my Garland impression could use some work.

"Whatever am I to do with you?" Maelor asked.

"We need to talk," I said, pausing. I wasn't comfortable with crowds and dead bodies. Which I suspected was a thing I was going to have to get over. "I would like to buy some goods. Special goods."

I'd remembered that Jon described him as a vendor. I really hoped this would pan out. Also, I really hoped once we were in private that he didn't go for my proverbial throat. Wait, no, not proverbial. Go for my literal throat.

Maelor's eyes brightened. "Ah! Why didn't you say you came here for business! Follow me!"

Jon leapt on my shoulder like a pirate's parrot before we followed him. "Well, this is slightly off-script."

Maelor went behind his bar and opened a trap door leading to a stepladder. We were heading into the cellar of the Black Cat.

"How so?" I asked.

"There weren't any Imperial soldiers during my loop, let alone a wizard," Jon said. "Someone is altering the story."

CHAPTER TWELVE
I CAN QUIT ANY TIME I WANT TO

The Black Cat's cellar wasn't really any different from a typical basement. There were more casks, some crates, and straw on the flagstone but I was still unnerved. Probably because I was going there with a vampire. It didn't help that strigoi noblemen were always at least rated for 10th to 12th level characters in the previous games, if not full bosses. It was pitch black except for the light streaming in from the open door to the bar above.

"Someone should light a candle," I said, absently.

Maelor snapped his fingers, and the room suddenly had a dozen lanterns burning across it. It was a sign he was a sorcerer as well as a vampire, which I probably should have suspected.

"Oh, neat," I replied.

A rat skittered across the floor before Maelor grabbed it with one hand and bit its head off before spitting the head to the side and pouring the resulting blood into his mouth. A row of shark-like teeth was visible, very different from your typical Bela Lugosi fangs. Maelor promptly threw the rat to one side. "I'm sorry, would you like something to drink?"

The trapdoor behind me slammed shut of its own accord.

I stared. "So, we're not going to even pretend, are we?"

"Why?" Maelor asked in his seductive voice. "Garland knew what I was, and you are Garland. Aren't you?"

I narrowed my eyes. "So, yeah, what have you got?"

"Why don't you consult that little pretty piece of jewelry?" Maelor asked, walking up to a nearby support beam and crossing his arms.

I did so, wondering how much Maelor knew, exactly.

MAELOR'S SPECIAL INVENTORY

* *LEATHER ARMOR +1*; 500 GP
* *LEATHER BOOT +1*; 250 GP
* *CLOAK +1*; 250 GP
* *LEATHER VAMBRACES +1*; 300 GP
* *ALCHEMICAL POTION* [Health]; 150 GP

I stared at the numbers and shook my head. "Yeah, I don't think I'm going to be able to afford any of this. Blame the castle upkeep."

"You can try selling me the items you took off the late Skull King," Maelor said, absently. "I suspect they're worth a pretty penny."

I wondered how pretty penny translated as: pretty ceramic piece? Coinage was rare in the books with it being mostly for foreign trade and higher value goods. It was why the prices in the game were ridiculous, even with devalued coinage. Garland was apparently always getting ripped off by the locals who knew he was carrying a bunch of treasure looted from monsters. It really made me wonder why he bothered with helping the townsfolk in the first place. Oh, right, because it was the 'good' and 'noble' thing to do.

Pardon my inner Jon Snowan coming out there.

"Yeah, I guess I should examine what that's worth," I said, once more consulting my bracelet. I was starting to feel like a *Fallout* protagonist with their PipBoy. Either that or my sister when she first got her phone as a teenager.

I went to the equipment menu and looked up the stats on the Skull King's armaments:

* *GHOST SWORD +5* [Witchfire Status Effect, Necromantic Damage]; Value 7,500 GP

* *GHOST ARMOR* +5 [Heavy, Immunity to Fear, Necromantic Effects]; Value 10,000 GP
* *GHOST HELMET* +5 [Bonus to Intimidation Checks, Immune to Critical Hits, Ice Damage Halved]; Value 10,000 GP

"Wow, these are way overpowered for the starting area," I muttered. "Do the bonuses even go over +5 in these games?"

"Nope!" Jon said, staring. "This is endgame content stuff. Skull King was bringing a gun to a knife fight."

At least it explained why I was able to kill two guys with a sword despite never having wielded one in my life. Funny how that bothered me no more than blasting the skeletons and zombies apart did.

"How much will you give me for them?" I asked.

"A hundred gold each," Maelor said, absently.

I stared at him. That wasn't even enough for a one to one with the already overpriced starting equipment here. "Really? You couldn't throw in some shiny beads? I've been cheated less by my internet provider."

Maelor shrugged, ignoring the anachronism of my comment. "You can't wear most of it as a sorcerer anyway. Magic is fundamentally the stuff of unreality and steel arms are made from iron, the antithesis of the Otherworld that provides all the magic to the world. That is why you must keep your armaments to a minimum."

"Nice justification for a game balance rule Gary Gygax came up with," Jon said, snorting. "Explain Darth Vader then! He was all iron!"

I shook my head. "I think I'll wait for a better vendor or to use these to arm someone else. Maybe I'll have a Warrior companion later."

"Every bit of armament you have is a potential salvation for your life," Maelor said, subtly threatening. "Can you really put a price on that?"

"Yes," I said, annoyed. "You literally just did."

Maelor nodded, acknowledging the point. "There's another option for you to potentially turn your limited funds into something worthwhile, Garland."

"And that is?" I asked, hating being referred to by that name.

Maelor conjured a deck of cards in his hand, waxy slips of hard paper. "A friendly game of Pwiffle."

"Yes!" Jon said, flapping his wings enthusiastically.

"And what if I *hate* Pwiffle?" I asked, staring at him. I *really* didn't want to get back into playing that game.

"Then you'd have undergone an extremely large change, Garland," Maelor said, lowering his sunglasses onto the bridge of his nose. "You *love* this game."

"Yeah, there's a lot of that going around lately," I said.

"Perhaps you've forgotten how easy it is to win. Pwiffle is a very easy game to master," Maelor said. "I can explain the rules to you if you want. A refresher if you've suffered one too many blows to the head."

I stared at him, fury in my eyes. I really didn't want to be dragged into this black hole of a game again. "I know how to play goddamn Pwiffle. It's a variant of poker with 52 cards based on a typical deck but with the four elements: Earth, Air, Fire, and Water standing in for Clubs, Diamonds, Spades, and Hearts. The Jokers are replaced with Collectible Cards that you can only spend in that session. You can insert one of five collectible cards you've picked each hand in a typical game that lasts five hands. Which is only relevant for tournament play. These cards have ridiculous abilities like making you change the value of a 2 to an Ace or the opponent must throw away one card. The collectible cards existing to justify *meaningless side-questing* in the video games and buying endless amounts of disposable packs of cards that maybe have a 1% chance of containing a genuinely rare Pwiffle card."

Maelor blinked, which I hadn't seen him do until then. "Yes, I suppose that is, in fact, how you play Pwiffle."

"Damn, Aaron, did a deck of Pwiffle kill your dog?" Jon asked, looking at me. "Did you go on a John Wick campaign of vengeance afterward?"

I sighed, dealing with painful memories being dredged up by the prospect of another round of the world's most addictive card game. Well, after *Magic: The Gathering*. "No, it's much-much worse."

"How?" Jon asked.

"Yes, how?" Maelor asked.

I did a double take as did Jon. "Wait, you can understand him?"

"Yeah, I never would have done so much trash talking if I'd known you were hearing other than squawking," Jon said. "That might be dangerous."

"I'm a vampire, he's a raven, so yes, I can understand him," Maelor said, rolling his eyes. "I can also understand rats and wolves."

I nodded. It made about as much sense as anything else in this world. "So, when you hear things like video games…"

Maelor sighed, which was the first act of breathing I'd seen him perform. "Yes, I'm aware you're not actually Ser Garland, that you're from another world, and you're part of the ridiculous war between Veles and Perun's Chosen."

"Weis is Perun's Chosen?" I asked, only now picking up on that. Earlier, Skull King had called him Perun's Voice, so it made sense, I guess. It seemed the Wise Man had been holding out on us.

"Yes," Maelor said. "Quite a bit of loyalty to a dead god. Veles defeated his brother decades ago and scattered his essence. The Wise Man has been undermining Veles rather than engaging in open warfare ever since. I don't have one of those magic bracelets you all sport to hold back the magic, but I don't need one. Creatures of Veles or the Underworld don't get affected by the spell Weis cast to make us all think Garland is still alive."

That was a lot to process. "So, you're a creature of Veles? Did you take part—"

"No," Maelor said, quite sharply. "I had nothing to do with the attack on Crossroad. This is my home after all, and the Dark Undermasters were my best customers. You'll find that quite a lot of us 'creatures of darkness' consider our god's cosmic temper tantrum to be embarrassing. I'm not even sure why he wants to destroy the world. Maybe because Perun created it as a gift for Mokosh and she chose the Sky Lord over him."

Jon stared. "The Dark Lord wants to destroy the world because of a girl he liked?"

"Yes, pathetic, isn't it?" Maelor asked.

"It is *so* relatable," Jon said. "Like Raistlin Majere, the greatest fantasy character of all time."

"Clearly you misspelled Arya Stark," I said, pondering Maelor's words. I had to admit, that put an interesting spin on things. "So, not every creature of darkness, err, no offense, is going to be an enemy? Some just want to live their lives doing, uh, creature of darkness-y things?"

I wasn't a great believer in absolute good versus evil, White alignment run or not, so it was reassuring that I wouldn't necessarily have to take a genocidal war to the bad guy's faction. Maybe we could even make some friends.

Maelor scrunched up his nose as if smelling something bad. "I wouldn't necessarily go putting too much faith in the neutrality, let alone goodness, of my compatriots' hearts. Some of the strigoi nobles, death lords, and zmei are powerful enough to resist our god's commands but most of the rank and file are near mindless horrors. Driven mad by their time in the Underworld or monsters created specifically to destroy humanity. Others are working for Veles and his lieutenants because of payment or a belief they will be spared."

I'd have pointed out how stupid a person had to be to let themselves be bribed into helping destroy the world, but you only had to turn on the news to see someone who would. "Got it. Not all of Sauron's forces are evil but most of them are."

"I don't know who that is," Maelor said. "You still haven't explained why you hate Pwiffle."

Lestat here was taking this awfully personally. They were like drug dealers from the old 80s PSAs. I'd been surprised to find in real life that you had to go to them if you wanted weed. They weren't handing out free samples. "Why do you care?"

Maelor looked embarrassed and adjusted his smoked glasses with one finger. Yes, that one. "I'm a *vampire*."

"Yes, and?" I asked. Which is a weird way to talk to a walking dead man but here we were.

"We're obsessed with counting," Maelor explained. "Sunflower seeds, blades of grass, coins, and more. It's one of our direst weaknesses. I wouldn't share it with you if not for the fact I, mostly, have it under control. However, it means that I love card games. The more numbers the better."

I cocked my head to one side. "That's a real vampire weakness? What the Count from *Sesame Street* suffers from?"

Maelor looked annoyed. Obviously, he had no idea who that was.

"Man, let me tell you about the rules this world functions on," Jon said. "So many stats, you wouldn't believe it. Attributes, hit points, armor class, modifiers—"

"Please don't," I said, suspecting we'd be here all day (or all night as the case may be), if I let Jon explain how tabletop games worked.

Maelor stared at me, and I felt the hairs on the back of my neck rise up. "Just indulge me, Garland."

"It's *Aaron*," I corrected.

"But for everyone else, it is Garland and since the real one isn't coming back any time soon, you should get used to it," Maelor said. "The people have very little hope and a lot of it is tied in folk heroes like him. They'll need that hope more than ever now that the Dark Undermasters are effectively destroyed."

That was a gut punch as a longstanding fan of the books as well as someone doing the basic math that a world that was being overrun with demons no longer having any demon hunters was probably in serious trouble. "Yeah, it's like Luke's Jedi Order being destroyed. All the effort to rebuild it by Garland has gone poof."

"The sequels don't count," Jon explained. "We only count the original movies and, I never thought I'd say this, the prequels. Only because the Clone Wars cartoons were awesome. George Lucas' stuff counts and maybe the Thrawn Trilogy."

"Uh—"

"So why do you hate Pwiffle?" Jon asked, switching subjects rapidly. "Enquiring ravens want to know."

I sighed, realizing I wasn't going to get out of this. "Fine, I don't like to talk about it but if I'm cornered, I'm cornered. I had a Pwiffle problem."

"A Pwiffle *problem*?" Jon asked.

This was so embarrassing. I raised my voice and glared at both individuals interrogating me. "I was an addict, okay? About three years ago, I started getting into the card game. Like really-really into it. I found out I had an employee discount at Epic Dungoneering™'s online store. Soon, I was card hunting and sneaking time to do online games. My relationship with Nightchilde suffered and I was doing online bids that I couldn't really afford. I wasted three months of my life trying to get a Witch Queen of Angho'horak nude and not because I was a pervert but because she gave a redraw upon defeat perk until they errated it out."

"Uh huh," Jon said, acting like he hadn't spent our entire relationship talking about how important the game was to him in this universe.

"What happened?" Maelor asked, sounding surprisingly interested.

I pinched the bridge of my nose. "I must have blown like $10,000 on my card game habit and that wasn't money I could afford as a suffering office drone. Finally, Arwen and my cousin, Alek, intervened when I started hitting my parents up for rare card money. Money that should have gone to my rent. They got me some online therapy and to go cold turkey. I ended up donating my entire collection to my nephew."

"Wow," Jon said. "I did not see that part of your past coming."

I frowned. "Little Georgie traded them all for Pokemon cards. Oh, and a month's supply of green tea Kit-Kats."

"Fascinating and tragic," Maelor said, putting one palm against the side of his face. "Now we *have* to play a game of Pwiffle."

"Like hell we do," I said.

SIDE QUEST(S) ADDED:

PLAY GAME OF PWIFFLE (0/1)
REWARD: 200 EXP, Pwiffle Card (Garland)

I growled, literally growled, at my bracelet. "It's a *SIDE QUEST*, it's *optional*."

"You need the experience, dude," Jon said, showing no sympathy whatsoever to my tragic backstory. "We're almost to level 3."

"I also revealed vital details about Veles to you," Maelor said, pointing at me in a thoroughly modern gesture. "In the words of the Wise Man, *you owe me*."

I wasn't sure that was something Weis had ever said but the old urge was still waiting there, hungry for colorful pictures and numbers. "Fine, one game. You'll have to provide the deck."

"Of course."

This was a terrible idea.

CHAPTER THIRTEEN
UNLUCKY AT LOVE, LUCKY AT CARDS

Playing Pwiffle with Maelor was, in fact, a terrible idea because I can't tell you what happened next. I literally have no memory of the next few hours because I regressed to a strange dream-like state where the world became nothing but numbers and overly sexy fantasy art. Cleavage sporting sorceresses, beefy guys with hefty swords, semi-nude half-human monsters, and the occasional landscape. It was a universe I lost myself into every bit as all-consuming as this one. Mind you, I was severely hampered by using someone else's deck and having no collectible cards.

ACHIEVEMENT UNLOCKED: Breaking the Bank
(A) 25 - Completely clean out an opponent at Pwiffle

I blinked. "What in the world?"

Maelor was sitting across from me, the two of us playing over a barrel of ale with several cards between us. He had removed his smoked glasses and was looking defeated. Indeed, his expression was one of sheer disbelief. Notably, beside me, was the entire contents of his "Secret Stash" while my purse felt a great deal heavier.

"Holy crap," Jon said, stunned. "That was like watching Ali box."

"Did I win?" I asked, blinking.

Maelor looked up, his expression one of disgust. "*Did you win?*"

SIDE QUEST(S) COMPLETED:

PLAY GAME OF PWIFFLE (1/1)

+300 EXP
+ 562 GP
+ YOU HAVE RECEIVED PWIFFLE CARD (GARLAND)
+ YOU HAVE RECEIVED STUDDED *LEATHER ARMOR* +1
+ YOU HAVE RECEIVED *LEATHER BOOTS* +1
+ YOU HAVE RECEIVED *CLOAK* +1
+ YOU HAVE RECEIVED *LEATHER VAMBRACES* +1
+ YOU HAVE RECEIVED *ALCHEMICAL POTION* [Heath]

Level 2 to 3
4500/5000 EXP

I checked my bracelet and noticed the in-game clock said it had been about three and a half hours since we'd started our game. My carrying capacity was also close to being full again, even with the alchemical stone, which made me wonder if I should get rid of the Skull King's armor and helmet anyway. Instead, I decided to hold onto it for a bit since obviously Maelor wasn't going to be able to pay for it.

I took a deep breath. "I should have warned you, I'm really-really good at Pwiffle."

"You hustled me," Maelor said, nodding in respect. "I would be furious and going for your throat right now if not for the fact I run a business that is hardly going to be running out of money. That and I have all those dead Imperials' possessions in their rooms to cover the loss."

"Right," I said, still feeling a little guilty. "Well, all this equipment will go to helping protect the people of Ledziania."

"I could not care less," Maelor said, packing up his deck. "Still, a deal is a deal and I'm not one to imp on one."

I wondered if that was a slur against Imperials or literal imps. "Right. Sorry."

"Never be sorry for winning. Take your winnings and go. Though I wouldn't mind if you decided to waste some of that gold upstairs on my girls, or boys. I could give you the four-course meal. Only 200 GP."

"Ooo," Jon said.

"I wouldn't even know where to begin," I said, before amending. "No, no just no. I'm strictly a one-woman kind of guy except for that one time at DungeoneeringCon 2017 because it turns out geek girls get wild at those, and they were cosplaying as…you know I'm not going to bring that up. Let me just say that if there's anything I can do to make it up to you, I'd be happy to do it."

Jon slapped his beak with his wing. "Dammit, Aaron."

"What?" I asked, confused.

Jon stared at me with his beady little eyes. "Think about your words."

Oh right, I just offered to a do a favor for a vampire crime boss pimp dude. Probably not a good idea.

Maelor smiled. "There is something you could do for me, Garland."

"I'm going to regret this, aren't I?" I asked.

"Yes," Maelor said.

I tapped my bracelet several times and my preexisting armor transformed before my eyes to become a sturdier black leather while the rest of my clothes became firmer. It was another magical display of the Mark of the Champion that wasn't really necessary. I could just pull on and off my own boots after all, though I was grateful not to change in public.

AC 1 is now AC 5

I stared at the bracelet. "Seriously? The leather armor only adds a +1 total? I mean the others add to the total, but you'd think a full suit of armor would do more than just leather bracers. What is this?"

"You're only covering roughly the same area," Maelor said, surprisingly insightful. "After all, why should leather armor that doesn't cover your feet add to the protection of your leather boots?

Really, every part of your body should have a separate protection score. However, that's magic for you."

"You seem awfully well versed in how my mark works," I replied, shaking my head. "Just how much do you know?"

"Enough," Maelor said. "Now are you going to do me a favor to make up for all the money and supplies you took from me or not?"

I narrowed my eyes. "Wait, did you let me win?"

Maelor gave an enigmatic smile. "Any answer I give would probably be a lie so you should treat them as such. I am, after all, a vampire."

He had a point there. "Alright, lay it on me, Pimpula."

"I wish you to rescue my son, Kragen Bloodstorm," Maelor said, frowning at my name for him. "He's in trouble again as you may have seen on your way in."

"You want me to rescue a guy who betrayed the town and murdered a family?" I asked.

"Will that be a problem?" Maelor asked.

"Eh, maybe?" I asked, surprisingly indecisive on this. After all, we were dealing with the apocalypse and every hand helped. On the other hand, the bracelet had probably been programmed by Larry C.C. Weis and I owed that guy (in the words of *Army of Darkness*' Ash) jack and shit and jack left town. If he wanted me to recruit Bloodstorm, maybe I should stay as far away from him as possible.

Maelor shrugged. "I am thoroughly biased on the man's behalf, but I should mention that the townsfolk are entirely wrong about his deeds."

"He didn't kill children?" I asked.

"Oh no, he did but they were evil children," Maelor explained. "Hollowed. That's what happens when Veles reanimated the corpses of stillbirths, substitutes them as changelings in the homes of couples, and proceeds to send them as sleeper agents into the world of men."

I stared at him. "That is *messed up*."

"Indeed," Maelor said. "Bloodstorm figured out that the late merchant, Borys, and his two boys were cultists of Veles. Individuals who opened the gates for Veles' forces. Bloodstorm couldn't prevent their actions before it was too late but punished their misdeeds. Admittedly, it probably didn't help his reputation to be found looting the man's house during the invasion, but all adventurers are entitled to the possessions of their defeated foes."

I'd have argued the point, but I'd have been a massive hypocrite. "So, he's innocent."

"Of sorts," Maelor said. "My son is still an individual with a berserker's fury and a history of intemperate decision making. He possesses both the blood of a vampire and the Little Grandmother running through his veins. Both naturally draw him to evil and darkness, but he's made it his point to try to direct that against people society would be better off without."

Great, I was recruiting Angel from *Buffy: The Vampire Slayer*. I tried to think of anything else. "Oh, wow, you were with Baba Yaga, huh?"

Okay, bad decision on what to think about instead.

"And she's black, huh?" Jon asked. "Because Bloodstorm certainly doesn't take after you looks wise."

"I'd avoid mentioning her name," Maelor said. 'The Little Grandmother might hear it and eat you or members of your family."

I paused. I made a key turning gesture in front of my mouth. "Right."

"As for her race, she is older than humanity and came with the first humans into the Rus lands on both worlds, back when travel between them was easier," Maelor said. "As for the circumstances of his conception, I was spectacularly drunk on blood and wine."

"Those beer, or should I say blood, goggles will get you every time," I said, nodding.

"We should help him," Jon said. "When he was my partner, he was a really good boost to our party."

"You want to help your friend," I said, nodding.

"Hell no," Jon said. "I want to get the experience. We're this close to hitting level 3. I was here for days before I hit that."

I sighed. "Is there anything we can do to convince the locals to let Bloodstorm go?"

"Gold will help," Maelor replied. "Unfortunately, my son's chief tormentor is not someone who is likely to submit to the authority of a Dark Undermaster. Even one as well-respected and seasoned as Ser Garland of Nowhere. My son is in the hands of Father Adolf."

"Yikes!" I said, grimacing. "That is not a good name."

Maelor looked confused. "What's wrong with Adolf?"

Yeah, they wouldn't know about that name's history here.

"Let's just say that everyone with that name will prefer to go by Dolph after some things happened in my world," I replied, understating matters tremendously. "They'd rather share a name with a big Russian boxer than the other guy."

Maelor didn't press the issue. "Father Adolf is the local priest of Mythras. After the Mad Queen opened the Southern Kingdoms to the Empire's soldiers, the Imperials also sent their missionaries out to try and convert everyone to their Sun God. They teach the Old Gods are a bunch of murderous and insane monsters while everyone who serves them is a traitor to humanity."

I grimaced. "I mean, aren't they kind of right?"

"There's a few who aren't completely mad still," Maelor said. "But the Empire's interpretation of their god is a horror show to anyone who cherishes even the slightest bit of freedom. It oppresses women, demonizes the body, and persecutes all nonhumans as vermin. Father Adolf has been trying to drive me out as an elf for years. He has also sought the deaths of the local domovoy, rusalka, and ratkin alike."

"Yeah," I said. "I vaguely remember those from the games. So, local religious leader is also a bigot, and your son is part elf as well as part-ogre. Rescue him and we're square. Got it."

MAIN QUEST UPDATED:

RESCUE KRAGEN BLOODSTORM
Recommended Level: 3
Reward: +500 EXP, Companion
Description: Kragen Bloodstorm is the best at what he does and what he does isn't very nice. He may be a murderous rotten

scoundrel and berserker but he's our murderous rotten scoundrel and berserker.

SIDE QUEST(S) UPDATED:

FIRE AND FAITH
Recommended Level: 3
Reward: +500 EXP, *Token of Faith*
Description: Father Adolf is the kind of guy who gives the Cult of Mythras a bad name and that's saying something given its history of genocide and oppression. Shut down his operation before it gets even more Inquisition-y on the local nonhumans.

"Ugh, not this crap again," Jon murmured.

"Excuse me?" I asked.

"It's just since the 21st century, every piece of media seems determined to tell us that, ugh, prejudice is wrong."

"Someone clearly never watched 'Let this be our Last Battlefield' on the original Trek," I replied.

"Wow, you may even be a bigger nerd than I am," Jon replied. "Listen, I'm a bi Asian kid who got bullied worse than Daniel-san at school. I *know* prejudice exists; I'm just saying corporate media making Rey a Mary Sue isn't going to solve it."

"Daisy Ridley was good in *Murder on the Orient Express*," I said, pausing. "It was just a bad set of scripts."

"I *know* it was a bad set of scripts," Jon said, annoyed. "It's just you're way too nice about these things, Aaron. Embrace your inner hatedom."

"No thank you. Honestly, the handling of Mythras here is weird," I muttered, switching topics. "The original Mithras cults of the Pre-Christian Roman Empire involved underground rituals where an initiate would have sex with a woman covered in beer to symbolize their union with a God. It wasn't an uptight religion."

Jon and Maelor both looked at me strangely.

"My degree is in computer programming, but I got to take some fun classes in folklore and mythology," I replied.

"So, classes in useless," Jon said. "I bet your parents were proud."

"Sadly, they were," I muttered. "They were disappointed I didn't get my doctorate in it. Then I could teach at the Community College while taking over the family pot stores."

Another reason never to go to drug dealers for weed was the fact that family will always give you a big discount.

"In any case, I didn't have any trouble with Father Asshat," Jon said. "A little gold and some flattery, you'll be able to talk him down from killing Kragen Bloodstorm."

CHAPTER FOURTEEN
BURN THE WITCH! TOO BAD I'M THE WITCH

"Okay, that didn't go great," I said, struggling in the ropes that presently tied me to a large wooden stake with a bunch of straw and kindling at its base. A few feet to my right stood Kragen Bloodstorm, who was also about to be burned to death. They had him on his knees due to not having a sufficiently tall enough piece of wood to tie him to. We were both on a stone platform that had apparently been constructed for the purposes of public executions.

Wonderful people, these Crossroad villagers.

There was a large crowd gathered around for our witch-burning, or heretic-burning, or just general burning-burning. Not all the crowd looked enthusiastic about my execution, but others were swept up in the fervor and it was a universal truth that no matter who it was happening to, plenty of people loved it when someone else was suffering.

As you could probably surmise, I didn't do well in my negotiations with the insane priest, Father Adolf. Said priest was presently ranting to a crowd gathered around a bonfire in the shadow of his temple. Sort of a pre-burning light show. It was a little past noon and that was apparently prime sacrificing time to Father Adolf's sun deity.

Father Adolf had a long gray beard, wrinkled skin, and insane eyes that twitched with the kind of fervor that told you he was getting off on this. He was dressed in a hooded robe of a slightly different style than the wizard I'd killed in the Black Cat. Instead of a bull on the front, he had a glowing sun symbol sewn in. Adolf was still a sorcerer, though, which he'd demonstrated by knocking me cold with a SLEEP spell. Not my finest moment. Several glass vials of oil were tied to his belt, and I had no doubt those would be used to expedite my demise.

"Yeah, I'd say it went poorly," Bloodstorm said in a big baritone voice that was the most Slavic sounding thing I'd heard so far.

"Nice to meet you, Kragen."

"I prefer Bloodstorm," Bloodstorm said. "Nice to meet you too, Garland."

"I prefer Aaron," I replied.

"Sure, Garland," Bloodstorm said. "Whatever you say."

Ugh. I was about to die, and I was stuck in a Laurel and Hardy skit.

Jon flew up around the pole and sat on its top. "All you had to do was flatter the religious fanatic and pay him some gold but, no, you had to call him Father Asshat and try to cheap out on the bribe."

"The asshat thing just slipped out! Besides, 500 GP is way too much!" I snapped, feeling embarrassed how completely south this had all gone and quickly. "I have to buy a new drawbridge and castle door to impress Ania!"

"Screw the door!" Jon said. "You're about to become a raven and that's going to look terrible on my record!"

Jon had a point. He was a jerk, but he had a point.

"People of Crossroad, I show you the unbeliever! The blasphemer! Yesterday, our beloved community was attacked by the foul unholy legions of your old gods! Creatures of impurity and licentiousness."

"I'm pretty sure that skeletons aren't licentious," I said, making use of my *Taunt* ability. Presumably. I didn't know where it versus just insulting people really differed. Assuming there was a difference. "You need fleshy bits for that."

"I dunno, I knew this one necromancer chick who used bones to—" Bloodstorm said to me, proving he was joining exactly the right kind of group.

"Silence!" Father Adolf shouted back at me with the kind of shrill voice you might have given an Eighties cartoon villain. "The Dark

Undermasters rejected the true god, Mythras, Lord of the Sun, Warrior Defender of Mankind, and embraced the darkness of false deities! The Dark Undermasters have tolerated heathens, unbelievers, and the foul nonhumans among their ranks too long! Mythras sent the ill fortune and disaster that we suffered last night as punishment for the Undermasters' sins."

"I think Veles sent the hordes of skeletons and revenants," Bloodstorm added. "What with them being all raised by Veles and wearing his symbol."

"Mythras is all!" Father Adolf said. "His will is in every event that has transpired!"

"Well, that just makes Mythras look like a dickhead!" I shouted, trying to see if I could use my Arcane Fire to burn off my ropes. I could feel my bonds burning away but slowly. Apparently, Father Adolf didn't have any ways to suppress magic other than binding someone's hands as well as gagging a man. He hadn't done the latter because they wanted me to confess or something.

Father Adolf also probably thought I couldn't throw any spells around without him clocking on to them. However, my magic didn't require any of the stuff that everyone else's did. It meant I could get loose easily but escaping was another matter entirely, especially with this guy riling up the mob like he was.

"Aaron, what are you doing?" Jon asked.

"What sort of just god punishes mothers, fathers, sons, and daughters for the crimes of another!" I addressed the crowd. "What sort of god unleashes the horrors of the dead, dragons, and demons upon people anyway! Is not life miserable enough!"

"You, Garland, are the worst of them all!" Father Adolf said, shouting at me. "A creature of unholy false god blood that has polluted these kingdoms with their treason, murder, as well as incest!"

"Not blood siblings!" Jon said. "Anime has taught us that is perfectly alright!"

"Really?" Bloodstorm asked, looking at Jon. "That's messed up, friend."

I glared at him. "Your mother is a hag, and your father is a vampire. Which is why you can understand Jon, I assume."

"Yeah, but my parents aren't related," Bloodstorm said, offended. "Adopted siblings are still siblings."

I rolled my eyes before continuing to address the crowd. "I know not any false blood! Mine bleeds red the same as any man's! As for incest, you know the Rose family! A generation ago, they were noble and kind lords who were open handed as well as decent to all those under their command! It was the Empire and their treacherous puppet queen that sacked this town! They do not command the Old Gods and they do not hold the key to stopping your misfortunes!"

I managed to burn myself free but didn't immediately jump away. I could tell the crowd was listening and that was the important thing. Also, I wanted Father Adolf's attention divided between me and his audience.

"You speak treason!" Father Adolf shouted. "There is one true queen of the Southern Kingdoms, it is Apollonia—"

That turned the crowd against Father Adolf almost instantly as a chorus of jeers, boos, and profanity filled the air. As much as they might have been hesitant to speak in Garlands defense, they absolutely *detested* the Mad Queen.

"Silence! Silence! She is anointed by the One True God and called sister by the Emperor of All!" Father Adolf shouted, trying to calm them. He was ignoring me now.

It was the perfect opportunity to climb up and go to Bloodstorm's side, burning the ropes. "Want to help me deal with this?"

Bloodstorm grinned. "Damned right."

My distraction didn't last long as Father Adolf turned around to look at us both with a furious, well, even more furious, expression on his face. "Blasphemers! I will smite thee with the power of Mythras!"

"Needs to diversify his material," Bloodstorm said, standing up and looking more like a mountain than a man.

"You speak very strange for—" I started to say.

"For a half-vampire ogre? Don't make this a race thing," Bloodstorm said, charging at Father Adolf.

Father Adolf waved his hand and from it a glowing bull emerged. It was massive with thick horns and slightly translucent. "I strike thee down with the Golden Bull of the Empire! Send these fools back to their Dark God's Underworld!"

Bloodstorm switched targets to punch the spectral bull in the face, locking horns, literally, and starting to wrestle with it.

"Oh, come on, Mithras fought the cosmic bull! He didn't command it!" I muttered, shaking my head. "This is just bad mythology!"

"Not the time, Aaron!" Jon shouted, flying at Adolf, only to be smacked away with an offhand blow from the priest.

"I summon the fiery flames of the Sun to strike thee down!" Father Adolf hissed. "May it burn you from hair to—"

I interrupted him by throwing out my hand and shouting, "PUSH!"

Father Adolf flew over the crowd before landing with a thud on the bonfire he'd erected in front of the platform. Father Adolf screamed as the glass vials of oil cracked and exploded, one after the other, setting him on fire then expanding the blaze exponentially. It only took a few seconds of thrashing in the flames for him to be reduced to nothing more than another charred corpse.

MAIN QUEST UPDATE:

QUEST COMPLETED: RESCUE KRAGEN BLOODSTORM (1/1)
+500 EXP
SIDE QUEST(S) COMPLETED: FIRE AND FAITH (1/1)
+500 EXP
+ 1 *Token of Faith* (Mythras)
+300 EXP, Slay Father Adolf (Bonus)
+300 EXP, Win over the Crowd (Bonus)

YOU HAVE REACHED LEVEL 3

Level 3 to 4
100/10000

Jon looked at the dead priest's body that was still burning on the pyre. "Seriously, do they not have any knockback resistance? Spell resistance? I knew PUSH was overpowered but I didn't know it was *that* overpowered. They need to fix this in beta."

"Oh, shut up," I said, taking a deep breath. I was sick of the smell of burning people.

The crowd was stunned and didn't look like they knew how to react. After all, it was one thing to turn against your local spiritual leader when he was mocking the late Lord Rose and proclaiming allegiance to a hated tyrant, it was quite another to watch him burned alive before your eyes. Never mind that they were quite happy to watch me get torched just a few minutes earlier.

Thankfully, I knew how to handle this. Walking up to the front of the platform, I said, "People of Crossroad, the priest suffered a tragic accident. The Empire's mouthpiece has skimmed coin and labor from every one of you. He's filled your head with lies and easy answers that provide no true protection against the undead or monsters that have assailed you! I suggest you go forth into that temple over there and redress some of the wrongs that have been committed against you! Take the candlesticks, tithes, and food he's hoarded for himself. When agents of his faith come to investigate, blame the agents of Veles and claim he was buried with honors!"

If there was one thing that was bound to get people moving, it was the promise of free stuff and a good two-thirds of the crowd immediately moved to begin looting Mythras' temple. The remaining third seemed more hesitant but given Bloodstorm was looking down at them with hate in his eyes and me alongside him, well, they decided they had better places to be. The only person who stayed was an old woman who hissed and cursed me for an unbeliever. She hurled a rotten apple at me that I managed to duck my head away from before it hit. Then she scampered off herself.

"I have to admit that was some impressive oratory," Jon said, flying over to my right shoulder. "Some truly great speech-ifying."

"Thanks," I said, smiling.

"Also completely plagiarized," Jon said, pecking me in the side of the head. "That was Garland's speech from *The Heretic of Heidelberg*! You couldn't come up with your own shaming of the crazy zealot?"

"It worked, didn't it?" I grumbled. "The short stories are just as good as the main books."

That was when I felt a massive hand slap me on the back. "Glorious, glorious! I have not seen such lovely violence since, well, yesterday. Run peasants! Run back to your masters! Know that the Bull of the North has sent thee!"

"Hi," I said, not turning to the guy.

"The Bull of the North is me," Bloodstorm said.

"Yeah, I got that," I said.

"Because I have horns," Bloodstorm said, pointing to the top of his head and why he was eight feet tall rather than seven.

"So I surmised," I replied. "Your father sent us to rescue you."

"He didn't come himself, I see," Bloodstorm replied, sounding somewhat disappointed.

I shook my head. "I'm sure he had important stuff to occupy him. Running a brothel, err, eating rats."

"Teaching at the Scholomance, chasing maidens, chasing young men, and so on," Bloodstorm said, sighing. "It's fine. He's not likely to change in our next four hundred years together."

"You don't look a day over three," Jon said, softly.

"Your bird is funny!" Bloodstorm said, showing he was yet another individual who could understand Jon. I wondered if all my party companions could do so. "It reminds me of another bird of another Garland I knew. Or maybe it's the same bird. There's something my mother tried to tell me about reincarnation, other worlds, and cycles of magic."

"Really, what was that?" I asked, wondering just how many people suspected their world was operating under a kind of dreadful curse that made it function like an open world RPG.

"I have no idea!" Bloodstorm said, cheerfully. "I was drunk at the time. Also, hungry. A pity we can't eat the late Father Adolf, but he looks old and tough anyway. Not to mention burnt. Would you rather have lunch at my father's establishment?"

Bloodstorm seemed surprisingly affable but also not exactly 'good.' "I have a few things to take care of around the village first. Dark Undermaster contracts and all that. You understand, right?"

"Of course, of course," Bloodstorm said. "I should point out our weapons and equipment are in a chest next to the platform. We should probably collect them before we head out."

"We?" I asked.

The ogre pointed to the sky. "Fate has brought us together, dear friend! From the day I was born, I have ever known that it was destiny to kill, maim, and wreck. But this does little to endear me to the locals. So, I have done my best to kill, maim, and wreck people that offend others. It may not win me any more friends, but it pays much-much better."

"Super," I said, uncomfortable. "I suppose it would also work well for a half-vampire ogre to have a Dark Undermaster accompanying him, so people don't attempt to slay him as a monster on sight."

"There is that too," Bloodstorm said. "They see an ogre wandering alone, they think I'm going to spirit away their maidens or steal their cattle. Which is ridiculous. I prefer experienced women and a sheep or goat will fill me up just fine. Still, they pepper me with arrows and chase me on horseback. They see me with a Dark Undermaster, and they assume it is not their problem."

He had a weirdly mixed way of speaking. Sometimes it was very modern and sometimes very old timey. I supposed it was the Mark of the Champion translating someone with a lot of unusual idioms. Which is what you would get from a centuries-old ogre from Fantasy Viking Russia.

"Sounds good," I said, heading over to a nearby chest and reclaiming my equipment. It all magically appeared on me rather than needing to be re-equipped. "But you realize we're going to be killing a bunch of gods and possibly going against Veles himself."

"Fine by me," Bloodstorm said. "Uncle Veles is a quite annoying fellow. He never quite got over Mokosh choosing his brother. Did you know they both used to be married to her and traded her every year's halfway mark?"

"I did not. Slavic mythology, man," I replied, checking my bracelet for any updates. There was one.

KRAGEN BLOODSTORM HAS JOINED YOUR PARTY
Class: Rus Berserker Warrior
Level 3
Alignment: Black

"Hey, you want a suit of Skull Armor?" I asked, wishing I had a party with fewer evil members

"Would I!"

CHAPTER FIFTEEN
THE PEOPLE UNDER THE STAIRS

No one seemed overly concerned with the fact we'd just publicly murdered the local priest, crazy asshole or not, but no one had seemed particularly concerned about us killing a bunch of Imperial soldiers in the Black Cat either. The Dark Undermasters had been the local authority in the area for about fifteen years so perhaps that meant everyone was assuming I was legally justified in what I'd done. Alternatively, like Bloodstorm said, it was probable that they were operating under 'not my problem' syndrome.

Which was fine by me.

Equipping the late Skull King's armor on Bloodstorm resulted in a very different look. The armor magically fitted itself to him and took on a vaguely Mongolian appearance with his Skull Mask adjusted for his horns. Bloodstorm wielded two giant hatchets as his preferred weapons, both unenchanted. I could have given him Skull Knight's sword and he might have gotten more use out of it than me from a strictly min/maxing perspective, but I was pretty sure I needed all the help I could get in surviving this place.

Leveling up-wise, I took the time to note that I'd gained my first second level spell. There were things like INVISIBILITY, DARKNESS, FIRE ARROW, BLIND, and EMPOWER. In the end, I chose the classic WEB spell because I remembered that the webs were flammable to Arcane Energy in *Dark Undermaster 2* but not normal fire due to a bug.

I hoped that was still the case and I could continue exploiting the system. This world seemed rigged, and I needed every advantage I could get.

I also noted I had a silver medallion with the symbol of Mythras, a glowing sun, on one side and the Bull of the Empire on the other. This was what I presumed was the quest reward, "Token of Faith." I had to admit I wasn't exactly comfortable putting on the symbol of a god I didn't believe in, but it provided a 5% spell resistance. I also figured that Mythras probably agreed that his priest had been a dick.

I had an additional attribute bonus that I assumed would be applied every level, which was really overpowered but something I wasn't going to question as long as it was in my favor. I applied it to INT this time around because I wanted to up my Arcane Fire bonus. I had to wonder if this was really increasing my intelligence in the 'real' world, much the same as my WIS. I didn't feel any different, but it would hardly be the weirdest thing I'd experienced these past two days.

ARAGORN "AARON" BARTKOWSKI
LVL: 3
CLASS: UNDERMASTER SORCERER
ALIGNMENT: GRAY
AGE: 34
SEX: MALE
RACE: HUMAN
STR: 10
AGI: 10
CON: 9
INT: 17
WIS: 8
COM: 15
CHA: 13

ARMOR CLASS: 5

ATTACK: +1 (+6 to ATTACK, 1d10+5 DAM Sword [witchfire])
HEALTH: 15

FEAT: Taunt

SPECIAL ABILITIES: ARCANE FIRE (1d6+4 INT bonus, Eldritch Damage)
SPELL LIST (2/1): PUSH, CURE, WEB

STATUS EFFECTS:

* *Alchemical Stone* (Red): +50lb carrying capacity
* *Token of Faith* (Mythras): 5% Spell Resistance

Finally, there was the issue of what to do with the five hundred gold pieces I'd won from Maelor. A smart play would have been to sit on it for a while and see if I wanted to buy something more valuable in the long run. However, I'd always had an issue with money burning a hole in my pocket and that was probably why I hadn't developed much of a savings. That and the evils of capitalism as my grandparents (who I'd never met) would say. So, I ended up spending 300 GP on updating the castle drawbridge and front door. Hopefully, Ania would approve.

Yeah, I had it bad for her.

REBUILD DRAGON KEEP QUEST UPDATED (3/12)

I had 362 GP leftover that I assumed would cover most of my current adventuring costs. I planned to treat Bloodstorm after we did our next job anyway. I was hungry from almost being burned alive and hoped they had something nonalcoholic to drink that wasn't complete ass. I'd never been much of a drinker, and I suspected they didn't sell Mountain Dew in this reality.

"Ah, so what daring rescues and felonious assaults shall we be conducting today, Ser Garland?" Bloodstorm asked me as we walked through the village. "This quaint little village does not seem like it would provide much sport, but I have found it to be full of secrets most foul and dangers most dire! Perhaps a dragon to slay or a princess to pilfer."

Eloquent for an ogre. Wait, was that racist? Speciiest? Whatever the hell you were supposed to call prejudice against objectively nonhuman beings? How were ogres supposed to speak? The ones in the game usually just went, "Grrr, kill puny human!"

"Ah, Bloodstorm," Jon said, sighing. "Don't ever change."

"Rats," I muttered, checking the notices that had been copied to a notebook I'd only now found inside my bags. Seriously, this hyperspace inventory the Mark of the Champion provided was really weirding me out. Why provide so many causal bonuses and not, I dunno, a bunch of actual powers to save this world? Did the magic just work like this or was there a specific reason that Weis had designed things this way?

"We're doing the 'Rats in the Cellar' quest first," I replied. "It seems like a pretty good place to start."

"Rats," Bloodstorm said, disappointed. "I confess, I was hoping for a bit more panache than serving the same job as a village alchemist might."

"The other side quests include beautiful Rusalka babes, a hideous monster needing to be slain, and Farmer Grub's wife," Jon said.

Bloodstorm looked down at me. "You taunt me, sir. You taunt me."

"We're under-leveled," I replied, explaining my reasoning. "Despite the fact we're a level over the recommended one for the side quests, the game assumes we'd have Ania, or Ania AND Agata as part of the party. Probably you too since I am noticing four available spaces on the party interface. Don't ask me if we'll have to dismiss people when we finally get to six companions. Either way, it's just you and me until Agata recovers and her sister leaves her bedside. Honestly, I wouldn't mind simply waiting it out until Agata awakens from her sleep but I'm not sure Ania wouldn't abandon us in this village, or the quests won't fail due to a time limit. This world doesn't operate to strict open world logic after all."

Bloodstorm stopped walking beside me. "Ahem."

I stopped as well. "Ah, right. That probably sounded like a lot of nonsense."

"You have a magic bracelet that strengthens you to superhuman levels as long as you kill things. The Lady Roses are also here but one is recovering. You want to forge yourself a bit higher but cautiously," Bloodstorm said, showing he understood things quite well or at least could translate gamespeak to local terms. Which made sense because his stats listed his INT and WIS at 15 and 16 repetitively. It was just his physical stats were all 18 or 20. Dude was a genius bruiser.

"Yeah, that's about the long and the short of it," I replied, surprised at how easily he was following this. "So, what's the problem?"

"We will be having lunch after this, correct?" Bloodstorm asked.

I smirked. "Sure."

The location for the contract, at least according to my map was a large two-story farmhouse with a windmill to its side, presumably for grinding grain. It was a little off to the side of the village and had a large fenced off yard that didn't seem to have any animals present, which surprised me.

"Ah, millers," Bloodstorm said. "The rich jackasses of every village."

"What?" I asked, looking up.

"Trust me, no matter what village, if you have a mill then you are a complete narf," Bloodstorm said.

"Narf," I said.

"Someone so bad, I had to invent my own profanity for them," Bloodstorm said. "Millers are always making money hand over fist by cheating their fellow villagers. Damn flour dealers. Trust me, every peasant out here is thinking nothing but nasty thoughts about who owns this mill."

I blinked. "Huh. I suppose prejudices really do depend on time and place."

"Read some Chaucer," Jon said. "It turned out that Medieval types were every bit as dirty, horny, mean spirited, and satirical as the rest of us."

"You read Chaucer?" I asked.

Jon shrugged. "I have the History Channel. Same difference. By the way, aliens built all the ancient cultures except, for some reason, the white ones."

"You know, I liked it when I was the sarcastic one in the party."

Either way, I didn't mind our employers being rich. It meant they could pay. Walking up to the surprisingly tall door of their home, seriously, it could fit Bloodstorm with just a slight stoop of his head, I knocked.

"Dark Undermaster here to solve your rat problem!" I shouted.

That was when the door opened and I found myself standing before a six-foot-tall woman and about half as wide, built like a linebacker with an apron on over her Amish-esque clothes. Her blonde hair was tied in girlish pigtails, which contrasted to a face that was square and hard. In her right hand was a giant rolling pin. Her accent was quite thick and not at all like the other people I'd met so far, even among the Imperials. "You come to kill the rats, ja?"

"That's what I said," I said.

"Goot, Goot!" The woman said. "They in basement. Kill dem all and I pay money, ja?"

"I guess, yeah," I said.

"Goot, goot," the woman said, stepping aside. "Husband useless in killing them. Watch for spears."

I did a double take. "Spears?"

"Go!" the woman said, waving her rolling pin at me.

"Right," I said, entering the house that I realized was extra-large in virtually every way. I felt like a child in the place, and it was decidedly uncomfortable. Especially as the place was decorated less like a miller's home and more like a butcher's. There was a kitchen filled with a variety of meats and the family apparently had a side business in sausage making by the number of links hanging from the ceiling.

It didn't take long to find the doorway leading to the basement, though. It did, however, take an embarrassingly long time to open it, though. The door was, again, ogre-sized and had a hoop for a handle that I pulled on for about twenty seconds before Bloodstorm reached over to pull it for me. It pulled back for him just fine.

The door opened to a long sloping cavern tunnel instead of a staircase with the walls covered in a glowing fungus that didn't provide quite enough light to show the bottom. A gust of wind proceeded to blow up from below as there were the sounds of skittering and chittering far louder than any normal rat could produce.

"I see this side quest is going to be influenced by HP Lovecraft," I muttered before looking at Jon. "What did you do when you did this quest?"

"Procedural, my friend," Jon said. "This is as new to me as it is to you."

"You got a torch or light spell?" Bloodstorm asked.

"Nope," I said, sighing. "Got to put that on my list."

"Well, I do," Bloodstorm said, pulling out a large stick with a weird honeycomb like top. "However, I'm not going to be able to fight with it unless I use it to smoke out some rats."

"Let's give it a shot and hope this doesn't end like *A Plague's Tale*," I said.

"I did some work on that game," Jon said. "They didn't appreciate my attempting to rename it *Medieval Girl Gets Eaten by Rats*."

"Ignis!" Bloodstorm said, causing the honeycomb at the end of the torch to burst into flame. I had no idea whether he knew magic or the torch itself was magic. I'd have asked him, but I was more focused on the fact I was descending into a cavern filled with giant rodents I'd stupidly agreed to exterminate.

The trip down the cavern tunnel was not that long but still felt like an extensive one. The place was unseasonably warm and damp with slime dripping from small stalactites while pooling on the ground in puddles that bubbled ominously. The rat noises only got worse as we reached the bottom, and I stumbled across large amounts of bones.

Lots and lots of bones.

Animal and otherwise.

One of the piles of bones was an eight-foot-tall man who had been stabbed with what looked like a dozen tiny spears in his back. He was dressed in a chef's hat, apron, and had his dead eyes vacantly staring outward.

There was also a large stone brazier full of twigs, straw, and smelling of oil. Possibly going to regret it, I gestured for Bloodstorm to light it up. Tossing his torch into the brazier, the room lit up like someone had turned on a light switch. I immediately saw we were surrounded by three- to four-foot-tall rats everywhere. There was at least a dozen of them with more sticking their heads out of tunnels built into the side of the football-field-sized chamber. All of them had red eyes that were looking at me.

In abject terror.

Yeah, the rats were afraid of me. Their little rodent faces were possessed of human-like features that could express themselves in a noticeable way. They were also all wearing clothes sized for them, pants and dresses that looked to have been made from stitched together castoffs. The smaller rats were clinging to the larger ones and probably the children of the group. Only a few of them were armed.

This wasn't a rat infestation.

It was a *rat colony*.

Everyone looked like they'd escaped a children's book too. You know, the ones where the animals look real enough but are humanized so they're kind of cute even when they're badgers or whatever? *The Wind in the Willows*? I'm reaching here. I don't recall any humanoid rat stories outside of *Warhammer Fantasy* and those guys were terrifying instead of adorable.

"Uh, hi," I said, feeling awkward.

One of the rat women burst into tears, hugging three smaller rats to herself. "Please don't kill my children, sir!"

I was starting to hate this world.

CHAPTER SIXTEEN
ALWAYS CHAOTIC EVIL ISN'T ALWAYS EVIL

I remembered when I first played *Keep on the Borderlands*, one of the original *Dungeons & Dragons* modules from way back when. During our expedition to the Caverns of Chaos, a typical dungeon, I came across a bunch of young orcs and goblins. Really young orcs and goblins. I chose to spare them but some of my party had argued that as creatures of pure evil, we should kill them. Others didn't care because they weren't there to roleplay and thought moral dilemmas had no place in a 1st Edition dungeon crawl.

Apparently, this had been a common reaction over the decades. The "Kill Orc Kids or Not" dilemma had been the first *Dungeons & Dragons* controversy as more than a few players felt going into the homes of green people to murder their families felt like hate crimes rather than epic fantasy heroics. Normally, I didn't spare much thought to this subject even on internet forums. It was, after all, just a game. Unfortunately, it seemed Weis' world was one of those places that loved introducing moral quandaries into what was otherwise straightforward monster slaying.

These were obviously not rats, something most people didn't object to the mass slaying thereof, but rat*kin*. Ratkin were a race of hobbit-sized underground dwelling humanoids that roughly occupied the place of kobolds in the setting. Nobody liked them in-universe but all indications were they were just another people trying to make their way in the world. You know, when not stabbing people in the middle of the night and stealing their stuff.

Great.

Well, I guess I wasn't going to fulfilling this contract. I might not have been the nicest person in the world, and I'd already committed a few good-natured murders (self-defense!) but wholesale slaughter of innocents wasn't going to happen. I didn't care if they did look like the guys infesting my apartment's nightmarish cousins.

"Die monsters!" Bloodstorm said, lifting his twin hatchets. "When you reach Veles' realm, tell them Kragen Bloodstorm sent you!"

My ogre companion began to froth from the mouth, and I suspected he was about to enter the kind of insane battle trance that the books described Viking Rus doing before their massacres. Something that, if you didn't have a foe in front of them, could easily result in them killing their own comrades.

I grabbed hold of Bloodstorm's belt and pulled him back. It required me to use both hands and push with my feet to get him to stop. "Hold on there, Jason Voorhees. There are children here."

"So, what you're saying is I should swing low," Bloodstorm said, clearly not getting my meaning or pretending not to. Still, he wasn't charging into the ranks of the ratkin to begin a massacre. Yet. I could tell by the hungry look in his eye that Bloodstorm's inner dhampyre-ogre was a wild beast and needed to be let loose every now and then or bad things would happen.

"I'm really starting to hate the writer here," Jon said, shaking his head. "This is like that old *Keep on the Borderlands* nonsense my old DM tried to pull on me."

I did a double take at the raven. Strange minds apparently thought alike. "I don't know what you mean."

Yeah, I loved screwing with Jon.

Could you tell?

"Well, you see, way back in 1st Edition *Dungeons & Dragons*, Gary Gygax wrote a module where you went to the Caves of Chaos—"

"Please, Ser Undermaster, we are a peaceful people," an elderly gray furred ratkin with a spear he was using as a staff walked up to me.

"We had already built our burrow when the Millers came and demanded tribute."

"Tribute?" I asked, wondering what sort of weird ass situation I'd wandered into. "They knew you were living down here?"

I mean, stupid question, I saw the dead body of the man I presumed to be the giantess upstairs' husband just a few feet away. Maybe there was a translation issue going on but clearly, she knew what was down here and had just expected me to carry out a slaughter. On the other hand, it explained why I was being paid a hundred gold for this. According to the books, plenty of the Undermasters would have just taken the money and gotten to the rat killing. They weren't exactly an organization noted for discrimination when it came to contracts. If it wasn't human or elf, it was fair game.

"One of our ranks a month to be sacrificed to be made into meat," the elder ratkin explained. "We hunted animals to fill the tithe as best we could but sometimes, we had to do it."

I stared at him, processing what he was saying. "The tithe is…people."

"Soylent Green is people," Jon said, imitating Charlton Heston. "People!"

The ratkin didn't react to Jon and just stared at me with his inhuman red eyes. "Yes, gifts of blood and flesh for our community's survival."

So, the people upstairs were killing ratkin and selling them as meat.

That was *messed up*.

"See? What did I tell you," Bloodstorm said, seemingly calmed down from his coming battle rage. "You can't trust millers."

"I think this is more their butcher side hustle," Jon said. "Still, ick. Seriously, rat meat? Gross."

"Talking rats," I said, feeling like he was burying the lede.

"I said it was gross!" Jon said, defensively.

"Unfortunately, I fear that bargain no longer holds," the elder ratkin said. "The giantess and her husband have received an offer of coin far greater than the value of their mill. So, they must eliminate us from the caverns beneath to sell. The fact that this town is subject to so many attacks from Veles' forces also encourages them to depart. I fear we slew her husband when he attempted to drive us out directly. He did not care for our offer to simply brick up the entrance to the land above. We have other exits."

I had a headache coming on. "This is a real estate scam? Who the hell writes this crap? Weis is much better than this."

Of course, there was no answer.

"Don't listen to these guys," Bloodstorm said, turning to me. "Ratkin are all liars. You might as well trust an ogre."

I stared at him.

"What?" Bloodstorm asked, grinning.

"Okay, so Bloodstorm has a sense of humor about treating people as irredeemable monsters," I said, aloud. "Good to know."

"This is probably one of those 'no win scenario' moral dilemmas," Jon said. "Like if you let the ratkin go, they'll turn out to be a plague on future generations. Game developers love making you feel bad about making any sort of ethical choice in games."

"They have children," I replied. "I know which side I'm choosing."

"If you so say so, Aaron."

"Betrayer! False one!" The giantess shouted behind me. Apparently, she'd followed me down. "You have broken deal and will pay penalty!"

"Ah, hell," I muttered, turning around.

The giantess was standing there with a pair of glowing goggles that I recognized as being modern night vision ones from my world. That incongruity was matched only by the fact she was holding a WW1 era flamethrower.

"Mothersucker," I muttered, staring at the decidedly non-Medieval weapon in my midst. It seemed she'd planned to help us out in our elimination of her rat problem. She probably should have mentioned that, as well as where she got that thing.

"Now, the rats burn! Husband be avenged!" The giantess hissed.

I dodge rolled out of the way as she fired a burst of fire that illuminated more of cavern around us and sent the ratkin scurrying in every direction. They were *fast* little bastards; I've got to tell you.

"I've got her!" Bloodstorm shouted, clearly just happy to have something to kill.

Bloodstorm charged at the giantess with his hatchets, howling with a mad look on his face. The giantess lifted her flamethrower and blasted my companion in the face. Instead of killing him, it just caused him to fall backward. Either because of the Skull Helmet or the fact that he was now a companion leveling up alongside me. Either way, he thrashed on the ground.

I'd already used up my PUSH for the day, magic seemed to function on Vancian rules (or at least spell slots), and I wasn't sure I wanted to see what Arcane Fire would do to this place if I hit a flamethrower with it. I knew that while it was cool to see them go up in video games, Bloodstorm was awfully close to her, and I wanted to keep my team-killing to a minimum.

Instead, I pointed at her and shouted, "WEB!"

I admit, I made the Spider-Man 'throw up the horns' gesture as I did it. As much as I wanted to take this world seriously as a place with real consequences for all I was doing, I was still *doing frigging magic* in a fantasy world. That meant that I was allowed to have a little fun with it.

The explosion of gooey glue-like strands out of my hand was a lot larger than anything Peter Parker had produced in the movies, though. Instead, it covered virtually the entirety of the cavern's back. It enveloped both the giantess, who I noted I'd never gotten the name of, and Bloodstorm both. That, unfortunately, prevented me from trying out whether webbing was flammable to Arcane Fire. If I wasn't willing to risk it with a flamethrower, I wasn't willing to risk it for the possibility of exploding webbing *and* a flamethrower.

The giantess clawed at the webbing covering her face, making various profane shouts that I was pretty sure were universal in their meaning. Bloodstorm was just as badly off, though, he quickly resolved it by removing his helmet with his mostly-free hands.

"Warn me next time before you throw spells, Garland!" Bloodstorm shouted, struggling with his arms and legs against the prehensile strength of the webbing.

"I hate these area of effect attacks," Jon said. "They utterly ruin any use from your melee builds."

"Help Bloodstorm!" I snapped, pulling out my sword and starting to chop the webbing to get him out. The witchfire, thankfully, didn't ignite it. Which was something I probably should have been worried about but didn't think of until after I'd taken a few swings.

"How?" Jon said, flying up in the air.

"Claw off the webbing or something!" I shouted,

"Fine!" Jon said, flying up to the webbing and clawing on it. After a few seconds, he was totally entrapped in the webbing against Bloodstorm's leg. "Great plan, Aaron! I can see why you were chosen to save the world!"

"Low WIS!" I shouted.

That was when there was a ripping, tearing, and growling noise from the place where the giantess had been trapped. There, she had been replaced by an even taller stooped over furred humanoid with a wolf's head. It was a mountain of muscle and only vaguely identifiable as female anymore.

The giantess was a Vulkodlak.

A werewolf.

Bloodstorm stared at the monster as he broke free of the webbing. "Finally, a worthy challenge!"

"Run!" I shouted.

"Oh come on!" Bloodstorm said. "I love punching werewolves! At least let me gore her!"

"Now!" I shouted, running out of the webbing.

"Fine," Bloodstorm muttered following me.

The Vukodlak attempted to pounce on us with a leap on all fours, only for her hind legs to get caught in the webbing and it to prevent her from killing us all. As soon as they were out of the webbing, Jon still stuck to Bloodstorm's leg, I threw a ball of Arcane Fire behind me. It struck the werewolf in the face.

And nothing happened.

"Dammit, they patched the WEB exploit!" Jon hissed. "It's like you can't be allowed to have fun in these games anymore!"

Before I could come up with another strategy, a series of spears flew through the air and slammed into the Vukodlak's chest. It fell back further into the webbing, only for more spears to be tossed. The creature thrashed and hissed before bleeding out beside the webbed up remains of her husband.

A series of cheers came from the ratkin behind me, who had taken advantage of the fight to reposition themselves. The spear hurlers turned out to have been able to deal with the giantess just like they'd dealt with her husband.

SIDE QUEST(S) COMPLETED:

RATS IN THE CELLAR (1/1)

+ 1000 EXP
+ 300 EXP (Vukodlak)
+ 300 EXP (Spare Ratkin)
+ *Cloak of protection* +1
+ 100 GP

Level 3 to 4
1700/10000

"I feel like we're getting rewarded, for doing very little," Jon said, pausing. "Also, who gives a reward for sparing monsters? You know who is responsible for this? All the whiny internet activists who don't know good clean fun—"

I closed Jon's beak with my fingers. "Hush."

Bloodstorm puffed up his chest. "We can still kill the ratkin. I'm just saying."

"No," I said, firmly. "We'll kill something else later."

"Fine-fine," Bloodstorm said, shaking his head. "Do you mind if I look the upstairs? That meat they had set up looked especially appetizing."

I made a mental note to switch out my companions as soon as possible. "You do you, Bloodstorm."

Bloodstorm gave me two thumbs up.

I turned around to address the ratkin. "You are now free! Go forth and live your ratkin lives in peace, no longer having to worry about the terrors of the werewolves! Know that your children will be able to—"

No one was there.

"They're gone," Jon said, flapping up after the webbing disintegrated back into wisps of magical smoke.

"Yeah, they scurried off!" Bloodstorm said, bellowing. "Like some sort of small rodent-like creature."

"You like pretending to be dumber than you are, don't you, Bloodstorm?" I asked, shaking my head.

"When you look like me, no one will believe you are a graduate of Kalizov University," Bloodstorm replied. "Not that I was but that's just because the dean takes a poor view of killing three fellow students during a bar fight."

"I'm sure they had it coming," I said, shaking my head.

"Yeah, they ran into my fists!" Bloodstorm proclaimed. "They were supposed to be smart too!"

I walked over to the body of the dead werewolf. Beside her body was the damaged and broken flamethrower next to the shattered night vision goggles. A pool of chemical fluid was leaking out of the former.

I picked up the broken night vision goggles and noticed there was a sticker on the side that had a very familiar logo with text underneath. The logo was a red shield with a white dragon breathing fire and the words were EPIC DUNGEONEERINGtm.

"The plot thickens."

CHAPTER SEVENTEEN
HORSE MOUNT RULES

The revelation that Epic Dungeoneering™ was active in this world and selling military grade equipment was something that should have bothered me more than it did. Instead, I just thought it made sense. I already knew my employers were evil, after all. It filled me with a perverse kind of hope since if they were arming werewolf millers then the travel between worlds had to be pretty common. It was my first real sign that returning home was a possibility.

"So, Garland, where are we headed next?" Bloodstorm said, walking down the village streets beside me. He was chewing down on his twelfth sausage taken from the millers and seemingly unconcerned about the meat's origin. He was also sporting the *cloak of protection +1*, which I'd given him rather than take for myself since it only came with a 5% spell resistance that didn't stack with my Mark of Faith.

"You know those are probably made of people, right?" I asked, letting Jon perch on the top of my head.

"Never question what goes into sausage, Garland," Bloodstorm replied. "If this is made of people, ratkin, and horse meat then it is probably a higher quality product than what most butchers sell."

I didn't have a good argument for that. "Hold on, I have to sit down."

One thing that open world RPGs tended to underplay was how damn exhausting it was to travel continuously across vast distances.

Or, in this case, fairly short distances. I sat down on the porch of a burned-out house and took a moment to catch my breath.

"You should probably get yourself a horse," Bloodstorm said, taking a drink from a wineskin that he'd filled up at the millers as well.

"I have a horse," I replied, looking at the demon steed rune on my hand. "Of sorts."

"Then why aren't you riding it?" Bloodstorm asked, confused.

I wasn't sure the answer, 'I have no idea how to ride a horse and it looks like it would hurt your balls' would be satisfying. So, instead, I went with, "I killed its previous rider and I'm not sure it's going to be that well-disposed to accepting me as a replacement. Oh, and it's from the fiery pits of Hell."

"The Underworld around here is actually pretty cold," Jon said. "Also, dark. So, it's more Northrend than Mordor."

"Thank you, Jon," I said, sarcastically.

"It's in the codex!" Jon said. "I read a couple of the entries by mistake while trying to figure out how to use the Mark of the Champion. Whoever wrote those should really learn to get a life. Who cares what the ethnic minorities of the Southern Kingdoms eat?"

"I do," Bloodstorm said, piping in. "It affects the flavor!"

I shook my head. "I was hoping to get promoted to writing those entries. Anyway, Bloodstorm is right. I should use a mount if I have one."

"It's not so bad when you have legs," Jon said. "I admit, I never got beyond the regular horse. Once you unlock fast travel, though, you'll never look back. At least when you're not exploring a new region for coin and cleavage."

"Fast travel?" I asked. "That's a thing in-universe?"

I didn't know why I should be shocked that teleportation would be a thing, but it seemed genre breaking. At least, I assumed fast travel would be a form of teleportation. I didn't know how any of this stuff worked and should probably have been paying more attention to Jon's lessons. They were just, well, physically painful.

"Why wouldn't it be?" Jon asked. "It's not unlocked until 5th level, though. You also can't go to any new locations, only past ones."

"I wonder if it works for Ania," I thought, speculating. "She's been all over the continent."

Jon shook his head. "That's what I don't get about you, Aaron. You're roleplaying one minute and the next minute you're trying to game the system. Pick a lane."

Sucking in my breath, I stood up and proceeded to touch the rune on my hand. "Uh, demon steed, I choose you!"

"Really, dude?" Jon asked.

"How do you do it!" I snapped.

Whether it was a silly way of doing it or not, it worked as the demon steed appeared seconds later in an explosion of smoke. The creature had shrunk considerably from where Skull King had been riding it and was now more properly proportioned for my size. It made me wonder if Skull King had been a giant back in his old life or had somehow managed to grow in this world. The demon snorted in my face and looked annoyed.

Much to my surprise, none of the locals seemed to pay the newly summoned monster any mind. You'd think they'd have been a bit more cautious around a creature of Veles after last night. However, the Dark Undermasters had been here for a decade and a half so maybe they'd gotten used to their black magic.

"It's probably hungry," Bloodstorm said, offering me a sausage.

"You want me to feed it probable human flesh?" I asked. "Or ratkin?"

"What do you think demon steeds eat?" Jon asked.

He had a point. "Fine."

I took the sausage and held in front of the monster mount before the creature greedily gobbled it up. I stroked its snout, and it whinnied happily.

My bracelet pinged and displayed a new message.

MOUNT APPROVAL INCREASED

"Huh," I said, nodding. "I guess demon steed maintenance is going to be one of the things I have to consider in the future."

"Be sure to let it graze on bodies," Jon said. "Probably out of sight from townsfolk."

"No kidding," I said, shaking away that mental image. I was rapidly becoming conditioned to accepting horror.

"What's its name?" Bloodstorm asked.

"I dunno," I said, blinking.

My bracelet pinged again.

NAME MOUNT (DEMON STEED): _____

"Oh, come on," I muttered, staring down at the bracelet. "Really?"

"What?" Jon asked. "It's no weirder than anything else here."

The demon steed stomped its front hoof against the ground and made a little flicker of witchfire where it struck.

That gave me an idea for its name. "Alright, demon steed, I name you Stompy!"

Silence prevailed over our group.

"Uh huh," Jon said, skeptically. "Stompy. Really?"

STOMPY HAS JOINED THE PARTY

"I thought you'd name him Witchfire," Bloodstorm said, looking to one side as if embarrassed.

Stompy whinnied appreciatively, clearly approving of the name.

"See, he likes it!" I said, happily.

"I bet Skull King had a badass name for it," Jon said.

Stompy made a noise that sounded halfway between a snort and a growl. It was a very un-horse-like noise.

"I don't think he cared much for his previous owner," I said.

Stompy bobbed its head up and down before stomping one foot on the ground. Perhaps doing a 'once for yes', 'twice for no' sort of thing.

"Oh, it's one of those Mr. Ed-style intelligent horses," Jon said. "Just what we needed. Listen, pal, the talking animal quotient of the party is already filled. Get your own thing."

"It doesn't talk," I replied, looking at where to mount onto the creature. It came fully saddled and with the, uh, other horse stuff. The, uh, bridle? Listen, I wasn't an expert on these things. I was just a fantasy fan, not a fanatic.

"Also, a mount is actually useful, unlike you, little raven!" Bloodstorm said, pitching in.

"Et tu, Bloodstorm?" Jon asked.

I reluctantly put my foot in the saddle and threw myself over the side, immediately holding on for dear life. Everything started moving around me as if I was high, drunk, and concussed at once. Except not nearly as fun. If Garland, or anyone who knew him for that matter, could see me then he probably would have died from embarrassment.

Jon flew off my head and took rest on the top of Stompy's head, between his ears. "Are you okay? You look a little rough."

I stared down at the ground that seemed distressingly far away. "Just a little motion sick."

"You're not moving," Jon said.

"Funny, the ground looks like it is," I said, closing my eyes and taking several deep breaths. "I'm good, I'm good. On the other hand, I feel like a walk could do me good. Let me just climb off this stallion here and never ever summon it again."

"Ha!" Bloodstorm said, slapping Stompy on the ass. "You're hilarious, Garland!"

"Ah!" I screamed as the demon steed took off, extending out its wings and taking to the air. Apparently, the ability to fly was one of those high-level mount abilities that no one had told me about. "Ahhhhhhhhhhhhhh!"

I held onto dear life while the demon steed flew over the tops of houses and did spins around Crossroad, causing me to feel like I was going to fall over at any moment. I swear, even though it was out of genre, the bracelet started playing the ending theme from "The Neverending Story" where the luck dragon chases the bullies. Seriously, the Mark of the Champion was alive and trolling me.

"Halt! Whoa, Nelly! Stop! Land! Escape button!" I shouted before I felt the demon steed lurch and I fell off the side. "Eject! Eject! No, wait, don't eject!"

Thankfully, that was into a bundle of hay on the ground as the creature had come to a stop. After several long minutes, Jon flew down and landed on my forehead.

"Hi," Jon said.

"Quiet, I'm dead," I replied, not moving.

"You're not dead," Jon said. "I should know because you're not a raven."

"Gimme me a minute," I said, pausing. "Assume I'm trying to do the Monty Python sketch about the plague."

"See, you're already doing cheap references like *Family Guy*," Jon said. "You're fine. If the horse wanted you dead, it would have dumped you over like it did Skull King."

I tried to sit up and failed. "You think Stompy threw Skull King deliberately?"

Stompy whinnied and bobbed its head up and down.

"Huh," I said, finally managing to get up and not throwing up only because I'd already done so once today. "Well, that just goes to show you that you should treat your mounts better than you treat your..."

"What?" Jon asked.

"I lost the sentence," I said, shaking my head. "Hey, Stompy, let's hold off on any more flight until, uh, yeah, let's just say ever. Okay?"

I swear the demon steed grinned at me.

"Where the hell am I?" I asked, looking around to see a large barn as well as a waterwheel equipped mill alongside a large house next to the river.

"More millers," Jon said, making a hock spit noise. "We're at the farm of the Miller family."

"What were the ones we just left?"

"They were the other Miller family," Jon said. "Heretofore known as the Werewolf Millers. These are the Human Millers. Probably."

"Uh huh," I said.

"Frigging millers," Jon said, shaking his head. "But yes, these are the people that wanted to hire us to deal with their rusalka problem."

"They're the mermaids, right?" I asked.

"More like water spirits," Jon said. "They appear as sexy ladies, lure you to the lake or river then drown you."

"Why?" I asked, confused.

"I have no idea," Jon said. "However, if you pay attention to mythology, monsters come in two varieties. There are the sexy ladies who lure you in to murder you: banshees, mermaids, sirens, succubi, hags who cover themselves in illusions, vampiresses, sphinx—"

"I don't think sphinxes do that," I interrupted.

"Clearly you haven't seen the Aegypta expansion for Dark Undermaster 2's take on the monster. Huba-huba," Jon said. "And the other kind of monster: which is big burly ugly ass dudes who want to eat you."

"I think you're being a bit reductive," I said.

"Mythology was clearly written by a bunch of horny dudes is all I'm saying," Jon said. "Women are actually the same way. If you've ever read the urban fantasy or paranormal romance aisle, you'll find out every kind of monster is actually an incredibly mean but bangable dude."

"You have given this matter a large amount of thought," I replied.

"I may be a bit sex obsessed after my transformation," Jon said.

"No kidding," I said.

"There's also horses as monsters," Jon said. "The kelpie, the water horse, the unicorn, the hippogriff. Basically, dudes wanted two things in ye old times: ladies and horses."

Stompy snorted.

"You forgot dragons," I replied. "Usually guarding some sort of treasure."

"Ladies, gold, and horses," Jon said.

"Yeah, that about covers it." I turned to the water mill. "Well, I guess this will be our next side quest."

"You're a work horse," Jon said, staring at me. "There's no need to do all the side quests today. We can take a break. Wait until Agata is awake and we have a party healer. Also, Ania. Because we won't have a party rogue otherwise. Think of all the locked chests that you might end up missing!"

"No," I said, softly. "I'm going on."

"Why?" Jon asked.

I took a deep breath. "Because I need to become more powerful if I'm supposed to survive this place. Better equipment, more health, and stronger powers. If I'm going to get out of this place alive, I need to level up."

I didn't want to admit that I also was getting a kind of weird thrill out of each of these encounters. I should have been terrified, but I admit I felt alive in a way I hadn't ever experienced before. Maybe it was insane, maybe I was risking my life recklessly, but I wanted to carry on.

"Just as long as it's not to impress a girl," Jon said. "There's a lot of fish in the sea after all. Or the river if you don't mind drowning, it seems."

I flipped Jon off.

"Ah, yes, giving the bird to the bird, very clever," Jon said.

Bloodstorm proceeded to jog up toward me. "Man, that was hilarious! You actually looked like you didn't know how to ride a horse."

"How the hell did you jog all this way?" I asked.

I shook my head and headed off to the water mill.

CHAPTER EIGHTEEN
THE PEOPLE VERSUS THE NAKED MERFOLK

Well, this wasn't going the way I expected.

It was at least a change from the previous side quests.

"So, by rescue your son—" I said, consulting the fifteen-page document in front of me. It was handwritten and almost impossible to read even if the Mark of the Champion translated written Ledzianian into English, it did so with its writing style instead. It didn't help that Medieval legal jargon was as impenetrable as in modern day. It was amazing even in small farming communities, they still had lawyers. Or, at least, had lawyers until they were eaten by the undead.

Bloodstorm was sitting over on a nearby tree stump, looking bored out of his mind while Jon sat on his head. Legal proceedings were not something that intrigued him, even when half of the participants weren't wearing any clothes.

Yeah, we'll get to that.

"I mean, you make him stop carrying around with that water spirit hussy!" Mrs. Miller said as she stood in front of her water wheel. She was a middle-aged blonde woman with a bullish frame as well as intense eyes. Mrs. Miller was standing next to her husband, who had barely said a word during the negotiation. Both were dressed the same as every other peasant in the town of Crossroad.

Just to the side was their younger son, a tall black-haired man about twenty years old, in linen clothes with a leather vest. I was pretty sure his name was Klaus.

"Uh huh," I said, looking down at the marriage contract. "Your elder son, Hans, is engaged to be married to Theresa Baker from the…baker family."

Just to Klaus' side was a blonde-haired girl in a long blue-white dress with a bonnet. She was about twenty-five years old, and this apparently qualified her as being an old maid. It seemed her previous fiancés had a habit of getting eaten, which was understandable given there'd been something like fifteen attacks on Crossroad.

"Yes," Theresa said, nodding. "The Millers were supposed to buy the mill owned by the Other Millers. It was to be our wedding present."

"My brother is a monster-chasing fiend," Klaus said, shaking his head. "He doesn't deserve Theresa."

"Hush," Theresa said, elbowing him. "He is my intended and to be respected, despite his many-many betrayals."

"And Hans wants out of this betrothal in order to marry his Rusalka girlfriend," I said, turning around to look at the second party that was waiting patiently just a few yards away.

There, standing absently, were King Vodyanoy, his two daughters, and the aforementioned Hans who were all stark naked. King Vodyanoy was a green-skinned black-haired toad-like monster who resembled King Hippo from the old *Punch Out!* games. He had a crown made of shale fragments and a pitchfork that he was using as a trident. Dude was also, uh, well, dude had a lot going on down there.

Gave a guy a complex.

His two daughters were exactly the opposite in appearance with similar green skin and long black hair but bodies that would have done well modeling for *Sports Illustrated*'s Swimsuit Edition. You know, if they were wearing swimsuits. I'm not trying to be crass here, really. They were very attractive spirits of the water is all I'm saying. Apparently, Jon hadn't been blowing smoke when discussing monster sexual dimorphism.

Hans was a perfectly ordinary looking man with a strong resemblance to his brother Klaus. He looked like he was lost in his own little world and not at all ashamed of the fact he was baring all. Indeed, the only thing I did notice on the guy was his silver glowing ring and that was because I was happy to be looking anywhere else.

"I am destined to be with Summer Breeze!" Hans said, practically singing. "We are in love, and I will go to their magical kingdom to live out my days making love while enjoying the wonders of fairyland!"

"Uh huh," I said. "Said magical kingdom being...the moat. Which currently does not exist."

King Vodyanoy spoke up with his thick baritone. His speech was less sophisticated than the bracelet usually translated people's speech as, which might just be a matter of the Rusalka not having many contractions in their language. "Castle moat refill. Gotta wait for a few rains or magic use bracelet."

Did everyone know about the Mark of the Champion? "Sorry, refilling the moat isn't listed on my objectives."

MAIN QUEST(S) UPDATED:
PAY FOR NEW CASTLE MOAT ~~2000~~ 800 GP
Reward: 500 EXP, Bonus to Keep Upgrade Score

I stared down at my bracelet. "Yeah, well, that's not happening any time soon, even with the discount. Just so we're clear, Summer Breeze is your eldest daughter?"

One of the two incredibly hot water spirits raised their hands.

"Yes," King Vodyanoy said. "Winter Chill is youngest daughter. Offer her to second son."

Klaus looked horrified, intrigued, then horrified. "I don't want to drown!"

"Keep away from my sons!" Mrs. Miller said, walking up and grabbing Klaus by the arm.

"Don't drown breeders," King Vodyanoy said. "At least until they are done seeding. Best to do mating against beach so human's heads can be kept above water and—"

Hans interrupted. "I have a *ring of water breathing*!"

"And where did you get that?" Mrs. Miller asked. "Did you waste money from the wedding on that Dark Undermaster nonsense? You know they get everything they own from murdered people! I heard one killed the village priest today!"

"Ahem," I cleared my throat loudly.

Mrs. Miller looked embarrassed. "Not that I don't appreciate your arbitration, Lord Garland."

"Right," I muttered. "Just so we're clear, I take it the primary problem here is fiduciary?"

Everyone looked at me strangely.

"Money," I explained.

"Yes!" Mrs. Miller said, before pausing. "No! I don't want my boy throwing his life away on some nonhuman slattern!"

Summer Breeze hissed at Mrs. Miller, displaying shark-like teeth which would have given me pause about letting her mouth get anywhere near something sensitive.

"I love Hans!" Theresa said, sounding utterly insincere. "Besides, my family is putting up a large amount of money to buy the other mill and we need someone who knows how to make flour!"

"I know how to make flour," Klaus muttered under his breath.

"Yeah, I have some news on that," I muttered, thinking back to the werewolf giantess and her flamethrower. "So, what is your take on this, Summer Breeze? Do you wish to marry Hans?"

"Human men are dumb but virile and I wish to bear children," Summer Breeze said. "The next Rusalka den is forty leagues away. Hans is acceptable as a mate."

"Human men are good for only one thing and sometimes not even that," Winter's Chill added, her voice a bit huskier.

"What a ringing endorsement," I muttered. "Are you sure you want to join this family, Hans?"

"I was made for more than being a mere miller! I was meant to explore the sublime and surreal worlds that beckon those who dare to tread in places normal men do not!" Hans said, spinning around like he was high on acid.

"He means underwater levels of Dragon Keep," King Vodyanoy explained. "Which are not presently underwater. Dragon fire makes real hash of the place. Glad my race can turn into elements."

"Is your son...okay?" I asked Mr. Miller.

"No, he likes to eat ergot," Mr. Miller finally contributed to the conversation. "That's the fungus that grows on rye. It will give you witch-visions according to my grandfather. Personally, I just use it when I need to relax."

"Well, that explains a few things," I said, shuffling the papers. "I have made my decision."

Bloodstorm raised his hand like we were in school. "Does it involve killing the Rusalka?"

"No," I said, dryly.

"Does it involve killing the Millers?" Bloodstorm asked.

"What?" Mrs. Miller asked.

"No!" I snapped.

"Trial by combat! Theresa vs. Summer Breeze!" Bloodstorm suggested.

"Now, that I'd watch!" Jon said, suspiciously silent during the entire affair. Maybe he'd just been looking at the Rusalka the entire time.

"I can take her!" Theresa said, rolling up her sleeves.

"You and what army, human?" Summer Breeze asked, glaring at Theresa.

"No, sister," Winter Chill said, holding her arm. "That is not our way."

"You're right," Summer Breeze said.

"We can send our brother to lure her someplace private and drown her there," Winter Chill tried to whisper but was just a little too loud.

"No," I said, raising my voice. "I think I have come to an equitable decision that will leave all parties satisfied."

"Yeah, fat chance of that," Jon said.

Everyone else looked equally skeptical.

"Oh, ye of little faith," I replied. "First of all, the Other Miller family has left Crossroad and bequeathed their mill to the Order of the Dark Undermasters."

"What?" Theresa said.

"That's outrageous!" Mrs. Miller said.

"It's also a big fat lie," Jon said.

"They did leave it behind," Bloodstorm said, shrugging. "Certainly, they don't need it anymore."

"Which we are donating as a wedding present to Klaus and Theresa," I replied.

"Wait, what?" Klaus said, looking hopeful to the point of ecstasy. "You mean it?"

Theresa narrowed her eyes. "What's the catch?"

"But Klaus is terrible!" Mrs. Miller said. "At everything! Hans was our chosen heir! He was always an exceptional boy."

Hans was still dancing around like a fool.

"Which is why he's gotten airs about being a fairy tale character," Mr. Miller said. "Shame. I knew we shouldn't have taught him how to read."

"Mom!" Klaus said. "I can do this! I think."

Theresa rolled her eyes but seemingly fine with settling.

"Trust me, kid, I'm doing you a favor," I replied. "Everyone deserves a chance to get out from under their parents' thumb."

"They do not!" Mrs. Miller said, offended. "By what right do you have to interfere in our affairs?"

"The fact I was called to arbitrate this dispute?" I pointed out.

"I was hoping you'd kill the Rusalka!" Mrs. Miller snapped.

"Yeah, well, you're getting a free mill out of it instead," I said, pausing.

"With a slight rat problem," Jon pointed out.

I was very glad no one in this group could understand him but me and Bloodstorm. "Please note that it does require a bricking up of its cellar for reasons of…appeasing the local something-something magic-magic blah-blah-blah."

"What was that?" Theresa asked, clearly trying to follow my conversation points.

"Do not question the Great and Mighty Garland!" I said, throwing my hands outward. "I have seen and faced things you would not believe!"

"Mostly in the past two days!" Jon added.

Bloodstorm sniggered.

"What about me?" Hans asked.

"You should put some pants on," I muttered before shaking my head. "Listen, I gotta ask, did you buy that magic ring with the money set aside for your wedding?"

Hans looked guilty, turning his head to the side. "Maybe. But it was for a good cause! Love!"

"You mean sex," I said, skeptically.

"That too!" Hans said. "I didn't buy it from the Dark Undermasters, though, but at the Black Cat!"

"Why were you at a brothel?" Mrs. Miller asked, scandalized.

"Obviously, to buy a magic ring," I said, sarcastically. "Well, I'm sorry but I'm going to have to rule that you're on the hook for some form of compensation to your parents for this. Actually, no, forget I said that. Since I just gave up a mill, you're on the hook to me."

"That can't be legal!" Mrs. Miller said, horrified.

"I will make it legal," I said, doing my best Darth Sidious voice. Honestly, the woman rubbed me the wrong way with her casual speciism and desire to control her sons' lives. Even if Hans was probably an idiot who would end up drowned or naked in the streets after being kicked out of the moat someday.

King Vodyanoy lifted his pitchfork and slammed it down against the grass, making absolutely no noise because it was wet dirt rather than stone. Up in the sky, storm clouds gathered. "I will pay husband price to Dark Undermasters in rain. By tomorrow, moat shall be replenished."

I narrowed my eyes. "So, you could have done this all along?"

"Yes," King Vodyanoy said. "But why do that when you can get other guy to pay for it."

Okay, points to the naked toad man.

MAIN QUEST UPDATED:

UPGRADE DRAGON KEEP 4/12
+ 500 EXP
+ 300 EXP (Get King Vodyanoy to pay for it)

SIDE QUEST(S) COMPLETED:

WET AND WILD GIRLS COMPLETED 1/1
+ 1000 EXP
+ 500 EXP (Peacefully Resolve Dispute)
+ 1 *Ring of protection*
+ 50 GP

Level 3 to 4
4000/10000 EXP

"Well, that was easy," I muttered.

"You can't be serious!" Mrs. Miller said. "You really just expect us to let our son walk off to go sire a bunch of mer-babies?"

"Rusalka, not mer," King Vodyanoy said.

Mr. Miller took her by the arm. "Let's go, dear. We have to plan for our son's wedding."

Theresa sighed. "It's better than nothing. I suppose Klaus will do."

"Thank you!" Klaus said, delighted. He was the only one who seemed entirely happy about the event's proceedings.

"At last!" Hans said, spinning around and taking Summer Breeze by her arms. "We are free to wed."

"Do not speak," Summer Breeze said. "We must go mate now."

Well, I could tell who wore the pants in that relationship. You know, if either of them wore clothes.

Bloodstorm got up. "I'm heading back to the Black Cat for lunch. It's about to rain and I don't fight in the rain unless I have to."

"Same here, Aaron," Jon said, shaking his feathers. "You should come join us. I assume there's food at the tavern."

I wasn't sure I was done side questing. "Sure, maybe. I'll catch up."

Soon, everyone left but for Winter Chill.

I looked over at her, trying to keep my gaze centered on her eyes. "Uh, hey, what do you want?"

The Rusalka stared at me. "Sex."

I blinked.

CHAPTER NINETEEN
THE SEXY PWIFFLE CARDS

YOU RECEIVE 2 HP IN DAMAGE; YOU SUFFER STATUS EFFECT
(WATERLOGGED)
+ YOU HAVE RECEIVED 1 PWIFFLE CARD (RUSALKA)

I was utterly soaking wet from head to toe. My boots sloshed as I moved through the front door of the Black Cat, feeling the warm heat of the hearth. The brothel was still as full as it had been in the morning, even a little more so, as the torrential downpour continued outside. Mind you, that wasn't why I was completely drenched.

Ania Rose was sitting on a wooden stool at the bar next to Kragen Bloodstorm. A bowl of meat had been set aside for Jon that he was happily pecking at. Maelor the Black was tending to the customers but looking at my arrival with a bemused look on his face. It was an expression matched by the others, though there was a hint of disapproval in Ania's eyes.

"So, she tried to drown you, huh?" Ania asked. "Every man in the Southern Kingdoms knows the stories but men keep falling for it."

I picked up my cloak and started wringing it out in front of the fire. "I used to be a lifeguard, so I managed to hold my breath."

"But here's the real question," Jon asked, looking up. "Did you finish?"

I glared at Jon.

Bloodstorm turned around and chuckled. "There is a valuable life lesson in this."

"Which is?" I asked, my voice absent of any humor. I was not in a good mood.

"You should have killed the guy and taken his *ring of water breathing*!" Bloodstorm replied. "Remember, if you think killing doesn't solve your problem then you obviously haven't killed enough."

"Uh huh," I replied, staring at him.

"Allow me to offer you a free pint. Unless you would like something stronger?" Maelor said, lifting a metal stein and putting it on the counter for me. There was a single seat open in front of Jon and they'd apparently been saving it for me. Which was a kind gesture from a small business owner like Maelor. Either that or no one wanted to sit next to Ania and Bloodstorm.

Pulling off my boots and emptying their contents before putting them back on, I walked over to the free bar stool and sat down.

"The weakest spirit you have, please," I said.

"That is an unusual request," Maelor said. "Garland."

Garland had been a legendary drinker in addition to lover and fighter. That was another area where we differed. The booze part at least. Given my addiction to Pwiffle, I tended to avoid just about anything else I might find habit forming. I hadn't had any complaints about the love part from my girlfriends and given some of my breakups, it would have come up if there had been. As for being a fighter? Well, that was a work in progress it seemed.

"Blame my 10 Constitution," I replied, sighing.

"I hope that wasn't shown in your performance," Ania teased.

My face flushed with embarrassment. "It's not like, mmm, err—"

Maelor put a warm frothy mug of brown liquid in front of me that I presumed to be beer. I sipped the result and got a strange look from both Bloodstorm as well as Ania. Apparently, this was not the way to drink a light booze. Not that they seemed to be having any trouble downing their much harder looking stuff.

"You don't owe me any explanation, Imposter," Ania said, using the title almost affectionately now. "It's like a cookie. One is put down before you, you eat it."

"Except instead of a cookie, it's p—" Jon started to say before I gave him a light smack.

Truth be told, I was regretting the entire encounter and that was because of Ania. It was weird to even think about courting her (for lack of a better term) but I had to admit a powerful attraction. The fact I'd tried to have a one-night stand with a water spirit, cool as that sounded in theory, left me feeling sort of ashamed. It was also a ridiculous notion since, forty-eight hours ago, she'd been a fictional character and considered me a guy walking around in her brother's clothes. Her brother who she'd been romantically involved with.

Okay, yeah, that would never not be weird.

"How is Agata?" I asked, deciding to switch subjects.

Ania's expression darkened. "Not good. She's suffered through a lot of violent and terrible nightmares."

"Past loops?" I asked, referring to the previous adventures she'd had with other Garlands. While a fantastic concept, the actual reality was horrifying to think about. Imagine being forced to repeatedly witness your hometown being sacked by monsters and dealing with people claiming to be your lost brother.

"Yes, and also her own past," Ania said. "You know she was married to the Queen's Brother, right?"

"Ivan Crookback, yes," I replied. "I always liked him."

Ania shot me a glare.

"What?" I asked. "He was always very clever and wasn't terrible to her in the books. It was Jorg who was the mean one."

Technically, the two queens had two brothers with the eldest being their half-brother, Jorg the Bastard Knight. Ivan Crookback was the physically disabled younger sibling of the twins who was a genius, sarcastic, and cynical. He served as a kind of audience stand-in for commenting on a lot of the idiocy and mayhem going behind the scenes at the court. Jorg, by contrast, was a terrifying warrior who laid waste to everything he touched. Because he was good-looking, though, he had plenty of fan girls.

"Whatever his personal qualities, he was an enemy of my house," Ania said, sighing. "What little is left of it."

Yeah, her marriage to Ivan Crookback was just the beginning of her issues.

"Well, I have every hope she'll get better," I said, trying to cheer her up.

"Why?" Ania asked. "You don't know anything about magic. I don't know much about your world, but I know it doesn't have much in the way of sorcery. For all you know, my sister could spend the rest of her life in a sleep or die tomorrow."

I paused. "I think she's stronger than that."

"You don't know her," Ania said.

"No, I don't," I said. "But I know you and you can't be that different."

Ania snorted then paused. "I've been with my sister in two cycles. The first one with Valentin was bad, worse than her husbands. He was... vicious to her. She was finally broken by that. The second cycle, she was a heroine. A far better person than I was. Strong and confident. You know what those two women have in common?"

"What's that?" I asked, feeling like I was stepping into a minefield.

"They both no longer exist," Ania said, finishing off her beer. "Both persons were created by their circumstances that have been erased from their minds by a deranged wizard that has decided we are supporting characters in a story about a dead man."

"I'm sorry," I said, genuinely sympathetic.

"You seem like a better person than the other imposters I've met, Imposter," Ania said, lifting the arm with her Mark of the Champion. "Mokosh knows I always wanted to throw Father Adolf onto a pyre. But you can't fill Garland's boots. It doesn't matter how many monsters you slay or what sort of magic you get out of these gaudy little bracelets."

"I just want to get home," I said, not entirely truthfully. "Maybe help a little along the way."

"I don't know who the new person will be that emerges out of that sleep she's trapped in or even if she will. I do know that freeing her from the fate of this ridiculous farce of an adventure is all I can do for her," Ania said, getting up from her bar stool. "You should take what pleasures you can out of this place, Aaron. It will kill you eventually and then all you'll have is memories. That and whatever carrion your master will feed you once you're turned into a crow."

Jon looked up from his bowl. "Well, that's just rude."

Ania tossed a small coin purse to Maelor, who caught it with one hand, barely moving. "I'll be taking Alfred."

Maelor nodded.

Ania proceeded to go up to one of the shirtless men and took him by the hand, leading him up the stairs with a sad, almost resigned expression on her face. He, on the other hand, looked quite happy to be with her.

"Yeah, I can see how she's burning with desire for you," Jon said, watching her go. "You're making a real solid impression on her."

"Jon..."

"You bought her a room, a repaired castle door, and even got her a moat," Jon said. "What more could she ask for?"

"Jon..."

"Oh, you also killed the evil knight guy who was threatening her village," Jon said. "I'm not saying that entitles you to a roll in the hay but maybe a little consideration."

"Shut up, dude," I said, sighing and going back to nursing my beer.

"Are you sure you don't want milk?" Maelor said. "Honestly, that is just pathetic, and I know you can afford better."

"Ah leave Garland alone," Bloodstorm said. "I don't understand or, care, really about all the nonsense they're talking about, but the guy is clearly having lady issues. Which there is only one other cure for than alcohol."

"Please don't say violence," I said, sighing.

"Violence!" Bloodstorm said, raising a fist. "You need to burn that extra energy out of you."

"I think that extra energy was already burned out of him," Jon said. "Or washed out of him. What's a dirty water-based pun?"

Bloodstorm pounded his fist into his palm. "Come on, let's wrestle."

SIDE QUEST(S) ADDED:
WRESTLE WITH BLOODSTORM 0/1
Reward: 500 EXP, Wager

I thought about my 10 Strength score and shook my head. "Yeah, that's not going to happen."

DECLINE QUEST? Y/N

"Hell yes," I said, annoyed. "I'm not in the mood to get my ass beat by a giant Viking minotaur guy."

"Ogre, not minotaur," Bloodstorm corrected.

"Whatever dude, the answer is no," I said, wishing my clothes would dry faster and wondering if I should just head back to the keep and hang them up on a clothesline in my room. We hadn't exactly hired a staff yet and I wasn't sure who would pay for it if we did.

SIDE QUEST(S) DECLINED

"Aww," Bloodstorm said, frowning. "You don't know what you're missing out on."

"Getting punched in the face?" I asked, glaring. "I think I do. You know this epic fantasy hero thing isn't all cool powers and monster slaying you know. There's some genuinely horrible stuff happening, and I don't mean people trying to kill me. There are real people getting hurt and I'm probably never going to see any of my family again either. Hell, even if I did see them, I'd probably be hunted for the rest of my life. It turns out my bosses are an evil conspiracy like, arms trafficking or something, here. It's like drilling for oil in Middle Earth. I'm sure they'd have me killed if I did get back home. Plus. I'm probably a psychopath? There's probably a legal limit on how many people you can kill for self-defense before it becomes murder. I'm like five guys in and you know these games will have you kill like hundreds before they're over. Plus, yeah, everyone seems to hate me except a ghost bird and a psychopath. No offense."

"I have no idea what you even called me," Bloodstorm said. "So, none taken."

"Aaron, are you drunk?" Jon asked, confused. "How much of a light weight are you?"

"He can't be drunk," Maelor said. "That's a sarsaparilla. I keep them behind the bar for children."

"You serve children in the brothel?" I asked, shocked.

"Yeah," Maelor said. "I am one of the highest paying employees of young mothers in town."

"Oh," I said, pausing. "I guess there's a lot of single mothers, what with all the deaths."

"Oh, no, most of them are married," Maelor said. "Their husbands get a discount obviously."

I blinked then went back to whining. "There's also the fact that this is a genuine responsibility. I didn't agree to become the only guy in the world standing between this world and oblivion but that's apparently the case now. Plus, there's nothing stopping Veles from coming to my world if he takes over this one as crossover seems possible. I was barely able to pay my rent back in my world. This is all just way too big for me."

Maelor nodded his head patiently and Bloodstorm gave me a friendly slap on the back that still felt like him punching me.

I drained my pint before sighing. "Sarsaparilla is actually from Southeast Asia and came to the United States in the 19th century. You really shouldn't have it as a drink here. It's like potatoes in fantasy novels. They really shouldn't exist in a historically accurate simulation of the times."

"I can't imagine why people think you might be on the spectrum," Jon said. "I mean that. Really."

"We have potatoes," Maelor said. "You need a hot meal, bath, and the love of a not-so-good woman."

"I already had sex today," I said, with a kind of dismissive attitude I never expected to have about it. "It ended with me being hit in the face with a bucket of water equivalent."

"An unusual experience during sex with a woman, I admit," Maelor admitted. "At least just with a woman."

I smirked. "Okay, that was actually funny."

"Thank you," Maelor said.

"The stress is finally getting to you, I get it," Jon said, nodding. "You pushed it down as long as you could with all the excitement. Believe me, man, I relate. Until I figure out how to release some of this insane tension I'm experiencing, I'll be there for you. We may have started as a familiar and guide but now you can count on me as a friend."

"Thanks, buddy," I said, feeling drunk but obviously not actually so. "You'll figure out how to masturbate somehow."

"Male birds pleasure themselves by rubbing their cloaca, the underside of the tail, on objects," Bloodstorm explained like a scientist. "Fun fact, if it's rubbing against your hand or shoulder, it's probably getting itself off."

Jon stared at him.

"What?" Bloodstorm said. "What do you think male birds talk about?"

"I'll be back in a few hours," Jon said. "There's a couple of patrons I need to..."

Jon flew away.

"And he was never seen again," I said, chuckling.

"I'm not sure what to charge him for that," Maelor said, dryly.

"I'm going to go beat some people up for money," Bloodstorm said, standing up. He slapped me on the shoulder. "Tomorrow, we shall kill more things and you will feel better. If Ania does not want you as a lover, you should sleep with her sister."

"This is not about Ania," I muttered.

"Sure, it isn't," Bloodstorm said, clearly not believing me. He walked off, shaking his head with a bemused expression on his face.

"Another please," I said, offering my empty stein to him.

That was when a beautiful curly-haired brunette with pale white skin, a diaphanous white gown, elf ears, and very prominent canines sat down beside me. She looked like she'd escaped an old Hammer Horror picture or a Clive Caldwell pinup painting for TSR's *Ravenloft* campaign setting. Like Maelor, she was an elf *and* a vampire.

"This is my daughter, Angelica," Maelor said. "She's the 50 GP service."

"Uh, hi," I said, nervously.

CHAPTER TWENTY
THE LITTLE LOST DRAGON PUP

YOU RECEIVE 2 HP IN DAMAGE; YOU NOW HAVE THE
STATUS EFFECT
(ANEMIA)
+ YOU HAVE RECEIVED 1 PWIFFLE CARD (FEMALE
VAMPIRE)

"You know, I'm coming dangerously close to respecting you, Aaron. When I was Garland, I just stuck with human women, but you banged two monster ladies in a single night. I think those are both Pwiffle cards I never acquired," Jon said, flying beside me. I was riding on the back of Stompy, clutching my legs to the side of the steed like a vice while Bloodstorm jogged behind us. Apparently, he didn't get tired as a half-vampire ogre.

"I thought you got the 50 GP service," I muttered, feeling like death warmed over as I reached into my bag and pulled out the alchemical healing potion, I'd won from Maelor.

I was still suffering from the Waterlogged status effect and earlier damage despite "resting" for the night. Apparently, that didn't count when you let a vampire feed on you.

I chugged down the drink and was surprised to find it tasted suspiciously like a Cherry Snapple.

YOU HAVE RECOVERED FROM ANEMIA AND WATERLOGGED. YOU HAVE RECOVERED 4 HP.

"Yeah, let's just say your 50 GP service and mine were a bit different," Jon muttered, sarcastically. "I'm lucky I didn't end up with a status effect of Fantasy Herpes."

"Hey, my father runs a clean establishment!" Bloodstorm said, shouting from the back. "You take that back!"

"Fine-fine!" Jon said, apologizing. "It was totally worth it and I'm just being an ass."

"You're a bird not an ass," I said, shaking my head. I was feeling much better physically but the seriousness of my situation still weighed heavily on my soul. It was becoming all too real for me, and I wasn't sure if I had the fortitude to endure it.

Mentally, not my crappy CON score.

"We should go hunting for the fifty collectible Pwiffle cards in the game world," Jon said, still acting like this was a game.

"We're not doing that," I said, shaking my head. "This is a main quest priority."

SIDE QUEST(S) ADDED:

COLLECT ALL UNIQUE PWIFFLE CARDS 3/50
Reward: 50,000 GP, 50,000 EXP, Divine Pwiffle Deck

"You have got to be frigging kidding me," I said, looking at the reward for that side quest. "That is *insane*. You could rebuild the Dragon Pit for that kind of money."

"I know, right!" Jon said, cheerfully justifying his own misguided adventures before his death. "Plus, the Divine Pwiffle Deck comes with its own special quest! If you get all fifty cards, you can do a Pwiffle battle with Veles himself."

My headache was starting to return. "Veles, the God of Darkness, will stop his campaign of world domination/genocide in order to sit down and play a game of Pwiffle?"

"Yes," Jon said. "It's sort of like the fact the Devil finds time to have fiddle contests in Georgia. If you manage to win, then you'll get a wish."

"A wish," I said, unsure how that would even work.

"You know, like genies and shit," Jon explained.

"And Veles would just honor that agreement versus blasting me for opposing him?" I asked, still stunned at the sheer stupidity of the plotline.

"I mean, you have to beat him first," Jon replied. "I assume Veles has a pretty wicked deck."

"Yeah, we're not doing that," I said, shaking my head. "I don't care how much we'd get paid for it. Decline—"

"Ah-ah-ha!" Jon interrupted. "What if I told you that you wouldn't have to go running around all the Southern Kingdoms chasing various side quests and engaging in dozens of Pwiffle battles against a variety of challengers. I mean, I had to crisscross the map and win a dozen tournaments and marathon games against people like the Witch Queen of Angho'horak but you don't."

"The Witch Queen of Angho'horak plays Pwiffle?" I asked, confused.

"*Everyone* plays Pwiffle," Jon said. "It is the national pastime of 9 out of 10 Fantasy Slavs."

"I am going to regret this," I said, saying something that I suspected was rapidly going to become my catch phrase. "How, exactly, would I avoid having to go card hunting across the continent?"

Why, why, why was I doing this? Was my lust for collectible cards truly so insatiable? Was it just the devil on my back that I couldn't kick? Or, in this case, the raven?

"I collected 47 out of the 50 cards," Jon explained. "They're presumably still on my body."

"You were killed by a dragon," I pointed out. "They're probably either burned to nothing or were destroyed when the dragon ate your remains."

"Not true, my friend!" Jon replied, cheerfully. "I found the body of a previous Garland in a giant flesh-eating amoeba the size of a Smart car. It had been in there for months and while it had been reduced to a skeleton, all its previous equipment was still intact. Apparently, we're meant to recover each other's equipment."

"That's horrifying," I said. "A giant amoeba?"

"I assume gelatinous cubes are copyrighted," Jon replied. "Either way, with the 47 plus these two new ones, we'd have 49."

"I can do basic math, Jon," I said, rolling my eyes. I hated to admit it but I was intrigued by the prospect.

"Let's just hope the final Pwiffle card doesn't require you having to bone a centaur lass. That's too much booty even for you, I think," Jon said. "Plus, bestiality. Wait, is it bestiality if they have a human top? Asking for a friend."

"You bang a centaur from the front," Bloodstorm said, as if speaking from experience. Which he probably was. "The men and women both have their parts down there, which is why Centaur men love human women. More options for positioning."

"Uh huh," I said, really wishing this conversation would end.

"It's the same with merfolk," Bloodstorm explained. "The art gives them fish tails but it's really split down the middle so you can get in real—"

"Please stop," I said, closing my eyes. "I have no idea why my day is turning into an anatomy of monster sex."

"I think you have a pretty good idea of why we're talking about monster sex," Jon said. "I'm not saying you should bang a dragon, but I tried to and died. Now I pass that quest to you."

Thankfully, a new objective didn't appear. "I'll think about it. That's all I'm promising."

"You alone can defeat Veles, Aaron!" Jon flew around in a circle above my head. "I've seen you play Pwiffle!"

"Yeah, I think I'd prefer to beat him with my magic or sword, thank you," I said, sighing.

"Okay, Bloodstorm, are you ready for our next quest?"

"Does it involve murder?" Bloodstorm asked.

"Maybe?" I asked.

"Then hell yeah!" Bloodstorm replied. "Some days I'm just so full of fury that I start hacking and slashing with no regard to friend or foe. All I'm seeing is red and it's such a glorious color. Then I awaken and am surrounded by the corpses of friends. Then I feel bad. Ever get days like that?"

"I can't wait for Ania to rejoin us," I muttered.

"Yeah, we need a thief," Bloodstorm replied, missing my point. "There could be traps, treasure chests, or pockets to pick."

"Plus, her sister was a good healer," Jon said. "I mean, I never listened to a word she had to say but that's just because she was a churchy-churchy type."

"A church that worships sex," I pointed out.

Jon flew down to perch himself on my saddle. He stared forward. "I admit, I might have benefited from paying better attention to my surroundings. Maybe not all dialogue should have been skipped. Mistakes were made. Lessons were learned."

"Did you actually learn anything?" I asked.

Jon beamed. "I didn't learn a goddamn thing."

Stompy made a snort that sounded like a laugh.

I laughed and shook my head. "We should do the monster-slaying quest next. I feel more confident about our ability to pull it off now that we've finished with a few other ones."

"Hell yes!" Bloodstorm shouted. "U-S-A! U-S-A!"

Both Jon and I looked back at him.

"I mean the, uh, United Southern Alliance," Bloodstorm said, sheepishly. "The group created for the purposes of fighting Veles before it sadly fell to in-fighting due to the machinations of the Mad Queen."

"Is it just me or does he not actually act like a person from this world?" I asked, looking at Jon.

"Your low WIS score is showing, Aaron," Jon said, shaking his head. "Anyway, I did learn one important lesson."

"Which was?" I asked.

"How to masturbate," Jon said. "Expect it to be happening all the time now."

"Ugh," I said, pulling out the *ring of protection* +1 I'd gotten from the last quest before slipping it on. "Just tell me when we reach the farm we're supposed to save."

AC 5 is now AC 6

"Aren't you the guy with the magic map?" Jon asked.

"I'm not talking to you. I'm leaving the travel plans to Stompy," I replied, holding up the ring to look at it. It was a gold band that resembled the one from the Lord of the Rings movies, complete with elvish writing. Since the Mark of the Champion translated everything, I knew it read, *ring of protection +1.*

Kind of disappointing.

Stompy whinnied.

The demon steed took us over the stone bridge leading into the farms surrounding Crossroad, this time to a deserted one on the edge of the community. Most of the crops had been burned down and there were a series of buildings that had been reduced to ruins. A plain wooden fence surrounded the place, and I saw a pair of individuals gathered at the gates.

The first of these individuals was a knight in red plate armor with his helmet under his right arm, held to his side. He had a kite shield with elaborate heraldry incorporating a lion, a dragon, and an eagle of all things. The guy was unfortunately also possessed of a Prince Valiant-esque haircut that I refused to believe had ever been fashionable and there was something about the guy that told me he wasn't going to be my friend.

The second guy was an ordinary looking farmer, at least for these parts, with a beard that reminded me of Weird Al from "Amish Paradise." They were both staring off into the burnt-out disaster of a farm and a single animal standing there among the ruins: a Pembroke Welsh Corgi. Which if you are not familiar with them are low-riding adorable balls of fluffiness that may not be the least intimidating dog breed ever but certainly come close.

"The dog is going to be the monster, isn't it?" I asked, sighing.

"At least it isn't a rabbit," Jon said.

"Yeah, I'm not sure this is that much of a defense against being derivative," I said as we approached the pair. "Forsooth, fellow travelers! It is I, Garland of Nowhere, come to aid thee in thine quest! How dost thou fair this day?"

The farmer looked up to me. "Why are you talking like that?"

I sighed.

"This is what you get for roleplaying," Jon said. "It's like those poor put-upon employees at Underland in Florida. They don't actually want to roleplay, and your customer information is fed to them via an earpiece. Just tell them your goddamn order and go wait for your mutton like everybody else."

"That was a curiously specific example," I replied.

"Four years as the guy cosplaying as Ivan Crookback," Jon muttered, giving a shudder that spread across his feathers. "All the time being told Ivan wasn't Asian. The horror, the horror."

"I'm here to kill the monster," I said, dropping the accent.

"You're too late," the farmer said.

"I'm what now?" I asked, blinking.

The knight in the red armor put on his helmet and pulled out his sword. "I, Ser Olivier de Valmont, Knight of the One True Queen have come here to slay the beast instead! You and your filthy order of Undermasters have preyed upon the good people of the Southern Kingdoms for too long, charging the peasantry for monster slaying that should be done in the name of chivalry and heroism alone! No more! The treasure of the Beast of Blackwood Bog shall be mine!"

I was a dedicated book reader and had no idea what he was talking about. "Do I need to read the glossary? Was there an NPC I was supposed to talk to first?"

"Have at thee!" Ser Olivier shouted, charging at the Welsh corgi.

The Welsh corgi proceeded to open its mouth and release a torrent of flame that proceeded to barbecue the knight in his armor worse than being hit by the giantess' flamethrower. It was particularly gruesome because it took him several seconds to die.

Bloodstorm watched the whole proceeding with a kind of fascinated awe. "I want to keep it!"

"No," I said, pausing. "Wait, maybe."

The farmer turned back to me after watching the entire proceeding. "Yeah, the dog is a baby dragon."

I looked at the dog who was doing doughnuts after killing the knight. "Uh-huh."

"It's true!" The farmer insisted.

"I believe you!" I said, gesturing to the late Ser Olivier's charred remains. The armor had melted around his skeleton. "I'm just assessing the situation!"

The farmer shook his head. "It must have gotten lost from its flight when the dragon attacked last night. Unfortunately, it got into old Karl's home, and you can see the results."

"What was all that about a treasure?" I asked, confused.

The farmer shrugged. "Supposedly, there's a dragon living in Blackwood Bog. Dragons have treasure. The knight thought this was the dragon and by killing it, he could claim it. He even said he'd forgo being paid because of it."

"How generous of him," I said, sarcastically. "Well, I'm not killing a baby. Dragon or not."

"Oh, come on, man!" Bloodstorm said.

I stared at him.

Bloodstorm lowered his gaze. "You're right, that dog is ridiculously cute. I want to name him Sparky."

Stompy whinnied in approval.

Jon looked between us. "You guys are all nuts. This could be an ancient monster that has just assumed the form of a fluffy puppy dog. You can never trust your eyes in the Southern Kingdoms. What if it's some wizard's foul experiment or part of a trap. A baby dragon is still a *dragon*."

I called over to the dog, relying on the bracelet to translate. "Hey, little one, do you know where your mommy is?"

"No!" the doggie responded, sounding like a six-year-old boy. "Will you help me find her?"

Jon covered his face with his wing. "If this is how I die for a second time, lie and say that it was an STD that did me in."

CHAPTER TWENTY-ONE
THE CURSE OF BLACKWOOD BOG

"Aaron, has anyone told you that you're an objectively terrible monster hunter?" Jon said, staring at me as I held the corgi. The corgi, which I was calling Sparky due to the fact dragon names were one long growl, merrily panted away as we rode to Blackwood Bog. It was a long shot that his mother was the titular Beast of Blackwood Bog, but we didn't have a lot of other clues to go on. Sparky wasn't all there, he had the dragon equivalent of something you'd medicate, and just described his home as wet and full of smelly trees.

It was already the afternoon as we finally left the confines of Crossroad village and into the wilderness beyond. Ledziania was a beautiful country with tall mountains, vast forests, and long stretches of tall green grass. The soundtrack really kicked in with the woman shouting in the background to the orchestra even as I bounced along on Stompy's back. I wasn't going to risk any attempt at flight until I'd taken a few lessons (which hopefully would never come). As before, Bloodstorm jogged behind us with no apparent difficulty keeping up.

"I'm just getting started as a monster hunter," I replied. "Frankly, for three days experience, I think I'm doing fantastic."

Jon somehow looked annoyed despite being a bird with no discernible face. "I mean you're supposed to be slaying monsters. So far, you refused to slay a den of ratkin, negotiated a marriage agreement with the water succubi, and now are taking the baby dragon home to its mother."

"Not to mention banged two monster ladies," Bloodstorm said. "That's how you get people like me."

"I'm just saying: what is this Disney Channel bullshit you're peddling?" Jon asked.

I covered the puppy's ears with my hands. "Don't use that kind of language in front of Sparky."

"I am a dog!" Sparky said. "You can't tell that I am a dragon when I am a dog. Did you know dragons could shapeshift?"

"I did not!" I said, playing with the thing like I did my nephew, George.

"I'm not supposed to eat the bird, yes?" Sparky asked.

"Hey!" Jon said.

"No," I said, petting him lightly. "Friend, not food."

"Aww," Sparky said. "You should always hold back your fire when frying knights because then you can't eat them. My mom taught me that!"

"I wonder if this world could be saved from hordes of marauding monsters if we introduced this world to Sesame Street," Jon said.

"Sesame Street is the puppet show with the cloth animals, right?" Bloodstorm asked, pretty much confirming he knew a lot more than he claimed.

"Okay, spill," I said, looking back at him. "Where the hell would you have ever heard of Sesame Street?"

"I admit, I have been to your world, Ser Garland, or whatever your real name is," Bloodstorm said. "I have journeyed through the dark magic portals in Death Mountain to the far-off kingdom of Mish-Eh-Gahn."

I blinked. "You…have?"

"Woah, I never knew this from our previous adventures together," Jon said, stunned. "There's so much more to this game than just card games and sex."

"You've taken your first step into a larger world," I replied, doing my best Sir Alec Guinness voice.

"I mean, I don't give a crap about any of it but it's cool to know it's there," Jon said, ruining the moment.

I rolled my eyes before shaking my head. "I hate to ask, Bloodstorm, but didn't you, uh, stand out?"

Bloodstorm nodded. "I admit, I had to file my horns down and wear a hat. Still, I got pulled over many times by your city guards. Apparently, I fit a profile. I assume you have a lot of ogre criminals in your world."

I paused before looking at Jon. "You know, I'm not touching that one. At all."

"Wise," Jon said, bobbing his head up and down.

"But the peaceful life of indoor plumbing, lightning powered devices, and easy women found on the Timber app was not for me," Bloodstorm said, sighing. "The hellish conditions of boxing up items at the Epic Dungeoneering™ warehouse was work fit for goblins, so I left it to them. It was good because the death lords came in and slaughtered the slaves there afterward and the warehouses are staffed by hordes of the undead."

I stared at him, waiting for some sign he was telling a particularly brilliant joke. It never came. "That is so stupid, it has to be true."

"It explains so much about how fulfillment centers work," Jon said. "If Bezos finds out about this, the purges will begin."

Jon and I both looked down at Sparky to see if he had any reaction to all this.

"I am a dog!" Sparky said, panting.

"Good boy," I said, watching us finally reach the edge of Blackwood Bog.

The place was covered in an eerie mist that raised a foot above the ground as glowing green lights danced in the distance of the twisted gnarled trees. Sunlight didn't seem to penetrate the canopy of the trees, and I could hear strange as well as unnatural noises mixed with the typical sounds of the outdoors. The music from the bracelet also took on an eerie tone with an emphasis on a single violin.

"This looks like the kind of place Artax would drown in," Jon said, surveying the place.

"I wonder if we'll find any ROUS," I said, staring.

"Rodents of Unusual Size? I don't think they exist," Jon said, absently.

"Blackwood Bog is the site of the Dread Dinner," Bloodstorm explained. "Lord Rose and his family agreed to meet with the Mad Queen in his summer hunting lodge under a flag of truce. It was a great party, and many kegs of ale were opened. That was when Princess Apollonia, turned into a dragon, was released upon Crossroad. The servants of the Rose family had their throats cut and were tossed into the bog where Veles claimed their souls. Maria Rose was captured by a handsome vampire lord who had long coveted her and transformed her into his consort, the lady of Dragon Keep trading her soul to darkness for a chance at revenge. A dreadful curse settled down upon the Bog and its surrounding forest, causing any dead man tossed here to arise as one of the dead as well as the animals to become fearsome monsters."

"Yeah-yeah, we've all seen season one's finale," Jon muttered. "Everyone could tell something was up because all the book readers had smug expressions on their face, including my then-boyfriend and his sister. Who I then left my boyfriend, her brother, for but we're not talking about that."

"TMI, Jon, TMI," I said, staring at the accursed place. "I don't suppose the vampire who turned Lady Rose was your father, was it, Bloodstorm?"

Bloodstorm shrugged. "Who knows? It could have been any number of strigoi noblemen living in the immediate area."

I wasn't even sure that was a deflection. "Right."

"I should warn you that this may be out of our league," Jon said.

"Oh, how's that?" I asked, not quite ready to go into the spooky haunted swamp. "Other than the fact it looks like Dagobah."

"Without Yoda," Jon said. "At least as far as I know. The place is meant to be visited by higher level characters. It's recommended for characters 4-12 and I barely got out when I visited at level 8."

"Ah," I said, pausing. "That isn't good. Wait, how did you know what sort of level it was recommended for?"

"Soul Gaze Feat," Jon explained. "I personally recommend picking it up early as it lets you know some basic stats about the environments as well as your enemies."

"I thought that only the people with the Mark of the Champion leveled up," I said, perhaps being foolish.

"The rules for champions and regular NPCs are different," Jon said. "Unless you're blessed by Veles or the Mark, you're probably not going to be above 5th level as a human. Which means stabbing people kills them. However, our problem is that we'll be dealing with monsters and plenty of people who are."

"I suppose that does explain how the game keeps its gritty realism," I muttered, thinking about coming back here with Ania or a full party if possible. If it was above our level, it was probably a good idea to gird ourselves for war before we investigated the haunted swamp.

"Home!" Sparky said, sitting up and turning into a hawk before flying into the swamp.

"Oh my God, he just flew in," I said, staring. "This is like Leeroy Jenkins all over again."

"That was staged," Jon said, watching him go.

"Save him!" I said, pulling on Stompy and pointing for him to go into the swamp.

Stompy proceeded to hover a few feet off the ground with his wings before following the hawk. I was immediately swatted in the face with branches, fleeing birds, and other creatures. I wasn't going to lose the dragon pup to whatever horrible things were inside it.

Unfortunately, my heroic attempt to save the little dragon pup was interrupted by ramming into a thick branch that slammed into my chest and knocked me off my steed into the brackish water below. I was up to my chest in the stuff but, thankfully, that was mostly due to having fallen on my ass. The mud was thick and nasty around me as the smell of the place was akin to rotting meat rather than any swamp I'd visited in my youth. FYI - I'd visited several because my parents were freaks who believed children should be outdoors and not on their computers. Given my former profession as a video game designer, you can see how that worked out.

My demon steed disappeared into a black miasma of smoke, which was a sentence I am so glad to have been able to use, before swirling back into the rune on my hand. Apparently, that's how summoned mounts worked in this world. If you weren't riding them or preparing to ride them then they went back into their Pokeball runes. Seriously, I didn't even like Pokemon that much and I kept using that metaphor. My nephew, George, had a lot to answer for.

"Aaron! Aaron!" Jon said, flying and landing on a nearby branch. "Are you okay, man?"

I was touched by my familiar's concern. "Yeah, I've been better. I may have taken a couple of health damage, but I don't think I'm too bad off."

"You gotta get out of here, man!" Jon said, sounding genuinely panicked.

I slowly climbed to my feet, my boots clogging with slime. "I'm good, Jon. But I need to summon Stompy again and get Sparky."

"Forget the dog!" Jon said. "You have bigger problems. When I say this is a cursed swamp, I mean it is a *cursed swamp*."

"I'm coming!" Bloodstorm shouted, trudging through the swamp with big steps that reminded me of a man going through a tire course at boot camp or at least what was shown to be boot camp in movies. "Just don't engage any bog men without me!"

"Bog men?" I asked.

"The cursed soldiers of House Poppy," Jon explained. "Nobody got out of the Dread Dinner unscathed. Also, behind you."

House Poppy was one of the most detested set of villains in the Dark Undermaster books despite the fact they were pretty much just henchmen of the Mad Queen. They'd been vassals to House Rose and kinsmen who had lost their own keep to the civil war afflicting the Southern Kingdoms after the Old King died. Boris Poppy had been named the castellan of Dragon Keep and it had eaten at him to the point that he'd been one of the architects of the Dread Dinner as well as the Mad Queen's ascent.

Violation of sacred hospitality aside, that might not have been so bad for the Poppy family if not for the fact that their massacre had been conducted in a natural spot sacred to Mokosh. There were also stories that Lord Rose had been the goddess' lover as a young man and that had been partially why the goddess had trusted Perun's final son to the family. She had been, in simple terms, *pissed off* by the Poppy's tossing her ex's body into one of her sacred pools. Thus, she'd withdrawn her protection from the region and let Veles' power run wild. The massacred Rose bannermen had become undead and the Poppy soldiers as well as the Queen's Guard turned into monsters with the worst fate reserved for the Poppy family itself.

Supposedly.

Larry C.C. Weis hadn't gotten around to saying what curse had happened to the Poppy family itself, Boris, Eva, or Little Alexi. Not that I really cared. That had been three books ago and seemed like one of those plots that had gotten lost in the ever-expanding narrative. I'd only known that it had resulted in them becoming some sort of hideous thing that was no longer human. I hadn't really given much thought to what that might have looked like until I got a good look at what Jon was pointing out.

"Nasty boy that escaped the Queen! Nasty boy gets eaten," the first of the bog men spoke through a mouth of rotted hideous teeth.

Rising from the mud around me were men at arms of House Poppy in rusted armor that barely hung from their bodies, their faces a horrific collection of cancerous sores and mutated growths. Living tree branches wove in and out of their bodies while injuries leaked crimson mud. They looked less like the undead, which I wasn't sure they qualified as, than some sort of Medieval David Cronenberg abomination. Their weapons were broken almost to pointlessness but if a man hit you with a wooden shaft in the skull, then you were just as dead.

There were four of the Bog Men and they radiated a kind of aura that made me nauseous just being in their presence. Well, more than just looking at the horrifically cursed individuals did naturally. Instead, it was like just being a few feet away weakened me in the knees and I could imagine something like STATUS EFFECT: NAUSEA -2. I wasn't about to pause to check my bracelet, though.

"ARCANE FIRE!" I shouted, aiming my hand at the closest one, striking it in the chest and causing it to rear back before immediately returning to take a swing at my head with a broken half-sword. Bog men turned out to be a lot tougher than ordinary skeletons and I had the feeling I was way outclassed here.

No sooner did I prepare for another strike then I had to dodge out of the way of a second blow from a bog man wielding a dagger long enough to be a short sword. I managed to get out of the way but my attempt to roll out of the way was stopped by the mud around me. Unfortunately, that left the third to come at me with a fresh shining ax with a glow of fairy fire about it. I moved my head out of the way to avoid having it cleaved in two.

"Flee!" Jon said, clearly terrified for me despite his inhuman state.

"Right!" I said, climbing to my feet and running away as best I could. Unfortunately, before I could, I felt a horrible stinging pain in my back. The fourth and final of the bog men had a short bow that he buried an arrow in the back of my shoulder with. My ring shined a bit as the magic protected me from being instantly killed but it was still more pain than I'd ever felt in my life. I couldn't help but fall to my knees.

Bloodstorm was still a long way away, charging through the muck.

"To Veles we offer the boy who escaped!" the bog man with the magic ax said, lifting his weapon to take my head.

"I am never forgiving myself for this," Jon said, charging and clawing at the bog man with the ax, buying me a few seconds extra of life. Jon was then battered out of the way and skipped like a stone against the waters of the bog.

"WWGD," I muttered, thinking about What Would Garland Do. Unfortunately, Garland was a demigod master swordsman and sorcerer while I was barely beginning my career as the latter. So, I decided to act like Aragorn "Aaron" Bartkowski instead. "PUSH!"

Just like in *Dungeons & Dragons,* I'd regained my ability to do magic after a night's rest and the spell slammed into the bog man with the ax. Much to my surprise, he bashed into the other three behind him and they went over like bowling pins. It only bought me a few seconds, but

I cast another spell. The agony from my shoulder where an arrow was still buried burned terribly but webbing shot out of my hand and covered the four bog men as Jon managed to get out of the way just in time.

I somehow managed to climb to my feet and cast Arcane Fire repeatedly, blasting one of the creatures to pieces then moving onto the next. Three were finally destroyed before the fourth, the one with the magic ax got free. That was when it had two hatchets buried into its shoulders before it was headbutted to the ground by an enormous bull man. Bloodstorm pulled out the hatchets from its shoulder and then it was sent to its final death by a pair of blows coming down on its head with them.

Bloodstorm looked back at me. "Okay, we need to talk about all your kill stealing."

Chapter Twenty-Two
Talking with the Mama Dragon

I opened my mouth to make a pithy comment at Bloodstorm accusing me of kill stealing before collapsing on the ground. I checked my bracelet, and the results were...not good.

Health: 5/15 (Major Injury, Poisoned)

I reached up to pull the arrow out of my back.

"No, wait!" Jon said, walking on the mud in front of me.

I ripped the arrow out of my back only to feel even more horrifying pain as the wound became worse.

Health: 3/15 (Major Injury, Poisoned)

"Yeah, don't remove arrows when they're stuck in you," Jon said, looking away.

"Now you tell me!" I said, reaching up and shouting. "CURE!"

Health: 10/15

"Cure?" Bloodstorm asked, looking at Jon. "That's how he does magic?"

"Yeah, he one-words it," Jon said. "I'd say that it was a violation of storytelling, but Garland used to do little hand signs and just say the name of the spell."

"Yeah, but he said the name of the spell in the Old Tongue," Bloodstorm said, looking down at Jon.

"I'm not sure saying Fireball in Latin is any more magical than saying it in English," Jon said, pausing. "Especially since everyone here is speaking old timey Polish."

"Which is what you're speaking," Bloodstorm said. "Don't you just love magic?"

I slowly climbed to my feet, still feeling like crap. "Will you two shut up? I got lucky in that fight."

LOOK AT THE BONES QUEST UPDATED:

+1600 EXP [Bog Men]
+40 GP
+1 *Battle ax [Frost]* +2

Level 3 to 4
5600/10000 EXP

"400 EXP each," Jon said, shaking his head from side to side. "See? What did I tell you. These are just the mooks of the swamp. You aren't going to be able to take this zone until later."

"We need to find Sparky," I said, pressing myself up against the side of a nearby tree. "I'm not going to abandon a child in a place like this."

Jon flew up and landed on my shoulder. "Oh God, please, Aaron, don't tell me you're actually falling for it."

"It?" I asked.

"The hype!" Jon said. "The Song of Ice and Batman! You can't let yourself convince yourself that you're a hero or you'll end up getting yourself killed. You have to be strategic about these things."

"Jon—" I started to say, noticing Sparky had turned back into his dog form and was at my feet.

"Seriously, you have to accept the dog dragon thingy is gone. Dead. Doomed. Some quests are going to be failures," Jon said, looking down. "I, too, tried to do the right thing sometimes in my quest for the next Pwiffle card. You know what happened every time I did? Bad things! We'll mourn the little murderous fire ball thrower, light a candle in his honor, but we'll live to fight another day."

Bloodstorm picked up Sparky and petted him.

"I know it's hard…" Jon turned his head and saw the dog. "Okay, I hate you both."

"I found my mommy!" Sparky said, cheerfully.

"You did?" I asked, both happy and afraid. I wasn't sure that Sparky's mother would be any happier to see us than the bog men. "Where is she?"

Sparky again transformed into a bird and flew out of Bloodstorm's arms before heading toward a specific light in the mist.

"Come on," I said, starting to walk through the swamp and making short jumps from the tiny islands spread throughout the bog.

"You sure?" Bloodstorm asked. "I hate to say it but the raven is right. You need more strength if you're going to survive in this world. You're not Garland."

"No," I said, continuing. "Garland's dead."

I managed to avoid collapsing by the time I reached where the light was gathered to find a surprisingly pleasant-looking grove with bright bushes of roses spread with poppies as well as other flowers. Sunlight streamed through a break in the treetops and the oppressive aura of Blackwood Bog broke, even if just for twenty or third yards.

There was a cave entrance nearby as well built into a hilly outcropping that was utterly black inside. It was in front of this cave that Sparky was barking in his dog form, which attracted the movement of *something* inside it. It slithered and moved with a tremendous volume, and I heard the sound of a great rumbling.

Jon took a perch on the side of a nearby tree branch encircling the beautiful garden grove. "Now would probably be the time to leave.

You've managed to get the dragon pup to his mother. However, if you're here to slay the dragon, I'm going to tell you this isn't *Eldritch Ring*. You don't come back from the dead."

"Hi!" I shouted at the cave. "I'm here to return your child! He was lost outside in the village, and I wanted to make sure he was safe."

"I never thought in my wildest dreams, I'd prefer Brave Ser Robin over Lord Low WIS," Jon said, sighing. "It was nice knowing you, Aaron. Though, once you're a raven, please understand that I hope you're cursed with someone every bit as stupid....and hello, nurse!"

Jon's response was to the arrival of a spectacularly beautiful honey-skinned woman with long dark hair held in a faux crown braid decorated with poppies. She didn't look particularly Slavic, but I think we'd long since passed the point where anyone cared about that, and this was an alternate universe fantasy world anyway.

She was also dressed in a form fitting crimson dress that accented her generous form as well. I'd say it was another example of female monsters being unnaturally hot, but I was pretty sure she was a shapeshifted dragon. If you could assume any form you wanted, why not look like Rosario Dawson at *Medieval Times*?

In the dragon woman's hands, she clutched Sparky tightly. "You have come a long way to die, Ser Garland. Even if I appreciate you looking after my child. Sadly, I know you are prone to trickery and treachery in your hunting of *zemi*."

Well, that wasn't good. "I'm not here to slay anyone."

"Why do I find that hard to believe?" The woman said. "You know who I am and that this is the place where your destiny was forged. It is here the curse was laid upon our household for our role in the doom of House Rose."

I blinked. "You're...Eva Poppy?"

Jon stared. "Wow, that is totally not how I imagined her looking. Also, the Poppy family got cursed into being shapeshifting dragons? That's not a curse at all! At least when Polly was cursed into being the dragon queen, she was stuck being a dragon until Garland broke the spell! This is like *The Mummy*! Who curses a guy with incredible power?"

Eva Poppy, I was certain of it now, seemed confused. "As if you didn't know, Ser Garland. Also, your raven is speaking nonsense."

"That must make Sparky the Poppy heir, Alexi," I said, surprising myself by still being invested in book plot points after being this far into the game.

"Yes," Eva said, cocking her head to one side.

"Well, that explains a few things," I replied. Alexi had been treated as suffering a variety of ailments and that had been part of why Boris had decided to betray Lord Rose. Now I felt kind of terrible about always thinking Alexi was a little shit and wishing him dead. He was infinitely more likable as a dragon dog.

"You seem awfully calm for one who is about to die," Eva said, her voice low and threatening.

"Would you believe I'm not actually Garland?" I asked. "That I'm actually a guy from another world who people just keep mistaking for Garland?"

"No," Eva said.

"Then I died recently and have come back with amnesia," I said, not missing a beat. "All I want to do is see your kid home safe because I have a nep...because I like kids. I'd like to leave here peacefully but if I must do that riding on demon horseback for dear life, I will. Just make sure that he stays safe. There are some people out in town that were looking to hurt him and some of them might have succeeded."

Eva looked confused. "You didn't come here to slay me in order to avenge your family and take back the treasure here?"

"No," I said. "Besides then your son would be an orphan. Can't have that."

Eva looked down at her puppy dog child then nodded. "No, I suppose we cannot. I will take your word at face value then, Ser Garland and both spare your life as well as give you a reward."

"Thanks," I said, shrugging. "Just doing my job."

Eva gestured to her cave. "Come within. It is here you will receive what has been in my care too long."

My bracelet started pinging wildly.

ACHIEVEMENT UNLOCKED: Keepers of the Peace, Not Soldiers
(A) 25 - Solve three problems non-violently

ACHIEVEMENT UNLOCKED: Befriend the Baby Dragon
(A) 25 - Remember, they get bigger

SIDE QUEST(S) COMPLETED:

LOOK AT THE BONES (1/1)
+ 1000 EXP
+ 3000 EXP (Restore Alexi to his mother)
+ 1 *Boots of speed*
+ 50 GP

Level 3 to 4
9600/10000 EXP

NEW SIDE QUEST ADDED:

BREAK THE CURSE ON BLACKWOOD BOG
Reward: 5000 EXP, Rose Shield +3
Description: By either slaying the Lady of House Poppy or showing you are not a complete piece of crap like the real Garland was in her mind, you have discovered a way to make this world an objectively better place. Don't screw this up.

I looked at Jon. "What the hell does that mean?"

"Don't look at me, man," Jon said, spreading out his wings. "This is completely out of my comfort zone. I never really bothered to explore the non-combat options for this game. Hell, I didn't even know there were persuasion checks."

"I didn't make a persuasion check," I said, dryly.

"Didn't you?" Jon asked. "Also, where the hell is Bloodstorm?"

"Somewhere, I'm sure," I said, turning around and walking into the cave.

The interior was not what I expected, assuming you could expect anything from a dragon's cave. Heading down a tunnel, I emerged into a large underground grotto that was half-submerged as you might expect a cave in the middle of a swamp to be. It wasn't horrifying or dark, though, but illuminated by glowing crystals as well as bioluminescent fungus. There was also a nearby desk, shelves of books, and a collection of chests as well as collected arms. Presumably, this was meant to be the Treasure of Blackwood Bog.

Sparky jumped out of his mother's arms into the water where he transformed into a North American beaver and began paddling about. It caused me to wonder about why there were beavers in Fantasy Poland, but I reminded myself to turn off my brain because, otherwise, again, that way lay madness. If Tolkien can have hobbits eating potatoes in Middle Earth, then beavers could be found in Medieval Europe.

Now if it had been a Eurasian beaver...

"Come," Eva said, gesturing me down a side cave into another room that was illuminated by candlelight.

"Boom shakalaka," Jon said. "This could be where you're getting a Pwiffle card I don't have!"

I followed Eva into the room and was stunned at the sight that greeted me: a makeshift mausoleum. Laid out on a seven-foot stone slab was the skeletal remains of Lord Tomas Rose. He had been dead for fifteen years, but I recognized him by the Rose shield that was placed over his desiccated body. He hadn't been armed for battle but was wearing the formal attire of a man attending a party. Still, he'd gotten to his sword and shield with the latter present here and the former having been taken by Garland after his father had been cut down.

"Lord Rose was a good man who took us in after we'd been on the wrong side of the Old King's War," Eva said, staring at the body. "Unfortunately, our cousin's charity only enflamed my husband's jealousy and hatred. I spent years looking for his bones among the monsters of the swamp but when I finally found them, I realized I could not take them back to his home. My husband can leave the swamp due to his pact with Veles and my son because he was an innocent in all of this, though he still bears our curse. Would you bring Lord Rose home to his family's crypt?"

I didn't need to look at the quest being updated to know what had to be done. "I will. For Ania and Agata's sake if not my own."

"Thank you," Eva said, nodding her head. "As for your reward, it is a bit of information. My husband was here with his master, Valentin, and my sister, Cordelia. They were the dragons that have repeatedly sacked Crossroad. They are at the Great Temple of Chernobog. It is where said Old God rests. If you can gain the strength to do so, slay it, and end one of the dooms afflicting Ledziania."

My bracelet updated its in-universe map with the location of a main quest boss.

MAIN QUEST UPDATED:

JOURNEY TO THE EARTH TEMPLE AND SLAY CHERNOBOG (0/1)
Recommended Level: ???

I barely registered that because I was left with the knowledge that I'd be facing *two dragons* there. Yeah, this game had some serious leveling issues.

CHAPTER TWENTY-THREE
THE CRYPT OF THE ROSE LORD

Transporting the body of a man who'd been dead for a decade wasn't exactly a typical RPG experience, but I put the late Lord Rose's body in my bag before riding back to town on the back of Stompy. Bloodstorm joined me, not having been distracted by a monster or other horror but simply having had to use the bathroom.

I didn't know where I was supposed to take the body or what to do with it, so I just made the best guess I could and brought it to the chapel in Dragon Keep. There, I set him down on the altar. The chapel was half-flooded and had passages leading down to the moat that I'd recently restored with King Vodyanoy's help.

Whoops.

The Temple of the Old Gods was a strange mixture of a Christian church with an Olympian temple. It was based around a large central hall that used to hold pews but now only had a few broken ones scattered around the base of the altar. A large empty brazier used to be ignited during services but hadn't been for decades, especially with the six inches of brackish water on the floor.

Behind the altar was a broken statue of Perun holding a war hammer above his head. Half of the statue's face missing. Perun, at least the way Weis wrote him, was pretty much Marvel's Thor with all the nobility and wisdom of Odin but the lusty arrogance of Conan. Very far removed from the mythological Thor's more loutish behavior.

The version carved in the temple was dressed like a Frank Frazetta painting with just a loin cloth and straps.

Beside the statue of Perun to his left and right were statues of Veles and Mokosh. Veles looked like an evil wizard with the face of a dragon and honestly was not too far removed from my old 5th Edition Dragonborn character, Lord Blackscale. Mokosh's statue was topless, which would have been a commentary on sexism if not for the fact that Perun wasn't wearing much more.

Because the temple was in the depths of Dragon Keep, there were no windows. However, the walls had large Byzantium-style mosaics that depicted what I assumed was the collected mythology of the Southern Kingdoms' former religion. Perun and Veles creating the world with Mokosh, their marriage, the war between the gods, and some other incidents I couldn't interpret. Probably good for illiterate people to learn the stories but given this was the private chapel of the Rose family, probably a bit self-indulgent.

"You know I never understood religion," Bloodstorm said. "Why do a bunch of all-powerful beings care about what you do with your life?"

"Why does anyone?" I asked. "If you believe in anything values-wise, you want other people to share them."

"Woah," Bloodstorm said, blinking. "I never thought about it like that. You are a very wise man, Garland."

I stared at him, confused. "Err, if you say so."

"I can't believe I missed all this content during my playthrough," Jon said, sitting on my shoulder. "It just goes to show you that not every game is like the Elder Scrolls where the best stuff is the side material."

Adjusting Lord Rose's shield on his chest and stepping away from the altar, I took a deep breath. "Okay, I guess we wait and see if anything happens."

"That is a terrible plan," Jon said. "Seriously, there has to be a—"

That was when there was the sound of a ringing bell from the towers of Dragon Keep as well as the roar of dragons. A beam of moonlight streamed through one of the larger cracks in the ceiling despite the temple being underground. Where the moonlight struck, bushes of roses grew around the altar and spread throughout the chamber. The body of Lord Rose, skeleton really, vanished like Obi-Wan Kenobi and I saw the sight of his spectral form standing there in all his Timothy Dalton in Season One glory.

He nodded at me before walking away and vanishing.

ACHIEVEMENT UNLOCKED: Honor the dead rather than avenge them
(A) 50 - Choose to return Lord Rose's bones rather than slaughter the Poppy family

SIDE QUEST(S) COMPLETED: BREAK THE CURSE ON BLACKWOOD BOG (1/1)
+5000 EXP
+Rose Shield +3

YOU HAVE REACHED LEVEL 4

Level 4 to 5
4600/20000

"Okay, I'm just going to shut up now," Jon muttered, staring at the sight. "Mind you, I'm getting a little sick of this Paragon run you're doing. We could have at least slaughtered the ratkin. Maybe spare the ratkin children so you could kill them when they became adults. Sustainable ethical EXP farming."

"Hush you," I muttered.

"I'm not sure you made the right decision," a familiar voice spoke beside me. "I've devoted a lot of time to slaughtering the Poppy family. There were only three members left."

I turned around to see the sight of Ania Rose, wearing a white night gown that concealed most of her body but somehow, I still ended up checking her out. She had a long glowing dagger in her hands and had clearly come down here believing she'd have to murder someone.

"Yeah, well Sparky, err, Alexei, is a kid," I muttered, not really wanting to get into an argument about what choices I'd made.

The Achievement was specific that there were multiple ways to resolve the quest and it hadn't even occurred to me to do it the other way. Mind you, the other way sounded like suicide, but I could imagine eliminating the Poppy family one after the other before confronting the last at the Earth Great Temple. Honestly, that was probably what fans of the books would have expected but the thought made me sick.

"A dragon kid who murdered a bunch of people but apparently Aaron has a savior complex," Jon said. "Not that I approve of killing children. I'm against it. I just am noting that it doesn't count if you're not human, elf, or dwarf. If you're not, you're just walking EXP."

"That would include you, Jon," I said.

"Details, details," Jon said. "Also, I don't mean you, Bloodstorm."

Bloodstorm shrugged. "If you can take me, you deserve what I own. That's how morality works. By this ax, I rule."

I'd given Bloodstorm the *Battle ax +2 (Frost)* I'd acquired in Blackwood Bog even though I was feeling a bit uncomfortable about handing all the magic items over to him rather than dividing them among the party. However, most of the ones I'd acquired so far were useless for a Rogue like Ania or a Sorcerer like me, so it was really a matter of practicality. I still had the *boots of speed*, though, and wasn't sure how to divide those.

"I can get not wanting to kill a child but how did you figure out to return him to his mother in the first place?" Ania asked, surprising me by her words. I would have thought she would have had a bigger reaction to her father's ghost being liberated from his earthly prison. Then again, that might be one of those things you needed a minute to process.

I paused, thinking about how to answer that. "I was just thinking about the time I was at the mall with my sister about ten years ago. I'd just gotten my job with Epic Dungeoneering™ and she was still dealing with her divorce from her deadbeat of a husband. A mall is—"

"An enclosed marketplace, yes," Ania said. "I know."

Okay, that was weird. "Well, we lost four-year-old George for a couple of hours, and it drove Wendy insane with grief. We eventually found him in the ball pit, which is a horribly unhygienic place that I guess I was just seeing my nephew in the little guy."

"I would say I pity your family if a human BBQ maker reminded you of your nephew, but I already knew he traded your Pwiffle collection for green tea Kit Kats," Jon said. "Bleah."

Ania lifted her bracelet up and presented it to me. "I've got a strange request to make, Impost...Aaron."

"Thank you," I said, taking a deep breath.

"He much prefers to be called Aragorn by his loved ones," Jon said. "You should definitely call him that and nothing else. Even if he asks you not to."

I flicked Jon over my shoulder, and he fell in the water at our feet. "Help, I can't swim! I am a bird! Of the non-waterfowl variety!"

I picked him up and put him on a nearby overturned pew as he sloshed the water off. "You were saying, Ania?"

"Do you have 500 GP?" Ania asked.

"A little over that, why?" I asked. "I've spent most of what I earned on trying to fix the castle but—"

"Transfer it to me," Ania interrupted.

"Okie-dokie," I said, discovering that I could check out her equipment as a Companion.

ANIA'S EQUIPMENT
+3 *Vampire dagger of human slaying*
+3 *Katana of the Dark Moon*
Lightbringer [bow] +4/+5 **Undead [Holy]**
Cloak of protection +3
Bracers of defense +4
Boots of shadows +2
Ring of House Rose
Ring of backstabbing
Belt of regeneration

Dark Undermaster Master Rogue Armor +4
Token of Love [Garland]

4503 GP

"Wow!" Jon said, looking over at us from his pew. "What a haul! I now don't feel so bad about the fact that I emptied your equipment out during our tenure together!"

"Appropriate magic items for a 9th level Rogue," I said, nodding in appreciation before I transferred the 500 GP with a little coin jingle noise. "Even a little higher than normal with some end game material."

It seemed that Ania had been able to adventure on her own once she acquired her mark and maintain her equipment across the past two cycles. I tried to ignore the unseemly sense of jealousy that welled up in the pit of my stomach from seeing the *Token of Love*. Those were used in the books to represent betrothals or to symbolize true love. It was pointless of being jealous of a dead man, after all.

"Sometimes I wish the translation spell of our marks worked better," Ania said. "Other times, like now, I am very grateful that it does not."

"Okay, hold on," Ania said, tapping her mark for a moment.

"Wait, why did you give me such crap for the bridge money if you had 4500 GP?" I asked, remembering her annoyance at my fixing up her room instead.

"I made that over the past couple of days," Ania said. "I took a couple of short fast travels to the capital Poz'nan in order to assassinate some nobles serving the Mad Queen. Those always pay well."

"Ah," I said, not sure how to respond to admission of murder for hire. It at least confirmed that fast travel did exist in this world and apparently did work like teleportation since Poz'nan was 192 miles from Crossroad. Interestingly, Weis had put Crossroad roughly where Warsaw was located if you superimposed the Southern Kingdoms over Poland. Not that the maps of Mokosh were completely 1:1.

That was when she called up the REBUILD DRAGON KEEP quest and REBUILD CHAPEL requirement before paying the 5000 GP necessary to complete it.

The water slowly drained away from the ground around us and the chapel was transformed as if it was undergoing a construction montage in a television show. All the mosaics were restored to perfection, the missing pews were replaced, and the passageways leading to the underwater levels were no longer flooded. Hopefully, King Vodyanoy got a heads up about it if he was using them for anything and hadn't just been evicted.

The statues of Mokosh, Perun, and even Veles were also repaired. I could even see smaller shrines to the other Old Gods and some of the new ones as well. The Rose family had been nothing if not pious after all. Fat lot of good it had done them in the face of the Mad Queen's treachery and Veles's invasion.

A thousand candles were illuminated around the chapel, and I could feel the mystical power of the place grow several times over. I didn't know if religion had any supernatural ability beyond the fact most priests used magic in-setting but if it did then this location had a lot of it now.

MAIN QUEST(S) UPDATED:
UPGRADE DRAGON KEEP 5/12

"If I was Catholic and it wasn't blasphemous, I would do the sign of the cross right now," I said, nodding. "So, I will, instead, just offer up praise to Spider-Man and Princess Zelda that this is a beautiful place."

"It's a shrine to a dead god, one that hunts us relentlessly, and my father's lover," Ania said. "However, it was important to him and that's all that matters."

Bloodstorm raised his ax. "Good meat, good drink, good gods, let's eat. That's a prayer from your yellow god, Bart Simpson."

I blinked. "Right. You know, I am hungry. You want to have dinner delivered or whatever gets done around here?"

Ania smirked. "I think we can get something to eat, Aaron. I was sleeping off going without for three or four days but I'm rested now. This is time for a celebration, and I think we should consider starting plans on going after the Earth Temple's master."

I grimaced, not sure that 4th level was the right time to start planning deicide. The Mark of the Champion hadn't exactly given any recommended levels for going after the Old Gods.

"You should take the Rose family shield, Aaron," Ania said.

I looked down. "I couldn't."

Ania rolled her eyes. "It's not going to do him any good. Don't take this as an acceptance into our family either, Imposter. Its magical aura will benefit you even if you don't have much skill as a warrior. Undermaster Sorcerers can use shields and swords, they just aren't very good at using them."

That was a little too gamey for what probably should have been a deeply personal moment but who was to question Ania wanting me to take up her family's ancestral arms? "Thank you, Ania. I mean that. This is like giving me the family chain mail."

"Mail," Ania said.

"What?" I asked.

"Mail already means chain," Ania said. "You've been saying chain-chain whenever you mention it and it's weird."

"Yeah," Bloodstorm said, shrugging. "I just figured he had a stutter."

"Oh," I said, blinking. "Blame the Player's Handbook."

I walked up to the altar and proceeded to pick up the Rose shield that felt warm in my hands. I put it on my back over the sword.

AC 6 is now AC 9
Player will now be able to make use of the BLOCK ability
-2 penalty during combat for UNTRAINED (Sword and Shield)

That was when yet another figure surprised me by their presence. It was a feminine aristocratic voice I'd heard only once before at the Black Cat. "Praise be to the Goddess and her blessings! My father's bones have been returned to their proper place while the Temple to the Three is restored!"

I turned around to see Agata, wearing a nightgown like Ania's, holding her glowing staff as a little fairy hovered beside her shoulder.

Ania ran up and hugged her sister.

CHAPTER TWENTY-FOUR
COUSINS STILL COUNT AS INCEST

Agata Rose seemed deeply uncomfortable with her sister hugging her and, reluctantly, patted her on the back.

"Uh, hello," Agata said, taking a deep breath.

The books had depicted a typical adversarial relationship between the Rose daughters. One of them being the feminine girly-girl older sister while the other was the younger tomboy. Fairly typical stuff. The show had erred by forgetting that siblings typically grew out of that and depicting them as still hostile as adults. It was just one of the reasons why I felt that they should have relied heavier on Weis' writing rather than trying to do their own thing.

Still, by the look of things, Agata and Ania hadn't developed a close relationship in this world either. That was probably because of Weis' magic, though. From Ania's perspective, she'd been through numerous cycles of Agata being at her side fighting against the forces of darkness. From Agata's perspective, Ania and she had been estranged since they were teenagers with little interaction thereafter. Now the spell was broken by both women having the Mark of the Champion, and time would move on. Their relationship could progress naturally.

Presumably.

"You're awake!" Ania said, looking up and examining her eyes like an optometrist. "What do you remember? Do you see anything different? Were there visions?"

"Dearest sister, I love you, but if you don't back away then I will turn you into a toad," Agata said, stepping backward.

"Can she do that?" Bloodstorm asked, looking at me.

"No idea," I said. "The Agata of the books never stopped being a deconstruction of damsels in distress. Now she's throwing spells around like she's Terra Branford."

"Kudos on the *Final Fantasy IV* reference. Most people forget the series existed before VII. Well, if Agata is a PC now rather than an NPC then who knows what her present status is, game wise," Jon said. "Agata would normally level up with you because she was a part of your party, but Ania kept her pre-you levels due to having the Mark of the Champion. Agata presumably was the same level as you, level 2, when she joined the party at the Black Cat but maybe she might receive some levels from her past loops."

Bloodstorm nodded. "That was just complete gibberish to me."

"I sadly understood every word." I checked my bracelet's interface. "It says she's 7th level."

Jon stared. "Pfft. That makes no damn sense. Boo, Weis! Boo! Write better rules! Take some advice from your fans!"

Agata stared at Jon. "The raven is talking."

"Yes, it does that," Ania said, dismissing her concerns. "I suggest you ignore everything that comes out of his beak."

"That is harder than it sounds," I said, feeling awkward I was inserting myself in a conversation three books in the making. "I'm very glad that you're awake, Lady Rose. We've got a lot to explain, and I hope you're—"

Agata strode across the chapel and proceeded to give me a passionate kiss on the mouth, including tongue. That would have been awkward enough but, uh, I'm going to be honest, she also got pretty handsy. Then she got *really* handsy and I realized that public displays of affection in Ledziania was apparently very different from Michigan. Seriously, this was the kind of behavior that would get you kicked out of a theater.

"Woah," I said, pulling away. "Listen, this is definitely not—"

"I know that I have to be rude with you in public but, sister, I need you to know something," Agata said, turning around. "Garland and I are married."

"What," Ania said, staring.

"What," I said.

"Plot twist!" Jon said. "It turns out it was neither Betty nor Veronica! Archie marries Cheryl Blossom!"

I stared at him, confused. "What?"

"It was neither Mary Jane nor Black Cat, it was Silver Sable?" Jon suggested another analogy.

"See, now that makes sense," I said, still confused. This was clearly something new and I had to wonder if it had happened in a previous cycle, which had horrifying implications on its own, or if Agata had just never gotten around to explaining the marriage until their father's spirit was laid to rest. It seemed like the kind of thing that would have come up. Maybe Ania had been ignoring the signs because her sister was brainwashed. Still, Garland and Agata? That was a longshot. Everyone had been a Garlestyne or Gania shipper. You know, the ones who didn't ship him with Jorg or Ivan.

Agata turned to address Ania. "I know it must come as a great shock, sister."

"Yeah, a little bit," Ania said, making the understatement of the decade by her expression. "I guess I was too busy trying to save the world to pay attention to the signs you were in a secret marriage *with my lover*."

"Do not be jealous, sister. It was destiny." Agata took my hand as I tried to figure out how to explain what was going on. She ignored my obvious discomfort and continued, "After I escaped my second husband, Radu the Impaler, I traveled far and hard through the dark forests at the foot of the Death Mountains. I would have died if not for Garland who saved me. That was when I realized that my feelings for my brother were not actually brotherly but that it was entirely justified because we were not blood related. He was actually the son of Perun with father's sister."

"Lots of god banging in this family," Jon said. "Wasn't there a theory that Ania was Mokosh's daughter while possessing her mom or something? Wait, does that make it more weird or less weird?"

"Yes," Bloodstorm answered like a mathematician.

Agata elbowed Jon in the beak, sending him over. "Half-mad from the tortures I'd endured and knowing he was only my cousin, I was willing to be his bride."

"Is cousin banging okay among humans? Because I think that's still gross," Bloodstorm said. "It's family tree not family bush."

"It's legal but frowned upon according to the books," I said, absently. "Lady Rose, Agata, there's never going to be a good time to explain this—"

"So, we married under the sacred trees of the Zoryas and I pledged myself to the sisterhood despite marriage being forbidden by both our orders," Agata talked over me. "Garland became my third and last husband. I swore then to study the secrets of sorcery so that I might help you, sister, someday reclaim our family hold. Which you have now that Garland is its lord. You are, of course, welcome to stay with me and my husband."

Ania facepalmed. "This is going to be awkward."

"Yeah, no kidding," I said, turning to Agata. "Listen, this is a hard thing to tell you but—"

"What is that?" Agata said, pointing at the silver medallion dangling from my neck with Mythras' symbol on it. I barely remembered equipping it this morning.

"Oh, this?" I asked. "Well, when I burned—"

"How could you?" Agata said, taking a step back from me as if I was revealed to be sick with covid. "After all the Cult of Mythras has done to persecute and ravage our lands? You are the son of the gods, Garland, and yet you betray our father as well as the Goddess to side with those intolerant monsters! Men who force women to work as slaves, treat the demihumans as vermin, and crowned the Mad Queen as their champion."

"Err, Agata—"

"I see some terrible pact must have been formed in my absence," Agata said, looking down. "Yes, I see it now. You were forced to accept the faith of the Bull God—"

"Hey, he is not my god!" Bloodstorm shouted. "Dude kills bulls, he doesn't worship them. Aaron said so."

"Perhaps as part of some odious pact to save our lives," Agata said, reaching over to me. "Do not worry, Garland, we shall find some way to unbind you from this faith of fire and restore you to your proper place as—"

Ania put two fingers in her mouth and whistled.

"Yes, sister?" Agata asked, turning around. "Is something amiss?"

"Goddamn, I forgot how much you liked to talk," Ania said, shaking her head. "First of all, he's not a worshipper of Mythras. He just wears it for the spell resistance."

"I feel really bad about it, though," I said, wondering where Ania had heard that. Probably from Bloodstorm. It turned out party members chatted behind the scenes. I didn't think anyone outside of Bioware had them do that.

"Next, he's not Garland," Ania said, sighing. Her shoulder slumped down and all the previous joy she seemed to take in the restoration of the family chapel as well as the return of her father's remains departed. It was like watching a balloon deflate.

"He's not Garland?" Agata asked, looking between us as if a fog was lifting from her eyes. That kind of, 'I'm not quite awake yet but I'm getting there' look. Unfortunately, I was pretty sure we didn't have any coffee from the Turqish lands.

"No," Ania said. "Our brother, your husband apparently, is dead. Aaron is kind of a distant cousin."

"Which is still weird to want to bang," Bloodstorm said. "I mean, I have hundreds of cousins and I don't want to bang any of them. I mean most of them are hags, but they can shapeshift into hot ladies, and even just saying that wants me to take an ax to my face."

"Not even the prostitute vampire?" Jon asked. "The vampstitute?"

"*Especially* Angelica," Bloodstorm said. "Who is my half-*sister* not my cousin. Seriously."

"So even less acceptable," Jon said.

"No, because multiplications of zero are still zero," Bloodstorm said, continuing to show he was smarter than the average bull-man.

"I'm really sorry about Garland," I started to say. "He was a great hero and deserved—"

SLAP

The sound reverberated through the chapel as Agata stared at me with undisguised loathing before turning around, tears in her eyes. I barely felt the strike but I'd been magically enhanced over the past few days. Still, I had the perverse image in my head of being on my last hit point and her strike killing me. That had actually happened to me during a game of *Eldritch Ring*. You really shouldn't let Mila Corpse-Lover give you a hug, no matter how cute she was.

"Do you think she left the party?" Jon asked.

"No, there'd be a message that AGATA ROSE HAS LEFT THE PARTY on my bracelet," I said, checking the bracelet just in case.

Nope.

Small mercies, I guessed.

"See? Now this is why you should have just banged the hot dragon MILF in the swamp," Jon said. "You're not going to get an opportunity like that again."

I wanted to say, "Maybe if I had a *ring of fire resistance*" but I wasn't in the mood right now.

"Well, that went better than I expected," Ania said, staring off at her sister.

"It did?" I asked, disbelieving. "What the hell were you expecting?"

"Her to stab you," Ania said. "Fireball you. Fireball me. Burn the castle down. Go into denial. Degenerate into blithering insanity."

"Oh," I said, pausing. "I guess it did go better than you expected."

"Do you think it was the real Garland that married your sister or one of the Imposters that was assuming his identity that she's only remembering through her affected memories?" Jon asked.

I stared down at Jon. "Jesus, man, really?"

The *Token of Mythras* glowed orange and I felt nauseous.

YOU HAVE RECEIVED A -5% VULNERABILITY TO MAGIC FOR BLASPHEMY.

"Oh, screw that," I said, pulling off the token and hurling it across the room. It bounced against one of the chapel walls and landed against the ground.

YOU HAVE REJECTED YOUR PATRON GOD, MYTHRAS, AND NOW NO LONGER RECEIVE HIS BLESSINGS OR CURSES.

"Yikes," I said, blinking. "Apparently, they are really serious about oaths and wearing the right gear in this world."

"Yeah, you gotta swear by the right gods," Bloodstorm said. "It's the most common form of prayer."

Ania, however, was focused on the question Jon raised. "I think sorting that out is the kind of thing we'd need the Wise Man for. I'm going to choose to believe it was the real Garland, though. My brother was a great man, but he was also pathologically incapable of staying faithful to one woman. He would have eventually betrayed her too, I think. After all, he betrayed me."

"I thought you had an open relationship," I said, observing.

Ania's eyes widened then narrowed.

"Which is not a thing I should say as it implies creepy levels of insight into your life," I said, cursing myself.

Ania shook her head. "I need to get myself a copy of those fucking books."

"They're overrated," Jon said. "There's only one true Weis in fantasy and her name is Margaret."

Ania reached through her nightshirt neckline and removed an amulet with a obsidian piece of jewelry that was shaped in a black rose bloom with crossed silver swords at the bottom. She walked over and put it my neck. "We did. But hurting my sister was never part of the deal. Find someone you love to give this to, Imposter. You may not be the genuine Black Rose but you're the closest thing we've got. Who knows, you may actually someday be a hero in your own right."

"See? This is what I'm talking about," Jon said. "It's like Sapkowski naming Geralt the White Wolf and stealing from Moorcock's Elric. Larry C.C. Weis is stealing from Dragonlance's Lord Soth by calling Garland the Black Rose."

"It's an homage, dude," I said, looking at Jon.

"Like hell it is!" Jon said.

"You have an author in your world named Moorcock?" Bloodstorm asked, sniggering.

I tried to figure out something to say to Ania that would make her feel better. Also, to let her know that maybe there was already someone I liked I wouldn't mind giving a love token. "Err, yeah, well, uhm, err, yeah."

Oh, yeah, that was smooth.

13 Charisma, my ass.

Ania gave me a kiss on the cheek and walked to the stairs leading out of the chapel. "You should finish up your remaining business here in Crossroad before we head out. The journey to the Earth Temple is a long one. We'll have to leave Lesser Ledziania and head down to Kalizov. Much of the region has been sacked by the Mad Queen's Army or the Dragon Queen *requisitioning supplies*. Bandits and the undead run freely."

The Southern Kingdoms were five nations, most of them named after their capital cities with Akoa, Kalizov, Lesser Ledziania, Poz'nan, and Mal'bork. Most of them obviously named after real-life (I needed to stop thinking of it like that) locations. Akoa, the Krakow equivalent, was the Imperial capital city and presently in the hands of the Mad Queen along with most of the other nations that had once been united under the Ledzianian King.

"Got it," I said, wishing I could voice my objection to the idea that defeating a few local monsters made us qualified to go *hunting down a god*. I spent twenty hours grinding my sword and armor drops before I even thought about going after the boss of Stormnight castle in

Eldritch Ring. Even then, I *still* got my ass kicked hundreds of times before I finally broke down and called in some multiplayer friends.

Either way, I watched Ania leave. I admit, I was mostly watching her backside. I may not have been the pervert that Jon was but that didn't mean I wasn't one.

"You know, I'm like ninety percent sure that if you just asked her to share your tent, she'd let you," Bloodstorm said. "Women are only ten percent more complicated than men as a general rule."

"You learn that in university, Bull?" Jon asked.

"I have mathematical proofs," Bloodstorm said. "The fools will rue the day they rejected my research like they did the man who proved the Sun revolved around Mokosh."

"I guess I'll be eating in my room." I said, shrugging. "I'm suddenly very tired. I think I'll eat, struggle with the privy a bit more, and read the glossary before bed."

"You're not going to level up first?" Jon asked.

"It'll keep," I said, though I already had some controversial ideas about where I was going to spend my next points.

Jon would not approve.

Admittedly, part of the reason why I would be doing it.

As I left the chapel, I couldn't help but notice the eyes of the Veles statue were rubies and glowed with a brilliant inner flame.

Watching me.

CHAPTER TWENTY-FIVE
A CERTAIN POINT OF VIEW

I dreamed of a giant face staring at me. It was a dream because I'd gone to sleep and now was somewhere else, though I perhaps should have questioned that logic given I'd been magically transported to a fantasy world where book characters were fighting it out to stop the end of both of our worlds.

Anyway, I was looking at the stone giant face that was on its side and connected to a body that was roughly the size of the Statue of Liberty. That's three hundred feet for you laymen.

The body was cracked into about fifteen separate pieces, but all of these were gigantic pieces of stone by themselves. We were also in some sort of valley with green foliage and flowers at the bottom while the peaks above us were covered in ice.

Oh, and there was a hundred-foot-tall war hammer sitting head down nearby with its shaft pointing to the sky. It took me a second to figure out where the hell I was and what I was looking at because it wasn't from the books, or at least any location that had been mentioned in them. Instead, this was a location from Eldritch Ring: The Skyfather's Body.

In very rough terms, it was the corpse of the god of those video games. It also looked suspiciously like the statue of Perun that I'd found in the Rose family chapel. In Eldritch Ring, though, it was the literal body of the Skyfather after he'd been slain by the Lord of

Darkness. If that meant this was Perun and the Lord of Darkness was Veles, then Larry C.C. Weis had clearly never had an original thought in his life.

"What in the world?" I heard Jon's voice speak beside me. Looking to my side, I saw a Eurasian man with black hair and a soul patch dressed in ripped blue jeans, a Larry Elmore Dragonlance art t-shirt, and a dirty hoody.

"Jon?" I asked.

"Yeah? What..." Jon looked up at me. "Holy shit!"

"I know!" I said. "You're human again!"

"Okay, dude, I need you to turn around," Jon said, moving his hands down to his pants.

I closed my eyes and shook my head. "Didn't you get that out of your system when you were a bird?"

"It's not the same!" Jon said. "Be glad I'm not asking for help."

"I am going to walk away now and by walk away, I mean run," I said, jogging toward the giant severed head of Perun. "Wow, I'm not sure that having proof positive that gods can die should make me feel more religious or less."

"Depends on the religion," I heard another familiar voice attract my attention. This one, at least, came from above my head.

Turning to look, I saw Larry C.C. Weis sitting on top of Perun's head with his legs dangling over the edge. A few ravens were sitting around him with one sitting on his head. "Hello, Mr. Bartkowski! A pleasure meeting you again."

"Hi, Mr. Weis," I said, pausing to make sure I was still armed. I was. Unlike Jon, I still looked like my fantasy self. "Would you do me a favor and come down here so I can stab you?"

"I'd prefer not to," Larry said.

"It's okay," I said, summoning some Arcane Fire. "I'm pretty sure I can hit you from here. Just give me a second to aim."

"I understand if you're a little upset..." Larry said, trailing off.

"You sent me to your dark fantasy series!" I said, looking up. "I'm in a hostile environment, I'm totally unprepared, and I'm surrounded by people who probably want to kick my ass. It's like I'm back in high school."

"I think you're overdoing the movie quotes," Larry said. "They're fine in moderation but Johnny Cage from the first live action Mortal Kombat movie is probably a bridge too far."

"There's another one?" I asked.

Larry sighed. "Simply put, Mr. Bartkowski, it was a matter of life and death. The world of Mokosh needs heroes and you're the closest thing we've got."

I briefly gazed back at where I'd left Jon before immediately regretting it.

"Oh Liv Tyler, how I've missed you!" Jon proclaimed.

I turned back to Larry. "Have you considered you simply have absolute garbage taste in champions?"

Larry pinched the bridge of his nose as if he had a migraine. "I'll be honest, Jon is about the third best of the champions. Card chasing or not, at least he made it out of the starting area and didn't fall prey to the powers of darkness. One of you actually killed a major character and took over their life."

"Wait, who?" I asked.

"Not important," Larry said, quickly. "But yes, it's basically you and Francine at this point."

"Francine is alive?" I asked, remembering how Ania had dealt with her. I'd just assumed I was the only champion left alive who wasn't working for Veles. Well, alive, not working for Veles, and not turned into a bird.

Larry nodded. "I chose as many champions as I did because I thought you'd work together but it seems multiplayer mode has a few bugs in it. I admit, I didn't see Ania harvesting the discarded eldritch rings of dead players coming, though. It's a reminder that a good writer doesn't control their characters, they just record their actions."

"That's not so much a metaphor as being literal," I said, climbing up the side of Perun's head and plopping myself on the side of his cheek so I could talk to Larry without hurting my neck. "This is a real world, thought, right? It's not something you created. It exists outside of your books."

"You sure you're up for exposition?" Larry said, smiling.

I frowned. "It's about the only thing keeping me from stabbing you, so yes."

Larry chuckled, either unafraid or assuming I was joking. "Yes, this is indeed a real world. Perun, Veles, Mokosh and the other Creator Gods helped construct this world back in the early days of the multiverse. Earth was created almost at the same time and there used to be a lot more crossover between the two."

"What kind of crossover?" I asked.

"Old gods working on both places, fairies, monsters, and the like," Larry said. "Also, sex tourism."

I facepalmed. "How did I know that was coming?"

"Perun was like most of the skyfathers of his time and loved getting laid. I mean, who doesn't? He had Garland as his last child, but he left quite a few bastards behind on your world as well. Those people had kids and sometimes they had kids with each other."

"What is with all the incest?" I asked, shaking my head. "Seriously, see a psychologist. Preferably one who isn't a fan of Freud."

"Be grateful for it in this case as that made you about 1/14th god," Larry said. "That's better than most of the champions. Mind you, Valentin was the only one who was better at about 1/7th but that's because his uncle was also his—"

"Stop," I interrupted. "TMI dude. Besides, he's dead."

"Not anymore," Larry said, softly. "Valentine killed a few of my champions and took their marks. As such, he's still in Veles' good book. You can expect him to make another appearance soon."

Great. I doubted the PUSH trick would work again. "Go on. Please continue explaining, then you can get to transporting me back to Earth."

Larry looked disappointed. "The thing you need to realize about magic is that it's a semi-renewable resource. It takes time to replenish itself with prayers, offerings, and stories. I'll get to that. Eventually, Earth's pantheons exhausted themselves fighting and fornicating until they were all driven away with the only magic left a fraction of its former power. Veles suggested a fraction of them move here to a fresh and live world."

"I'm following you so far," I said. "This is all a big global warming metaphor or maybe colonialism."

I was glad Larry was occupied or he probably would be throwing a fit about my reading too much into these books.

Larry rolled his eyes. "It's not an allegory. Tolkien talked about this. Allegories mean orcs are standing in for the Germans in WW1. Applicability means you can use orcs to talk about WW1. Whatever the case, the local gods weren't too happy about this, but Veles slaughtered them all with the help of his fellow Old Gods. All except Perun who married Mokosh and agreed to defend her as well as the last of her daughters."

"How did that work out?" I asked.

"Not well since Veles was already married to her," Larry said. "All girls love bad boys, I guess."

I sighed. "So, they ended up being married for a while and try to make it work but eventually Veles kills Perun."

"Something like that," Larry said. "But it was more environmental than romantic. It's taken a while but Earth's magical reserves have recovered. So much so that Veles now intends to come back to the Earth and double his power. What better way for a god to demonstrate their power than mass death and destruction?"

"What, was he behind WW2 and Hitler?" I asked. "The atomic bomb?"

"No, that would be stupid," Larry said. "He was, however, willing to finally kill Perun off. It took all his might, but he managed to put my former deity in the ground. It exhausted him, though, and has forced him to delay his invasion of Earth. He needs to strengthen himself by draining Mokosh, the world and the goddess, of its power before opening a portal for his forces. He's also speeding up the process by increasing the amount of death in this world to feed on."

"Now it sounds like you're ripping off Warcraft," I said.

"The lore of those games was ruined by executive meddling," Larry said. "In any case, to try and stop him, or at least delay him, I used my mastery of ring lore—"

"Do you have a single original idea in your head?" I asked, sarcastically.

"To harvest the power of Perun's heart," Larry said, patting the dead body. "Each bracelet contains a fragment of his former power. It means the wearers can theoretically slay the Old Gods and free all the life essence they've accumulated. Maybe even destroy Veles and force him back to his domain for a few millennia."

"And you think the best guy for that is a computer programmer from Michigan," I said, staring.

Larry conjured a stack of papers. "You lifted the Curse of Blackwood Bog. I've already got the next Garland short story ready for an anthology with Jim Butcher and Kevin J. Anderson. Even if you die, which would suck because I don't have any more bracelets, you've made a permanent change to the cycles."

"As much as I'd love to read that, I've already lived it," I said, sighing.

"You sure?" Larry asked. "I've already got talks with the FANT channel and some offers from Netflix. Apparently, they really screwed up the other great Polish fantasy series."

"One thing I don't get—" I started to say.

"One thing?" Larry asked, teasing me.

"One of *many* things," I admitted. "Why all this nonsense to begin with? The book series, the video games, and the television show. If this is all real, and I'm going to assume it is, then what's the point of making it all a series in my world?"

"Magic is powered by stories, Aragorn," Larry said.

"Aaron," I corrected.

"Aragorn," Larry said. "It's not just the name that you were born with, those can be changed. It's the name of your true self. In terms of raw power, no one is going to be able to beat Veles, but gods are made of stories and magic is the way they manipulate belief. If you create enough stories around a hero then they might be able to slay a god just because that's the way the tale goes, no matter how impractical."

At this point, it seemed we'd gone from Tolkien, Sapkowski, and Martin over to Pratchett and *The Neverending Story*. Complaining about that wouldn't do any good, though, especially since it wasn't like I could point to anyone who knew how magic really worked in my world. At this point, I was ready to just go with it no matter what he claimed about how the world worked since reality seemed to be on his side.

"And that's why you've brainwashed an entire kingdom into thinking Garland is alive?" I asked.

"'Fraid so," Larry said. "People might believe Superman could beat General Zod but that's not happening with a random guy off the street. Unfortunately, the amulets need at least some small amount of Perun's blood to channel the power. Just about everyone in Ledziania has a little but that runs the risk of attracting Veles eye. So, I decided to recruit people from Earth."

"This is the dumbest plan I've ever heard in my entire life," I said. "Also, wait, does this mean Jon and I are related?"

"Let's just say that Jon's mother and her Polish tennis instructor were closer than his father thought," Larry said.

"Ah," I said, nodding. "Say no more. Did you have to turn him into a raven?"

"Resurrection magic isn't my forte," Larry said. "I did the best I could for the people I got killed trying to stop this situation. Unfortunately, all my plans have gone pretty askew by now. Epic Dungeoneering™ was supposed to find the people with the qualities I needed for proper champions but they've been suborned by Veles' agents."

"So, I wasn't selected because I was the best man for the job," I said. "I was selected because they thought I'd fail miserably."

"No," Larry said, surprising me. "I did my own research. You're my pick."

"Why?" I asked, genuinely perplexed. "Or is it because I'm the last remaining noticeable sprog from Perun's loins in my world."

"The internet," Larry said.

I grimaced. "We're doomed."

"No, seriously," Larry said. "I was on DarkUndermaster.org and really liked those essays you wrote. Figuring out that the mother of Garland was Lilandra, Lord Rose's cousin, rather than the bar maid, Zelda, was a sign of your genius."

Weis seemed to think being able to pick up on basic foreshadowing was a great skill. It was also the author covertly complimenting himself.

"*Everyone on the internet* figured that out before the television show," I said. "At least who read the books."

"Yeah, but you were also the only one working at Epic Dungeoneering™," Larry said. "That hadn't died already. Believe me, you are the only person left who meets the minimum standards I put out for my champion."

Wow, for a professional writer, he utterly sucked at giving speeches. "Send me home."

"I can't," Larry said, sighing. "The buck stops here, Aragorn. We need you. The Southern Kingdoms need you. Ania needs you. Agata needs you. Hell, Jon the raven needs you."

I shook my head. "Ania is a better qualified hero than I'll ever be. Agata doesn't want anything to do with me and with good reason. You've put that family through hell. Why not reincarnate Garland? Why settle for the discount off-brand version?"

"He's gone," Larry said, sighing. "For good. In order to resurrect someone, you have to get their permission, and you only get one chance."

"Who made that rule?" I asked.

"I have no idea," Larry said. "Death, I guess? I'm privy to cosmic secrets of the universe but even I don't know all of them. The fact was that Garland chose not to come back after he was betrayed by his brothers. Too many quests, too much killing, and too many failures. Maybe I pushed him too hard or maybe he knew he couldn't pull off the quest I wanted him to. Either way, he's off the table for good."

"Maybe you killed so many of your characters, the audience wouldn't accept a Gandalf the White-esque return," I said.

"Don't get too meta on me," Larry said. "Even if that ship has sailed."

I looked down. "Listen, I can't do this. It's too big. Call my cousin or the Special Forces or—"

That was when Weis got a terrified look on his face then vanished in a swirl of mist.

I paused. "That's not a good sign."

"No, no it is not," I heard Valentin say from the back of a red dragon descending from the sky. "I owe you a broken neck."

Well shit.

CHAPTER TWENTY-SIX
GREAT. NOW I HAVE AN ARCHNEMESIS

Valentin was very much alive, which was impressive since I'd dropped him off the side of a cliff. He'd changed his mount from Stompy to a dragon that resembled how I imagined Maria Poppy's dragon form but was somehow sleeker and meaner looking. While I wasn't sure how you sexed dragons, I had to say this one seemed more feminine somehow than I'd imagine a Smaug or Glaurung sort of creature.

Valentin didn't just exterminate me with a blast of dragonfire, though, but stepped off the dragon once it settled on the side of Perun's head. He'd managed to replace his armor, including his Skull Mask, though it was now the color red. On his back, I noticed an enormous maul, which looked like a block of rune-covered granite on a large metal pole. Valentin then reached up and removed his skull mask to expose his human face.

He should have kept himself covered.

I'm not going to body shame anyone, but the guy looked less like the badass warlord I'd expected him to and more like he'd slaughtered an army of Twinkies on his way here. He was white, bald, and had cheeks that made him look like a giant baby. Some guys could pull off the look like Vincent D'Onofrio's Kingpin or even Mike Myers' Doctor Evil, but he didn't have the presence for it.

"Been hitting the local mutton and goat a bit, have we, Valentin?" I asked.

"Skull King," Valentin said. "Valentin was my human name."

"Uh huh," I said. "Is your last name actually Velesson and you lucked out in terms of your destiny or is it something like Perriwinkle? Focker? That's a real Dutch name. They didn't just make it up for the Ben Stiller movie."

Valentin pulled his maul off his back with telekinesis, summoning it to him like Thor and his hammer before a blue glow surrounded him. "I will end you in the most painful manner imaginable, Bartkowski."

"Now you just look like a discount Shao Khan," I said. "Not the video game version either. The Brian Thompson one from *Mortal Kombat: Annihilation*."

My present plan was to get him so pissed off that he charged at me then cast PUSH to knock him off the side of the giant stone head we were presently sitting on the side of. It was pretty much the exact same plan as before and would do nothing to deal with the dragon, but I didn't have much in the way of ideas.

"Halt!" A figure said, appearing beside me with the same kind of black smoke that had teleported Larry away.

Both of us turned to see a bearded man of immense power and dignity standing there in a midnight blue robe that had a large glittering black gemstone at the base of his neck. He had a well-trimmed beard and a terrifying gaze. In his left hand, he was holding a staff with a coiled gold horned dragon at the top of it. It took me a second to recognize him.

"Peter Stormare?" I asked.

"No, you idiot," Valentine said. "This is Lord Veles, God of the Underworld and Rightful Ruler of the Universe."

"Seriously, man, I loved you in *American Gods* and *Until Dawn*," I said, looking at him. "I mean, I could take or leave your performance as Satan in Constantine but that's really the whole movie. As an urban fantasy film, it's fine, but as an adaptation of *Hellblazer*—"

Veles snapped his fingers, and I started throwing up snakes. Writhing black things that crawled out of my throat onto the ground before me. Each of them having all too human-like faces and eerie black eyes like their master.

Yeah, that's a thing.

"Forgive the rudeness, Aaron," Veles said, sounding, again, totally like Peter Stormare. "However, if I had to deal with your endless nattering as a means to buy time to figure out a way from your predicament, we'd have been here all day."

I stopped vomiting up snakes and fell on my knees. One of the snakes hissed at me and snapped at my face before I fell back, almost slipping off the side of Perun's face. Any joke or response died in my current state of pants wetting fear.

"Just let me kill him," Valentin said.

"That wouldn't make a very good story, would it, Valentin?" Veles said. "The Wise Man had an incredibly stupid plan to defeat me by shaping the Earth's poor desperate masses with his stories. These stories have fed me almost as well as conquering the Earth. All the frustration and anticipation of the audience soothing my injuries as I crush the dreams of millions waiting for a champion to distract them from the meaningless of their lives. My recovery time has been halved each time one of his noble champions comes to Mokosh and meets their end or chooses a new master."

I tried to speak but just ended up dry heaving for a few seconds, then blasting the snakes on the ground with my Arcane Fire. Watching them burn, I cleared my throat. "So, what you're saying is that Weis not being able to finish his books has been bringing about the apocalypse?"

"Yes," Veles said. "The final season of the show was particularly delicious in the suffering it caused. Plenty of parents named their children Celestyne or Dragonia. I bet they're feeling regret at said choice."

I stared at him. "I'm sure Weis is smart enough to not make one of his central characters into a villain."

Veles stared back, unblinking.

"Really? Crap," I said, frowning. "That's disappointing."

"I hate those books," Valentin said, sneering. "Real men watch football. American football."

I stared at him. "Wow, this must be hell for you."

"I adapted," Valentin said. "Now I can do whatever the hell I want to whoever I want whenever I want. There's no law, rhyme, or reason. When you're the strongest guy in the room, they let you get away with it. I'm now the strongest guy on the continent."

I stared at him. "You are more disappointing in-person than I expected. The speech you gave at the keep was at least cool. This is more like Al Bundy, Sith Lord."

"Valentin was the first of Weis' chosen champions," Veles said. "He came closest to defeating me by cleansing two of the temples and casting two of the Old Gods back."

"Then I got smart," Valentin said, ignoring his master referring to him by his human name. "I saw that I'd become a living god."

"Demigod," Veles corrected. "At *best*."

"And I switched sides," Valentin said, lifting a completely different bracelet than the one Ania had taken from his body. "Some of the other champions were smart like that. Others…weren't. You stole from me, man, and I'm going to have it back."

Great, he was another guy who thought this was a giant video game. "Sorry, Ania is using it."

"Ania and Agata are part of the property I'm referring to. I think I'll take it all back with interest," Valentin said.

Except he was playing it like those private servers from the old WOW days. The ones that were non-stop deluges of, actually, no need to go into it. You can pretty much imagine what they were like by thinking of your typical multiplayer online shooter and then putting it in text form. We were all little shits online when we were teenagers but it's a certain kind of asshole who never grows out of it.

"Dude, you realize Immortan Joe wasn't the protagonist of that movie, right?" I asked.

"Just more garbage from Hollywood trying to make men feel bad about themselves," Valentin said. "It's all w—"

"Stop, please, no, we're not getting political," I interrupted him. "We can all agree the first *Ghostbusters* reboot was terrible."

"There was another reboot?" Valentin asked. "I've been here a while. Please tell me it was an R-rated gorefest. Proper Eighties nudity too! Disembowelments and decapitations galore!"

I stared at him. "You're like an evil Jon. Eviler."

"Don't compare me to that—" Valentin prepared to say something that would start a fight I absolutely could not win.

"I am here to make you an offer, Aaron," Veles said, ignoring our patter.

"A chance to get yourself out of the hole that the Wise Man has dug for you," Veles said. "He was never going to return you to your home. He's never going to stop using you. Even if you were to somehow succeed in this insane quest of his, which doesn't have an end point, then he'll just find more work for you. Garland was sent to my halls after his betrayal and feasts with the other heroes, but do you know what makes a hero? Death. Any man who is alive and a hero is eventually bound to disappoint his fellow mortals."

I was scared but talking with the bonehead beside me got me to recover at least a little of my courage. "I dunno, I think this quest has a pretty clear ending. Go destroy your avatar and save the world. It's like getting rid of the One Ring. The Scouring of the Shire isn't really necessary if you're doing a movie."

"I felt that lost a lot of the poignancy Tolkien was going for," Veles said. "It's a way of showing veterans can't really return home. It changes while they've left, just as they, themselves, are changed."

I really wasn't expecting that sort of insight from the God of Evil. Nor for him to be one of my favorite Swedish actors. "So, I just say yes, and you'll send me home?"

"Yes," Veles said. "I could also offer you a substantial check and a proper position in Epic Dungeoneering™. Manager. Vice President. You can escape from the indignities of wage slavery and live as an executive. You'll have enough money to live like a lord and pass it down to whatever offspring you may someday have. Inherited wealth has always been the basis of nobility after all."

I stared at him. "And what if I want to stay?"

Veles chuckled. "I've been watching you, Aaron. You don't like killing. You're capable of it, Father Adolf and the storm knights at the Black Cat prove that, but it's not something you take joy in like Valentin or Little Ania Rose."

"Not so little anymore," I muttered.

Veles nodded. "I saw what you did with the dragon hatchling. You are too kind for this world. Killing people like Valentin won't warp you—"

"Hey!" Valentin said.

"But this is a world of violence and desperation," Veles said. "What happens when you have to kill bandits trying to steal food for their children or the peasant levies sent to hunt you for saving a demihuman family from a purge? What about when you have whole villages burned to get at you. When families are put to the sword to make the people inform on your location? Because that is the hero's path here. It will gradually chip at everything you hold dear until you realize you've become like those you fight."

"Is that what happened to Garland?" I asked.

"Here's a revelation, Garland was never Garland," Veles said. "Just a man. Better ones died trying to replace him. Better ones than you. In the end, they all end up like my brother, dead and forgotten by an ungrateful populace."

I had a feeling Veles was telling the truth, at least as he saw it. Much to my surprise, a Medieval string version of "Short Change Hero" by the Heavy started playing on my bracelet. It was another sign the bracelet had a sentience of its own. Except, I was pretty sure it wasn't Larry's consciousness directing it.

"Everything is shit in my world too," I said, coldly. "You know, I was all ready to leave before you came along and convinced me otherwise."

"You are aware of the consequences of your refusal?" Veles asked, sounding more amused than angry.

"Yeah," I said, calmly. Which was surprising because I was scared beyond anything I'd ever felt before in my life. I just didn't show it because I'd entered a kind of fear-induced shock where everything seemed distant and unreal. I was going to die and there wasn't a damn thing I could do about it. Well, there was. I could take the deal but if I did, I'd be party to murdering an entire planet. The equivalent of, "The Resistance HQ is right down that street, Mr. Nazi. Have a nice day." Doing nothing was not nothing and I was genuinely surprised I had it in me to say no to Veles. It didn't feel heroic, though. It felt stupid. I guess doing the right thing was dependent on Low WIS somehow. I just didn't hoped it didn't hurt too much.

"Are you *sure*?" Veles asked, dragging out the last word.

"Can we get on with it?" Valentin said. "I have an appointment with the Slavers Guild in an hour."

Veles stared at him.

"Sir," Valentine said, lowering his gaze and muttering. "Err, my lord, your godliness…"

"Yes, I know," I said, talking to Veles. "But if I said yes then I'd have to live with that for the rest of my life. So go fuck yourself."

Veles nodded, seemingly impressed. "It's good to see at least some of my brother's bloodline maintains of their dignity in the face of death. Goodbye, Mr. Bartkowski. You were at least a man of principle and that was more than most mark wearers could say. You may kill him, Valentin."

"Finally," Valentin said, lifting his maul.

Veles vanished in a swirl of smoke as the dragon watched the both of us, hungrily.

"PUSH!" I shouted, holding my hand out.

The blast washed over Valentin, who managed to stand there with only a couple of inches difference from where I'd struck him.

"*Boots of Unyielding Force,*" Valentin said, chuckling. "It's amazing what you can commission these days."

"Ah hell," I said.

"Anime martial arts attack!" Jon shouted as he ran up the side of Perun's head and did a spin kick that would have done Street Fighter's Ryu proud. It caused Valentin to stagger before Jon unleashed a bunch of punches, kicks, and even a throw that bounced him across the ground. It would have been pure awesome if not for the fact he wasn't wearing any pants.

I fired a blast of Arcane Fire at Valentine, but it landed against his armor like a water balloon. "What in the world?"

"I took the Bare Fisted Monk specialty when I hit 9th level!" Jon shouted. "I'm 18th level in this form, man! Pwiffle made me strong! Run!"

"Where would I run?" I said, not ready to abandon my friend.

That was when the dragon reared its head back as a glowing fire gathered within the back of its mouth.

"Dammit," I muttered, tackling Jon over the side of Perun's head as the top of it was covered in flame.

That was when I woke up in my bed in Dragon Keep. Jon was sitting on his perch, shaking his wings out.

"Okay, did that just happen?" I asked, seeing sunlight stream through the windows.

Jon looked at me. "Yeah, I'm afraid so. Weis likes communicating with dreams, but it seems that's no longer a safe way to do so. Veles has found his chat room. I doubt we'll be receiving any more invites any time soon."

I shook my head. "Why did he go through the whole song and dance? Veles, I mean. Why doesn't he just send an army to kill us every time? I mean, yeah, he did send Valentin, but he's not supposed to—"

"Simple, Aaron," Jon said, looking defeated. "Veles gets off on it. He'll kill us well before we become a threat to him. He'll also finish the job of killing you if he thinks he hasn't done a thorough enough one in the first place. I know that because that's what happened to the woman who mentored me. I don't know where ravens go when they die but I haven't seen her at any of the NPC helper parties since."

Suddenly Jon's aversion to heroism was a lot less funny.

"So, Liv Tyler?" I said, switching the subject.

"It's not hard to figure out who you spend your private time thinking about," Jon said.

"What do you…" I trailed off because I saw Ania at the door in full adventuring gear.

"We ride at noon," Ania said.

CHAPTER TWENTY-SEVEN
FARMER GRUB'S WIFE

"So, what was her name?" I asked, riding on the back of Stompy as the others prepared to depart Crossroad. Jon was sitting on the front of the saddle, in a foul mood ever since the previous night.

We were heading to the last remaining side quest in my journal, though more for lack of anywhere else to go than a desire to complete it. Especially if it was just a sex quest like Jon thought. I'd told the others I wanted to get myself lunch at the Black Cat first but, truth be told, I needed a bit of time to get my head on straight after dealing with Veles.

"I don't want to talk about it," Jon said, staring forward.

"Are you sure?" I asked.

"Do you want to talk about the cutscene?" Jon asked.

"Cutscene?" I asked.

"Yeah, I mean your meeting the Big Bad and his Dragon," Jon said. "Who just so happened to have a dragon of their own."

"I don't religiously read TVtropes.org but I assume you mean Veles and Valentin," I said.

"Yes, I mean Veles and Darth Bonehead," Jon said. "It was a cutscene. Hence why I was suddenly awesome, and you managed to just barely survive a dramatic near-death experience. It explains the villains plan, followed the end of Act One, and sufficiently raises the stakes for the conflict."

"I don't think it's how that works, Jon," I said, softly. "But if you don't want to talk about your raven, I understand."

I didn't understand at all, actually. I wanted to know everything about Jon's guide back when he was an adventurer rather than a guide himself. It seemed like it had ended tragically but I hoped it would provide insight not only into my friend but how this insane world worked. It wasn't a nice thing to do to Jon, but I felt like I needed every insight I could get if we were to survive this. Well, I was to survive this. Jon had already died, and I wasn't sure there was a way back from that.

Jon sighed. "Her name was Rebecca, I called her Becky."

"You dated a girl named Becky?" I asked.

"Do you want to talk about the guy who looks like an adult Cartman almost killing you?" Jon asked, referring to Valentin.

"Sorry."

"We didn't date," Jon said, sighing. "What with her being a raven and all. However, Becky Chang was a receptionist at Epic Dungeoneering™ in life and fully embraced the whole 'save the world' nonsense."

"It's not nonsense," I said, immediately regretting it.

"Don't you think I know that?" Jon asked, spinning around on the saddle. "But she wanted to be a hero. To escape the boring humdrum nature of her life and do something important with her life. She tried to join the Army after high school but got rejected for injuring her ankle during basic training. It turned out another trainee tossed her off the side of a wall for not wanting to suck him off."

"Yikes," I said.

"As you said, our world is crap too," Jon said. "It just has less zombies. Rebecca made it to 5th level before she died trying to save a family from a giant. The giant was way too high level for her and knocked her into orbit like that glitch in *Skyrim*."

"She died heroically, I guess," I said, not at all sure that Jon would find that statement comforting rather than infuriating.

"Screw heroism," Jon said, confirming my suspicions. "I later tracked down the giant and found out said family had massacred his herd of sheep before cutting his eight-year-old son's throat. The six-foot-tall kid had been tending the herd. Becky forgot the cardinal rule of Ledziania: everyone here is an asshole.

"She tried to make you a hero, didn't she?" I asked.

"You're damned right she did," Jon said, sighing. "We fought like crazy, but I was determined to level up myself by finding all the cards and then tackle the main quest with no chance of losing."

"That was your strategy?" I asked, realizing there was possibly more than met the eye regarding Jon's quest for more cards.

"Yeah," Jon said. "I did some smaller quests, don't get me wrong. Clearing out bandit lairs, laying to rest ghosts, and rescuing a young woman from a hideous lion man that had been promised her to secure her father's release. Man, was she pissed off after I killed her lion lover."

"You killed the Beast from *Beauty and the Beast*?" I asked, disbelieving.

"He had it coming!" Jon said. "Seriously, that story has some messed up implications."

"What happened next?" I asked.

"I tried to take out Skull King at the Temple of Earth," Jon said, shaking his beak back and forth. "I thought I had the equipment, party, and skill to take him down. Everything went wrong. I didn't even get to Chernobog. I ordered my companions to retreat, and Becky went to claw out his eyes. It gave me the distraction to get away, but it cost her, well, her second life. After that, I just focused on getting laid and my card games."

Wow, I had not expected Jon to have a reason for his behavior. "You didn't seem to treat Skull King as the kind of man who murdered your friend when I faced him."

"I thought he was an NPC!" Jon said, pausing. "Not a real person. No offense, Stompy."

Stompy snorted and blew fire from his nostrils.

"They're all real people, Jon," I said, not sure what else to say.

"We'll see how well that attitude holds after you've killed your hundredth or so person," Jon said. "All the ale doesn't silence the screams of the men I killed nor does all the beautiful company make up for the lovers I failed to protect."

"That's from *Goldeneye*," I said.

"First of all, I rephrased it, and second of all, Sean Bean said it so it's fine to put in a fantasy setting," Jon said. "Next, I'm the James Bond in this relationship. You're more like…Samwise."

"Samwise is the one who actually finished the quest and destroyed the Ring," I pointed out.

"That is a lie, Gollum did!"

"So, what are you going to level up as?" Stompy asked, suddenly speaking in deep demonic reverb.

I pulled on the reigns. "Hold up, what? You can talk?"

Stompy turned back to look in my direction. "Yes. I just chose not to speak until now."

"But why now?" I asked.

"I got sick of hearing you talk about idiocy," Stompy said. "To be fair, I was testing to see if talking to you would be better than talking with Valentine. He kept trying to insist the reason that he was putting on the pounds was that he no longer had access to the rhinos horn powder that he put in his energy drinks."

"How did he end up eight feet tall?" I asked.

"Growth potions," Stompy said. "He got them from a traveling peddler who preached that the dwarves were secretly controlling the world through banking and comet-based spell launchers."

I blinked. "Do you think Weis wrote that or is this world just stupid?"

"Could go either way," Jon said. "He should stick to dark fantasy instead of comedy, though. Ser Terry shall not be imitated."

"I should level up now," I replied. I called up my character sheet and began assigning points as well as cycling through both the feats as well as Spell Lists.

I decided to raise my INT to 18 and max out that stat, eighteen being the human maximum from previous games, rather than address either my low CON or WIS. Indeed, I was afraid of raising my WIS now since I was afraid it would make me realize how stupid I was being.

I made a controversial choice that I was certain Jon would give me shit for by choosing a Sword and Shield Feat from my free feat for level 4. In the previous games, it was always better not to distribute up your points between melee and sorcery but pick one lane or the other. However, I was getting the impression that being a jack of all trades might be better than being very good at one thing. This might well be the only fantasy world outside of *The Bard's Tale* where I wished I could be a bard. Plus, the Rose Family Shield gave me the option to block in combat and I suspected I'd need that without the complications of a -2 penalty.

For the spell list, I decided to get JUMP as my additional 1st level spell. It was a choice between that and GENTLE FALL, but I figured I would need to be able to get out of the way of people more than jump down pits. For my 2nd level pick, I chose ANIMAL SUMMONING as assist characters were always the crutch of those who couldn't fight worth crap.

Interestingly, hitting 4th level bestowed a couple of benefits I didn't expect. I noticed my attack score was now up to +2, which was a bit more forgiving for a pure Sorcerer run in the previous games. Certainly, it wasn't as good as an additional +1 every level like with a Warrior, but it meant I was at least progressing.

Finally, I noticed the LESSER MAGIC special ability had been added to my repertoire. I pulled that up on the Glossary.

LESSER MAGIC

Description: An ability that belongs to both Sorcerers of 4th level and Warriors or Rogues who take an Arcane Specialization. Lesser magic represents the ability to do unlimited small-scale magical effects like lighting candles, dancing lights, low-level telekinesis (limit 10lbs per level), conjuring flasks of water, and cleaning yourself in the morning. These can be performed an unlimited number of times per day.

"Wait, what was that?" I asked, looking down at the description. "Cleaning myself? Yes!"

"This is just flavor magic, dude," Jon said, annoyed. "Don't get so excited."

"I used the sheepskin and oil today, dude," I said, looking at Jon. "Never again."

ACCEPT CHANGES Y/N?

I hit Y.

ARAGORN "AARON" BARTKOWSKI
LVL: 4
CLASS: UNDERMASTER SORCERER
ALIGNMENT: GRAY
AGE: 34
SEX: MALE
RACE: HUMAN
STR: 10
AGI: 10
CON: 9
INT: 18 (MAX)
WIS: 8
COM: 15
CHA: 13

ARMOR CLASS: 9
ATTACK: +2 (+7 to ATTACK, 1d10+5 DAM Sword [witchfire])
HEALTH: 20

FEAT: Taunt, Sword and Shield

SPECIAL ABILITIES: ARCANE FIRE (1d6+5 INT bonus, Eldritch Damage), BLOCK (requires shield), LESSER MAGIC

(unlimited times per day)

SPELL LIST (3/2):
[1] PUSH, CURE, JUMP
[2] WEB, ANIMAL SUMMONING

STATUS EFFECTS:

* *Alchemical Stone* **(Red): +50lb carrying capacity**
* *Token of Love* **[Unpledged]: No Effect**
* *Boots of speed*: **Double Movement Speed, Dodge Roll Bonus**

"Hey, they changed the spell interface," Jon said. "I guess they patched the magic bracelets."

"I'm wondering about that," I replied. "It seems to have a mind of its own."

"Who could possibly imagine the rings containing the essence of a dead god might have some quirks," Jon said. "I really question some of your choices here too."

"I knew you would," I said.

"You look like you're moving to get the Master Ranger specialization," Jon said. "Which is very stereotypical for a man named Aragorn."

"Says the guy who went bare fisted monk," I replied. "You know weapons exist for a reason, right?"

"I once punched a dragon in the face," Jon said. "Envy me."

"Was this the dragon that subsequently incinerated you?" I asked.

Jon sighed. Which I wasn't aware ravens could do. "Listen man, just focus on relaxing. Mrs. Grub looks a little like Jennifer Connelly in *Dark City*. You know, after she grew from cute teenager in *Labyrinth* into a super-hot babe. You remind me of the babe. What babe? The babe—"

"Stop. I'm doing the quest without sex," I replied. "I'm not interested in your sloppy seconds, dude."

"That's a very sexist attitude, Aaron," Jon said. "After all, if you don't want seconds then you need to go after virgins and you know who goes after virgins? Terrorists. Terrorists and cultists. Terrorists, cultists, and—"

"I'm stopping this conversation before you say another word," I said, grabbing his beak and holding it closed.

We arrived at the farm, a small one-story house that looked considerably more run down than either of the Miller homes. The front door was open with a trail of blood leading into it. I let go of Jon's beak.

"Well, that's new," Jon said. "Probably not a good sign. We're here to save you, Mrs. Grub! Maybe your husband if we have the time!"

I charged in with my shield and sword drawn.

CHAPTER TWENTY-EIGHT
JON SLEPT WITH A HAG

The interior of Farmer Grub's home was horrifying as it was littered with the remains of what I assumed to be Farmer Grub. The place was a bloodbath and just describing it would raise the content warnings of my future biography to include WARNING - GRAPHIC VIOLENCE. Given we were already skirting the line with sexual content given how horny everyone seemed to be in the Southern Kingdoms, I'm going to err on the side of caution and only describe it as bad.

Lots and lots of red and pieces of meat.

Some black too.

Smelly too.

Don't think about that too hard.

In the center of the room, I saw the individual that was responsible for this horrific murder, and it put a different context on what Jon as well as other champions had been up to. Leaning over the largest chunk of meat on the ground was a female creature that was vaguely humanoid but with a hideousness that was difficult to put into words.

If I had to describe it, I would have gone with the idea of the Wicked Witch of the West, except much wrinklier (like tree bark), as well as naked with claws that looked like something out of a *Resident Evil* Boss fight. The creature's teeth were also like sawblades and its hair hung loose from its head like it was seaweed. It was a hag, the female counterpart of ogres, but a lot nastier.

Now if you had low WIS like me, you might not immediately have concluded that they were probably a disguised Mrs. Grub. However, I had genre savviness to compensate for my general lack of foresight (or hindsight for that matter). What would be more Larry C.C. Weis in terms of writing than the woman that was so willing to sleep with random adventurers was really a monstrous cannibalistic hag?

"Yeah, not Jennifer Connelly," I said, lifting my shield in one hand with my sword in the other.

The hag stood up and was now too tall for her cottage, stooped over. "I recognize that voice, little bird. You were one of my lovers. You thought I was so lovely."

"In the words of the great Ash Williams, honey, you got real ugly," Jon said, quoting *Army of Darkness*.

Whether or not Farmer Grub had it coming would be a question for the ages as I was about to say more when the witch lifted her palm and conjured a purple powder she blew in my face. I coughed as suddenly everything became exceptionally wavy, like I'd gone from zero to sixty in terms of baked on the good stuff. The hag spoke some words that resounded in my ears but had a reverb that made them unintelligible. Like Charlie Brown's teacher, they were nonsense, but I barely noticed because the room was spinning around me as I found myself unable to do anything but step back.

"What is going on here," I said, sounding like my voice was in slow motion and moving up and down in volume. I almost stumbled on the ground from the weird hallucinations I was experiencing. Big huge white letters appeared in front of my face like they were holograms projected in the sky above a football game.

WIS SAVING THROW FAILURE; YOU NOW HAVE THE STATUS EFFECT (Enthralled)

I mentally cursed myself for forgetting that low WIS didn't just mean that I was prone to making an ass of myself and stupid stands on principle. No, it also meant that I was more vulnerable to magic. I was, sadly, what Obi-Wan Kenobi would term the "weak-minded." Which was not the sort of thing anyone liked to think about themselves but explained my years of quiet acquiescence to Epic Dungeoneering™'s exploitation. Still, I had to wonder what it meant because I certainly didn't think I was enthralled. I knew Mrs. Grub was a monster and that I had to get the duck out of fodge.

That was when Monster Jennifer Connelly stepped through the smoke toward me. Listen, I'm not going to be weird about this, but she was a very attractive woman who had a place in my heart growing up. Also, I may have watched a couple of movies where she was, uh, taking advantage of those qualities. Monster Jennifer Connelly was the hypothetical succubus version of her with red skin, horns, and the kind of proportions that she hadn't needed in life to enthrall us, but my teenage self might have exaggerated.

Intellectually, I knew this had to be some sort of illusion and the fact the hag chose to appear as something distinctly nonhuman had me wondering if I had a secret fetish for monster women. However, I wasn't quite so into the issue that I was willing to go along with this. Not the least because hag women used human men to procreate and then either ate their babes or switched them with human women's before eating theirs. If that sounds messed up, welcome to actual fairy tales versus what Walt Disney made of them.

"Kiss me, Garland," Mrs. Grub said, her voice echoing in my ear. "I will let you live if you please me."

I struggled to pull away before slumping over. "Whatever you say, lady. What do you need me to do?"

Mrs. Grub kissed me on the lips and bit my lower lip, drawing blood across my mouth. "I need you to blame an incubus for my actions here. Find a human male to blame for my husband's death as the monster in disguise. Kill them and claim me an innocent. I have fed well here in Crossroad. I am not yet ready to leave. I will reward you in a way that will be the last joy you will ever need to explain."

I paused. "Sorry, enthralled here, could you repeat that?"

Yeah, I couldn't resist what she was doing but I could ask for specifics that would hopefully give me time to resist the spell.

"Go kill a man and claim he was an incubus who killed my husband," Mrs. Grub said. "Then I'll mate with you and eat you."

"Ah," I said, nodding. "Sounds good. I'll get right on that. So, do you have any specifics about the guy I'm supposed to kill?"

Mrs. Grub lifted one of her hands to slap me and I briefly saw her true form again before she paused. "Ha. That was very clever. You almost had me fooled. You are smarter than your reputation suggests when it comes to a beautiful woman."

I wasn't inclined to defend Garland, having never met the man, but I had to admit the short stories and what I'd learned about the latest novel inclined me to think he would have fallen for this hook, line, and sinker too. There was a scene in *Conan the Barbarian*, the John Milius one not the remake, where Conan bangs a witch but finds out she's like a werewolf or something midway through. He ends up tossing her on a fire and she turns into a will-o'-the-wisp before flying away.

"He's really not," Jon said, having been flying around the room this entire time. He went right to my face and poked me in the eye.

"Ow! Mothersucker!" I shouted, grabbing it as my head cleared enough to see I was once more surrounded by gore as well as an eight-foot-tall hag.

WIS SAVING THROW SUCCESS; YOU ARE NO LONGER ENTHRALLED

Any gratitude I might have felt or wisecracks I might have made were interrupted by the hag raising one of her eight-inch-long claws and pointing it at me. She hissed something in a language I didn't understand but the result was clear: PUSH. I was sent flying backward through the wooden shutters of her house before bouncing across the ground, rolling at the foot of Stompy.

"I know, I know," I said. "You told me so."

Stompy looked at me sideways, as if to say, 'What? You expect me to talk? That's silly, I'm a horse.'

Jon flew out of the cottage behind me, only for the side of it to explode as Mrs. Grub exited like the Incredible Hulk's evil grandmother. Secrecy was apparently off the table for the hag, and she was fully capable of tearing me apart. Hags are all descendants of Baba Yaga you see and whatever the hell she is, god or monster, they're a lot more powerful than their male counterparts.

If you want a classical literature comparison versus a *Monstrous Manual* one: Grendel was the biggest badass that ever lived but Beowulf managed to take him out. Grendel's mother made him look like a toddler crying at the supermarket. It made sense this adventure was recommended for a level-four party.

A party I was absent from.

"Die, you impudent wretch!" Mrs. Grub hissed and started slashing down with her claws like my sister's cat did her couch.

I barely managed to raise my shield up to block the attack. Sparks flew from each blow as I was forced down onto my knees by the sheer power of the attacks. I considered attacking with Arcane Fire but if the wizard at the inn had been able to absorb it, there was no way it would do much here. Instead, I tried to time my attack with my sword to strike at her chest—and failed miserably, having the +5 sword knocked from my hands.

YOU HAVE BEEN DISARMED

"No shit!" I shouted, watching Mrs. Grub leap ten feet in the air to come down on me. I remembered I had *boots of speed* and proceeded to run to the side before making a dodge roll out of the way at the end, which was twice as long as it had been before. Even so, I barely managed to get out of the way. It turned out Mrs. Grub had the JUMP spell too.

Stompy snorted, apparently having no interest in joining in on this fight on his own.

"WEB!" I shouted, pointing at her.

The tendrils of spider-silk flew outward, and the hag merely growled another spell out from her lips and caused them all to evaporate into nothingness.

YOU HAVE BEEN COUNTER-SPELLED

"Oh, come on!" I said, confused. "This is some boss-level bullshit! Counterspell is like a 7th level ability!"

"I have forgotten more about the Craft than you could ever know, Garland!" Mrs. Grub hissed. "I am not merely one of the distant descendants that have a dozen generations from the Crone but I am her very own daughter! I was part of this land when it was still a part of the Mirror World before the Pact of Veles moved it with the Forest of Secrets. Centuries have passed from when I was born—"

That was when Bloodstorm buried his ax into the back of Mrs. Grub's head. "Why is it that my family is so consistently awful? You're like the third sibling I've had to kill this year."

Unfortunately, Bloodstorm's attack didn't work like it would have on a human and Mrs. Grub responded by knocking him away like a fly. That was when she found a light arrow buried into the side of her head and another into her chest.

"We just can't leave you alone for a single afternoon, can we?" Ania said, pulling back another energy blast from Lightbringer. "Why can't you do something normal and go to the brothel to get your wick wet?"

"Can we focus on the monster, sister?" Agata said, aiming her staff like a pool cue and shooting out a blast of glowing green energy that struck Mrs. Grub again.

All it seemed to be doing was pissing the hag off.

"Yes, less talking, more fighting!" I said, raising my hands. "SUMMON ANIMAL!"

There was a chime noise followed by the appearance of three astral wolves, glowing translucent beings summoned from the Sky Kingdom of Perun. They immediately started charging at Mrs. Grub, clawing and biting at her. That provided a distraction for Bloodstorm to charge at her again and start hacking at the hag with his ax, only for her skin to resist his blows like steel. There were a few bloody wounds opened, her inner essence more like tree sap than blood, but it was slow going. She also clawed him good, somehow managing to penetrate his incredibly potent armor.

"Get back!" Agata shouted as she raised her staff. "By the light of Zorya of the Light, Lady of the Dawn, I bring forth the wrath of flame as well as righteousness! Be cast down, evil one, to Veles domain through the power of my words: FIREBALL!"

I didn't have time to contemplate why I now understood the weird language she'd been using earlier that the bracelet hadn't previously translated.

"Oh shit!" Bloodstorm, clutching his wounded side before running away like a football player trying to catch a pass.

Mrs. Grub snarled as she finished slashing the last of my wolves back to astral dust, sending them back to their home dimension. She started to counterspell, only for another arrow to strike her in the head, stopping her cold.

That was when the entire area around her for ten feet exploded into a circle of flame and the hag screamed like, well, someone just hit with a fireball. Mrs. Grub was singed from top to bottom and collapsed to the ground, her bark-like skin now scorched like she'd been a tree in the middle of a wildfire. All her claws had been burned, leaving only branch-like stumps.

That was when she got up.

"Oh, you have got to be kidding me," Ania said, staring in disbelief. "I thought you said your magic was powerful!"

"It is!" Agata said, embarrassed. "Apparently, hers is more so!"

Mrs. Grub raised her hands. "You think you're the only one who can summon fireballs, girl? I can bring a whole storm of them down on you! In fact, I think—"

"JUMP!" I shouted, having used my boots to grab at my sword.

My plan had been to leap into the air, raise my sword up, and slash down like a Jedi Master or wuxia swordsman doing an epic bit of magic. Unfortunately, it turned out I was more Wile E. Coyote than Li Mu Bai and I landed with a thud on top of the witch. It was like jumping twenty feet in the air and landing on a tree stump. However, much to my surprise, I'd at least managed to keep my sword pointed down and it had buried itself through the hag's torso. The necromantic power of the witchfire did the rest of the necessary work and Mrs. Grub disintegrated into fine grayish powder underneath me.

"Aaron!" Ania said, running up to my side. "Are you okay?"

"Fuck no!" I shouted, feeling immense pain across my entire body but especially my leg that was bent the wrong way.

HP: 1/20 (Major Injury)

"Hold still, this is going to hurt," Agata said, pulling the leg into place before starting to cast multiple CURE spells.

They hurt too.

SIDE QUEST(S) UPDATED: MY KID LOOKS LIKE THE MILKMAN (1/1)

+5000 EXP
+3000 EXP (Greater Hag)
+400 EXP (Uncover the secret of Mrs. Grub)
+0 EXP (Failed Objective- Did Not Save Farmer Grub)
+500 GP
+1 Pwiffle Card (Hag)

Level 4 to 5
13000/20000

Jon settled down beside me. "Huh, I always wondered what the failed quest objective meant about never finding out Mrs. Grub's secret."

I stared at Jon.

"What?" Jon asked, staring back.

CHAPTER TWENTY-NINE
ON THE ROAD AGAIN. I JUST CAN'T WAIT

"Oh, come on, Aaron!" Jon said, perched on Bloodstorm's shoulder instead of mine. "How was I supposed to know that her secret was that she was actually a cannibalistic hag? It could have been anything! Like, maybe she was a missing princess or was secretly part of the resistance against the Empire!"

I wasn't speaking to Jon after my experience with Mrs. Grub. Instead, I'd just hopped on Stompy's back and joined the rest of the group as we departed through the South Gate of Crossroad, departing the town and leaving Dragon Keep in the hands of the locals until we could make our return.

All four members of our group were riding demon steeds, which surprised me but there had been an entire herd of the creatures inside the keep's stables. They were the signature mounts for the Dark Undermasters and perhaps one of the reasons why the order of monster hunters wasn't in line with Mythras cult orthodoxy.

Amusingly, I'd tried to talk to all the steeds and Stompy only to get stonewalled. I got the sneaking impression that they were all having a great deal of fun at my expense. Certainly, Ania and Agata didn't seem to believe they could talk back even though demon steeds were demons rather than equines and we had a talking raven.

"*Then you investigate,*" Ania said, shaking her head. "There were like forty corpses in the basement and some of them were Dark

Undermasters. The gods know how long she'd been carrying out her cannibalistic feasts under the order's nose."

"To be fair, that's more on them than Jon," Bloodstorm said, riding alongside me. "Obviously, the Dark Undermasters weren't investigating the disappearances in the area very thoroughly. Also, my sibling's witchcraft was very powerful."

"Those who supplement their magic with the arts of desire are extra powerful with it," Agata said, having freely embraced her new religion's peculiar doctrine. "I doubt she had any difficulty luring men into her bed for sacrifice, meals, or supplementing her connection to the forces of nature."

"I'm sure Aragorn struggled mightily against whatever buxom slattern she chose to appear as," Ania said, sounding surprisingly cross.

"Hey, don't talk about Ms. Connelly that way!" Jon said. "She's one of three reasons to see *The Rocketeer*! The other two being jetpacks and Timothy Dalton. Even if he's a Nazi in that movie. I know, spoilers for a thirty-year-old film."

"I was enchanted!" I said, continuing to ignore Jon's speech. "It was traumatizing not sexy."

"I mean, it can be both," Bloodstorm said, nodding. "Either way, it was a powerful monster we managed to put down and the sign that this group has the potential to achieve great things together."

"A greater hag is a far cry from a god's avatar and that's what we're up against," Ania said, staring forward.

"Yeah, we could use a little level grinding ahead of time," Jon said. "Like a couple of months' worth to get Aaron up to speed with you, Ania. Maybe a few weeks for you, Agata. I'm not saying levels are everything, they certainly didn't help me, but it couldn't hurt to press the scale to the swim part of the sink or swim scale."

"That analogy makes no sense," I said, unable to resist responding.

We were heading in the opposite direction from Blackwood Bog and were now heading in the direction of Kalizov. I'd been able to gather that the farmlands and townships along the way were mostly abandoned now. The fighting between the Mad Queen and the Dragon

Queen had been stretching on for years now with the remainder of Celestyne's forces under siege.

It didn't take long to confirm this was true as the territory to the south of Crossroad included a bunch of burned homesteads, cracked stone roads, and signs of battle that were a few months old. The sun was hanging over our heads with clear skies as far as the eye could see but there was an ominous sense about the road ahead. The Earth Temple where Chernabog rested was past Kalizov and we'd have to dodge the greater bulk of the Mad Queen's army as it prepared to crush the last pocket of resistance to her reign.

"I'm afraid time isn't on our side," Ania explained. "Each of the Temples of the Elements are linked to a specific Old God that is feeding on most of the ambient energies of the world while passing the rest on to Veles. The world becomes darker, more severe, and more corrupt each hour their magic is active."

"Like strigoi, they're draining the Earthmother dry," Agata said, using a much more accurate analogy. "If we wait to be strong enough to destroy Chernobog as he is now then the disparity between our power is likely to grow rather than shrink. The world will also be far darker and more perilous."

"The only way we can buy time for humanity is to dam the river of magic flowing to Veles," I said.

I paused, not sure how much of my vision to share. "Veles, err, Valentin is said to have defeated two of the Old Gods. Shouldn't they, I dunno, be dead?"

Ania rubbed the side of her head. "My memories for all the cycles aren't exactly to be trusted but I remember Valentin's cycle well. He did defeat two of the Old Gods with our party. We managed to relight the sacred fires as well. It required vast amounts of power from Veles to re-summon his allies from the void they were banished to and set things back on track. It may have cost him years off his plans and he wouldn't have been able to pull it off if we'd defeated all of his lieutenants."

I followed that logic. Barely. "So, we need to destroy all four Old Gods and relight the sacred fire thingies or he'll eventually be able to ruin things again."

"We need to kill the Old Gods, relight the sacred fires, and then kill Veles," Ania corrected. "Veles' temple lies under a mystical shield in the Death Mountains near by the fallen body of his brother, Perun. Bald Mountain, specifically, is where it is located. No one can get anywhere near him until the magic of the Earthmother is no longer reinforcing that barrier."

"You've got to give Weis some credit," Jon said, surprising me. "As derivative as an author he may be, the guy certainly knows how to design video games. There's a definite A to B plot here as well as good open world design. Lots of in-universe justifications for why we can't just head to Bald Mountain immediately."

Honestly, it was a little *too* well-designed and I had to wonder about whether anyone had tried to color outside the lines. Had anyone tried digging under Veles' magical barrier? What if Veles' avatar was destroyed before the other Old Gods? What if the reason all the previous champions had failed was because Veles knew exactly where they were going and what to do? It gave me the mental picture of a rat in a maze with the end having some cheese in a trap.

"Even then, he's guarded by a massive army of the dead," Agata said. "The Mad Queen and other armies would be needed to join together to destroy it. If only the Twin Queens would put aside their differences to stand against the horror affecting the world."

"Yeah, that's not happening," I muttered.

Ania nodded. "The Mad Queen has almost won. Why would she stop now?"

"One problem at a time," I replied.

"We should kill the Mad Queen and end the civil war," Bloodstorm suggested.

That almost stopped our ride.

"What?" Bloodstorm asked, looking at Ania. "You're an assassin."

"I don't think it's that easy," I replied. "It's not that kind of story."

The plucky band of rebels and misfits with their own dragon as a monarch had been unable to overcome the Imperial-backed forces of Queen Apollonia. Ironically, the fact that the country was riddled with undead horrors and cultists worshiping the God of Darkness had probably kept the war from being a complete loss by Celestyne. As much as Celestyne would love to unite the people against Veles' forces, the fact was the Mad Queen had most of the territory under her control and was the one being forced to defend it.

Unfortunately, it seemed the civil war was about to come to an end, and it would soon be a bunch of tyrant religious fanatics working with a corrupt nobility against the literal forces of Hell. At least that had been the state of things last book. That had been written ten years ago and the people of the Southern Kingdoms had been dealing with Weis' loops ever since.

"I'm not a friend of the Dragon Queen," Ania said.

"She is the superior candidate for rulership," Agata said, simply. "Have you forgotten that it was the usurper who destroyed our family?"

Ania narrowed her eyes. "I have forgotten nothing. Have you forgotten that Garland's affair with Celestyne and breaking her curse is what started this whole civil war in the first place? Your so-called husband is the reason the land is being ravaged when there's an evil god invading the universe."

"Two universes!" Jon piped in.

"Stop helping," Ania said, showing again to have picked up some of the modern speech of the champions.

"I'm just glad people are distracted from my screw ups for once," Jon said.

"So-called husband?" Agata said, looking appalled. "How dare you? Just because he chose me—"

Ania's hand moved down to her dagger before she paused. "Aaron, I'm appointing you leader of this group."

"What now?" I asked, doing a double take.

"I agree!" Bloodstorm said, raising his hand. "We can vote like the High Grecian Empire."

"Democracy is the worst idea ever conceived by man," Agata said, sharply. "Imagine how foolish the average person is and then assume that a good half of them are even dumber. Then ask yourself if their numbers should be what determines policy."

"Then we can go with the older rule of divine right," Ania said.

"Agreed," Agata said.

"Aaron is the leader or I'll fucking smite you," Ania said. "See, just like how the gods do it."

"Why am I getting put in charge?" I asked. "Do I get a say in this?"

"No!" Agata and Ania said simultaneously.

"Why are you trying to pass off the leadership of the most important quest in Ledzianian history to some homeless vagabond?" Agata asked, appalled.

"I have a home," I said, annoyed. "Admittedly, I rent but—"

"He *has* a home," Ania said. "It's our home. Lord Emberly appointed him as the Lord of Dragon Keep."

"He did *what*?" Agata asked.

I swear the horses we were riding were not only not disturbed by all the fighting going on top of them but enjoying it.

"There may have been a case of mistaken identity," I tried to inject.

"Yes, I know!" Agata said. "You will renounce your claim to Dragon Keep immediately!"

"He will not," Ania said. "He's also leading this quest because I don't trust your leadership and I hate people. Also, Bloodstorm is someone who would probably just start us on a quest to kill whoever is paying us."

"I'm just along for the ride," Bloodstorm said, cheerfully. "This armor is enough to pay for my services for a decade. We also get a chance to kill a god. Possibly multiple gods. What more could anyone ask for?"

"I dunno, I can ask for a lot more," Jon said.

Ania was just trying to create a buffer between her and her sister. There was no question that we were all on the same page here: no one wanted the world to be destroyed after all. It was kind of insulting that she thought anyone would fall for the fact she was just assigning the task of minding her family to me. However, a part of me, a very small part, was honored that she thought of me for the task. The other part, the much larger part, had no interest in playing referee for a family squabble that had been going on since I was a teenager.

"I'll pass," I said, shaking my head. "Our goal is to get to the Temple of the Earth and slay Chernabog. It's what's in the quest journal. We don't need anything else."

Ania seemed surprised I'd turned down her fake job offer. "It's a bit more complicated than that. We're equipped for a week's journey down past Kalizov but even if we ignore the Mad Queen's armies—"

"Which we absolutely are," I said, pointing out that was a whole different questline.

Ania nodded. "Then we will run out of supplies before we reach the Black God's Woods."

"Hey!" Jon said. "Call him by his name. He may be our enemy but no need to be racist."

Ania narrowed her eyes. "Chernobog means Black God, you nitwit. Before he was corrupted to evil by Veles, Chernobog was just the god of the latter half of the seasons. He had black hair."

The actual specific mythology of Slavic folklore had never been, as far as I know, codified the way, say, Greek had been by Bulfinch or Norse by Jack Kirby (womp-womp). There were a lot of differences of opinion and stuff that had never been written down. Plus, shockingly enough, some countries had different traditions regarding the gods of Pre-Christian Eastern Europe. The religious equivalent of whether Legends or Disney sequels were the true *Star Wars*. Larry Weis had ignored that in his writing and made an entire pantheon of consistent roles for all his gods as well as demigods.

Four of the most important deities in the Dark Undermaster version of things were the Quadruplets. Two pairs of identical twins that had been born to Mokosh one enchanting evening during the Solstice. There was Belobog the God of Good Fortune, Chernabog the God of Misfortune, Zorya the Goddess of Dawn, and Zorya the Goddess of Night. Yes, there's two goddesses with the same name. It happens.

Supposedly, all four of the children shared fathers in Perun and Veles. How did that work exactly? Because they're gods and fuck you. I was pretty sure Belobog was going to be in one of the other Elemental Temples, but I wasn't sure about the Zoryas. There were plenty of other gods that could be inhabiting the temples, and I was curious about researching them before we made it a point to kill them. Assuming anyone had anything other than hearsay and sermons to draw from.

"I know, I know, I'm just being an ass," Jon said. "I got the full lecture from Agata the first time we went after Chernabog."

"What do you mean, first time?" Agata asked, confused.

"No, you're being a raven, Jon," I said, shaking my head before looking at Agata. "It's a long story and I'll try and fill you in when we make camp, Ms. Rose."

"*Lady* Rose," Agata said. I was just glad she didn't add 'peasant' to the end of that sentence. I'd checked her stats during our trip here and she had a 15 Comeliness score but an 8 Charisma, which explained a few things. Unfortunately, it wouldn't pay to alienate our healer during our whole quest to save humanity thing. Still, if she tried to bully her way into leadership, she'd find out I wasn't nearly as easygoing as appearances suggested.

"Sure," I said, biting my tongue. "So, we have to find a place to bunker down before we make our assault. It's not going to do us any good to be dehydrated and starving when we need to kill a god."

Surprisingly, Agata decided to contribute more than spells, sass, and inappropriate groping. "The Abbey of the Twins is a two-day ride on demon steeds before the Black God's Forest. They were the people who gave me refuge against the Impaler's forces. They also taught me the many sacred arts of Mokosh as well as defending myself."

"You then broke your oath of chastity to them to marry Garland," Ania said, digging deeper.

"I thought they were sex witches," Jon asked, confused.

"The Priestesses of Mokosh are sworn never to get married but take many lovers for their rites," I said.

"Many-many lovers," Agata said, as if taunting me. Then she dropped the pretense. "But not you, Imposter."

"So, you can go to town but never fall in love," Jon said. "Like Jedi."

"That is not what Lucas meant in the prequels," I said, annoyed.

"He totally did," Jon said. "He said in the interviews."

"I will not be renewing my magic with your patron, raven," Agata said, raising her nose and ignoring that we didn't care. "I shall find another to make the wind and rain as well as make flowers bloom. To cause the honey to drip from one's hair."

"My patron?" Jon asked, confused.

"She means she's not going to enjoy Aaron," Bloodstorm said.

"I mean, yeah, I thought that part was obvious," Jon said. "Wait, is it not obvious? I got lost in all the metaphors."

I rolled my eyes. "It's obvious. I think. Just to be clear, those are all double entendres, right?"

"Yes, Aragorn," Ania said. "My sister has developed a positively filthy mouth since our separation."

"Aaron," I corrected. "Okay, sounds like a plan, Agata. Hopefully, the sisters are going to be okay with our deicide plan."

"When Veles is defeated then the madness will pass from the gods minds and the Old Gods will be restored to their former selves," Agata said. "A new Golden Age will come to Ledziania."

"Or the Empire will force us all to worship Mythras," Ania said. "Or the Old Gods will start their own plans of domination."

"Or the Turqs will invade," Bloodstorm said. "The Rus Kingdoms are busy fighting each other but invading the Southern Kingdoms has always done wonders for their unity."

"Plus, Epic Dungeoneering™ has a way to visit this world," I pointed out, even though they were probably unfamiliar with the group. "If they lose Veles' patronage, they might still be able to come here. Who knows, maybe they'll sell the method to certain resource hungry governments from my world. Next year, we could have tanks rolling in to 'liberate' the kingdom while drilling for mana. Like a fantasy version of Avatar. The James Cameron version, not the airbender one."

That was enough to depress everyone in the party from the sudden silence.

After a long pause, Jon said, "So who is up for a game of Pwiffle?"

CHAPTER THIRTY
TRAVEL TIMES ARE A BITCH

It didn't take long for the luster of being in an epic fantasy adventure to wear off. My time in Crossroad may have been terrifying but it was never boring, and I'd never had to deal with saddle sores, digging latrines, and eating things that only barely qualified as food.

There was perhaps a reason for that since I didn't know anything about riding horses, hunting game, gathering firewood, or preparing meals that didn't come with microwave instructions. I was able to blast monsters but even that was a specific skill that hadn't gotten much use as we stuck to the main roads.

Both Ania and Agata attempted to teach me some of their skills, but this proved to be an unmitigated disaster. My biggest weakness with swordplay and shield work was the fact I wasn't strong, quick, or full of endurance. Also, I knew how to fight with a sword and shield just fine. I just didn't know that I knew how to fight with a sword and shield or how to explain that I did.

If that didn't make sense, let me explain. Ania tried showing me the basics, but my reflexes kicked in every time that I was able to do what she needed me to do. The Mark of the Champion apparently functioned like Neo learning kung fu in *The Matrix*. It had been downloaded into my brain just like how to channel magic. That meant I was in the unenviable position of being unteachable since I could do all the positions but didn't necessarily know when to. I didn't have a warrior's mindset (or even a rogue's).

The same thing had happened with Agata only with even less success. She'd spent five years studying the arts of sorcery at the Abbey of the Twins. She'd learned philosophy, spirituality, meditation, and the natural principles behind it all. Much to her extreme irritation, I seemed to know more about the theory of it than she did whenever she asked me questions. Again, I knew kung fu, plus an 18 INT.

This did little to improve our relationship. Agata had taken up with Bloodstorm to renew her magic and seemed determined to be as loud as humanly possible in the camp, specifically near my tent. Jon had suggested that it was an attempt to make me jealous, but I had no idea why she'd even want me to be jealous. I wasn't interested. I mean outside of a purely aesthetic appreciation.

Ania, herself, had retreated into her guarded self that had little to talk to anyone about except how it related to the mission. All the progress we had made seemed to have evaporated as soon as we were away from Dragon Keep. Perhaps it was the presence of her sister or the fact we were on our way to almost certain death but the most I could say was she'd turned to calling me Aragorn over Imposter.

It didn't help that our surroundings were depressing as Hell. Ania hadn't been exaggerating about how nasty the civil war had gotten. Both sides had burned whole villages to the ground, strung up people to starve in cages, and stripped the fields bare to make sure they were fed through the winter. The fact that the two armies' efforts meant no one would be eating next winter didn't seem to occur to the people in charge or they didn't care. Several times, we found groups of wandering stray dogs that I found somehow more depressing than the bodies abandoned in the road needing burial.

One thing I gave Larry C.C. Weis credit for was that he didn't present a particularly romantic view of war. The Dragon Queen may have been the "good" guy but that didn't mean that the people serving her were better or the men conscripted into the Mad Queen's army were any worse. Both sides liberally employed mercenaries and if the Imperial storm knights were more prone to atrocities, then it was just because they were in a foreign land rather than the locals in theirs'. Combining this with the punishing pace we were setting on our tireless demon steeds, I started to appreciate Jon's inane chatter as a distraction.

"Dina Meyer or Rose Leslie for Ania if they do a remake?" Jon asked. "I am torn."

"I'm not doing this," I said, feeling queasy from my sixth hour on Stompy. I checked to see if there was anything I could do.

YOU ARE SUFFERING STATUS EFFECT [NAUSEA]; -1 PENALTY
YOU ARE SUFFERING STATUS EFFECT [EXHAUSTION]; -1 PENALTY

Nope!

Unfortunately, I'd been queasy from my sixth minute and was determined to push through without asking for a break every twenty minutes like I had been earlier. "Also, Dina Meyer is in her fifties now."

"Oh, like you wouldn't crawl through broken glass to date her still," Jon said.

"You have a point," I said, having just enough strength to pretend to be in the mood to joke around.

"Anyway, I'm saying *Dragonheart* and *Starship Troopers* Dina Meyer," Jon said. "Rowr. We settled on *Underworld* Kate Beckinsale, *Legend of the Seeker* Bridgit Regan, or *Agent Carter* Hayley Atwell for Agata, right?"

"You settled on them. Also, Hayley Atwell is way too nice for Agata," I said, admittedly glad for the distraction. I was about ready to lose my lunch for the second time in our journey. Something that wasn't going to make my companions respect me anymore.

"Excuse me!" Agata said.

"You don't know who those people are!" Jon called back.

"I am nice!" Agata said.

Bloodstorm burst out laughing.

Ania burst out laughing to Bloodstorm's laughter.

"You will never see me naked again," Agata said, sneering.

"I sincerely doubt that," Bloodstorm said, chuckling. Say what you will about the man, but he had plenty of confidence. Justifiably so by the noises Agata made.

Assuming she wasn't faking.

"I think we should pause for Aaron to take another break," Ania said, moving up to my side and taking Stompy's reins. "He looks like he's about to start hallucinating his horse talking again."

"That happened," I said, staring at her. "Jon was there."

"I have no idea what you're talking about man," Jon said, lying. "Anyway, how long exactly did you last with the Rusalka? If you were holding your breath, it couldn't have been very long. It's okay, it happens to everyone."

"Rusalka women only drown the men after they reach their pleasure," Ania said, citing Dark Undermaster lore. Which, apparently, included monster sex practices because of course it did. "Then they explode into water."

Jon stared at Ania before looking down, apparently torn about how to respond. "There is a very-very obvious dirty joke I could be making but it would be wasted on Aaron since he's the hobbit of our group and looks like he could use a Second Breakfast."

"Please don't mention food," I muttered.

"Also, a nap," Jon said. "Or three."

Ania brought our group to a stop.

"Garland, I have to say I expected more from you," Bloodstorm said, crossing his arms.

"He's not Garland," Agata said, annoyed.

"He's not the Garland but he's a Garland," Bloodstorm said. "I've met a couple of others over the years. You don't need the magic bracelets to remember if you're aligned with the powers of darkness."

"You're helping us, so you're with the powers of light," Agata said, as if she was trying to convince herself more than him.

"Then why is your sister black in alignment and Aaron listed as gray?" Jon asked. "I expected him to be lily white by now, but his point score is even more Gray than his White and Dark points put together."

I didn't bother speculating on that because I was still too miserable. "How the hell did you make these kinds of journeys when you were a human, Jon?"

"Well, obviously I put some points in Endurance," Jon said. "But really, every night I just fast traveled back to the Keep and slept in my bed then fast traveled back to where I'd traveled furthest in the morning."

I didn't respond for a second. "What."

Ania looked away. "I mean, that's theoretically possible but—"

"We could be teleporting back and forth *this entire time*?" I asked, madder at him than I'd been when he'd not bothered to tell me that Mrs. Grub had some sort of secret that he'd ignored in his attempt to get me laid.

"You'd have to hit 5th level first!" Jon said, flapping his wings a bit. "I mean, Ania could probably do it but I'm sure she knows that."

Ania looked to one side. "I don't trust the Wise Man's magic."

"It's not the Wise Man's magic," Agata said, lifting her bracelet. "The Rheingold artifacts are the holy power of the late god, Perun, and shall guide us to the secret for returning him from death!"

"A god coming back from the dead?" Bloodstorm asked, rubbing his chin. "Sounds kinda Mythras-y to me."

I shook my head. "I'm good guys. I'll push through. I'm not slowing you down."

Bloodstorm burst out laughing in the same way he had with Agata. "Oh, Garland, I love you man but you're absolutely slowing us down. There's a reason we're not flying on these things and that's because I've ridden with guys who had consumption who looked better than you."

"What happened to them?" Jon asked.

"They died," Bloodstorm said, absently. "Garland insisting on boiling our water would have saved the Monster Regiment from the bloody flux if we'd known about it. Mind you, both he and Agata can just make fresh water too."

"I can?" I asked, blinking.

"Yeah." Bloodstorm said. "You're a wizard."

"And that has what to do with it?" I asked, confused.

"We'll rest for a few hours," Ania said. "Then we'll resume if Aragorn is up for it."

"The more we rest, the more people will die," Agata said, explicitly blaming me for this and I wasn't sure I disagreed.

"I'm good," I said, sucking in my breath. "No matter what, I want to press on."

Ania pushed me gently and I almost fell out of Stompy's saddle.

"Oh for Mokosh's sake," Agata said, pulling out her staff and waving it over me before speaking several magic words. I saw her bracelet display several words in Ledzianian that translated to English in my brain.

AGATA CASTS LESSER MAGIC: REFRESH ON AARON "ARAGORN" BARTKOWSKI

Immediately, I felt like someone had just given me an injection of the syrup they use to make Mountain Dew to the brain as all of my aches, pains, as well as tiredness vanished. I no longer felt like I was about to dry heave on my demon steed either.

YOU HAVE RECOVERED FROM STATUS EFFECT [NAUSEA]
YOU HAVE RECOVERED FROM STATUS EFFECT [EXHAUSTION]

"There," Agata said, tapping my head with the end of her staff. "Can we get back to riding?"

I paused. "That was lesser magic?"

"Yes," Agata said. "I'm surprised you didn't do it to yourself."

I didn't know *it could do that*. Yeah, I needed to go over the various effects that I was capable of. It seemed I knew kung fu but I didn't know that I knew specific moves. It would have been extremely helpful, for example, to know how to do this REFRESH cantrip. So, I decided to check just what I could do with Lesser Magic.

AVAILABLE LESSER MAGIC EFFECTS (Level + INT Bonus, 8): CLEAN SELF, CREATE FOOD, CREATE FIRE, CREATE WATER, MINOR ILLUSION, REFRESH, TELEKINESIS (1 Kilo per INT bonus), VENTRILOQUISM

"Yeah, okay this was on me," I said, feeling somehow even worse than when I'd been suffering status effects. I wondered if it was possible to die of embarrassment in this world or if I should just run into the spears of the nearest group of goblins.

"None of them are particularly useful in combat," Jon pointed out.

"Yeah, but they would have made this trip a lot easier," I muttered. "My bad, guys! Sadly, they don't have a spell for learning how to ride better."

"We could strap you to stompy," Bloodstorm said. "Maybe rope you down and have him carry you like cargo."

"That's not a terrible plan," Agata said, rubbing her chin. "What are your thoughts on that, Ania?"

Before Ania had a chance to respond, I saw a group of soldiers coming down the road toward us. They didn't sport any banners, which was a bad sign, and were primarily wearing chain mail (sorry, mail) and mismatched tabards. I had no experience with Medieval warfare but, generally, the books implied that was a sign that whoever was wearing them had been a militia man or peasant levy who'd killed the previous owners.

There was a scene in the *Seven Samurai*, the original Kurasawa one, where the samurai find out the village they're protecting has a bunch of armor as well as weapons. This is because after some of the battles nearby them, the peasants had gone out and murdered any lone samurai or wounded ones they'd come across. A not-so-subtle bit of moral ambiguity that got lost in most adaptations. Basically, the peasants weren't the friends of the hereditary nobility and eventually would get rid of them in the Mejii Revolution.

"Bandits?" I asked, looking at them.

"Worse," Ania said. "Noble hunters."

"Noble hunters?" I asked.

"Deserters and scum," Agata said, growling.

"War is the best time to muddy your relationship to the noble houses," Ania said. "Usually by stabbing some poor fool and claiming his identity."

"It doesn't work," Agata said. "Often."

Poland, even Fantasy Poland like Ledziania, had a slightly different relationship with their feudal overlords than Medieval Japan or even Western Europe. Whereas, generously, about 1% of the populace and often 1% of 1% of the population were aristocrats elsewhere, a good 10% of Ledziania's people were technically nobility. Very technically. In practice, this meant there were just a lot of dirt-poor nobles, but it did mean the social divide wasn't quite as severe as it was in, say, Westeros or Gondor. Still, where there was class divide, there was going to be people who wanted to jump the fence to do some social climbing. Possibly involving stabbing.

"In my world, identity thieves just ruin your credit rating," I muttered. "Are you sure these guys are imposters?"

The leader of the group came up on his ordinary black horse wearing a black cloak with a dead black rose in his lapel. "Hail travelers, I am Ser Garland of Nowhere, Lord of Dragon Keep and defender of the Southern Kingdoms! Please come back to our camp for libations as I come to ask your help against the evil forces of Veles."

He notably did not have a bracelet.

"Yeah, he's going to drug us, slit our throats, and defile our corpses, isn't he?" Jon asked.

I smiled. "It sounds great, Ser Garland!"

Ania and Agata looked at me strangely.

Bloodstorm just smiled.

CHAPTER THIRTY-ONE
NEVER BET AGAINST A MICHIGANDER WHEN DEATH IS ON THE LINE

The noble hunters turned out to be an amiable bunch of guys. You know, for complete scumbags. I say this because we were brought back to their camp and offered hospitality while they planned to drug us then either kill or enslave us. What exactly they had planned for us I figured out primarily by the chains I spotted on our way into their ruined fort base next to some blood.

Subtlety went out the window by the time they brought out our drugged food with them openly discussing what could be done with us without lowering our price on the slave market. They were apparently speaking in Imperial and didn't think we spoke that language (or had bracelets that could magically translate the local language).

My original plan for dealing with them had been to get them to lower their guard before escaping but hearing their rather graphic details, I decided to be a bit more final in my approach. That involved using my newly discovered Lesser Magic to fake drinking and eating while switching out the poisons involved. If you think this would prove difficult and worthy of description, you'd be wrong since the moment I explained it to Ania, she said she'd take care of everything. When a 9th level rogue tells you that, you believe her, and it fell to me to try to keep everyone as distracted as possible.

I managed to do that by reciting a bunch of stories that I filed the serial numbers off from. I admit, their reaction to *Star Wars* was the strangest one but it may have been in the telling. They were really interested in the fact that Luke Skywalker and Leia were siblings, for example. Like pruriently interested.

Still, I had to admit that their leader was quite charismatic. He was a one-eyed ex-knight named Black Tom Marigold and an actual member of the nobility who had managed to find himself the respect of a small army of cutthroats who had lost all faith in their aristocrats. As I sat around his fire under the light of Mokosh's moon, I found myself wishing he wasn't a guy trying to kill us.

"Sorry about the Garland business," Black Tom said, removing his false eye and pulling down his eyepatch. "You understand that is how this sort of business goes. There are not many people worth robbing on the road these days except nobles and they're usually pretty well armed."

"Of course," I said, pretending to drink from my wineskin.

"So, obviously, we have to lure you back to the camp then drug you with black lily," Black Tom said, slurring his words. "Then we rob you while you're out of it."

"Then you let them go, huh?" I asked, not believing that for a second.

"Of course!" Black Tom said, smiling. He was already feeling the full force of the drugs they were going to feed us. "Except the ones we can ransom and the witnesses. Oh, and sometimes the prettiest ladies or lads. They fetch the highest price on the Imperial slave markets. Can you believe people fetch more money than their possessions these days."

"It's a seller's market," I said, looking around to the rest of the group. Most of the bandits looked worse than I did after that one time I took cold medicine and my mother's home remedy for pneumonia. I ended up hallucinating a Balrog in my closet after Arwen and Eowyn had a pillow fight. "One thing I'm curious about, Tom, isn't all this a violation of sacred hospitality?"

Black Tom snorted. "You listen to too many bard's tales, Arry. Who is going to punish us? The gods? Perun is dead, Mokosh's priestesses are a bunch of harlots, and Veles is already planning to kill us all. Maybe Svarog. He's usually off hammering something in his...hic...cavern."

"Yeah, he's kind of conspicuously absent from the narrative for such a major god," I said, making a note that we might want to seek out some divine help that wasn't from Veles. Presumably not Mythras since I'd unwittingly become an apostate to him.

"Anyway, you're deserters from the Mad Queen...err Queen Apollonia's army?"

"Mad Queen, Dragon Queen, Empire, and even some of the Rus sellswords," Black Tom said. "It turns out all the lower ranks have a fundamental thing in common: we're all just arrow fodder for the officers. So, I decided to become a heroic bandit for the poor."

"Really?" I asked, staring.

"Yeah, I'm poor," Black Tom said. "So are they. I was eighth of nine brothers and seven of them are dead. The ninth is...the ninth is..."

That was when Black Tom passed out. He wasn't the only one. That was when I gave the signal to the others or tried to. We hadn't agreed on one, so I ended up doing the wave and they got the message. Bloodstorm got up and began cleaving people's heads left and right as a few struggled to resist. Ania stabbed the latter in a ruthless fashion before moving to the disabled. Even Agata used Arcane fire on a few snoring away. I picked up my sword, lifted it, and pushed it down into Black Tom's chest while he lay before me. It was a ruthless act, but I was surprised how easy it had proven to be.

Maybe Veles was right about this world.

RANDOM ENCOUNTER ENDED: DANGEROUS DESERTERS 1/1

+ 2200 EXP [Bandits]
+ 3000 EXP [Bandit Lord]
+ 50 EXP [Cook]

+ 300 EXP [Switch Poison Ruse]
+ 551 GP
+1 *Alchemical eye of seeing*
+ 1 *Dagger +2*
+ 1 *Belt of Protection*
Level 4 to 5
18550/20000

"Alright, who killed the cook?" I said, getting up. Cooky had been a ratkin with a chef's hat and I felt bad they'd offed him. It was the kind of local color that added to the world, and I hated that we'd killed Ratatouille.

"The cook was the worst one of them!" Bloodstorm said, lifting his bloody ax over him. "Who do you think prepares the black lily?"

"I'm not sure why we had to bother with this," Agata said, looking disgusted at the camp around us. "We could have defeated them in honorable combat."

"Screw honor," Ania said, looking around. "These guys all had it coming."

"I do not disagree," Agata said, sighing. "Though I think we could have taken them in battle."

Bloodstorm shrugged and walked over to me. "You're just upset because it turns out that the Fake Garland is some sort of evil mastermind."

I frowned. "Thanks, Bloodstorm. I think. Where is Jon?"

He slapped me on the back. "Off scouting, I think. He said something about this being near where he died."

"Ah," I said, wondering if it would be a good idea to make a detour to try to recover his equipment.

The bandits' camp was significantly off the road, in the nearby woods, next to a ruined fort that they'd taken over despite the fact it had been burned badly by a fire. Still, in terms of fortification, it wasn't a bad location, and it gave us a place to spend the night. That was, assuming that we wanted to spend the night nearby the twenty-four or so people we'd just murdered. I had to admit I wasn't exactly comfortable with the way this had gone down. I'd hoped we could just slip away from them

"I'll go start moving the bodies," Bloodstorm said, making an offer I was grateful for. "We'll pile them together for a pyre in the morning. Best not to signal our presence until we're about to leave. You don't want to attract any unnecessary attention."

"You think they have any friends out there?" I asked.

"I think that there'll be some uncomfortable questions if a group of knights come across us over a bunch of bodies," Bloodstorm explained. "People tend to assume that I'm the bad guy whenever they come across me standing over dead people."

"Ah," I said, nodding. "Can't imagine why."

Bloodstorm laughed heartily and started to work. "You are a very small and puny human, Garland, but I like you."

I stared at him. "You know I'm someone else, Bloodstorm. Why do you keep calling me Garland?"

Bloodstorm looked at me. "You'll find, Aaron, that it is a lot better for you to have an identity separate from the one you use as a hired killer. It may become necessary to disappear into another identity someday, which is an option I didn't have. I used to be Kragen the Bull Man, a curiosity for the various men who kept me as a slave to work their fields or have garbage thrown at me. It was only when I became the Bloodstorm that I gained power over my life. But to be the Bloodstorm has its own perils and sometimes I wish I could have just been Kragen the Free."

I was shocked by this sudden bit of emotional honesty. "You were a slave?"

Kragen paused, clearly remembering a time he'd prefer not to. "We'll talk about it later, Garland. But you may someday be able to return to the life you had before. Whether or not it will still be waiting for you or it is your life to return to is the question."

A picture formed in my mind of Bloodstorm being born and substituted for a young Rus man like so many other changelings born from hags. His look wouldn't have been an issue given how diverse the people of the Southern Kingdoms and beyond seemed to be, but his inhuman heritage would have eventually shown itself, probably at puberty. I imagined him getting sold into bondage and the trauma that ensued. Trauma some enterprising old merc had seen potential in and used to make Bloodstorm a weapon with. Bloodstorm would find his freedom and wealth in bloodshed but getting out of being a warrior would prove more difficult than expected, leading to things like his failed attempt to attend university. It was basically the movie version of Conan's life but he had no Thulsa Doom to direct his rage at.

"Sure, man, whatever you say," I said, wondering if I was making assumptions but suspecting I had a pretty good idea of just who my companion was now. If everyone was going to treat you as a rampaging monster, then you might as well be one. It was better than being a victim.

"We should extinguish the fires and cover up the bodies," Ania said. "There's enough hay to cover up the bodies. The enemy has spies in the air as well as on the ground. Getting the horses spread out would be useful as well to cover up our presence here."

"We can't just release the horses," I said, staring at her. "They'll end up starving after they throw a shoe or worse."

Ania stared. "You're worried about the horses starving?"

"Yes," I said.

"After poisoning a bunch of people then murdering them," Ania said.

"I like horses," I said, pausing. "I don't like *riding* them but I like animals in general more than people. Besides, you could use your teleportation power to take them back to Crossroad where they can be a benefit to the village."

Ania stared. "You want me to make like twenty trips to Crossroad just because you want to slow us down to care for some animals?

"You could probably bring Bloodstorm and other members of the party with you but yes," I said, staring at her.

Ania pinched the bridge of her nose. "Sure."

"What, really?" I asked.

Ania stared at me. "I would normally call you soft and spoiled, like some of the other champions I've dealt with but you're not, Aaron. You have a big heart and while that will get you killed someday, you're also smarter about your tactics than most. We could have taken this group of noble hunters or fled but you arranged it, so we had the best advantage possible. It was a bit crude, unplanned, and should have been consulted with us first—"

"Stop, your praise is overwhelming," I said, sarcastically.

Ania gave a half-smile. "What I'm saying is that you have won my respect. For what you did in the Blackwood Forest and tonight."

I wasn't sure how I felt about the fact that poisoning a bunch of bandits was something that had won her respect. I couldn't help but imagine a big ANIA GREATLY APPROVES in the upper left-hand corner of my vision when carrying out this murder plan. The thing was that it didn't really influence my reasons for doing it. I had never much cared for the way some video games treated relationships. In a lot of RPGs, they were treated like a vending machine where you put in a sufficient amount of money then you got candy as a reward.

While no great expert on relationships, my love life was proof of that, I knew they didn't work like that in real life. You could do everything a person wanted and still find out they weren't interested. Hell, there was a very good chance that if you did, you were only going to make things worse for the both of you. Real relationships were give and take. Also, sometimes it flat out didn't work out and you had to take it on the chin.

"I may not be the strongest, I may not be the most magically powerful—"

"You're not the cleverest," Ania added.

I rolled my eyes. "But I like to think I know how to think outside of the box."

"What box?" Ania asked.

"The box," I said. "Hopefully, that'll keep us alive long enough to put down Veles and company."

Ania looked down. "Truth be told, Aaron, I don't have much faith we'll be able to beat any of the Old Gods."

I blinked. "You don't?"

"Veles is toying with us," Ania said. "That's the only reason we're still alive."

"Classic villain mistake," I said. "One we'll take advantage of."

I had to wonder what being trapped in a continuously repeating *Groundhog Day* loop of fighting against an evil god would do to a person.

Ania snorted, looking over to the fire pit that was now smoldering. "I wish I had your confidence."

There was an awkward pause and both of us looked away. I got the impression neither of us were particularly good at emotional stuff.

"So, yeah, we have about 1000 GP, do you want to repair the alchemy lab or replace the tapestries?" I asked, trying to figure something else to talk about.

Before Ania could respond, she looked over my shoulder into the sky and grabbed me by the arm before pulling me to the side. I was confused until I saw a red dragon flying through the air with a tiny figure on its back.

Valentin.

"Mothersucker," I whispered. "That bastard is cheating."

Valentin circled around several times, seemingly looking for something that he didn't find. I wondered if he'd seen the campfire earlier. The horses had to be visible from the sky but that worked in our favor as we'd dismissed our demon steeds and he was looking for us, not an encampment of bandits. If he was closer, he might have seen they were all dead, though.

That would probably attract the attention of even someone as thick as Valentin. In the end, the next five minutes or so were spent in abject terror that reminded me of the scenes with Frodo and the Ringwraiths. There was nothing we could do against a dragon at our present level, let alone a Valentin who wasn't easily knocked off the back of a rearing stallion.

In the end, Valentin turned his dragon mount around and flew off into the distance.

We were safe, for now.

Ania watched him depart. "I don't think the God of Evil feels the need to play fair. Still, you know he could have killed us at Crossroad. Valentin didn't write that speech he recited. Veles wants us playing by his rules. We need to figure out a way to break the rules and catch him off guard. Otherwise, we're going to meet the end that all the other Imposters…champions have."

"I agree," I said, admitting it. "No offense but it strikes me that you and your sister are being put through hell, specifically, but never so much that you're permanently killed."

Ania looked at me. "The same thought had occurred to me. Veles wants us, the characters from Weis' books, my family, alive. Which sadly doesn't apply to you or the other people. I don't know why."

"Yeah, I got that impression." I nodded and explained my dream to her.

Ania looked deeply into my eyes. She seemed skeptical. "You were willing to die rather than betray us?"

"Err, yeah, I guess?" I asked, shrugging. "Let's not make a big deal about it."

"Do you want to have sex?"

CHAPTER THIRTY-TWO
LOOTING ANOTHER PLAYER'S REMAINS

The two of us snuck into the cellar to get away from the, well, massive number of corpses that were lying around the fort above. That was a major turnoff. No, I'm not going to share any details, but it had been a brief moment of joy for the both of us. Well, not so brief. That's not bragging, that's liberally exploiting the REFRESH spell.

Unfortunately, even that had limits and the two of us were dead asleep until the afternoon when I opened my eyes and saw Jon staring down at my face. "So, someone has been busy."

"Gah!" I said, knocking him off as I bolted upward.

I was still in the fort's cellar, surrounded by rotting sacks and straw on the ground. A wooden ladder led up to the trapdoor in the fort above. The bandits hadn't had much in supplies and what little left had been devoured last night. Still, it had been cool despite it being sweltering above and I felt reasonably refreshed even without my magic. Okay, no, I felt fantastic.

To my side, I saw Ania was already getting dressed with her back turned to Jon. "I'm glad to see a hawk didn't kill you last night, Jon."

"No problems there," Jon said. "Though I did meet another crow who wanted to mate with me. You'd think I'd be okay with dating a girl who didn't want to talk but it turned out that's just not my style."

I wrapped my blanket around me. "Get out."

"No," Jon said.

I shook my head. "Hey, Ania, do you want to get breakfast?"

"In the context that this is a camp, and we should have breakfast before we leave?" Ania asked, surprisingly harsh. "Yes, yes I do. We can eat with the others."

"Okay," I said, confused.

Ania's expression softened but only for a moment. She walked over and kissed me on the lips then patted me on the cheek. "This was fun, and we should do it again when we have the chance. However, you should understand this is just a soldier's rest."

I blinked. "A soldier's rest."

"Try not to make too much of it," Ania said, looking uncomfortable. "It's good to have someone in the party to seek comfort with but I have others. You should too."

I didn't respond to that.

Ania turned away from me and went up the ladder. I didn't bother to watch her go, feeling like I'd been slapped.

"Huh," Jon said, watching her depart. "So, you're the *girl* in this relationship."

"Shut up, Jon," I said, gritting my teeth. "I mean it."

"You're a booty call before the telephone was invented," Jon said, raising a single wing. "I'm not sure what you're so upset about. In the words of the great George Costanza, this is like discovering plutonium by accident!"

"Shut up, Jon," I said, growling. A rat scurried across the ground, and I aimed my palm at it before causing it to detonate with Arcane fire. It made a brief squeaking noise before becoming a charcoal briquette.

Jon saw the rat burn before looking at me. "So, we're kind to horses and ratmen but not people or rats? I'm just following your weird logic. The kind that sees an important difference between American and European beavers. Which is the set up for a dirty joke right there that I'm not doing because I respect you so much. Okay, I can't resist. You see, American beavers—"

I stared at him.

"Right," Jon said. "I'm shutting up."

"Thank you," I said, sighing. I performed the CLEAN SELF spell and felt like I'd taken a warm shower before I started putting on my clothes. I ended up repeating the cantrip because my clothes were soaked in sweat. I was starting to pick up why every man smelled of cologne in this place since regular bathing wasn't really a habit. Same for the women who notably all wore very noticeable perfume, even Ania.

Jon didn't keep to his silence. "It was never going to work out, Aaron. She's a fantasy character that's seen this all before. She was in love with her stepbrother and an elf girl in the books. She's also seemingly had a couple of rounds with other protagonists, I'm sure. It's like that scene in Westworld—"

"I never watched Westworld," I said, lying. I wasn't in the mood to have my life compared to pop culture.

"Maybe she'll come around," Jon said, finally sounding sympathetic.

"Maybe," I said, sighing. "Maybe this is all there is to it as well."

"And maybe she doesn't want to start something because you could die tomorrow," Jon said.

"You think?" I asked, realizing by my hope that I'd fallen for her hard. I couldn't just back away even if Ania could.

"I think you should bang the sex witch to make yourself feel better," Jon said. "But I'm pretty sure Bloodstorm would want to join in and I'm not sure that's your bag."

"Where were you last night?" I asked, deciding to switch topics.

"Locating my corpse," Jon said, shutting me up.

"Did you find it?" I asked, uncomfortable.

"What's left of it, yeah," Jon said, surprising me. "The Dragon Queen's camp was attacked not soon after she fried me. They were forced to retreat without burying any of their dead and the Mad Queen's forces didn't bother. Animals have picked over the place and—"

"I'm sorry," I said, lowering my head.

"I don't care," Jon said. "Like a Klingon warrior, I believe my body is just a shell, especially as I'm currently flying around. Anyway, that's not what's important."

"What's important?" I asked, having a bad feeling about this.

"The deck is intact!" Jon said. "All of my beautiful cards survived the dragon's fire!"

I stared at him. "Super."

"Think of the EXP, Aaron!" Jon said. "Fifty thousand will level you up a couple of times in one go!"

"I think strategy makes more of a difference here than sheer numbers," I said, remembering my embarrassment yesterday. "Just learning how to do something doesn't actually tell you when to do it. It's probably why Weis starts everyone off at level 1. It's a way of educating people on how to master their abilities."

"And we saw how that's worked so far," Jon said. "Dude could have just given the bracelets to a team of Navy SEALs and a fantasy nuke to take to Bald Mountain."

"I don't think it's that easy," I replied.

"You're the kind of guy who makes up excuses as to why the Eagles didn't bring the Fellowship to Mount Doom, aren't you?" Jon asked.

"Secrecy was their best ally," I muttered, embarrassed.

"Oh, for fuck's sake," he said.

"That was my parents' explanation at least," I said, suddenly missing them terribly. I hadn't seen them in over a year before this and was unlikely to see them ever again. I was almost willing to forgive them for being the hippie tree hugging pothead fantasy nuts they were. Almost. Almost willing to forgive them for naming me after their favorite fantasy character. Wait, no, I was nowhere near ready to forgive them for that.

"In any case, help me do this because you're my bud," Jon said. "There's some other goodies spread among my bones as well that you might be interested in."

"Such as?" I asked.

"Are we negotiating? Just agree," Jon said.

I sighed. "Fine."

"Good," Jon said. "Now what did you get last night from the bandits? Any goodies I might be interested in?"

"You're a raven, Jon," I said, staring at him. "What possible interest could you have in magical items?"

"One, I'm a raven," Jon said. "That means I'm attracted to all sorts of shiny things."

"That's magpies," I said.

"You're doing it again," Jon said, stretching out his back. "No one cares but you."

"I'm just saying that crows, ravens, rooks, magpies, jackdaws, jays, treepies, and nutcrackers are all different breeds of the Corvidae family," I said, once more highlighting I could be on the spectrum.

Or a biology nerd.

One of those two.

"No, there wasn't anything you'd be interested in," I said. "Just a belt, a dagger, and an eye of seeing."

"Wait, what was that last one?" Jon asked.

"An eye of seeing," I said.

"Is it an *alchemical* eye?" Jon asked.

"I think so, why."

"Gimme," Jon said, opening his mouth.

I stared at him, not moving. "Black Tom had it. It won't fit in your eye, and I hope you're not stupid enough to cut out your eye to put it in. It's not the Eye of Vecna."

"Ever hear the urban legend of the Head of Vecna?" Jon asked. "My Dungeonmaster actually pulled that off with us. Total Party Kill via voluntary decapitation."

"How did the last guy cut his head off?" I asked.

"Not important," Jon said. "But just gimme the eye."

"How?" I asked, confused.

"I said gimme!" Jon said.

"Fine," I said, wondering what the hell Jon planned to do with the eye. I put the thing in his mouth. "I should warn you that I haven't had time to wash it…and you're eating it."

Jon swallowed it in one gulp. He then looked like he was getting a power up. "Oh, hell yes."

I stared. "Is this a crow thing? I asked.

"Raven," Jon corrected me.

"You shut the hell up!" I snapped, staring at him.

"It's an alchemical eye," Jon said, ruffling his feathers up and down. "That means it was always meant to be swallowed. Idiot seems to have been using it as a prosthetic. Anyway, it shrinks down for your stomach and now I have my insight powers back!"

"Your what now?" I asked.

Jon sighed. "My ability to look at people and determine what level they are as well as class, race, etcetera."

"That would be useful, I guess?" I asked.

"It is when we're trying not to get killed," Jon replied. "Anyway, I can feel it kicking in."

YOUR FAMILIAR HAS GAINED INSIGHT ABILITY

I sighed, thinking about Jon whispering in my ear about whether or not to fight every little creature. "Anyway, I'll go get your remains. If nothing else, the gold would pay for most of the needed repairs to Dragon Keep."

"Ugh," Jon said. "A man has the possibility of finding a literal mountain of gold and he wants to use it to flip his castle. Veles is only going to wreck it again."

"I don't think so," I said, pausing. "I don't think there's any more bracelets to be made."

Jon looked up. "What makes you think that?"

"Just a feeling," I said, getting the impression from Weis that this was the last round available. "I think that's why Veles is so eager to end this."

"Well, that sucks," Jon said.

"Yeah," I said, sighing. "Let's get going."

"Yeah, there's one more thing worth discussing," Jon said. "We're pretty close to the area where my body was located but it's a much-much higher-level zone than this."

"I don't think reality comes with zones," I replied.

"You say that after Blackwood Bog," Jon said. "There's a lot of unpleasant things roaming around the ruins of the Dragon Queen's camp. Still, I trust you to be able to kite your way in on Stompy and get out."

"What sort of things?" I asked.

"Things I'd probably need a glossary to identify," Jon said. "Whenever there's mass death, there's creatures of Veles attracted."

I nodded. "Okay, then."

"That's it?" Jon asked.

"No pain, no gain," I said, looking down at Jon.

"Are you being stupid because Ania just wants to be bed buddies or because you're scared that Valentin is going to kill us all unless we have a WISH spell to kill him?" Jon asked.

"Yes," I said, climbing up the wooden ladder.

The sun had risen with the ruined fort having been cleaned up enough that you would never have known it had been the home of a contingent of thieves as well as murderers. Agata was in a corner praying while Bloodstorm was preparing breakfast on an iron skillet, eggs and bacon. There was no sign of Ania as I walked outside of the fort, summoned Stompy, and proceeded to start riding away.

"What are you doing?" Ania called out, having been on the rooftop surveying the landscape.

"I'll be back soon!" I called out.

I let Stompy take me to the location that had been marked on my map as I rode through the ruined and deserted grasslands of Southern Ledziania. Several times, I passed shattered statues of Perun and villages that had been reclaimed by nature in the past three years. About the only time I ever felt less surrounded by people was when I'd traveled through Kansas on my way to Undermastercon.

Eventually, I came to what looked like a deserted fairground. There were large colorful tents spread around everywhere with most of them trampled to the ground. A storm gathered in the sky above and a rainstorm began as I saw the many skeletons spread throughout the ruins, the results of their bodies being left to rot. There were a lot of rats spread throughout the place, gnawing on the dead even as I saw countless overturned banners showing the Dragon over the Ledzianian crown.

"She did not do well here," I muttered.

Jon, who landed on my shoulder and crawled under my cloak hood, shook his feathers of water across my face. "Yeah, she's been losing the war pretty consistently for the past year. Lots and lots of losses that normally would have been easy for her to win. In any case, we're almost there."

"You see any monsters?" I asked.

"Not yet," Jon said. "But they're here, I promise you."

Much to my surprise, I saw the Dragon Queen's Royal Tent was still erect, a few arrow holes on its sides but still intact. It had probably been enchanted to be more resistant and to stay up when the rest of the camp hadn't been. I urged Stompy on and we entered to find nothing but mud as well as a few broken tables. It may have been kept up, but they'd gotten away with as much of its contents as possible.

"Yeah, this is where I died," Jon muttered. "The attack wasn't long after, like minutes as I understand it, so I wouldn't be surprised if my remains are here."

I stepped off Stompy, surprisingly not feeling any pain or nausea after our long ride, to look for Jon's remains. It didn't take long to find a set of bones and a pile of ash among the mud and broken furniture.

"Is that you?" I asked, unwilling to rifle through the remains just yet.

"Yes," Jon said. "Alas poor Jon, I knew him Horatio. Something-something, *Hamlet.*"

"Not funny, dude," I said, disgusted.

"It's my body, dipshit," Jon said. "Go get my stuff."

It felt morbid to go through his burnt bones like this, but I had his permission so, I sucked in my chest and pushed down my disgust to start looking. Thankfully, I had gloves. Eventually found three intact objects next to the rib cage under the charred remains of a *cloak of protection +3*.

"Bingo," Jon said. "We are in business."

An almost complete deck of collectible Pwiffle cards.

An undamaged Mark of the Champion. It was white gold as opposed to yellow gold in appearance and had a different set of runes on it. I couldn't help but feel sad looking at it and wondered what stories it might have told. Well, I didn't have to wonder since Jon had already told me most of them.

Also, there was a small black book-sized computer tablet that had a bunch of ash on it but was otherwise unharmed. It was an Epic Reader from Epic Dungoneering's website.

"Sweet!" Jon said, staring at the iPad knock off that had Amazon, Barnes and Noble, and other bookstore apps for reading their books. "It's still intact! See if it works."

"There's no way this still works, Jon," I said, tapping the device that had soot on it. It immediately popped to life. "You've got to be kidding me."

"It's magic," Jon said, "I got it from a genie. Strictly lesser wishes from that guy, though."

I stared at him. "Uh huh."

I pocketed the Pwiffle cards before staring at the Mark of the Champion. That was when a new message appeared on it that I'd never seen before.

WOULD YOU LIKE TO ABSORB DIVINE ESSENCE? Y/N

CHAPTER THIRTY-THREE
THE ROAD TO DIVINITY

Jon looked down at the bracelet and its message about absorbing divine energy. "Okay, my bracelet, which that is, never said that."

"Maybe it's unique to collecting previous champions' marks," I said.

"Valentin was the only one who was doing that," Jon said. "Yet, he never collected anyone's power. Believe me, he would have too."

"No kidding," I said, pausing. "Maybe it's not possible once you switch sides."

"Maybe it's just that you don't know how any of this works and we should leave it alone," Jon said.

"Right," I said, hitting the Y button on my control.

"Goddammit, Aaron," Jon said, covering his face with a wing.

That was when I felt my entire body go rigid before I fell on my back into the mud, staring at the tent's interior canopy. Bright lights flashed before my eyes, and I began to foam at the mouth before everything vanished around me.

I found myself in an immense void, staring outward into a universe that was still forming. There was the sound of a hammer pounding against an anvil followed by the molding of metal as my attention shifted to a small corner of a distant galaxy.

"Behold!" a male voice spoke as I saw him as a translucent ripped black bearded man who looked like if you somehow combined Gimli the Dwarf with

Arnold Schwarzenegger. Like Perun, he was bare chested and looked like a barbarian hero. He was just sort of squat and square shaped. His interior was made of galaxies, nebula, and stars.

Next to him were two beautiful female statues that were simultaneously women as well as planets. Listen, I'm not even going to try to explain how that worked. Just understand that it was true, and I could see seas in their hair as well as rolling mountains in their, uh, well you get the picture.

"Are you that lonely, Svarog that you have decided to build your company?" the voice of Peter Stormare spoke with an almost Disney-like hiss. A giant horned snake made of stars forming a constellation was speaking. Veles, I presumed.

"They are not company for me," Svarog said. "But company for you and Perun. We are not alone among the gods but have done little to populate our realm with peoples. I shall bring these two to life and they shall be your brides. We shall populate their worlds with our children and raise great civilizations in our image."

Perun, me, nodded in agreement. "Yeah, it's been something of a sausage fest these past few billion years."

I had the feeling this dream wasn't exactly literal.

"I have some ideas for combining reptiles and birds," Veles said. "I think it'll be fantastic."

"We should stick with hominids," Svarog said. "But I suppose we could give you some time to try it out."

"What are their names?" Perun asked.

"Mokosh and Mat Zemlya," Svarog replied. "Twin worlds that will exist entwined between this universe and the most immediate close one. That way they can share the power of both universes."

Yeah, that was gibberish to Perun as well as me.

"I just have one question," Perun asked, using my voice.

"Yes?" Svarog asked.

"What if one of the twins doesn't like one of us?" Perun asked, clearly referring to his brother. Perun, I could feel his emotions as if they were my own, wasn't concerned about his ability to win over either of the twins.

Or both.

Veles glared.

I woke up with the sensation of someone licking my face with a long-forked tongue. Blinking, I opened my eyes and saw a dragon licking my face. It was far more the Spyro or adorable anime type over the terrifying Vermithrax Pejorative kind. Also, random aside, but *Dragonslayer* is the darkest, most messed up, Disney movie ever made. Even the princess died in that one.

"Uh, what the hell?" I asked, looking over to see Jon looking down at me from a nearby perch. The rain had stopped.

"Don't look at me, you've been down an hour and I'm pretty sure you pissed yourself," Jon said. "Sparky here showed up just a few minutes ago."

I cast CLEAN SELF again just in case. "Sparky?"

Sparky, if this dragon he was, was small for a dragon. I mean, I didn't really have any sizes to judge him against except Valentin's and the ones who had attacked Dragon Keep but they were about the size of small houses. Sparky, by contrast, was about the size of a pony verging on full grown horse.

"Hi, Mr. Bartkowski!" Sparky said in his familiar voice, showing a lot more awareness than most of the people here. "Mr. Jon told me all about you."

"What are you doing here?" I asked, shaking off the vision I'd had.

"I want to be a hero!" Sparky said.

"Oh crap," I said, realizing he must have followed us from Crossroad. "We need to get him back to his mother."

"Good luck on that without fast travel," Jon said. "We're almost a week out. It's not like the fate of the world is at stake."

Yeah, that wasn't good. "Well, I suppose we can figure something out when we get back to camp."

ALEXI THE DRAGON AKA "SPARKY" HAS JOINED YOUR PARTY
CLASS: Dragon Scout
ALIGNMENT: Grey
LEVEL: 12

"Dammit!" I cursed under my breath.

"How the hell is he 12th level?" Jon asked. "This game is so poorly designed."

"Hero!" Sparky said, looking up with his big bright all-too-human eyes.

"What happened with the bracelet?" Jon asked, landing on my shoulder.

"Are we really changing the subject?" I asked.

"You just passed out after absorbing part of a dead god," Jon said. "You're damn right I'm changing the subject."

"You swore!" Sparky said. puffing out some flame with his words.

I sighed and checked my bracelet for updates.

YOU HAVE GAINED DIVINITY SCORE 2

"Divinity score?" I asked, having no idea what that was. "Do you have an idea?"

"No clue," Jon said. "As far as I know, you're the first guy who ever grabbed another champion's bracelet other than Valentine."

"Gods!" Sparky said.

"Is he a boy, a dog, or a dragon?" Jon asked.

"I have no idea," I said, tapping on the divinity score in hopes it gave an explanation.

YOU HAVE RECEIVED THE FOLLOWING BENEFITS:

+ 1 to Attack Rolls
+ 1 to Saving Throws
+ 1 to Attribute
+ Attribute Maximum raised to 20
+ Your maximum level has increased

"That seems pretty weak tea for absorbing god powers," Jon said.

"I dunno, I feel like the raised Attribute Maximum has a lot of potential," I replied. "Plus, the attack roll bonus is effectively a free level of Warrior. Given my low WIS, the saving throw bonus is also a godsend. They don't list what the maximum level is, though."

"Twenty was the human maximum in this world," Jon said. "But I always assumed they'd sell DLC to get you to level 30 and maybe 40 if they don't screw it up and have to spend three years debugging like they did with Cyber Dragons."

"I wonder if this is a one-time thing or if this is a thing we can do with all the bracelets," I replied.

"Yes, well, I'd rather you not get into hunting your fellow champions," Jon said. "Assuming there's any left."

"This isn't *Highlander*," I replied. "There can be only one isn't a rule that is in effect."

"That's what you're saying now but once you introduce a PVP element to a game, it's suddenly Thunderdome," Jon said, surprisingly less than enthusiastic. "It might be possible to recover more of these bracelets from the already dead champions but I'm not sure that is a good idea. We don't know what collecting these things will do to you or if any other champions are still alive."

Ania had indicated that Francine might still be alive, and Larry C.C. Weis had said someone was impersonating a character in the world, but I hadn't been paying as close attention as I probably should have been. The prospect of recovering the bracelets from dead champions or the ones that turned evil was interesting, though. It might provide an edge that was previously nonexistent. It would mean killing the ones who had turned "evil", though. People from my world. It shouldn't make a difference in how I felt about it but it did.

"Ania and Agata have their own but that might ruin their immunity to the setting's magic," I replied, thinking on how to work this out. The vision I'd had was one that transcended conventional reality and, I had to admit, I wanted more. As addictive as collecting Pwiffle cards was, this was a whole different level of high.

"See! See!" Jon said, flapping his wings on my shoulder. "You're already falling into the trap. Not even your simping for Ania is stopping you."

"Say that again and I'll feed you to Sparky," I said. There were some things a man didn't say to another man off of an internet forum.

"Hmm?" Sparky asked, turning his head sideways.

"Don't confuse the dragon dog boy thing!" Jon said. "Anyway, I wouldn't have thought you'd be the kind of gamer who wanted to become a god. You struck me as the kind of guy who gives up power at the end of *Baldur's Gate*."

"I don't want to be a god," I said, under my breath as my eyes darted back and forth as if I could see everyone seeing through the transparency of my life. "I prefer a quiet humble life of service."

"You know who aren't humble?" Jon asked, clearly reading my true feelings on the subject. "People who get worshiped as gods."

"The Buddha and Jesus would disagree," I pointed out.

I wanted another bracelet already. I wanted to see the cosmic secrets of the universe and if the power growth was exponential.

"The exceptions that prove the rule," Jon said. "Besides, they're not the fun religions."

I hope this wasn't in Weis' next book because then I'd be responsible for offending 2/3rds of the Earth's potential readership.

"Okay, fine, I'm not a humble hero," I said. "I would do terrible things with the One Ring of Sauron."

"All gamers would, my friend," Jon said. "Within each of us beats the heart of a potential supervillain."

"Want to be hero, not villain," Sparky said.

I patted the dragon on the head. "Sure, kid, sure. We'll make you a hero. But we need to talk about bringing you into battle. I'm not comfortable endangering the life of a child."

"He was like eight when the massacre at Blackwood Bog happened," Jon pointed out. "Which was fifteen years ago in-universe. That's also ignoring that he fried like a dozen people at that farm."

"So, mean!" Sparky said. "They were mad I ate their sheep. Sheep are good."

Well, that explained the massacre there.

"So, he's less a child dog dragon person and more a psychotic child dog dragon person," Jon said. "Which I am happy to point at our enemies."

I checked the Quest Journal to see if there was any more information there.

MAIN QUEST(S) ADDED:
THE ROAD TO DIVINITY
Description: Gather all the Marks of the Champion to absorb their power (2/15)
Reward: Alternate Ending
SIDE QUEST(S) UPDATED:
COLLECT ALL UNIQUE PWIFFLE CARDS 49/50
SIDE QUEST(S) COMPLETED:
RECOVER JON SNOWAN'S REMAINS 1/1

"No new EXP," I said.

"I think that stuff dealing with the quote-unquote real world doesn't count," Jon said, "Hence you only got story EXP for killing Valentin."

"You are obsessed with that," I said.

"You're damn right I am," Jon said. "You should have gone up like five levels there."

"Tell me something I don't know," I said, dryly.

"The *Dungeons & Dragons* cartoon is the greatest isekai of all time," Jon said.

"Uh no," I replied. "I mean, I watched it and liked it but the answer is obviously Super Mario Brothers."

"That's not even true in all continuities!" Jon said.

"You could argue *A Connecticut Yankee in King Arthur's Court*, *The Wizard of Oz*, and The Chronicles of Narnia were all isekai but nothing will equal the Mushroom Kingdom's greatness. I even like the weird cyberpunk movie version from the Eighties."

"Do you ever wonder what the hell they're talking about?" Ania asked, walking through the tent flaps.

"No," Bloodstorm said, following her in. "Not really."

"Me neither," Ania said.

Agata rounded out the group.

"Hey, guys, we've got a dragon!" I said, unsure how to respond to them tracking me down.

Ania stared at me. "Good, because we're about to have an army of the dead descend upon us."

Well crap.

CHAPTER THIRTY-FOUR
THE VERMIN LORD STRIKES

"Great job," Jon said, looking at me. "You've led the entire team into a trap."

I did a double take. "You were the one who led me here!"

"I know!" Jon said, shaking his head. "How could you be so stupid as to listen to me!"

Ania walked forward. "Just get on your demon steed and be ready to move. Valentin didn't find us last night but that doesn't mean he didn't think we were somewhere in the area. He's dispatched a death lord to summon a small army of undead to deal with us."

"A friggin' death lord? At level 4? Oh, we are screwed," Jon said, shaking his head.

"I agree," Bloodstorm muttered.

Death lords were the copyright friendly version of liches, which were themselves the copyright friendly version of Sauron as well as the older myths that inspired Tolkien like Koshchei the Deathless. The very short version was they were wizards who pledged themselves to Veles and received immortality (the undead skeleton kind) as well as a great deal more free will than most undead.

Now you might ask why someone would trade their souls to become a creature that couldn't enjoy food, sex, or even sleep but if that was your primary concern then you probably weren't the kind of guy Veles was looking for anyway. If a death lord ever needed an itch to scratch, as Garland found out in "A Night on the Town", they could steal the skin of a peasant to wear for a night of revelry. You could destroy their body but as long as their soul object existed, you know how those work, they come back unless you destroy the ring, needle, egg, whatever.

About the only good news was that death lords weren't necessarily the top of the pyramid. They were under the Old Gods and Veles in terms of power but if you were second tier because the first tier were literal gods, well, I wasn't sure that was actually that much of a downgrade. Discretion was the better part of valor here.

"Only a cutscene deus ex machina can save us now. I don't care if you are eating god fragments!" Jon said.

"What?" Ania asked.

"Long story," I muttered.

"He totally wants you to give up your bracelets so he can eat them," Jon said.

"You are not taking my bracelet!" Agata said, horrified.

"I do not want to eat the bracelets!" I said, pausing and looking to my side.

"You do!" Agata said, horrified. "I can see it in your eyes."

"Yay! Combat!" Sparky said, bouncing up and down while swishing its tail from side to side. "Go burn evil!"

Bloodstorm walked over to Sparky's side and put his hand on the dragon's head. "You're a little on the scrawny side to be a proper dragon but I accept your squiredom to Lord Garland. You shall be the first dragon Dark Undermaster."

"Ooo," Sparky said.

"We have minutes before they arrive, *Aaron*," Agata said, managing to speak my name as if she was dry heaving it up. "Get on your demon steed and let us gallop away as fast as the winds will take us. Fly if you can manage it."

"No argument from me," I said, muttering. "Though I may have to WEB myself on top of the horse."

Stompy made a whinnying noise that told me he didn't think much of the plan.

"If only you could talk to object to said plan," I said, staring at him. I really didn't like the demon pretending he couldn't talk.

"What about the dragon?" I asked.

"Can you turn into a hawk again, Sparky?" Bloodstorm asked.

"Yes!" Sparky said. "But want to fight."

"Fight later," Bloodstorm said, patting it again on the head.

Unfortunately, any plans that we might have had went out the window as soon as a shrill booming voice spoke over the battlefield. "Fools, blunderers, imbeciles! I am accursed with a knave that has sent me to deal with the trash of the Southern Kingdoms! A man who dares call himself the Skull King! Know, Garland, that I consider your band of pick pockets and whores to be beneath my efforts. Today you will be torn limb from limb by the armies of the hungry dead on the orders of an odious fool who considers himself not only my equal but superior!"

"Do you think he's referring to Valentin?" Jon asked.

"Vecna Junior here seems to have an issue with being sent to deal with our ragtag band of misfits," I muttered.

"Wouldn't you?" Jon asked. "If you're a lich, you've got shit to do. Making dungeons, filling them with traps, kidnapping princesses, and cursing kingdoms."

"It bothers me that your last sentence makes perfect sense," Ania said, peering out the tent flaps. "Yep, he's out there on the back of a white demon steed. It's Hellmaster Pollux the Vermin Lord."

I stared at her. "Gee, no wonder this guy is pissed off, he's been sent to do the evil overlord equivalent of fetching coffee. You don't take a name like that unless you're fourteen years old or the guy who would go on a shooting spree."

Agata looked at me. "I believe he was born with it."

"At least his parents knew what kind of career he was going to pursue," Jon said, dryly. "Either that or they were putting their finger pretty heavily on the scale to encourage an unlife of evil wizardry."

"Damn and I thought Arargon was weird," I muttered, trying to think of a way out of this.

"What's weird about Aragorn?" Agata asked, confused.

I didn't bother to respond and turned to Ania. "Can you fast travel us out of here?"

"It doesn't work when you're in danger," Ania replied, because of course it didn't. "Also, no, I don't know why. It's magic and magic doesn't make any goddamn sense."

Agata frowned at that statement. "Magic makes perfect—"

"And he's raising his army," Ania interrupted, her tone becoming acidic. "If only we weren't on a *battlefield full of unburied corpses*."

"Arise my children of death, come forth upon my command!" Hellmaster Pollux shouted. "Ravage the land and slay the living! Your dark lord commands you and understand you shall never know the peace of the grave again unless thy brings me the heads of Garland as well as his whores!"

"I feel insulted," Agata said. "Even though I believe prostitution to be a far too disrespected profession that is vital to the survival of a functioning society."

"Do you think whores includes me?" Bloodstorm asked. "I've only taken money a few times at my father's establishment. The kind of people interested in me aren't really my type and it's much easier to make money by taking it from corpses."

It started raining much more intensely as I felt the air ionize around us while there was a terrible crack of thunder followed by the exterior being illuminated by blue lightning flashes. My stomach turned at the presence of an energy that reminded me of the ghostfire effect around my sword. I'd accidentally touched my finger against it once and almost passed out from the sensation of being drained. It had taken Agata and my own CURE spells to heal it that evening. This wasn't quite as bad, but it felt like the energy was all over and around us now.

"I'm going to die here," Ania said. "Which wouldn't be so bad, I've expected it for a long time, but the latest Imposter has turned everyone into a wannabe court jester.'

"Sorry!" I said.

"Fight them as they come through the tent flap," Ania said, shaking her head. "Undead are usually dirt stupid and we can hold them off for a bit before they overwhelm us. We can winnow their numbers enough to get a break in their ranks large enough to ride past them. From there, we'll fly and hopefully stay ahead of Hellmaster Pollux."

"Any plan that involves the word hopefully is not a good plan," Jon said.

"Come up with your own then!" Ania snapped.

That shut Jon up and I still hadn't figured out how to get us out of the jam I'd put us all in. "If the lich, err death lord, goes down then do the forces he's summoned?"

"Usually, but that's why—" Ania started to explain.

Any chance her plan was going to work vanished just like the royal tent above our heads, no matter what magics had been worked into it. It was blown away as if by a stiff wind and we were suddenly caught up in the massive storm that was raining down upon us. Battle music started playing on my bracelet and I had to say I wished it would knock it off. It also exposed our enemy and let me know just what we were facing.

Hint: It wasn't good.

"Hiding like rats? A foolish gesture when you face the Vermin Lord!" Hellmaster Pollux shouted. He was a guy who, I had to give credit, looked awesome. The death lord seemed like he belonged on a metal album more than your more traditional fantasy art. He was wearing the luxurious robes of a king and had a literal crown made of jagged pieces of iron that reached into the air twice the size of his head. The guy had a skeletal face but it wasn't fully bone but a mixture of flesh and muscle with actual eyes (albeit white milky ones) that provided him enough of a human expression to be extra-horrifying.

You know, the whole uncanny valley effect. Long white hair trailed down his shoulders and flew with the wind as he did circles around the camp on his demon steed from about twenty feet in the air. His staff had a human skull on the top with blue crystals growing out of it and witchfire glowing out of the head piece's eye sockets. In another fantasy series, he would have been the archvillain versus a mini-boss that would, nevertheless, probably kill us all.

Hellmaster Pollux's steed was only slightly less Metallica meets Blind Guardian. The demon steed looked a great deal nastier than

Stompy and my demon steed already looked awesome. The sickly pale horse was almost translucent, showing its bones within its thin emaciated flesh. It, too, had white milky eyes but a face that was malformed with bony growths coming out of its body in a form of natural armor. It had wings that looked like bones with a thin see-through membrane that almost made the creature look slimy, reflecting the dim light of the day through the storm clouds in a way that would have been beautiful if not for the fact it was so terrifying.

Compared to those two, the army that was rising from the dead all around us was almost mundane. Still, that was a horrifying sight on its own. The rat-gnawed skeletons assembled into their original forms with the missing bones replaced with spectral replacement parts and their eyes glowing like jack-o-lanterns. Their armor was in a state of disrepair and their weapons shattered but the magic gave them repairs to that too. It was the sheer numbers that gave me pause, though, as I saw not ten or twenty or even fifty but well over a hundred.

More were rising too.

"FIREBALL!" Agata shouted, conjuring the blast without the lengthy chant she'd done earlier and sending a streaming blast forward. While the bracelets might have a diminished effect on the Rose sisters compared to me, they seemed to be definitely having some sort of effect.

Unfortunately, the blast was knocked away like a cat batting away its owner's hand. Hellmaster Pollux had a ring glowing on the hand he'd used that sparkled with more white-blue light as he did so. "I have forgotten more about the Art than you will ever learn in your pitiful mortal lifetimes, concubine of Mokosh! The games the gods have been playing with your family end today!"

"Well, I got nothing," Agata muttered.

The first of the skeleton warriors started charging as Ania and Bloodstorm attacked and fought them as best they could. Even then, they would have been instantly overwhelmed if not for the fact that it was taking a moment for the horde of undead to position themselves. We were about to be dogpiled by an army of the dead that would have given George A. Romero a run for his money. That was when I decided to do something stupid. Which, to my credit, had the benefit of making sure I died trying to do *something*.

"Super Mario Brothers, Muthersucker!" I said, casting JUMP and hurling myself in the air at the guy who was presently conjuring a gigantic blue-white witchfire fireball in his hands. By gigantic, I mean it was bigger than himself and his demon steed combined, appearing above his head like a spinning globe. I hadn't expected to jump quite as high as I was presently hurtling through the air and wondered if my *boots of speed* had accidentally turbocharged my spell. Maybe it was also a function of having recently ingested some godhood.

Either way, the idiocy of my action as I sailed directly toward the fireball became obvious even to my Low WIS self as the demonic skull-faced wizard grinned at me while continuing to speak his weird incantation that I couldn't quite translate despite the magic of my bracelet. This is where I enacted the second part of my stupid plan.

Having only a second to make a react, I cast PUSH without bothering to say the words. Apparently, it was something that just required the will to do it. Instead of aiming for the wizard, who had absorbed Agata's fireball like it was nothing, I cast the spell at the demon steed's underside as I was about to pass by. Preoccupied with his fireball, Hellmaster Pollux didn't stop the spell, and it caused his demon steed to spin upside down. It turned out that massive blasts of gravity could disrupt the flight of mystical mounts, it seemed. That prevented me from flying into the fireball, albeit I missed it by inches, and I sailed about forty feet in the air.

What followed was a wholly unexpected series of events occurring in rapid succession like dominos falling that I will lie to you now and insist I completely had planned from the beginning. The first of these actions, was the fact that Hellmaster Päləks was suddenly upside down while preparing to hurl his fireball at me. Instead, it struck the ground (due to his fireball being taller than the distance from the upside-down lich to the ground).

The second was the fact that hitting the skeleton soldiers below triggered the nine- or ten-foot fireball (I didn't exactly have a tape measure) and resulted in its detonation. White flame exploded outward from the Hellmaster Pollux's hands and blew up a not insignificant chunk of his army then and there. I'd say just about everything for thirty feet in every direction, which was a 706-foot total blast radius.

Hellmaster Pollux, himself, was at the epicenter of this conflagration and while he didn't take any more of the blast than his minions, it sure as hell wasn't good for him. It seemed that necromantic energy wasn't any better for undead abominations than the living. Which was a good thing to note as it probably meant that casting CURE spells to harm them wouldn't have worked. I didn't know if it killed the death lord, but it did lead to event four, which was the spells animating all the other skeletons present going poof. The spirits animating the corpses around us collapsed, sometimes with audible sighs of relief, and our situation became far more survivable. Except, for, sadly, event six: I was now falling into a gigantic conflagration of witchfire.

Balls.

"GENTLE FALL!" Agata shouted, aiming her staff upward and causing me to slow down in my descent.

It was like falling through water but that didn't really resolve the primary problem as I was now about ten feet from the ground and feeling the towering blue-white witchfire flames licking my backside. If you asked if I screamed like a toddler, I'd tell everyone that I kept my stoic dignity but we both know that's a lie. It hurt, goddammit (godsdammit?) and was only going to get worse when I landed in the fiery inferno.

That was when Ania, of all people, cast a spell. "SHADOW HAND!"

The description of the spells that Mark of the Champion bearers used may not have been detailed but they were accurate, and a large six-foot-long abyssal black hand shot forth from her fingertips to grab me by the legs. It jerked me over the entirety of the flames, and I landed with an enormous thud on the ground. I felt like I'd just suffered the world's worst sunburn as well as a week of the flu in one go.

HIT POINTS: 5 out of 20 (Grave Chill)

"That was awesome, Aaron!" Jon said, praising me. "Stupid, but awesome!"

"The gods protect fools and the rich," Ania muttered. "I guess we know which one you are."

My response was less than gentlemanly to the woman I still wanted a relationship with. It involved giving her the bird and I don't mean Jon.

Ania smirked.

"Insects! Mice! Peasants!" the shrill voice of the death lord said as a naked skeleton emerged from the witchfire flames that it started stumbling through. It still bore its iron crown and the glowing ring on its finger. "Did you really think that I would be undone by my own sorcery? My death is sealed elsewhere! I will send you to the Shadow Realm or turn you into stones! I think I will keep the men as slaves and have the women eaten by goblins!"

"May I burn him?" Sparky asked.

"Yes," I said.

Hellmaster Pollux tried to use his ring to block the dragonfire that poured over him as he stood in the witchfire that was still eating away at him. It didn't work because Sparky's came from a good old fashioned chemical reaction (I think). It was magical enough to affect the lich, though, and he fell to his...well not knees but kneecaps. He continued to rant while Sparky blasted him with a second blast, but it became unintelligible gibberish towards the end. The third blast caused him to disintegrate completely.

Jon looked down at the defeated wizard before looking at me. I had to wonder if he saw any commonality with the way they'd both died. Instead, Jon asked, "So, who wants lunch?"

Bloodstorm raised his hand.

CHAPTER THIRTY-FIVE
SANCTUARY, AT LAST

Jon was singing Salt-N-Pepa's "Push It" badly, much to the confusion of everyone else.

"Please stop," I said, glad to be away from the battlefield and back on the road. Technically, we weren't on the road, though. Having been already caught once by Valentin's forces, we had set the demon steeds to a gallop and then a low flight before allowing them time to rest. We were now merely walking, using the cover of trees to take a sideways trek toward the Abbey of the Twins.

"I'm just saying you have developed your signature move," Jon said. "Like Ryu and his Dragon Punch, Ken and his Hurricane Kick, or Chun Li and her Lightning Legs. You are Push Dude."

"I am not Push Dude," I said, dryly.

"I dunno, you are pretty pushy," Bloodstorm said. "Three times may not sound like a lot but most people get through life without pushing anyone to their deaths."

"Plus, it was a lich!" Jon said, cheerfully. "I mean, it's bullshit that we have to deal with it at our current levels, but we got him."

"I wouldn't overly congratulate yourself," Ania said, once again playing the role of kill joy. "Hellmaster Pollux is the least of the Thirteen. You managed to score an incredible victory but that doesn't mean that it was the hardest foe you're ever going to face. Chernabog and Valentin are both tougher foes. As would a dragon be."

"I'm a dragon," Sparky said, having reverted to corgi form. He was sitting on top of Stompy with seemingly no difficulty staying on even during high speeds.

"Yes, we know," Ania said.

"He'll be back," Agata said, cursing. "Even before Veles started using the Earthmother's stolen powers to bring back his followers, the death lords keep their soul items in Bald Mountain. It may take him a month or a year, but he will eventually regenerate."

"I dunno, maybe Veles will be like Darth Vader and say he's failed him for the last time," I said, feeling a surprising amount of optimism about events.

"He brought back Valentin," Jon said, surprising me with his pessimism.

"Yeah, but you can only show mercy so many times in a corporate structure," I said, shrugging. "You have to make an example of failure if you don't want people slacking off. Imagine trying to explain that the guy lost to an infant dragon and a computer programmer."

"Ahem," Bloodstorm said.

"It becomes less impressive when there's a demigod half-vampire ogre, sorceress, and master assassin involved," I pointed out.

Bloodstorm laughed at that one.

"I am not an infant," Sparky said, unhappily. "I am a squire now."

"Sure you are, buddy," Bloodstorm said. "The best damn squire there is.'

"No arguments from me," Jon said, jumping in the air and flapping his wings to avoid a tree branch. "That was the finest dragon burning I've seen since, well, me."

Well, that killed the mood quickly. Even if it was meant as a joke, it wasn't very funny. Still, the lull in the conversation gave me time to check my bracelet for the details of our battle.

SIDE QUEST(S) UPDATED: DEFEAT THE THIRTEEN (1/13)
+ 10,000 EXP (Death Lord)
+ 20,000 EXP (Undead Army)
+ 450 EXP (Demon Steed)

+ 1 *Iron crown of domination*
+ 1 *Ring of abjuration*

YOU HAVE REACHED LEVEL 5
Level 5 to 6
29000 out of 40000 EXPERIENCE

Going up another level should have been something that pleased me, and it did, but I felt like I wasn't getting the kind of job experience necessary to fully make up for my failings as an adventurer. Still, we'd almost been slaughtered back at the camp, so I wasn't about to dismiss any advantages. After all, I could practice with my new abilities even if it frustrated Ania and Agata to no end.

The interface had updated again and was now displaying my Lesser Magic effects. I'd gained an additional 1st level spell as well as a 3rd level one. Now, the obvious choice for a third level was a heavy damage-dealer like FIREBALL or LIGHTNING but I was noticing this "game" wasn't one that rewarded traditional styles of play. I decided, instead, to get SUGGESTION in hopes I could lean into my ability to talk my way out of problems. It also was as close to the Jedi Mind Trick as I could probably get out here. I gained one additional cantrip and chose MEND, which I would use to fix my battered armor and clothes.

The addition of the Divinity score also confused me and I was glad that Jon mentioning it was something that had been forgotten in the wake of the death lord's attack. Now that the high had passed from getting a look at the cosmic origins of the universe (possibly two universes), I was iffier about wanting to absorb more Marks of the Champion. It seemed like it could be a poisoned chalice, no matter what the benefits it provided. After all, when had the desire for human beings to take the power of the gods *ever* worked out in myth?

Which left Attributes to raise. Hmm, I had two points to spend. One from going up a level and one from the rush of divine power I'd gotten. I was tempted to raise my WIS more, but I figured that might convince me of how hopeless this all was. Instead, I decided to put both points in CON, which hopefully would make me less likely to throw up. It would also, if I was reading how this worked right, give an additional HP for all my levels.

ARAGORN "AARON" BARTKOWSKI
LVL: 5
CLASS: UNDERMASTER SORCERER
ALIGNMENT: GRAY
AGE: 34
SEX: MALE
RACE: HUMAN
STR: 10
AGI: 10
CON: 11
INT: 18
WIS: 8
COM: 15
CHA: 13

ARMOR CLASS: 9
ATTACK: +3 (+8 to ATTACK, 1d10+5 DAM Sword [witchfire])
HEALTH: 30
DIVINITY: 2

FEAT: Taunt, Sword and Shield

SPECIAL ABILITIES: ARCANE FIRE (1d6+5 INT bonus, Eldritch Damage), BLOCK (requires shield), LESSER MAGIC (unlimited times per day)

SPELL LIST (9/4/2/1):

LESSER MAGIC EFFECTS: CLEAN SELF, CREATE FOOD, CREATE FIRE, CREATE WATER, MINOR ILLUSION, REFRESH, TELEKINESIS (1 Kilo per INT bonus),

VENTRILOQUISM, MEND
[1] PUSH, CURE, JUMP, ARMOR
[2] WEB, ANIMAL SUMMONING
[3] SUGGESTION

STATUS EFFECTS:

* *Alchemical Stone* (Red): +50lb carrying capacity
* *Token of Love* [Unpledged]: No Effect
* *Boots of speed*: Double Movement Speed, Dodge Roll Bonus
* +1 to all Saving Throws [Divine]

I accepted all my changes and took a moment to relax as I felt better for all the benefits I'd gained. I was about three quarters of the way toward my next level after this as well, which meant things were not looking nearly as hopeless as they had when we first started. I mean, they were still hopeless but less hopeless, y'know?

The side quest saying that I was to defeat the Thirteen implied that Hellmaster Pollux was probably gone, at least for the duration of our quest. I didn't know much about the Thirteen but understood they were the Sith Council, so to speak, of Veles priesthood and all death lords. Unfortunately, even if we did kill them off, it'd be like eliminating the generals of a modern military. Veles would just promote some more.

"Speaking of improbable victories, do we have any strategy for killing Chernobog?" Jon asked.

"Nope," Ania said. "I've managed to infiltrate the temple three times, at least as far as I can remember, and Valentine was the only one who was able to destroy him. He did so by hitting him a lot with his sword."

"That worked?" Agata asked.

"It did for him," Ania said. "You were there."

Agata stared down. "I don't remember."

"Probably for the best," Ania said, clenching her teeth. "He was very fond of you and annoyed you didn't seem to want to be with him."

Agata looked horrified. I mean, I would be too.

"Don't worry, nothing happened," Ania said. "Valentin had some scruples left before he sold himself to Veles."

"I find that hard to believe," I said. "He strikes me as the kind of guy who would go on to be a shooter at his place of work."

"The thin veneer of civilization that held him back from his worst impulses was always a facade," Ania said, sounding surprisingly philosophical. Usually, she was very monosyllabic about matters unrelated to the mission. "However, that thin veneer did hold him back for quite some time. It was only when he realized that he would never get what he really wanted from us that he realized he might as well join the Lord of Bald Mountain."

"Walt Disney got the god for that sequence wrong," Jon said. "Fantasia had Chernabog in charge there."

"The way of the warrior eventually reveals who you are," Bloodstorm said. "Either that or it kills you. Or both."

"Each time I went to the Temple of the Earth, it got better guarded and the previous methods we used became impossible," Ania said. "As Aaron so eloquently put it, Veles is cheating. We'll have to figure out a wholly new strategy to destroy the Old God's avatar and relight the sacred fire. It'll also require us getting past all the corrupted nature spirits, mercenaries, and undead defending the place."

"We can figure out what to do at the Abbey of the Twins," Agata said. "The blessings of Mokosh and the Zoryas keep that place from being overrun by Veles' forces. It is also far enough from the civil war that the Empire hasn't attempted any of its purges of the Mother Goddess' religion."

"We can't stay long but it might be worthwhile to consult with their High Priestess too," Ania said. "As Agata shows, they wield a lot of magic. Magic we could definitely use in our quest."

"Yeah, I can think of a few reasons to stay with a bunch of sex witches," Bloodstorm said. "Right, Aaron?"

I didn't immediately respond. The person I wanted most, and I needed to establish some expectations and boundaries. "As long as we can avoid any more bandits trying to drug and enslave us."

"Agreed. Those guys deserved what happened to them. I mean, who drinks black lily? You smoke it, dammit. Preferably with a bag of Doritos and a large sandwich. Man, I miss Doritos. Hell, I miss sandwiches."

"They don't have sandwiches in Ledziania?" Jon asked.

"The sandwich was invented in 1762 by the Earl of Sandwich," I said, absently. "Weirdly, pizza used to be rolled up like a taco and dates back to Roman times."

"How have you ever gotten laid?" Jon asked.

"Tongue," Ania said.

Jon did a double take.

"What?" Ania said.

"The Sisters of Mokosh give classes on these things," Agata said, nodding. "Most men need instruction. Also, practice, much-much practice. I can arrange classes for him if you want him to please my sister."

"I'll instruct him," Ania said, sharply. "If he needs instruction. Which he doesn't"

"Ah," Agata said.

Ania glared.

Interesting. Maybe there was a spark of possessiveness there after all.

"I'm guessing it was the Refresh spells," Bloodstorm said. "It's why a wizard never lacks for company."

"Anyway," Jon said, sounding annoyed at all the sex talk that wasn't coming from him. "I'll be glad to have a place to sit back and relax. I need to show Aaron how to use my Epic Reader. I have every single *Dungeons & Dragons* novel downloaded on it plus several other favorites. I intend to educate him on classic lighthearted fantasy. We'll start with the Legend of Drizzt and should have that done in a couple of years. Then on to the Wheel of Time. That should be completed before Aaron is forty."

"I think the charge has probably run out on it, Jon," I said. "Even if it did survive dragonfire."

"Dragonfire!" Sparky said.

"It's powered by magic!" Jon said. "I asked for that in my wish. Mind you, since it can download books from another reality, I probably should have requested the ability to send messages back."

I shook my head. "I'm not even surprised at this point."

With that, our demon steeds broke out from the edge of the forest and came onto a grassy field leading up to a beautiful stone structure rising in the distance. It had majestic statues, twenty feet high, of two identical beautiful women in front of its doors. The first one held the Sun above her head and the other one held the Moon at her waist. It was the size of a castle and there was a great power radiating from it.

It had also recently been attacked.

Crap.

CHAPTER THIRTY-SIX
OH YES. THIS ISN'T A TRAP

Well, the Abbey of the Twins wasn't going to be able to serve as a refuge. The enormous structure had been thoroughly gutted by fire and there were signs of magic having been used extensively to defend against its attackers. The walls were scorched with blast fires, places still covered in ice like the interior of a poorly maintained freezer, and electrical scars.

It was a shame because the interior of the Abbey was one of the most luxurious places that I'd experienced so far in my journey through the Southern Kingdoms. It was a reminder that in a world with magic that the sorcerers were a license to print money (or mint it since they used metal coins). There were fur carpets, beautiful works of art, and ornate glass windows that drew a sharp contrast with even Dragon Keep. This had been a place of safety for the people here and it had been devastated by someone or *something*.

One thing that was lacking, though, was bodies. After having dealt with the undead and seen hordes of corpses abandoned alongside the road, it was strange to see so many signs of battle but not the slightest sign of actual death. Whoever had attacked had either managed to kill no one or gone to elaborate lengths to clean up after themselves. They hadn't bothered to loot the place either, which was even more unsettling as gold candlesticks and silver artifacts were left where they lay.

Only the people were missing.

Agata was obviously upset and spent her time exploring every room, nook, and cranny for signs of survivors. Ania was doing the same, except I expected she was looking for traps or remaining enemies. It was an interesting contrast that said more than a great deal about both women. Bloodstorm just shrugged and helped himself to the full pantries of meat, fresh fruit, and other magically preserved supplies.

Me?

I just sort of hung around with Jon. I'd had to cover poor Sparky's eyes several times going around the place as the art, damaged as it may have been, often was of the explicit variety.

"It seems the Zoryas aren't sisters if some of the art here is to be believed. Either that or they're just into that shit," Jon said, looking at one of the portraits with his head tilted sideways. "I thought the internet had to be invented for that position."

"Could you be any more inappropriate?" I asked.

"Yes," Jon said. "Like, why don't you get a Pwiffle card for sleeping with Ania? I mean, it's probably because her collectible card is in the base deck. However, you should get a special one for the romance being completed. Is it completed? Anyway, I figure the reason she doesn't get a sex card is that she was like fifteen in the original book and people would be weirded out even though that was fifteen years ago in-universe. It's like Hailee Steinfeld, she's a very hot lady now but you can't unconditionally lust after her because, hey, she was a kid in *True Grit*. Strangely, I never had that problem with Drew Barrymore. Probably because I was a kid too when she was."

"Yeah, that's fucking inappropriate," I admitted, not in the mood for funny banter while we were at a potential massacre site.

"I can get worse," Jon said. "Like, did you assume this abbey would be like the one from *Monty Python and the Holy Grail* full of horny young women tempting Sir Galahad the Chaste? Naughty Zoot!"

"Leave," Agata said, walking in with Ania behind her. "Come back in an hour and maybe I won't kill you."

Jon nodded, clearly understanding she was serious, and flew off.

"He copes with the horrifying situations we encounter with humor," I said, trying to explain on his behalf.

"I don't care," Agata said, on the verge of tears.

"I'm sorry," I said, taking a deep breath.

Agata glared. "I don't need your pity."

I decided just to shut up because nothing I said was going to make anything better.

"They're not dead," Ania said. "Yet."

"They aren't?" I asked, suspecting that whatever happened wasn't going to prove any better.

"They've been taken," Agata said. "The spell of protection woven around the Abbey is one that had to have been taken down from the inside. I can return it to its former prominence to guarantee our safety for the night, but we should leave in the morning."

I wasn't too concerned about that but that sounded like a good idea. "I saw the basement was fortified. Maybe we could hide out there. Who took them?"

"Veles' forces. Probably from the Temple of the Earth. They had a bit of unexpected help, though," Ania said, lifting a holy symbol of Mythras. "I found this next to some coagulated blood. The kind only undead shed when they're injured. There's other signs too that point to an alliance of the Empire and Lord of Darkness."

"Crap," I said, staring at that. "That's not good. You'd think Mythras would object."

"I'm not sure Mythras is still alive, assuming he ever existed at all," Ania said. "The elves believe that the gods of many cultures are usually the same deity operating under a different name. Perun and Mythras were both warriors of light as well as Skyfathers."

"It is a highly offensive and stupid idea that demeans the gods as well as their worshipers," Agata said, shrugging. "But what do you expect from elves?"

Ania grimaced and bit back whatever response she was thinking of. After being separated from her family, Ania had ended up being adopted by a bunch of all-female elvish assassins who had taught her their ways. Which is why she was a moon-worshiping ninja in Fantasy

Poland. I didn't know why so many groups were all-female in the Southern Kingdoms and sometimes wondered if it had just been an excuse for Larry Weis to write one-handed.

"A little bit racist but not important right now," I muttered, uncomfortable. "So, our quest to kill Chernabog just became a rescue mission?"

"We can't afford to focus on rescuing civilians," Ania said, showing her usual cold-blooded logic. There was a kind, caring, and decent person underneath all the hard edges but it was buried deep. Really deep.

"The Sisters of Mokosh are one of the few sources of magic that is still opposed to Veles," Agata said. "If we're to bring down Veles' barrier around Bald Mountain, we need to have them at our back."

"And I suppose the fact they're your friends has nothing to do with it?" Ania asked, sharper than I expected.

"Of course it does!" Agata said, appalled. "They're my sisters too, every bit as much as you."

Ania glared. "I think they're a lot more so."

I knew better than to get involved in an argument between siblings, especially one as heated as this, so I slowly backed away into a corner in hope that they couldn't see me. Like that scene in *Jurassic Park* where they hoped the T-Rex needed movement to know where they were. Ironically, even as a child, I thought that was ridiculous and assumed they got away because it had already eaten two hundred pounds of lawyer.

"Why are you being so difficult?" Agata asked, throwing her hands up in the air. "We can't win this war without saving the people endangered by it."

"We can't win this war period," Ania said. "But we can make sure Veles and company pay a bloody price along the way. What do you think, Aaron?"

Crap.

"Don't ask him!" Agata said. "Your evening's fancy is an idiot!"

"Evening's fancy?" I asked.

"He is not an idiot," Ania defended me. "He saved our lives."

"By putting them in danger in the first place!" Agata said. "He dropped Pollux on top of his army like boiling oil but his fireball came within three feet of us! We could have been consumed too."

"I didn't see you coming up with any plans," Ania said. "What matters is that it worked."

"Can I speak up?" I asked, raising a finger in protest. Sadly, not the middle one.

"No," both women said simultaneously.

I sighed. It seemed I was in a Polish anime. "We should try and rescue the hostages. Not only is it the right thing to do but we need all the help we can get against Chernabog."

NEW SIDE QUEST(S) ADDED: RESCUE THE PRIESTESSES 0/1
Recommended Level: 12 to 14
Reward: 10,000 EXP, Bonus to Assemble Armies mission, *Priestess of Mokosh Set*, *Paladin of Mokosh Set*, 10,000 GP
Description: The priestesses of Mokosh have been taken by the Empire and Chernabog's forces. Get 'em back, hopefully in one piece.

Agata didn't look happy that I was agreeing with her, and I had to wonder if she was just determined to hate me since I was wandering around with her husband's identity and whatever the hell I was with her sister.

Ania looked equally irritated, having clearly expected me to back her up because we were closer. She shook her head and walked out. "Well, I hope if you manage to rescue a few and ruin our chances to save the world that they give you the typical Mokosh reward for your heroism. Because you're certainly not getting it from me tonight!"

Agata stared at me. "Also, elves aren't a race. They're a species!"

She then departed the room, leaving me with Sparky, who was curled up in dog form on a warm blanket he'd taken from a nearby bed.

"Yeah," I said, pausing. "That was adults talking about some things you're too young to know about."

"You were talking about sex and how the witches would sleep with you if you rescued them," Sparky said.

I paused. "Oh, right. Then yes."

"They talk a lot like my mom and my aunt," Sparky said, showing slightly less childishness than before. The guy had been like eight when he'd been turned into a dragon and was a mixture of under-socialized, advancing at a different species' maturity rate, as well as whatever condition he'd had before it all happened. I made a mental note to not underestimate him even if I wasn't about to treat him like an adult either.

"Yeah," I replied. "It reminds me of my fights with my sister. I'm going to miss her if I never get home but, honestly, not many other people are waiting for me back there."

"That's good because you're probably going to die here," Sparky said, nodding his head.

I stared down at the dog, not sure how to respond to that.

"Heroically!" Sparky amended.

Bloodstorm popped his head in through the door. "Hey, I found a survivor."

"You did?" I asked, doing a double take.

"Yeah," Bloodstorm said, chewing on a sausage. "She's in the courtyard of High Grecian art."

"High Grecian art?" I asked.

"The naked dudes section versus the naked ladies or naked dudes and ladies section," Bloodstorm said. "You know there's a men's dormitory here for acolytes? They can't be priestesses, but they can live here to help with their rites."

"Nice work if you can get it," I said, shrugging.

"You sure you don't want to get the others?" Bloodstorm said.

"They're having sister problems," I said, shaking my head.

"Ah," Bloodstorm said. "You know if the thing with Ania doesn't work out, my sister is looking for someone to share blood with. The vampire not the hags. I don't speak with them. Usually."

"I'm not really interested in becoming a fly-eating brainwashed henchman," I said, not sure if they had Renfield equivalents.

"Oh, hell no!" Bloodstorm said, clearly getting the context if not the specific reference. "You'd be a full-blooded vampire. Angelica's planning on opening her own place in the capital city of Akoa. Plenty of people paying to get drained."

"I'll hold off on becoming undead until we've failed to save the world," I said. "I also don't date the sisters of friends. It never works out."

"Suit yourself," Bloodstorm said. "I don't think we have much of a chance against the gods we're about to slay but I respect the ambition. I just think you might want to set your sights lower."

"Veles will come after me, so I might as well go after him," I said, walking to the general direction of the courtyard.

"So, it's a hate thing, huh?" Bloodstorm asked, following with the dog in the back.

"There's only three things I hate: Nazis, people who claim everyone they hate is a Nazi, and cottagecore enthusiasts," I said.

"Yeah, those cottage people freak me out," Bloodstorm said, making a mock shudder.

The courtyard of the abbey was indeed full of a bunch of Michealangelo's David-esque statues of men wrestling, or, well, yeah. It was also full of beautiful flower beds, well-trimmed grasses, and signs that the Abbey of the Twins hadn't exactly been running out of coin. You know, if all the other items of fabulous wealth on display hadn't been a clue.

There was an enormous twenty-foot-tall statue of Mokosh in the center of the place before bubbling pools that I assumed to be natural hot springs. Though, given this was a magical world, I wouldn't have been surprised if someone had used sorcery to create them the same way this place had ice spell-equipped freezers.

At the foot of the statue, kneeling before her in what looked like prayer, was a breathtakingly beautiful woman (I know, another one!) with a crimson hooded cloak. She had light brown skin the same shade as Maria in Blackwood Bog and if said woman reminded me of Rosario Dawson, this lady had some definite Zoe Saldana qualities. She was wearing another cleavage displaying dress and it didn't take a rocket scientist to figure out she was a dragon in disguise. Probably, Cordelia Poppy AKA Eva's sister and the "bad" sister who had gone along with Boris Poppy's plan to assassinate the Rose family to take over Dragon Keep.

Now you might assume I was being a bit premature in my judgment. Just because I was literally trapped in a fantasy novel by a hack writer didn't mean that everything was secretly trying to kill me. However, family resemblance aside, I had several reasons to believe my theory. Number One: I'd already been warned by Eva Poppy to be on the lookout for Cordelia. Number Two: I knew Valentine was looking for me with the help of a female dragon. Number Three: The Sisters of Mokosh had to have let someone in who could destroy them from the inside. I was pretty sure they would be more likely to let in a woman than a man. Number Four: Bonehead as he may have been, I was pretty sure that Valentin was smart enough to know that we would have gone to the Abbey on our way to the Temple of Earth. If nothing else, the guy was a fellow "Garland" and probably knew which way adventurers would tend to go on their quests.

Plus, again, all the dragon women I'd met, sample size of one that it may be, seemed to be unable to resist keeping themselves color coordinated with their true forms. Certainly, with her perfect makeup and attire, she didn't look like she'd been hiding from a bunch of raiders. Maybe I was making a ridiculous assertion, and it was a sign of my low WIS, but I was willing to bet this was a trap. The trick was to play it cool and not tip her off that I was on to her. If she was assuming a human body, then she probably had orders to identify us first and maybe report back to Valentin before executing us. The best thing to do was to pretend ignorance and see if I could get an advantage over her and, by proxy, Valentin himself.

"Good evening, madam," I said, stretching out my arms. "I am so glad to see someone of this abbey escaped unharmed."

The woman nodded. "I barely escaped with my life, milord. Are you truly the legendary monster hunter, Garland of Nowhere?"

I paused before answering, considering my next words carefully. It was possible that I might be killed right then and there but I had an exit strategy with my *boots of speed*. Bloodstorm, however, would be left in the lurch. I decided to play some word games first. "That depends on who is asking. You could be one of the Great Enemy's spies and—"

That was when Jon flew down and landed on one of the nearby Grecian statues, flapping his wings in a panic. "Aaron! I used my INSIGHT ability! She's a dragon! Run!"

Goddammit, Jon.

CHAPTER THIRTY-SEVEN
THE GODDESS IN THE FOUNTAINS

Well, I was screwed.

The woman, Cordellia Poppy, I was certain now, transformed before my eyes into the same feminine-looking dragon that I'd seen earlier. Somehow, without Valentin riding on her back, she looked even more intimidating. Perhaps it was the fact she didn't have to deal with the fact that her idiot manchild rider was holding her back.

Mind you, it could just be the fact she was a house-sized monster that was capable of breathing flame powerful enough to melt steel. I'd seen what Sparky's personal flamethrower could do and this creature was probably closer to a WW2 bomber dropping napalm. If I hadn't been overwhelmed by the sight, I might have taken advantage to run or attack during her transformation, but that opportunity passed.

"Garland of Nowhere, you are the enemy of Veles the Lord of Darkness," Cordellia spoke, her voice a sultry purr despite being a terrifying dinosaur with wings. "It is here you will meet your end and join the ranks of all the others who sought to end the final days."

"Well, it's been an honor!" Bloodstorm said, lifting his ax. "Barbarian Rage!"

Bloodstorm charged at the dragon, screaming, only to be slapped away with the dragon's tail and sent flying through the air into a trio of nude statues. He wasn't dead but I had to say that was probably not the finest moment in his career.

"Hold up a second," I said, setting down Sparky. "There are children present."

"Prepare to be burned from skin to bone," Cordellia said, moving her head like a snake about to strike.

"Go away, Alexi," I said, drawing my sword as its white-blue flames ignited. "I have to kill your aunt."

"No!" Sparky said, frowning and assuming his dragon form. "No fighting my aunt!"

"What?" Cordellia asked, confused.

"I'm not sure that's possible," I said, looking down at Sparky. "She seems like she wants to fight me really bad."

"Alexi, what are you doing here?" Cordellia asked, hissing.

"No fighting my new friends!" Sparky said, turning to Cordellia. "They broke the curse on the bog and now he is teaching me to be a Dark Undermaster."

"Yeah, sure, he's my dragon squire," I said, turning to her. "Kid's got real potential."

"You would threaten my nephew to protect yourself?" Cordellia asked, growling. Clearly, she thought I was holding the kid hostage.

"Lady, you're the one threatening us!" I said, turning to her. "I'm trying to get him out of the way!"

"I will be a great knight and you're ruining everything!" Sparky growled, glaring at her. It would have been comical if not for the fact I was still pretty terrified of dying.

"You will return to your mother immediately!" Cordellia said, growling at him.

"Mom knows I'm here!" Sparky said. "She's the one who sent me."

"She did?" I asked, wondering what the hell was wrong with Eva Poppy. "Oh wow."

Cordellia let forth a furious ear-splitting roar toward the heavens. That was when she took off into the sky above the courtyard and flew away.

"Huh," I said, staring up at the figure in the sky above us as she disappeared into the setting sun. "I did not think that was going to work."

"And don't come back!" Sparky shouted, blowing a bit of fire in her direction that stopped about six feet from his mouth.

"Don't be mean to your aunt," I said, frowning. I checked my bracelet after it pinged.

SIDE QUEST(S) UPDATED: RESCUE THE PRIESTESSES

+ 5000 EXP (Dragon Retreat)
+ 1000 EXP (Do so without violence)

Level 5 to 6
35000/40000
NEW OBJECTIVE: ENTER THE ANTECHAMBER OF THE GODS TO RECEIVE BLESSING

"What in the world?" I asked, confused.

Above our heads, a glowing Aurora Borealis shone with golden light between the abbey and the sky. It was a wild guess but I assumed that was the spell of protection that Agata said she would get back up. I was just grateful she'd managed to get it up after Cordellia had left and not before as I'd rather not have been trapped here with her. Hopefully, it would keep her from rethinking her choice to leave us alone.

"Did we win?" Sparky asked.

"Not all battles are won with swords or fire, kid," I said, patting him on the head. "Remember, knowing is half the battle. GI Joe."

Sparky stared at me strangely.

That was when Bloodstorm jogged up to me, carrying his ax. "Sorry, I needed to get out of a bunch of stone dicks. What did I miss?"

"Sparky is proving to be the MVP of the team," I said. "I think we're good for a bit, but I think we can officially say the abbey is compromised as a headquarters for the team."

"Yeah, the biggest benefit of staying at this abbey is off the table if there's no priestesses," Bloodstorm said, laughingly pushing me with his right hand. Unfortunately, he had the strength of a bull, and I was sent flying backward.

I ended up splashing into one of the sacred pools and thanks to the fact I had a sword and a bunch of other equipment weighing me down, I ended up sinking quite heavily into the water. I worried about drowning and that worry became worse as I kept sinking for far more than several feet but seemingly dozens before I emerged upside down in a pool that only came up to my chest.

I was very confused as I found myself in some sort of underground grotto that reminded me of Eva Poppy's lair, which made sense because Mokosh loved building her sacred pools in these sorts of places. There were altars built from natural stones, candles burning on them, glowing fungus, and more icons devoted to the Mother Goddess. There were also a few small statues of Veles, Svarog, Perun, and the other gods lying around.

Oh, and Mokosh, herself, was present.

Mokosh was a woman with long flowing fire-gold hair that would have required a mountain of hairspray to keep as poofy as it looked. Being a Mother Goddess, she was a bit on the mature side with her appearance being about her mid-thirties. Without putting too fine a point on it, she was a bit on the plump side but in a way that was curvier than any other descriptor. The goddess was wearing a loose sheer dress that opened to its sides and barely kept within the bounds of decency. You might question how I knew this to be Mokosh herself as opposed to any of the other gods, but I knew, just knew, the same way that I knew Veles was a god.

Also, when she walked toward me, her bare feet caused flowers and plant life to bloom out of the ground. That was probably a pretty good sign of divinity there. The woman had flowers growing in her hair and I had to wonder if they were actually growing out of her head, but I didn't want to make any statements I might regret, especially since I'd almost drowned by falling into one of her sacred pools.

I was unsure what the proper protocol was for meeting a deity that didn't want to kill you. I wondered if she would talk like one of the Aesir from the Mighty Thor comics or something more terrifying like the God of the Old Testament.

"Hi, Aaron!" Mokosh said, flashing a peace sign. "Whassup?"

Or Mokosh could sound like she was from California.

"Uh, hi," I said, feeling soaked to the bone by her sacred pool but not chilled due to the water being exceptionally warm. I could see literally rainbow-colored trout swimming in the pools beside me and felt the magic pulse from the place. "Nice to meet you."

Mokosh walked into the water, revealing she was a bit shorter than me as she came up only to my neck as her hair floated in the water behind her. She pointed at my chest and nodded. "You, sir, do not suck."

I blinked. "Uh, thank you?"

"The Wise Man has a really poor track record with his champions," Mokosh said, looking around as little pixie-like women floated around her head and just added to the feel of an R-rated Disney movie. "Some of them are brave, some of them good, some of them clever, and others talented. Unfortunately, we're not really batting four for four with any of them. Honestly, our average is terrible."

"You have baseball in Ledziania?" I asked, confused.

"Try and keep up, Aaron," Mokosh said. "Basically, we're out of divine essence from my husband's corpse and you were basically a Hail Mokosh pass, who is me. So far, you're doing good, and I wanted to give you a pep talk. Also, a divine blessing because without the EXP boost you're going to die at the Earth Temple."

"Oh," I said, blinking. "Yeah, that would be bad. Jon said we should grind beforehand."

"Yeah, well, Veles is cheating," Mokosh said, frowning. "Rotten jealous bastard. He never forgave my sister, Mattie, for becoming the Earth and the seven headed dragon goddess that Marduk slew. After she regenerated, she divorced his ass, and I was forced to pick up the pieces. Now she's known as every mean girl goddess in the hundred pantheons. You know her from that cartoon that Jon mentioned."

"Tiamat?" I asked, trying not to stare at the fact her already translucent dress had gotten more so in the water. Unfortunately, my body wasn't obeying, and I was very much obviously excited. Hopefully, she wouldn't notice.

"I'm a love goddess, dipshit, of course I noticed," Mokosh said, responding to my thoughts. "Anyway, Mattie pretends her new look isn't from *Dungeons & Dragons* by adding the extra two heads, but I know better. Gods claim all the time we're above the petty creations of humanity, but the truth is we love any mention we get. Thor? Loves the comics and movies. Hercules? Still has the '80s movies on VHS. The ones with the Incredible Hulk actor, the one from the TV show, not the MCU."

I was very confused. "Lou Ferrigno?"

"Yes, exactly," Mokosh said, turning around. "We all love the Wise Man's books and the spin offs. I think the last time my sons and daughters were mentioned was American Gods and the author added an additional Zoryas so they were a Hecate trio. Not our religion! Anywho, you're good-ish and cunning even if you're not wise. You didn't spill any blood in my sanctum and thus I don't have to curse you like Valentin planned."

"Wait, what?" I asked, now paying complete attention to what she was saying. Yes, I was distracted. Cut me some slack. Mokosh had a lot of Free Brittney energy.

"You think so? I always liked her," Mokosh said, once more responding to my unspoken comments. "Valentin sent his agents to kidnap my priestesses with Sleep spells, Tasers from your world, rubber bullets, and tear gas so they could avoid spilling blood. My priestesses fought back, you're allowed to when you're part of the clergy, but it didn't work. Valentin hoped you'd kill Cordellia and thus turn the abbey into a hellscape like Blackwood Bog. Either that or Cordellia killed you."

I blinked, processing that. "That son of a bitch."

"Much like you, Valentin is much smarter than he appears," Mokosh said.

"Err, thank you?" I asked. "Wait, you would know we were defending ourselves. Would you still have cursed us?"

Mokosh shrugged. "Divine rules. You let one guy get away with spilling blood in your sacred pools and suddenly everyone is doing it. I am very happy I didn't have to turn you into a werewolf or dragon or something."

"What is it with cursing people with cool powers, anyway?" I asked, finally having a chance to ask someone who might answer.

Mokosh, instead, pinched the bridge of her nose. "Aaron, you need to stay on topic."

"Oh, sorry," I muttered, embarrassed. "What's the topic again?"

"You need to keep doing what you're doing," Mokosh said. "Keep trying to avoid traditional ways of playing the game."

"The game?" I asked.

"The game of life," Mokosh said. "My first husband's blessings may resemble the fantasy boardgame that we all love but if you play like the others played, you'll die. You need to press every advantage you've got because Veles is not above pressing his finger on the scale to make sure he wins."

"Yeah, I got that impression," I said, sucking in my breath. "Any other advice?"

"Sleep with other women to make Ania jealous," Mokosh said. "But not her sister because that will just piss her off."

I blinked. "Err, I can't do that!"

Mokosh lowered her gaze and raised one eyebrow. "Really? Because it seems like you're doing a fine job as is."

I looked away, embarrassed. "Alright, fair enough. I'm just not sure if we have a thing or not yet. We're not dating so it wouldn't be wrong, but I'd like to date her, but she doesn't seem ready. I'm not sure where we stand."

"Neither is she," Mokosh said. "She was raised by an honorable pious father she knew cheated on her mother with me then among elves who consider sex about as intimate as a handshake. Her last two lovers are dead, one of whom was tortured to death by the Bastard Knight and the other who she just found out married her sister."

"And was her brother," I said.

"As a goddess, I should point out that's not as big a deal to me but sure," Mokosh said. "If you do want to win her heart, you need to be very patient and expect things to go in unconventional ways."

"Unconventional how?" I asked.

"I'm not telling you," Mokosh said. "Just know that you will find love here in your journey across the Southern Kingdoms. It may work out with Ania, or it may not. Cherish what you have without pushing too hard for more. Sex is a weapon that you may need to employ. It's just like your sword or magic and you may have to use all three to survive this."

"I'm not really comfortable with this line of—"

"Finally, you're right to absorb the other fragments of my first husband," Mokosh said. "But you need to level up first and keep your sense of self strong or Perun will reincarnate in your body, killing you. You might ascend to godhood, too, which is fine, but you'd be a piddly demigod, and we need someone with a bit more oomph. So, keep harvesting divine power until we can figure out what to do with it. We translate that into experience points with the bracelet. That's earned by stories and heroism."

"What was that?" I asked, trying to follow this insane conversation while being distracted.

"Sadly, we've run out of time, at least if I'm going to reach my second level," Mokosh said. "It's time for your blessing."

"Oh good," I said, even more confused now than when I started.

Mokosh slipped out of her dress and slid over to me, kissing me on the lips. If I had any other thoughts, they quickly vanished at her touch.

CHAPTER THIRTY-EIGHT
CELEBRITY ALL-STAR PWIFFLE

I woke up naked, barely conscious, and covered in bruises. I leave your imagination to fill in the blanks. It was nighttime now and I was in the shadow of Mokosh's statue in the courtyard. To my side, I could see my clothes, neatly pressed and folded. Which was probably not good for leather armor, but I didn't know anything about magical dry cleaning.

"Uhhhhhh..." I tried to speak.

What was it about Ledziania that made everyone so unrelentingly horny? I wasn't even upset but just curious. Usually, it took slightly more than a five-minute conversation to get to sex even when I was using the Epic Dungeoneering™ Timber App.

Either way, I couldn't move.

ACHIEVEMENT UNLOCKED: DIVINE CONGRESS
(A) 25 - Make love (or just get busy) with one of Ledziania's deities

"Oh, you've got to be kidding me," I said, staring. "They give an achievement for that? What are we, teenagers?"

"If I'd known you could get an achievement for it, I would have tried harder with the Zoryas," Jon said, settling down beside my head. "Mind you, I think I probably should have hit on both instead of one."

"Go away," I said, turning away from him. "I'm not in the mood."

"Your dick says otherwise," Jon said.

I looked down and saw that, yes, I was still at attention. "Huh. I think that's actually worth seeing a doctor over."

"Magical enhancement!" Jon said, cheerfully. "In any case, it answers the question I've been asking myself the most."

"I shudder to think what that is." I grabbed my armor and covered myself. When I sat up, something fell to the side and bounced against the courtyard's grass. "What in the world?"

It was a Pwiffle card. It had a nude Mokosh on, her naughty bits strategically covered with hair and the waters of her pond.

YOU RECEIVE 5 HP IN DAMAGE; YOU NOW HAVE THE STATUS EFFECT (EXHAUSTION)

ACHIEVEMENT UNLOCKED: DECKMASTER
(A) 25 - You have completed a Divine Pwiffle Deck

SIDE QUEST(S) COMPLETED:

COLLECT ALL UNIQUE PWIFFLE CARDS 50/50

+ 50,000 GP
+ 50,000 EXP
+ 1 Divine Pwiffle Deck

YOU HAVE REACHED LEVEL 6
Level 6 to 7
45000 out of 60000 EXPERIENCE

"Wow, you're rich," Jon said, looking at my bracelet. "Of course, you're going to spend it all on upgrading Dragon Keep to, I dunno, have a chocobo breeding pen."

"I was thinking the Dragon Pit," I said, pausing. "We need a place for Sparky."

Leveling up once more by completing the Pwiffle deck had been one of my plans from the beginning, but it still felt like cheating. It also proved not to be quite the game changer I'd expected in terms of experience. A single level when we were trying to kill a god and the 20th level Valentin with his dragon allies. Still, I wasn't going to look a gift horse in the mouth and Mokosh's help was better than just about anything else I'd received so far. Weis had just given me Jon and if this were *Clash of the Titans*, the original one from the Eighties, I would have preferred a mechanical owl and helmet of invisibility.

"Yeah, it's called a kennel," Jon said, referring to where Sparky should be kept. "Anyway, everyone else is asleep."

I was disappointed. "No one is concerned about my disappearance?"

I admit we sometimes had our issues, but I would have been searching the world over if one of the others had gone missing.

"Everyone was concerned," Jon said. "When Mokosh's statue said you were with her, Ania thought it was a trick of Veles while Bloodstorm was ready to go spelunking through the holy caverns for you. Agata was the only one who said we should trust the goddess but that just led to another fight with Ania. Sparky got distracted by one of the holy doves and let's just say that we should be glad no one likes pigeons."

"Oh," I said, feeling guilty for doubting them. "What about you?"

"Through our familiar-master bond, I was able to determine that you were alright," Jon said.

"You were?" I asked.

"Hell no!" Jon said. "I was worried sick, and you were off banging Aphrodite!"

There was a crack of thunder above the courtyard.

"I think they take mislabeling really seriously around here," I said, calmly. "But yes, it seems her blessing was very specific."

"Yes, who could have imagined the sex goddess would have sex as a blessing," Jon said. "So, I take it you and Ania aren't a thing-thing?"

"She said no but I don't know how this is going to go over," I muttered, getting up. "Mokosh said I should try to make her jealous, but I don't like those kinds of games. Also, that I had to be prepared for it not going anywhere."

"Mokosh gave you dating advice while you were having your divine congress?" Jon asked, looking up at me. "Also, seriously, put that thing away."

I looked away, embarrassed. "I'm not responsible!"

"I am one hundred percent sure that is not the case," Jon said. "Just, I dunno, go take care of it in one of the sacred pools or something. That's what hot tubs are for."

I stared at him. "Remind me never to get in a hot tub after you, unlikely as that scenario is to occur in fantasy Poland."

"You clearly weren't invited to the fun parties of Epic Dungeoneering™," Jon said. "The ones with all the drugs, hookers, and elves."

I absolutely hadn't. "What now?"

"So, what was it like?" Jon asked.

"No, Jon," I said, getting dressed as best as I could and glad that I was able to, uh, pull it back.

"Spoilsport," Jon muttered.

I felt really, uh, refreshed after the experience even if I was weirded out by how my clothes smelled vaguely like lilacs and there was a mild glow to myself. I meant the latter literally and saw I looked a great deal fresher in the reflection of the pools around me. Like I was prepping my Timber account picture. I checked my bracelet, which was still on me and hadn't left despite my earlier description of being naked (it felt like a part of me these days).

TOKEN OF LOVE HAS BECOME BLESSING OF MOKOSH
+1 to CHR and +1 COM until one sleeps with one's true love

"How does a polygamous sex goddess define true love?" Jon asked. "Jon!"

"That is a serious question!" Jon said. "Also, I would point out that I consider those two dump stats but I'm not going to risk pissing off the love goddess. So, I'm going to shut my mouth and keep all my snide commentary to myself."

"I think that's literally impossible for you," I said, calmly.

Jon sulked.

Three seconds later.

"So, since she's the goddess of motherhood, I'm assuming she's an older MILF-looking type with big boob—"

"Good evening," Veles said, appearing behind us.

"Mothersucker!" I said, almost falling into one of the sacred pools again.

"I was born from the primordial chaos of the universe so that's thankfully one of the few things I'm not guilty of," Veles said, dryly. "Zeus on the other hand was known to have banged Rhea and we've never let him hear the end of it."

Veles was wearing a white suit and Panama hat that made him look like a drug trafficker from an Eighties action movie set in some fictional South American country. He had a briefcase to his side that was identical to the one I'd received from Epic Dungeoneering™.

"Are you, uh, allowed to be here?" I asked, unsure what was about to happen.

"Given I'm the only greater god left in this universe, you'll find there's very little that I'm not allowed," Veles said. "But rules of hospitality mean that I'm not going to kill you with my bare hands or will you dead on my wife's sacred ground."

"So, you'll drain her magical essence and wage war on her people but not spill blood on her carpet?" Jon asked.

I glared down at Jon.

"Basically, yeah," Veles said, conjuring a table and chairs in the middle of the courtyard before putting his briefcase on it. The table was an ornate wooden one while the chairs were fine leather ones with extra stuffing.

"Uh, what's happening?" I asked, staring at him.

"I think he's pissed you banged his wife," Jon said, flying up to sit on the heads of one of the nearby statues.

"If I was pissed about mortals banging my wife, I'd have to kill most of the planet," Veles said.

"You *are* going to kill most of the planet," I pointed out. "Two planets in fact."

"Oh, right," Veles said, without a hint of humor. "Well, then, sucks to be you. But no, that's not the reason."

"So, what are you here for?" I asked, still trying to figure out why Sauron had decided to drop by for a visit.

That was when Veles pulled out a Pwiffle deck with the cards each pressed against solid gold backing with plastic coverings. "The ultimate Pwiffle match!"

I stared at him. "You have got to be kidding me."

"Nope," Veles said. "It's our national sport."

"Remember, you get a wish if you beat him!" Jon said, suddenly interested.

"And if you lose, you get your soul claimed!" Veles said.

"Wait, what?" I asked, horrified. "That's a thing?"

"No, not really," Veles said, showing a very dry, understated sense of humor. "I'm the God of the Dead so everyone on Mokosh goes to me anyway. I don't need to bargain for souls like Satan. Which, honestly, fuck that guy. He's not even a god, he's just a jumped-up messenger. Ahrimane? Now that was a guy who could wreck shit. No one remembers him anymore, though."

"Unless you've played *Prince of Persia*," Jon said. "The non-crappy-but-not-quite-as-good-as-the original reboot."

I stared at Veles. "Are you pulling my leg?"

"Obviously," Veles said, gesturing to the chair across from him. "But I'm not making up the part about everyone coming to the same Underworld. I reward the virtuous and punish the guilty accordingly."

"The God of Evil runs Heaven, huh?" I asked, sitting down in the chair across from him. It was incredibly comfy.

"More like Elysium," Veles said, smiling like a serpent. "It's why I was eventually able to overcome my brother. People's faith in the sky may fade as they learn more about space and the stars but they never lose their fear of death. It's part of the plan, really. Once everyone is dead, then we can bring some actual order to the universe. Good people will have good things and bad people will have bad things happen to them."

"Except for killing everyone first," I said.

"Yes," Veles said. "I think we have enough humans in the afterlife for a sustainable source of faith. Faith taking the physical form of golden apples, ambrosia, and divine mead. No need to be greedy by breeding generations of billions more humans. At least until I'm ready to invade other realities. You've got to pace yourself with these things, though."

Veles was being awfully free with details about how the universe operated but maybe he thought it didn't matter since I probably wasn't going to be alive much longer. Either that or this was Introduction to Gods 101 level stuff and I had enough divine essence to qualify for the Community college course on it.

"Close enough," Veles said, having that habit of reading my mind that all the gods seemed to possess.

Admittedly, I'd only met two.

"So, if I win, I get a wish?" I asked, making sure I had that correctly. "I can wish for anything?"

"Within reason," Veles said. "You're getting your wish granted by me, Veles, after all. I'm not going to grant a wish where I am asked to kill myself or stop my invasion. I would be willing to resurrect the dead, return you to Earth, or bestow immortality. Also, I'm going to point out that I'm not going to engage in any cheeky word games either. If you ask for immortality, I'm not going to turn you into a stone or give you eternal life but not youth. I may be a monster but I'm not a *dick*."

"That's very nice of you," I said, pausing. "Except for the fact you already offered to return me to Earth for free."

Veles smirked. "Can't blame a man for trying. I could also force Garland back from the realm of the blessed dead so he can take over your job as hero. After all, no one wants to see you here, do they?"

I tapped my fingers against the table. "You're aware I know about psyching out your opponent, right?"

Veles was trying to get into my head, and I had to admit that it was working. I had a hefty case of Imposter syndrome since, well, I wasn't a beloved fantasy hero adored by millions of people across the world. Well, two worlds. I'd managed to acquit myself well so far, winning two upset victories, but the fact was that I only needed to lose once. The fact I literally was an imposter to two of my party and causing them no end of pain was something that bothered me to no end. Veles knew all of this and knew that I was thinking all of this, so I had to push these thoughts out and focus on the game.

"Can't blame a man for trying," Veles said. "I also promise that I won't attempt to kill all of your friends while you're playing the game."

That was another thing I was worried about. "What is it with the games anyway? You could just tell Valentin where we are and send your entire army."

"My motivations would be as inscrutable as a god's," Veles said, with a soft hiss. "Oh, wait!"

I narrowed my eyes. "Try me."

Veles frowned. "It's more fun this way. But believe me, things have started to get boring."

I took a deep breath. "Bring it."

Veles smirked. "So quick to get back into your Pwiffle addiction, are we, Aaron? Well, I'm afraid tonight you've met your match."

CHAPTER THIRTY-NINE
EASY OR NIGHTMARE MODE

"I give up," Veles said, tossing his guards on the table and resting his chin on his palm with his elbow on the table.

"What?" I asked, looking up from my cards. My eyes hurt from focusing on them and I noticed it was now morning. Thankfully, I'd cast REFRESH a few times during the night. Jon was snoring nearby. I'd forgotten to cast it on him.

"We've been at this for six hours and you've managed to stalemate me despite the fact I literally can't lose. I made this goddamn game," Veles muttered. "I have places to go, people to kill. I forfeit."

"Oh, come on, man, I was about to deploy this card to reverse your use of the Death Lord suite," I said, lifting a card with Veles' picture on it. "That would have put me within an hour or two of total victory."

"Really?" Veles asked, looking at the card. "You were going to use the *Veles* card against me?"

"It allows me to take over all undead deployed," I said.

According to Jon, that required my little blackbird friend to infiltrate a tomb of a death lord and challenge him to a game of Pwiffle with his life as the stake. It put Jon's quest for the cards into perspective.

"I know what it fucking does!" Veles snapped, leaning back.

I unscrewed the top of a bottle of Snapple that had come with a cooler that Veles had provided. It was next to a plate of pizza rolls and a couple of empty bags of chips. Veles had brought a group of succubi waitresses, all of them dressed like MMA ring girls, to provide snacks during the competition. I had the impression that he had expected something a little harder in terms of requests for refreshment. However, I preferred to remain clear headed during matches.

Veles and I had agreed to go toe-to-toe with Marathon Pwiffle, which roughly speaking, meant you played until one party had ten more match victories than the other. It was a particularly punishing all night form of the game that favored long-term strategy over quick victories. You'd have thought that would favor the immortal god, but I figured I could outlast Veles.

I looked up from my notepad where I'd been calculating points and shook my head. "So, I win?"

"Yes, Aaron, you win," Veles said, dryly. "I would rather grant you a wish using my near-omnipotent power than continue trying to crack that computer brain of yours. Dustin Hoffman would play you in the Eighties."

I stared at him.

"*Rain Man* reference," Veles said. "Seriously, watch some movies made before you were born that don't involve samurai."

"I've seen the film, I just don't appreciate the reference," I said. "Not all neuroatypical—"

"Don't care," Veles said. "How the hell did you beat me?"

I pointed with two finger guns at him. "*Star Trek: The Next Generation.*"

Veles stared.

"There's an episode called 'Peak Performance' where Data is challenged to a strategy game against an alien and—"

"Don't care," Veles said. "I withdraw my question."

"He realizes the alien can't be beaten by trying to win but if he drags it out—" I continued, admittedly enjoying twisting the knife a bit more than I should. This was as close to winning a golden fiddle with Satan as anyone was ever going to get.

"I said I don't care," Veles muttered. "If I wanted to be bored to death, I would have had a conversation with Thoth."

That was an opening I had to learn something more. "Yeah, I'm confused by that, did you make my world or did other gods? Because you reference them existing, but the vision of the Earth's creation only showed you and the other main Slavic deities."

"Do you really want to waste time asking about religious trivia?" Veles asked.

"Yes," I said, automatically.

"Fine." Veles closed his eyes. "The very short version is that it shouldn't come as a great surprise that ninety percent of all religious doctrine in the universe is nonsense. However, it's the remaining ten percent that will trip you up."

"Uh huh."

"There are other gods than our pantheon, but popularity doesn't equal power. I'm a creator deity alongside Svarog and Perun. That's the highest level you can get except for overgod, which the three of us could become by combining."

"Like Voltron?"

"Yes," Veles surprised me by saying this with just a hint of sarcasm versus an entire boat load. "Exactly like Voltron, Aaron. We were called Triglav when we were one being and were as close to the capital G god as exists in the primal universe. Obviously, we're not doing that lately."

"Because you killed your brother."

Veles gave me a 'no shit, Sherlock' gaze that reminded me of shows like *Breaking Bad* and *Better Call Saul* where the villain protagonist is surrounded by idiots. You understood that feeling so you sympathized even when they were doing awful things. It was hard not to like Veles despite the fact he was a genocidal dark lord, odd as that statement may be. There was just a sense that his plan to take over the world had been driven by being done with humanity's crap. Which, given the timing of Perun's death was just around WW2, might have some basis in real-life events.

"Yeah, I figured between the invasions and earlier the Christianization of Poland, it was time to start over," Veles said. "I may be evil, Aaron, but I have standards. My brother, who fought in the Battle of Britain as a Polish airman and sired your grandmother, disagreed with my decision that we should wipe out mankind or at least cull it to manageable levels. Now I'm going to be harnessing the power of Mokosh as well as the other greater gods, the step below creator deities, to become the new Triglav. One will instead of three in one."

"And the other gods aren't interfering?" I asked.

"The other gods, on Earth and Mokosh at least, are all descendants of me and Mat Zemlya or selfish assholes themselves," Veles said. "There's a handful who want to protect mankind, but they have their own issues. Mythras' fan club utterly disgusts him for instance. My remaining brother, Svarog, doesn't care as long as it doesn't involve his dwarves."

"You're very forthcoming with information," I admitted.

Veles rose from the other side of the table. "You're family, Aaron. Idiot family like Valentin but family, nonetheless. It's why I'm handling you with kids' gloves. I'd rather you work for me than kill you but I'm not going to let you become an actual threat."

"I wish for fair play," I said, taking a chance.

Veles did a double take. "Excuse me?"

"You said I get a wish," I said, shrugging. "I wish for an actual chance at accomplishing this."

Veles stared down at me. "You're already getting a chance at this."

"A fair chance," I said, staring at him. "Valentin is hunting me down with his dragons, there's more storm troopers—"

"Storm knights," Veles corrected. "Soldiers of the bull, which I point out is what Veles translates as. It means oxen-haired, which I admit sounded more badass circa 700 AD or so."

"Is that a humble brag about how you're secretly the guy behind the Empire?" I asked.

Veles smirked. "There's nothing humble about it. Mythras really came to rue what I've turned his followers' empire into. It's worse than what happened to the Carpenter's religion."

I waved him off. "The storm knights you had in the inn waiting for us. I'm following the same script as the previous champions but you're putting your finger on the scale."

"Mokosh told you," Veles said.

"I'd already figured it out," I said, frowning. "I don't get it. Why go along with all these quests to begin with if you know when and where people will go? Why just up the difficulty from Easy to Nightmare mode?"

Veles chuckled and snapped his fingers, causing the table and Pwiffle cards to disappear. "As stated, gods are powered by stories and faith. It is as much our meat and drink as the souls of mortals is our herds of cattle. The Wise Man stood where you are now and is the only other person to have won against me in a card game. He asked for a chance to duel it out with champions, and I set the terms."

"Which you're now violating," I said, staring at him. "Didn't you used to punish oath breakers with disease and shit?"

Yay for my mythology classes.

Veles shrugged. "I'm not violating the oath, but I am well and truly sick of having to deal with the parade of idiots that Weis has sent after me and my followers. They mock my brother and his demigod son with their incompetence as well as arrogance. So, yes, I've been gradually turning up the heat, so no one notices. Valentin being a champion, however rogue, means he has free will so sending him after you isn't violating the rules of the agreement I made with Weis. Instead, it just means it's PVP."

I hated that the God of Evil was a gamer. It seemed like it violated some laws of reality but perhaps I shouldn't have been surprised given how people behave online. "And you said you don't play word games."

Veles frowned. His white suit disappeared, and he was once more wearing a black robe that made him look like Peter Stormare, Sith Lord. "Very well."

"What?" I asked, not having expected him to agree.

"You've made a successful argument that I have been missing the spirit of the game," Veles said. "You'll now have a chance to fulfill the quest and do battle with me. I'll lend my forces no more aid than is strictly necessary. It won't be until you directly challenge me in Bald Mountain, which I sincerely doubt you'll reach, that I'll cut you down like grain with a scythe. In short, I am restarting the game at Normal mode. You can even speak with the Wise Man freely without my listening in."

"Thanks," I said, not exactly happy about Veles letting Weis in my head again. "What about Valentin?"

"He's still free to kill you," Veles said. "But I won't bring him along to your dreams or tell him where you are."

It wasn't much but I wasn't sure what else I could ask for since I didn't know the limits of gods and he was also the guy who was making the promise. "And you swear by this?"

"I swear by myself, which is the most powerful oath a god can make," Veles said. "My brother's essence protects me from knowing your exact location and striking you down directly but I still have plenty of forces to do you in the old-fashioned way. Note that I will also be treating you as the last of the champions. I won't spare any of your party for the next time around because there will be no next time. The Rose family, Bloodstorm, and your little dog too are all on the chopping block now."

"Right," I muttered, not sure this was a good idea. "I guess we're done here, then."

"Indeed," Veles said, conjuring a large Medieval silver *zloty* (Polish coin) in his hands before flipping it to me.

I caught it. "What's this?"

"Recompense," Veles said. "You get one free extra life because, you're right, I wasn't living up to my promises of fair play. You can use it to bring back Jon, Garland, one of the other champions, or David Bowie for all I care."

"David Bowie is in the Slavic Underworld?" I asked.

"Focus, Aaron," Veles said. "Remember, my offer to bring you in on Epic Dungeoneering™'s upper management stands. The apocalypse is going to take some time before it gets going and you can live your entire life in luxury. Maybe an unlife afterward. The only people who don't suffer eternally among the slime and oath breakers of humanity are my followers."

"You must be very proud of your clergy," I said.

"They're a bunch of idiots, thieves, liars, and bullies," Veles said. "But it's better they work for me than against me. Besides, I don't have to care when I expend their lives for the destruction of humanity. A job that is hard to convince good men is justified. Still, I prefer to have people like you in charge. It took a lot of effort to get your family to come over to my way of thinking."

"Wait, what?" I asked, looking up.

With that Veles was gone.

"Son of a bitch," I muttered.

Jon yawned and looked around. "Okay, did you lose your soul? Did the Devil go down to Michigan?"

"No, I won," I said.

"What did you wish for?" Jon asked, suddenly excited. "Please tell me if it involved turning your close friend back into a human being."

"I don't think Stompy wants to be a human being," I said, looking at the coin in my hands. I wanted to bring back Jon, but it was too big of an issue to raise immediately, especially since the entire world (two worlds really) depended on us being able to survive this.

I also wanted to get a second opinion on this coin as I wasn't quite sure I bought Veles' statement that he was going to "play fair" now. If he was really interested in playing by the rules, he wouldn't have cheated in the first place. I got the impression the only reason I was still alive was that he really didn't think I was a threat to him right now. He was humoring us, and I hoped to change that opinion by slaying Chernabog.

I decided to take a moment to update my levels as well, already knowing what I was going to pick. In this case, I decided to pick the lesser magic of TORCHLIGHT and SILENT WALK that could be extremely useful if we went into a dungeon. I could have chosen CURE (II) or one of the attack spells but decided to go with LESSER CHARM instead. As a 3rd level spell, it could affect most humanoid individuals underneath my level. Which, if Jon was accurate, was probably most "normal" people in the Southern Kingdoms. I also decided to test my raised maximum Attribute levels by putting another point into INT.

It worked.

ARAGORN "AARON" BARTKOWSKI
LVL: 6
CLASS: UNDERMASTER SORCERER
ALIGNMENT: GRAY
AGE: 34
SEX: MALE
RACE: HUMAN
STR: 10
AGI: 10
CON: 11
INT: 19
WIS: 8
COM: 15 (16)
CHA: 13 (14)

ARMOR CLASS: 9
ATTACK: +3 (+8 to ATTACK, 1d10+5 DAM Sword [witchfire])
HEALTH: 36
DIVINITY: 2

FEAT: Taunt, Sword and Shield

SPECIAL ABILITIES: ARCANE FIRE (1d6+6 INT bonus, Eldritch Damage), BLOCK (requires shield), LESSER MAGIC (unlimited times per day)

SPELL LIST (10/4/2/1):

LESSER MAGIC EFFECTS: CLEAN SELF, CREATE FOOD, CREATE FIRE, CREATE WATER, MINOR ILLUSION, REFRESH, TELEKINESIS (1 Kilo per INT bonus), VENTRILOQUISM, MEND, TORCHLIGHT, SILENT WALK
[1] PUSH, CURE, JUMP, ARMOR
[2] WEB, ANIMAL SUMMONING

[3] SUGGESTION, LESSER CHARM

STATUS EFFECTS:

* *Alchemical Stone* (Red): +50lb carrying capacity
* **Blessing of Mokosh: +1 to COM, +1 to CHR**
* *Boots of speed*: **Double Movement Speed, Dodge Roll Bonus**
* **+1 to all Saving Throws [Divine]**

That was when Ania and the rest of the party entered into the courtyard to find me waiting, Jon taking rest on my shoulder.

"Where the hell have you been?" Ania asked.

I stared at her. "I was having a soldier's rest."

"With a goddess!" Jon said, cheerfully.

Okay, that was dickish of me, but I had to admit it felt good.

Agata looked shocked.

Ania just snorted. "Fine, don't tell us."

Okay, that worked out better in my head.

CHAPTER FORTY
THE FIRST DUNGEON

"So, I suppose the question we're all wondering is...how is sex with a goddess?" Bloodstorm asked, traveling alongside our group as we made our journey toward the Earth Temple through a backroad route that Ania had discovered while studying the abbey's maps.

The strange thing was the journey was longer and more dangerous, supposedly, than our trip so far but we encountered almost no opposition on our way. The ruined fortresses, the corpse-strewn battlefields, and the occasional hostile villages all were passed through without so much of a hint of a sword drawn. Indeed, right now, we were walking alongside the road just outside of the Earth Temple's location in some primeval forest.

If I was a man who believed in any kind of luck but bad, I would have just presumed we'd caught a break. Unfortunately, I wasn't, so I had to wonder if our lack of violent encounters was due to Mokosh helping or Veles trying to prevent us from leveling up any higher.

"That's not what we're wondering," Ania said, sarcastically. "At all."

"This could actually be important," Agata said, sounding disturbingly interested. "We could be receiving messages. What positions were involved? Did she ask you to perform any specific acts? How would you feel the blessing manifested?"

Ania stared at her sister in horror.

"What?" Agata asked. "Is this because of the rumor she's your mother?"

"She is not my mother!" Ania said. "My mother is the same as yours!"

"I'm just saying it's a legend I've heard," Agata said. "From the crow.

"The crow!?" Ania asked, appalled.

"I'm saying a lot of people have the theory from clues left in the books," Jon said. "It's up there with the theory that P+L=G."

That was Perun and Lilandra Rose being Garland's parents, which was something that everyone had figured out before the television show spoiled it.

"Mokosh is not my mother," Ania said, more softly this time.

"Yes, it's not like you have brilliant red hair while your supposed mother has black hair or the fact that your dad was known for having affairs with goddesses," Jon said. "Albeit we should both hope it's not true because then Aaron will have banged your mom and that's even worse than your sister."

"Oh God," I muttered, closing my eyes.

"He wasn't going to bang me," Agata said, frowning.

"Yeah, he has way too little tolerance for bullshit and head games," Bloodstorm said. "I, on the other hand, love both."

Agata glared at him.

"Ania's mom has got it going on," Jon started singing. "She's all I want and—"

He was interrupted by a rock knocking him off my shoulder.

"Ow!" Jon said, on the ground as we left him behind. "That could have killed me!"

"If I wanted you dead, bird, you'd be dead," Ania said.

"I'm not going to lie, I think you had that one coming, Jon," I said, pausing. "Perhaps we can discuss something else now?"

"Yeah, like what you're going to do with the resurrection coin that Veles gave you," Jon said, popping up and taking to the air before moving to the tree branches around us one by one as we passed them.

"What now?" Ania asked, blinking.

"Aaron beat Veles in a game of Pwiffle and got both a wish as well as a coin of resurrection," Jon said. "Also, fifty-thousand gold pieces that I'm sure he's going to spend on something stupid like military preparations."

"Shit, man, with that you can buy your own kingdom," Bloodstorm said. "We need to talk about upping my fee."

"I thought you said that the armor was enough to last you for a year," I said, dryly.

"That was before you became rich," Bloodstorm said. "Remember, money and friendship only don't mix if the rich one is stingy."

I laughed then shook my head. "Let me check on the castle situation first."

REBUILD DRAGON KEEP REQUIREMENTS (8/12):

* ~~Rebuild Ania's Room (cost: 100 GP)~~
* ~~Rebuild Garland's Room (cost: 200 GP)~~
* ~~Restore Drawbridge (300 GP)~~
* ~~Restore Tapestries (500 GP)~~
* ~~Restore Alchemical Lab (1000 GP)~~
* ~~Restore Moat (2000 GP)~~
* Restore Armory (2000 GP)
* Restore Blacksmith (2000 GP)
* ~~Restore Stables (5000 GP)~~
* ~~Restore Chapel (5000 GP)~~
* Restore Battlements (10,000 GP)
* Restore Dragon Pit (50,000 GP)

"Huh." I said, staring. "That's weird."

"Weird Al Yankovic and Goth Girl weird or, 'I have woken up in a bathtub with my kidney missing'?" Jon asked.

"The former, I think," I said. "The Tapestries and Alchemy Lab are paid for. So are the Stables."

"I'm responsible for those," Ania said. "The horses you forced me to bring back to Crossroad actually brought in a pretty copper. They were mostly warhorses, and I also noticed the bandits had a large chunk of viable arms as well as mail."

"I wonder where they got the postage for the latter," Jon said.

Ania rolled her eyes. "The stables were something I had to take care of before we left. I took out a 5,000-gold piece loan from Maelor the Black to cover them so we had demon steeds to transport us. He expects 10,000 gold pieces when we get back."

"You took a one hundred percent interest loan," I said.

"Yes, well, there's no dwarf banks in Crossroad," Ania said. "Usury isn't against their religion."

Jon looked over at me. "Ever wonder whether that's racist?"

"I don't know if it's racist," I said.

"Dwarves are a species not a race," Agata said. "Well, the underground miner ones."

"I'm just saying that we have actual Jewish people in Ledziania," Jon said. "Francine Dubois is, French Canadian Jewish, which is cheating."

"Cheating at *what*?" I asked, confused.

"I miss Francine," Ania muttered. "Can we get back to fixing the castle?"

"We have enough to make the Dragon Pit," I said. "Which, I assume is a pit for dragons."

"Congratulations on making use of that literally higher than humanly possible intelligence there, chief," Jon said.

"We should save that for last," Ania said. "I don't trust Dragon Keep to not be attacked again before we manage to assemble the armies to take down Veles."

"I don't think that's going to happen," I said. "Veles promised he was going to abide by the rules…and I just realized how utterly stupid that sounded coming out of my mouth."

"See, already you're making use of your 19 INT," Jon said. "Now you should put some more points into WIS."

"You think battlements will do better than dragons?" I asked, looking at Ania.

"If we had dragons, we would need a pit," Ania said, pausing, then looking at Sparky in dog form. "Dragons as in plural."

"You don't raise dragons in a dragon pit," Sparky said, surprising everyone. "That's the place you *make* dragons."

I looked at Ania.

Ania shrugged. "Dragon Keep was originally constructed when the Rose family had the job of being the Royal Dragon breeders. Dragon riding knights were able to keep the Empire and the Rus at bay as well as the demigods who rose up in Veles' name. That was centuries ago, though, and the Dragon Pit was already in ruins by our grandfather's time. If there's secrets of how to turn ordinary men and women into dragons, then the only people who know it are the gods or Queen Apollonia."

I was still confused as to how cursing people into nearly indestructible monsters that could shapeshift back into people was a curse but at least Celestyne had been unable to assume human form until Garland had helped her. Still, that seemed to be something that needed to be handled in-person. Instead, I spent the money to upgrade the Armory, Blacksmithy, and Battlements. That left us with about 36,000 GP toward fixing the Dragon Pit. Wait, no, we had to pay back Maelor, so 26,000 GP. Roughly halfway there.

REBUILD DRAGON KEEP REQUIREMENTS (11/12)

"We've made some progress in preparing for a counterattack against Veles," Ania said. "Though money and a restored castle alone isn't going to win us any wars. Still, it might keep the town safe against the next attack."

"I think you need soldiers for that and there's no more Dark Undermasters," I muttered, unfortunately bringing down her sense of accomplishment. The once-powerful order had been winnowed down to nothing thanks to the constant attacks on Crossroad. Piotr was the only one still alive, except for ones who had been on missions abroad when the attacks happened, and I doubted he would find much help against Veles with the Empire.

"One problem at a time," Ania muttered. "There are heroes out there willing to fight for the cause. There's also villains and monsters who know that their evil will be extinguished if Veles triumphs."

"You'd ally with fiends?" Agata asked.

"Yes," Ania said. "In the face of a god who wants to destroy all life on this world, any alliance is justified."

"I am starting to be more comfortable with the Imposter as leader," Agata said.

"You disagree?" Ania asked.

"The problem with allying with evil to defeat evil is that evil is an untrustworthy ally," Agata said. "It is also no stronger than good or competent. You will often find yourself betrayed and undermined at key points. Veles will always be able to provide more in bribes as well. He is, after all, the god of wealth."

Ania frowned.

"Yeah, back to the resurrection coin," Jon said. "I call dibs."

"You can't call dibs," I said.

"I call dibs," Jon said. "You need to use it to resurrect my friend, Becky."

I blinked. "You don't want to use it to resurrect yourself?"

"I'm not sure it would work," Jon said. "I'm reincarnated as a crow so I'm not technically dead. Would I like to be back to a human? Yes, absolutely. I would instantly become the ultimate badass of this group and make you my wacky sidekick."

"Uh huh," I said.

"You'd be my Robin," Jon said. "Not even Dick Grayson or the Red Hood Jason Todd but Tim Drake."

"Tim Drake is awesome," I said. "But you were saying?"

"No, you'd be Damien Wayne," Jon said, getting actually hurtful. "Anyway, Becky is dead-dead and if we bring her back then she'd be another—"

"Raven?" Ania asked.

"He just wants his friend back," I said.

"No shit," Ania muttered. "I think you shouldn't use the coin at all. Veles' gifts are poison, and I would hurl it as far as possible into the sunset."

"Uh huh," I said, pausing. I wasn't going to do that because I think we needed every possible advantage. Ania wasn't wrong, Veles couldn't be trusted. The coin was probably a trap of some kind. However, like the One Ring I'd speculated on possessing, I wasn't willing to give it up easily.

"You should use it as a backup," Bloodstorm said. "Keep it for you or one of us should things go to hell."

It was a simple but practical suggestion.

"We should use it to bring back—" Agata started speaking.

"Garland couldn't win this," Ania said. "As much as I love my brother, he was not a leader of men."

Agata looked away. "I know you're mad but—"

"We'll hold onto it for now," I interrupted. "There's no need to make a decision now. Maybe we can get someone to analyze it."

"Like a goddess?" Ania asked.

"Yeah, maybe," I said, shrugging. "I'm sure we're going to run into some more before this all ends."

"We should consult my mother," Bloodstorm said, looking at me. "You'll have to mind your manners, though. She's a daughter of Veles with his first wife but has no loyalty to her father."

"Veles is your grandfather?" Agata asked, shocked.

"My family is not a great bunch of people," Bloodstorm said.

I didn't want to put consulting with Baba Yaga on my SIDE QUEST list and was glad it didn't pop up on my bracelet. "We'll call that Plan B."

"I don't like the level of interest that Veles is showing in you, Aaron," Ania said, frowning. "I hope you know what you're doing."

"Not a clue," I admitted. "Let's just focus on the next step of our journey for now."

That was when I smelled something truly vile. It was a rancid chemical smell that made all the emptied chamber pots and death of post-siege Crossroad smell like perfume. It was also a distinctly unfantasy smell and reminded me of the time I'd gone to visit some of the still-active Rust Belt plants with my parents as a child. They'd dragged me and my sister to several protests during the Clinton years with the belief they could strike at everything from global warming to groundwater contamination.

As we passed through the last of the trees on our demon steeds, I came to a view that would have broken their hearts. There was a massive clear-cut forest with thousands of stumps spread before us. The stumps were each from trees at least a century old as modern logging equipment like bulldozers, cranes, and saw vehicles were being employed. There were several concrete buildings in the distance producing black smoke as a sickly polluted black river of sludge poured through the area, generating most of the smell.

What made the sight even worse than the kind of *Two Towers*-esque nightmare was the fact that there were also piles of bodies. Groups of elves, centaurs, satyrs, and more had been shot full of holes with modern ammunition before being burned with flamethrowers like the one I'd seen used by the giantess. There was even a couple of buckets around the bodies full of dead fairies, which would have been perversely funny if not for the fact it was a frigging genocide being carried out. Epic Dungeoneering™'s logo was on practically everything, showing they weren't just making video games these days.

The people operating all the equipment came in three groups. There were the Imperials, who were dressed in their uniforms and carrying guns around like they'd never held them before but understood the basic idea of "point and shoot." There were the actual workers with their hard hats and orange vests that didn't seem too broken up about looting fantasy land. Then there were the slaves and that was the only way I could describe them: goblins, ratkin, dwarves, trolls, and even the occasional human in chains doing drudge work. There was no sign of the elves or other massacred species, perhaps because they'd been executed as a warning to the others to stay in line.

Dominating this environmentally unfriendly vista was the one tree that wasn't harmed because it would have been impossible to harm it with tools. It was a mile tall, and no I'm not exaggerating, and as wide as a city. The Eldritch Tree reached the sky and glowed with a brilliant light that seemed somehow dimmer than it should have been. In its branches, knots, and alcoves, someone had built an extensive series of stone castles. At the base of the mammoth tree's roots, I saw a field of oil derricks at work. Somehow, I doubted they were just after oil.

"Huh," I said, staring at the sight. "I was joking when I suggested they were drilling for mana."

CHAPTER FORTY-ONE
PRISONER TRANSFER FROM CELL BLOCK 1138

"This is messed up," I said, staring at the sight of the devastated landscape. I could only imagine that it had once been a vast forest like Mirkwood or something out of a Disney movie, but it was now just an environmental horror show that made *The Lorax* look subtle.

"Each of the Elemental Temples is aligned to their specific element," Ania said. "Trees for earth, a lake for water, a cloud palace for wind, and a volcano for fire."

"Yeah, I played the first *Final Fantasy*," I replied. "It was in the break room. Francine managed to beat Chaos with four White Mages."

"Honestly, this feels more like VII, with Shin-Ra Power Company stealing all the life-stream's energy," Jon said, his tone suggesting he didn't find much funny about this either but was making the effort to joke around anyway. "It's a good thing Agata is our resident healing girl, that way we don't have to feel bad when Sephiroth kills her."

"She's alive in the reboot," I said.

"Shut up, those games do not count and will only ruin the story!" Jon said.

"This is ugly and gross," Sparky said, surveying the landscape. "We should burn all these people."

"Maybe later," I said, unwilling to take on an army even if they were scattered about the surrounding ten miles or so. "One thing I don't get, though."

"One thing?" Ania asked, clearly implying I didn't get a lot.

Which, fair enough, I didn't.

"Why is Veles doing *this*?" I asked.

"Defiling the temples is part of his plans," Agata said, shaking her head. "The atrocities he works here are necessary for him to claim the power that rightfully belongs to the Earth Mother."

"Veles is gathering all of the magic of this world so he can invade Earth," I said, making a guess. "He needs all of Mokosh's power and probably gets a boon from all the death he's causing here as well as being the god of evil."

"I mean, yeah," Ania said, sarcastically. "I thought that was obvious."

"Your obvious is probably a bit different to someone who grew up in a world where all mages are charlatans or alchemists," Bloodstorm said. "Knowing what the limits of Veles power and his ultimate aims are, though, is good. Even if we can't stop him."

I didn't much care for his defeatist talk even if, yeah, our chances weren't great. They probably hadn't been great when the first champion had been sent.

"Yeah, but wasn't Veles driven from Earth by, well, Christianity?" Jon pointed out. "I mean, not to give props to the Church but between Judaism, Islam, and Christianity's various flavors from nutty to creamy, I think capital G God has it covered for defending Earth."

"Veles implied it's a bit more complicated than that," I said.

"Which he would, because he's a fucking liar," Ania said.

"True," I conceded. "But I get the impression faith is the food of the gods but that doesn't strictly correlate to power. Veles, Perun, and Svarog were at the beginning. Way-way before religion existed and making planets so they didn't need faith to be badasses."

"So, being the most popular god just makes you the owner of all the Oreos on the planet," Jon said. "Useful but not necessarily enough to make you king."

"I dunno, man, Oreos are pretty awesome," Bloodstorm said. "I would have helped these Epic Dungeoneering™ people with their genocide for a crate of them."

I was smart enough not to respond to that. "In any case, I'm also not sure where a lot of gods fall in all of this. Veles may have led the Old Gods to Mokosh to keep their power, but they seem to be his henchmen now, crazy and working for him despite the fact they don't get anything out of it."

Veles had also implied that he, Perun, and Svarog had been the original creator deities, but I wasn't going to pay that much attention. I knew for a fact that Mythras existed because someone had been pissed off by me invoking the Christian God.

"He scammed 'em," Jon said, following my train of thought. "Still, it explains why the guy isn't invading New York with an army of skeletons. This plan has been in the works for a while, and he needs all the death as well as worship here before he goes looking for a fight on Earth with Optimus Prime."

"Optimus Prime isn't a god," I replied.

"I worshiped him as a child and even Michael Bay couldn't destroy his appeal," Jon said. "He's absolutely a god."

"Maybe that's why he's got Epic Dungeoneering™ on his side," I said, refusing to respond to that. "They could be the people he's recruited to work with him in taking over Earth from behind the scenes. Offer your average Silicon Valley oligarch immortality and you already have them on your side."

Taking over two worlds wasn't something that Veles was just doing with his army of the undead. Indeed, the army of the undead seemed to be just there as a direct instrument while he used more 'Annatar, Giver of Gifts' and 'Darth Sidious' moves behind the scenes. He didn't have to defeat the local gods of Earth, if we had any, if he killed everyone off with climate change or a nuclear war either. Hell, maybe all the zombie apocalypse movies were Veles prepping humanity for his Plan A.

"Peter Thiel is already a vampire," Jon said. "Dude drinks children's blood. But I thought Weis created Epic Dungeoneering™.

Also, I didn't think they were involved in arms trafficking or lumber. If I had, I would have invested more in their stock."

"Yeah, Karl Marx didn't mean workers buying stock in their company when he said they should seize the means of production," Bloodstorm said.

Jon shook his head. "You think too much dude."

"So, I've been told," Bloodstorm said.

"It seems Veles bought them out," I said, having already figured that out a while ago. "Though given how holding companies work, I wouldn't be surprised if it's just one part of a much-much larger empire that they're just keeping to one heraldry here. What do you think, Agata?"

"I think you are focused on trying to discern the plans of gods when the only thing that's important is killing the one nearby," Agata said.

"I'm surprised you didn't say the conversation was blasphemous," I said.

"Oh, it is, but you slept with my goddess so I'm not sure how I can make that accusation," Agata said. "Also, I think you may be on to something with Ania being Mokosh's daughter."

"Oh, fuc—" Ania started to say.

"I have a plan on getting in there," I said, looking up at the massive tree.

The Eldritch Tree was one of the legendary landmarks of this world, for obvious reasons, and the first of the plants brought by the gods from their domain. It had been the obvious focus of the Eldritch Ring games, and it was weird seeing how much Weis had included from them here as well as in the books. In addition to putting lies to any creativity he might have had, it meant that we should probably watch out for giant monsters that you can't fat roll from. It also meant I'd have to avoid Invaders and get some more Summons.

"I'm going to hate it, aren't I?" Ania asked.

I shrugged. "Depends on how much you like depending on your sister?"

"What?" Agata asked.

It took about three or four hours to really get it right, but we managed to decorate Agata as a death lord with minor illusions that lasted an hour when done by me (and about twenty minutes when done by Agata). We put the *iron crown of domination* on her head and did our best to turn her hair white, make her skin look saggy, her eyes sunken, and her Mokosh robes look like the tattered remains of royalty. She changed her staff to look like a sinister ruby-eyed serpent made of gold was crawling around her staff.

We had several uniforms of Veles-aligned mercenaries that Bloodstorm and Ania had managed to acquire from departing caravans. You could tell they were Veles aligned because they involved a lot of skull motifs and bone decorations. I tried not to think about the fact they'd probably killed a lot more people than the guards themselves but maybe they'd also released some of the slaves. Rather than substitute them for our actual armor, I decided to use them as a basis for our magic hiding our true identities. Basically, models for us to work from.

Several times, we'd had to start over since the minor illusions had started over, and we were trying to get the details perfect. There were also the slight issues that Bloodstorm and Ania were not the kind of people that the Empire recruited for their forces. Bloodstorm for being an ogre-elvish vampire hybrid while Ania was, and I know this is going to shock you, a woman. I remember many a forum conversation over whether this was realistic.

"So, I'm the Chewbacca here?" Bloodstorm asked, wearing a pair of illusionary manacles. We would have to start the illusions all over again soon, but I had managed to get the look I was going for down.

"Yes," I said, acknowledging Bloodstorm had seen *A New Hope*.

"Can I speak, or do I make bear growls?" Bloodstorm asked.

"Only snarl and look savage," I said.

"I'm just trying to get my motivation," Bloodstorm said. "Am I a resistance fighter or a savage animal? Am I going to be a gladiator or work slave? These details matter."

"No, they don't," Jon said, sitting on a stump. So far, we'd managed to sit on the edge of the forest for hours without being found.

"I am the Witch Queen Scylla, apprentice to the Hellmaster Castor the Doommaster, brother of Hellmaster Pollux the Vermin Lord," Agata said. "I am not a member of the Thirteen but related to the Hellmasters via their mortal relations in the previous Magyar royal dynasty of the Hellmasters. The ones overthrown for black magic and Veles worship. Like all Magyar royals, I am, of course, a snobbish bitch—"

"However, will you pull that off," Ania muttered, reading my Epic Reader. Somehow, she'd lifted it out of my extra-dimensional bag. The one that still needed enhanced carrying capacity for some reason.

"But this is just playing to stereotypes," Agata said. "Not all Magyars are bad, you understand, only its current royals who willingly joined the Empire and betrayed—"

"Can we stop the racism against Hungarians?" I asked, really wishing everyone would stop going off script.

"What's a Hungarian?" Agata asked. "Anyway, it's not racism because—"

"Magyars are absolutely a race," I said, pausing. "I think."

It was like having a conversation with my great aunt Hilda. I hadn't even heard of half the peoples she was prejudiced against.

"My dentist was Hungarian," Jon said. "So, I'm good. So, what books are you reading, Ania?"

"The Dark Undermaster novels," Ania said, dryly.

"Oh," I said, wondering if that was a good thing or not. "What part are you up to?"

"The part where I lose my virginity to Thistle," Ania said, incredibly annoyed. "It's very…descriptive."

"Ah," Jon said.

"I was sixteen," Ania said.

"Not as bad as Book Daenerys and Drogo," Jon said, nodding. "I'm shutting up now."

"I should point out I was a teenager when I read those books," I said, as if it made any difference.

"That reassures me you weren't using these books for sexual pleasure," Ania said.

No, that had been the fan art, but I wasn't going to say that. "They aged you up in the show."

"Halt!" a voice spoke nearby and made me realize we probably should have retreated deeper into the woods.

I turned around to see a group of Imperial storm knights on red stallions, the creatures treated with a variety of alchemical solutions and stones to the point that they looked barely like normal animals anymore and had been drugged to the gills to remove their fear of death. Maybe it was stereotypical that the bad guys abused animals (and it's not like castration was a particularly good sign of how normal people treated horses) but it offended the part of my brain that emphathized with animals more than people.

The leader of the Storm Knights was a sight to behold with golden armor seemingly molded around him, a flowing red cape, and laurels around his head that marked him as a Lord Centurion of the Emperor. He looked like he'd escaped from *Warhammer 40K,* and his eyes were full of the crazy that came from devoting oneself to the Imperial Cult. On his back was a greatsword that looked three times the size of a normal one and more at home in an anime than a grounded fantasy series like the one I was supposedly in. He was also larger than most human beings, almost the size of Bloodstorm without his horns, and I suspected he was on as many alchemical potions as his horses.

The Imperial Knights behind him looked considerably more "normal" as well as slightly nervous, as if they understood the man beside them only barely qualified as human. The Lord Centurions were the Empire's answer to the Dark Undermasters but had gotten themselves severely affected by something during their private rituals to Mythras and supposedly controlled the Imperial court from behind the scenes.

"I am halting," I said, raising my hands. Which I just realized might be considered a hostile act in a world with magic.

"I am Lord Centurion Gaius Andronicus," the man said, somehow managing to perfectly combine classicism and militaristic disdain in one sneer. "You have approached a special project area of the Holy Empire and must either retreat or face the wrath of our divine wrath."

The wrath of our divine wrath? Seriously?

"They have seen too much already, milord," one of the storm knights said. "We should take them to the slave pits or execute them here."

"They look *ridiculous*," another of the storm knights said. "Like troubadours pretending to be servants of the nonexistent god of these savages."

Wow, they had guys who didn't believe in Veles or the Old Gods working at one of their elemental temples. That was some Flat Earther bullshit.

"I am—" Agata started to do her song and dance routine that I expected would be a complete failure.

So, I decided to interrupt. I adopted an accent that I tried to do as English but ended up somewhere wandering from Boston to Australia to Victorian orphan waif. "Indeed, sir, we are troubadours that have been summoned by the Skull Masked Lord to create a play in his honor!"

I waved my hand and cast LESSER CHARM on the Lord Centurion, hoping my enhanced intelligence would give me enough bonus to overcome the fact this guy was a veteran.

"The Skull Masked Lord?" The Lord Centurion said. "You mean that idiot popinjay we're ordered to follow?"

I cast SUGGESTION by waving my hand. "Aiye, indeed, good sir. He wishes us to make a great story about the glories of his triumphs against the forces opposing the Empire."

"This man is an idiot and a liar, sir!" one of the lightning knights said. "He also consorts with nonhuman filth. I suggest take the women and—"

The lightning knight proceeded to hold out his hand, teleporting his great sword into his hand with some kind of magic before severing off the man's head in one blow. "I have given you too much leave to complain, grouse, and undermine my authority."

Okay, this guy apparently did go to the same school of leadership as Darth Vader. The other storm knights looked horrified as their comrade's headless body fell to the ground. No one made a move, not even the horses who just stood there as if mesmerized. The Lord Centurion rested the sword on his shoulder as it glowed with glowing runes that leaked snowflakes on the ground as if it was a miniature storm.

"I am a good friend with the local warlord, Valentin," the Lord Centurion said. "I am quite confident that you being hired to make a play for him is the sort of thing he would do. If you are not, then, well, you will find yourself bitterly regretting this lie. I will deliver you to the throne room directly."

All my group looked at me with anger.

Whoops.

CHAPTER FORTY-TWO
THE ILL-CONCEIVED RESCUE

Well, I done fucked up.

Just about everyone in my party was giving me the stink eye and I had to admit they were probably right to do so. I'd overreached by believing I should oversee the diplomatic elements of our plan and had cast aside all the ideas we'd been working on for an improvised Hail Mary plan. Said Hail Mary plan had been intercepted and now we were on our way to meet with Valentin and what was either his dragon or the army of elite soldiers in his ranks.

Great job, Aaron.

Right now, we were presently in an open carriage elevator that had a set of electrical controls affixed to a wooden cage. We were rising from the base to the top of what appeared equivalent to a five-hundred story building. Except, the 'building' was a giant tree. It was kind of funny to speculate on the fact that the Norse believed Yggdrasil was an ash while it was an oak tree in Slavic mythology. It looked like the Slavs won this one. Okay, maybe it was just funny to me.

We'd been forced to leave our demon steeds behind at the tree's base but that didn't really matter since they all disappeared into our hand runes. My charm magic seemed to be holding since that startled the Imperial storm knights, but Gaius seemed uninterested. Mostly, he'd spent the entirety of our journey lecturing us on local history from an Imperial perspective.

"The Peace Bringing Mission is one that I, of course, volunteered for once the Emperor declared that he would be supporting Queen Apollonia for rulership of these miserable peasant hills," Gaius said. "Many people believe the Queen's son, Cezary, is actually the bastard of our glorious ruler. However, I do not believe this, if not for the reason that it would put the succession of the Emperor's nephew in doubt."

"Yeah, I've heard that story before," I said.

Prince Cezary Piast-Jagiellon was known as the Demon Child and had future serial killer written all over him. Well, would have had future serial killer written on him if not for the fact he was already killing people as a child. He had six bodies to his name by the time he was twelve and had schemed to "deflower" Agata before she was forcibly married off to Ivan Crookback then Radu the Impaler. He was about seventeen now according to my calculations and probably even more of a monster.

One of the speculations in the fandom, because we had nothing better to do for the past decade, was that Cezary's inhuman and cruel behavior wasn't due to natural psychosis but being the son of Veles versus Emperor Constantine the Black. Personally, I questioned this theory after meeting Veles. Veles was undoubtedly evil, but I didn't see him as the sort of guy who pushed his nanny out a window at age eight.

"Did you?" Gaius asked. "Honestly, getting rid of their superstitious culture and replacing it with proper moral values is, of course, tedious work. The aberrant sexual practices and distorted bloodlines of these Southerners is something that will take many generations to breed out. My men, of course, are encouraged to help the process along. Mongrel Imperials are better than native breeds."

We were already close to a thousand feet high and still going. Strangely, it didn't seem to be getting colder or the air thinner as the Eldritch Tree warmed us with its light as well as fed us with its air. Still, I could see the light flickering at times like a bad lightbulb.

I tried to figure out which of my friends would react first. Agata looked like she was about to unleash on the Lord Centurion at any second now while Bloodstorm was still pretending to be a dumb prisoner. Ironically, it was Ania who looked the most comfortable with a completely even expression on her face. That was the one that made me nervous. It could mean she was keeping things professional or was about to go on a killing spree.

"And you're willing to take orders from Valentin?" I asked, making my first mistake.

Gaius grabbed me by the throat and held me above his head like Darth Vader. "We do not take orders from the Skull King. He is a pagan fool lost in his own sloth and gluttony."

"My apologies," I said, dryly, unable to add milord.

He dropped me on my knees.

"Apologies accepted," Gaius said. "Truth be told, my grandfather rode with Sulla Magnus. He was a man who understood the way to defeat the heathens at their own game. He allied with those who raised the banner of the Death's Head and harnessed the magics of the Twisted Gods. They spread plague among the inferiors and almost united the Southern Kingdoms."

The storm knights looked as nervous and disgusted as I must have. I got the impression whoever this Sulla Magnus was, he was not particularly well liked even within the Empire. "The Death's Head."

"Nazis," Ania clarified. "We had some of them in the 1940s too."

I was always confused why a society that didn't have Christianity used the Roman Christian calendar but that was the least weird thing I'd had to rationalize since my coming to Fantasy World. Seeing that Gaius Andronicus was in front of the open carriage of the elevator, I made a decision.

"PUSH!" I shouted, sending him back only a step.

Ah crap.

"Traitor!" Gaius shouted, summoning his sword again.

That was when Bloodstorm kicked him in the chest with enough force that I wanted to shout, "This is Sparta!" It proved much more effective in sending the Lord Centurion over the side of the railing. Given we were already a thousand feet in the air, I imagined he had quite a bit of time to cast a spell to save himself if he had one memorized.

He didn't.

I was promptly stabbed in the back by one of the storm knights with a gladius, which was a bit like being shot by a Stormtrooper in *Star Wars*. It was just embarrassing. Thankfully, the magic in my armor and the fact I was literally empowered by the bracelet to be harder to kill kept it from being a fatal blow. Still, it hurt like hell and wasn't helped when I banged my head back against the guy's face. Headbutts turned out to be terrible ideas in combat even if they were preferable to death.

"Arcane Fire!" I said, blasting the guy in the face and sending him screaming back through the other side of the elevator that was now rocking due to the fighting going on inside.

Two of the storm knights tried to repeat Bloodstorm's action with Gaius by tackling him over the side of the elevator, only for Bloodstorm to grab both by the necks then squeeze. There was a sickening crack as the two storm knights fell to the ground, both of their necks broken simultaneously. That left two more storm knights, but I shouldn't have been surprised to see their corpses on the ground with both the remaining troopers' throats slit by Ania. Blood spilled across the floor of the elevator and out the sides. The elevator was still a rocking bit but thankfully slowing down.

"Okay, a warning next time when you dramatically change plans," Ania said, turning to her side.

Agata threw up over the side.

"I guess not," Ania said.

"Just a little," Agata said, looking down and throwing up again. "I don't like heights or moving at great heights."

Jon, who was sitting on the top of the cage, looked down. "Do you think that will kill anyone that it hits? I mean, assuming Gaius and the other guy didn't land on them first."

I moved to the elevator's controls, which were a series of levers rather than buttons and pulled us to a stop. We stopped between floors.

"Thank you," Agata said, pausing. "Oh, right you're bleeding."

I'd barely noticed when Agata cast her CURE spell on me. One of the benefits of your HP going up seemed to be that you really did start to become a guy who could shrug off blows like an action movie hero. I cast MEND on my armor after she was done to seal up the hole.

"Was it the mention of Nazis who set you off?" Bloodstorm asked. "I asked because I need to know if you're going to go ballistic on any cottage core people we might find."

"I was improvising," I said, taking a deep breath.

"Yeah, well don't do that," Ania said, looking around. "Though I suppose that we're at least in the Earth Temple. Unfortunately, they're probably going to notice the bodies on the ground and probably want to bring this elevator back down. Then alarms will go up and we're dead. So, I guess what I'm saying is, good job, Aaron."

"We need to get to the Dungeon," I said, pausing. "The priestesses are our priority now."

"We need to slay Chernabog," Ania said. "Impossible as that may seem right now."

"The dungeon is three levels up," Jon said.

I looked up. "How do you know?"

"I've been here before," Jon said, looking away. "I failed in my run to stop Chernabog but I made it this far. There were no priestesses to rescue this time, though. I think I had the idea of organizing a slave revolt, but I don't think that ended well for anyone."

If a crow could express regret in his features, then he was doing it.

"I know how to handle this," Agata said. "Move us to the dungeon, Aaron."

"We need to regroup and—" Ania started to say.

"Trust me," Agata said.

It was clear Ania didn't. Instead, she just pinched the bridge of her nose. "Sure, why not. This is a disaster already. Let's have everyone decide they're a cunning mastermind."

"It gets funnier when you realize that due to divine tampering, Aaron is one of the smartest people on the planet," Jon said. "I know it makes me sad too."

"Yes, yes, it's Let's Shit on Aaron Day," I said, starting the elevator again.

"You should go by Aragorn," Agata said, adjusting her crown. "It sounds much nicer when spoken aloud."

I was hesitant to put my faith in any of the group other than Ania, or Bloodstorm, or Jon, or myself. Which, uh, okay, really narrowed it down who my actual problem was with. It was embarrassing because Agata had thrown down a lot out of magic smackdowns since I'd met her a couple of weeks ago.

Agata certainly wasn't the helpless damsel she'd been in the previous books but that had been when she was a child so why was I holding that against her anyway? Maybe her attitude toward me hadn't been the most welcoming but we were all making adjustments. Besides, she'd been noticeably friendlier since we'd left the Abbey. I tried not to think me banging her goddess was the reason.

"I'm going to trust you," I said, taking a deep breath. "How about you, Ania?"

"I trust her every bit as much as I trust you, planning wise, at least," Ania said, sounding like she was both paying me a compliment and backhandedly insulting at the same time. "So, don't screw this up, Agata."

The elevator arrived at the level that Jon identified as the dungeon, and it was one of the lowest levels of the tree branches that were capable of holding up a stone city. I knew that because it was the first level with a stone city built on top of it.

The interior was a long and depressing series of cells stretching forward from the entrance onward, little cubby holes that had once been rooms for individuals hoping for communion with the Eldritch Tree turned into cells with iron bars marked with magical seals. The seals looked like translucent heraldry made of blood and hung over the bars like a hologram projected into the air.

I didn't get a chance to look at the cells long, but I could see there were a lot of women in them.

It was noticeable that most of them looked, well, uh, like they'd stepped out of an anime convention. Blue, pink, and glowing hair was very common as was garments that seemed woven from starlight or mist. Magic was the great equalizer when it came to appearances, at least assuming you questioned why they all looked like models with rare exceptions.

Unfortunately, the sexiness was rather spoiled by the fact that quite a few of them also looked like they'd been through the ringer. A few had been beaten, others had their fingernails removed, and others were soaked in a way that suggested a primitive form of waterboarding (probably closer to witch dunking). Not all of them had seemingly been tortured but all of them had been stuffed into these cells for the past three days with no changes of clothing or access to their magic. Each of the women had iron collars around their neck, gags in their mouth, and their hands wrapped in iron wire that was designed to suppress their powers.

This wasn't a prison without guards, though. Worse, they were nasty guards as they were all Knights of Veles, black armored plate-mail wearing assholes who were infused with the power of undeath while still alive. All of them had helmets that had cross slits in them that peered into Stygian darkness. I'd never read about them in the books, but they were mini-bosses spread around *Eldritch Ring*'s levels.

The Knights of Veles were surrounded by a bunch of regular guards as well, but it looked like about twelve Darth Vader-looking guys next to dozens of regular guards, with the place having each cell with two or three guards. We were probably outnumbered, oh, say, 40 to one. Which, aside from being an awesome Sabaton song, meant we were utterly screwed.

Until Agata lifted her hand while pointing at them.

"Kill each other," Agata said, her voice filled with a horrific certainty. The crown on her head glowed and a black flame encircled a good half of the ones before us. The Knights of Veles seemed to mostly shake it off and drew their witchfire blades that were all too similar to my own. The ones around her, though, were not and immediately descended on their surrounding warriors.

"This is interesting," Ania said, pulling out her blades.

"Hold back," I said, holding my hand in front of her. "Domination spells get broken if you attack."

Ania looked confused.

"Kill each other," Agata said, repeated. "Kill each other."

The Crown of Domination was a powerful artifact, and it was interesting to see its power spammed repeatedly as the Knights of Veles eventually fell under its power. The ordinary guards died first, and the Knights of Veles killed half of their own before seemingly finally throwing off their mental control.

"Well, that was a good plan," Bloodstorm said, hefting his ax. "But I think we're still screwed."

I lifted my sword and pulled up my shield. "I'm prepared to fight."

"Don't fight, come up with a plan, idiot!" Ania said.

"Now that doesn't make any sense," Jon said. "If he's an idiot why have him come up with the plan!"

"Shut up!" Ania said.

"WEB!" I shouted, aiming not at the Knights of Veles themselves but the hallway between us and filling it with massive amounts of prehensile webbing. The knights started hacking through it with ease.

"That's not going to hold them," Bloodstorm said, frowning.

"It's not meant to," I said, looking at Sparky the dog. "Dracarys."

"What?" Sparky said.

"Burn em!" I shouted, pointing.

"Oh!" Sparky said, turning back into a dragon. His dragonfire opened just as the first of the knights got himself free and the hallway before us became an inferno. There were screams and shouts as the knights were cooked alive in their armor. For good measure, Agata released her lightning bolt that surged through three of them. The remaining two knights standing didn't bother to attack. They just sort of stood there motionless as Ania peppered them with light arrows until they died, perhaps just being determined to die on their feet. Bloodstorm shook his head, seemingly annoyed he hadn't gotten involved.

"I need a crossbow," Bloodstorm muttered. "Arrows are Ania's thing."

"How about throwing axes?" Jon said.

Bloodstorm looked thoughtful. "Yeah, or like an ax I throw, and it comes back."

"Or a hammer!" Jon said. "A small hammer you could fit in the palm of your hand and throw before it comes back to you."

"You don't think that's too cliche?" Bloodstorm asked.

Ania rolled her eyes.

"You know, I'm starting to miss the undead," I said, choking on the smell of burned flesh and covering my mouth.

Agata removed the Crown of Domination and tossed it to one side, disgusted. "That was everything it had. Let's get my sisters free. If they didn't know we were here before, they certainly do now."

"That was pretty brutal," I muttered, thinking about the girl who liked knights and fairy stories from the books.

"It's war," Agata said, stepping over the dead.

CHAPTER FORTY-THREE
LAST-MINUTE REVELATIONS

The dungeon was thankfully easy to seal off from the rest of the tree city (involving door locks and bars over its two entrances). Agata used Arcane Fire to send the elevator spiraling down to the ground when it started coming up with a bunch of reinforcements. Honestly, I had to check her Alignment Points to make sure she hadn't taken a turn to Black.

The results were...confusing.

Aaron (3rd Alignment Level, Grey)
Agata (3rd Alignment Level, White)
Ania (3rd Alignment Level, Black)
Bloodstorm (1st Alignment Level, Black)
Sparky (0 Level Alignment Level, Unaligned)

Apparently, Agata had gotten 30+ points on her alignment bar toward White for using the *iron crown of domination*. It was an indication that "White" alignment might not be a 1:1 with good anymore than Black was with evil. On the other hand, I wasn't sure what it was meant to represent and why I was so high with Grey.

I decided to check what my experience points were and hoped that I'd gotten enough from this horrifying massacre to reach level 7. At this point, I was desperate for every possible advantage we could get.

SIDE QUESTS COMPLETED: RESCUE THE PRIESTESSES 1/1

+ 10,000 EXP (Rescue All of the Priestesses)
+ 500 EXP (Lord Centurion)
+ 500 EXP (storm knights)
+ 12000 (Knights of Veles)
+ 10000 (regular guards)
+ *Priestess of Mokosh Set*
+ *Paladin of Mokosh Set*
+ *Greatsword of frost +3*
+ 10,000 GP

Level 6 to 7
58000/60000

Dammit, I was just below 7th level. The irony was that I was leveling up massively fast by any stretch of the imagination, but it wasn't enough to keep us alive. It made me wonder if I should have searched out more Marks of the Champion because that divine power would have felt really good right now.

"You should check to see if you've leveled up, Agata," Ania muttered, looking at her own bracelet.

"What now?" Agata asked, looking confused.

"It's a long story and I'll walk you through the quick version of it," Ania said, gesturing for me to follow. "Come here, Aaron, there's something I want to show you."

I tried to do so but as soon as I made a motion, it felt like I was carrying around a sack of rocks and each step felt like I was walking through water. It made me look like I was duck walking, which confused Ania and Agata both by their looks.

"I think I'm over-encumbered," I said, blinking. "No, I don't know why I didn't notice until I started moving."

"Give me the great sword," Bloodstorm said, offering his hand.

"You should also switch over to the *Paladin of Mokosh Set*," Jon said, speaking in a tone that suggested mirth. "That stuff is unique being a light armor that has medium armor protection. Plus, it's really good against spells."

"Drop the leather armor from my father's shop," Bloodstorm said. "We can pick it up later or not. We've got bigger fish to fry."

"Easy come, easy go, I guess." I adjusted my equipment on the Mark of the Champion's interface. I suddenly felt naked for a few seconds as I shifted between my current armor then the *Paladin of Mokosh Set*.

It was very…unique.

And tight.

Ania and Agata stared.

Ania looked like she was ready to burst out laughing while Agata tilted her head to one side. Jon did laugh and fell out of the air, rolling around on the ground. Bloodstorm gave a sideways glance at the others before shrugging as if he wasn't sure what was so funny about it.

The armor, if you could call it that, was extremely tight and made of a form-fitting molded substance that seemed designed to give the impression of a much shapelier physique than mine. It was very tight around certain areas, had a cowl, and came with a cape. After a few seconds of moving around and hearing the movement of my legs against the crotch area, I took a deep breath. It was still grey with, I kid you not, lots of purples worked into it.

"I'm Batman, aren't I?" I asked, my voice lowering an octave. "The Joel Schumacher one."

"Mokosh knows what she likes, I guess," Jon said, "Be glad it doesn't include bat nipples."

"It is very…" Agata said. "No, I don't know why my goddess is having you dress like this but you wouldn't be the first she has given a costume."

"Do I need to be worried?" Ania asked, taking valuable time from our rescue to make fun of me. A rare occurrence for her but one I doubted she could have ignored the opportunity for under these conditions. "Is your goddess going to be jealous?"

"The goddess is never jealous," Agata said, haughtily. "If he chooses to pursue the path of the Paladin of Mokosh, it will become his responsibility to pleasure as many women as possible."

Jon jumped back to his feet. "Okay, now it's not funny anymore."

Bloodstorm chortled.

"No," I said. "I'm not interested."

Everyone stared at me as if they didn't believe it.

I gestured to the cells around us, full of priestesses who universally shared a look of 'weren't you supposed to be rescuing us.' "I think we have more important things to worry about now. Also, it's the difference between liking a ham sandwich and eating them every day for every meal. It's a lot of responsibility."

"Wouldn't clams be a better metaphor?" Jon said, not helping our situation. "Also, only you would find a divine mandate to be a boy toy a responsibility not a privilege."

I shook my head. "I have a world to save. Two in fact."

Nothing against sex work, just not gonna making a profession from it.

Or religion.

"You've certainly found time to work and play," Ania said. "I'm sure you'll eventually get that dragon Pwiffle card."

"The dragon Pwiffle card isn't a sex card," I said. "You get it for siding with the Dragon Queen in the Rebellion Expansion."

Jon paused before releasing a torrent of profanity. "Dammit! I knew I was forgetting something."

Ania directed me back to where she'd been gesturing in the first place. It was, of all things, an office someone had set up in the dungeon with a set of computers as well as monitors. They didn't look like modern ones, the monitors being black and white while the computers were all big blocky ones like you'd have seen on old episodes of Seventies *Doctor Who*. However, the very fact it existed in a setting not too dissimilar to *The Lord of the Rings* was its own argument and probably confusing as hell for longtime readers of Weis' books.

There was a dead goblin in a white security guard's uniform and olive-colored pants sitting in a wooden chair. The goblin's skin was the shade of his pants, and a spear was sticking out of his chest. He looked like he'd stepped out of *Shadowrun* more than Weis' books, being an obviously fantasy-looking monster in an otherwise mundane profession. Guy had a bunch of keys on his belt and even the stereotypical rent a cop pot belly.

Goblins in Weis' world was something of a deconstruction of their role in other settings but not exactly a reversal either. They were green-skinned guys with canines that usually extended out in front of their slips from their upper or lower jaws that worshiped Veles along with the other gods of darkness.

Ironically, this didn't really make them that much worse than human beings. Goblin religion consisted of, "the gods are bastards. Don't piss them off." Which, as theologies went, wasn't at least internally consistent. They came in two varieties: the ones who lived underground while clashing with the ratkin or dwarves and those who were tribal peoples on the surface that struggled not to get their land stolen by humans.

The creation of the Death Mountains in the Eighties by Perun's death had done a lot for opening the goblins to having their own nation and much-wider interaction with the surface world. It also meant that Veles was directly controlling quite a few of the tribal councils and forcing them to participate in his war. Weis may have had put the goblins as the mooks for the Dark Lord, but he never forgot they were as much slaves as anyone else in his armies. The guy even had a little nametag that said, DAVI JO'HNSON. Which was ridiculous enough to make me laugh.

"What am I looking for?" I asked, trying to figure out where the power came from and whether it had a connection to any other systems spread throughout this gigantic tree.

I was confused as to why there weren't a bunch of klaxons blaring or trumpets announcing that Princess Leia was about to escape. I was half-expecting someone to detonate a bunch of explosives in the cells as well. Weis was just the kind of author to turn victory into ash whenever things were looking too good. It was possible that the city wasn't populated with nearly as many soldiers or personnel as it looked like from the outside and the dead bodies hadn't yet attracted the attention we'd expected. The computer here didn't necessarily mean they had, for example, cellphones or even walkie talkies. It didn't necessarily mean they didn't, though, and depending on slowness of communication among the enemy seemed like a very bad idea.

"I was curious if you knew anything about...this," Ania said, pushing the goblin out of the chair.

"I'm not a hacker," I muttered, sitting down and noticing that the security guard was still logged on. All the writing was in goblin, but it magically turned into English when I looked at it, which might have been a function of the computers or my bracelets. A few seconds later, all the blood runes on the cells vanished as well as the iron doors swinging opened.

"You sure?" Ania asked. "You seem to have hacked this problem to pieces."

It was a rare compliment. "There was a folder that said PRISON COMMANDS with MAGIC RUNS ON/OFF."

I didn't mention that it was right above PORN, which had a dozen subfolders sorted by GOBLIN, ELF, LESBIAN, GAY and GAY LESBIAN GOBLIN ELF. Mostly because Jon would demand we investigate. I mean, I had questions to but probably not the same ones as Jon would. Like, do they film it here and with what?

Agata and Bloodstorm immediately went to try to remove the collars off as many of the Sisters of Mokosh as possible. Almost immediately, they received a verbal tongue lashing for the length of time it had taken to get them loose. Honestly, I felt it was a tad ungrateful but was more concerned with figuring out what to do next.

That was when I saw something that caused me to stop dead in my tracks. Up on the top of the security station computer was a framed photograph. I grabbed at the photo with my hand like I was catching lightning and stared at the sight with an intensity that threatened to burn a hole through the frame.

"What's wrong?" Ania asked, confused.

Jon flew over to sit on my shoulder and peer at what I was looking at. "Son of a bitch."

The photo was the late Davi with three people I recognized. The first of them was Barbara Wojciechowski, holding up a dragon hand puppet on her left hand. Louis Tolliver was beside her, looking unhappy, possibly because Davi had his arm draped over his shoulder. However, it was the fourth person in the photo that drew my attention most.

Alek Bartkowski.

Alek Bartkowski pretty much looked like a slightly younger version of myself, about two years difference. A slightly younger version of myself who was convinced he was Solid Snake. He was wearing gray camouflage pants, a gray tank top, dog tags, and a bandana. He'd also grown a slight beard even as he was staring at the camera like he was about to stab it. I wasn't exaggerating either, since he was carrying a combat knife in one hand.

"My brother and cousin," I said, shaking my head.

"And you give me crap about incest," Ania said, disgusted.

"No, not like that," I said, annoyed.

"No offense, Aaron but there's not many ways to interpret brother-cousin," Jon said.

I rolled my eyes. "Short-short version. Yes, I'm adopted. My aunt, Elizabeta, or Betty as she preferred to be called, got knocked up at sixteen. She wanted to go to university. That was fine with me. My parents adopted me instead. They were much older and financially stable as well as going to America. They also wanted kids. Two years later, she got knocked up again, but it was with her husband. She dropped out of college to be a trad wife. By then, I was living in America. My sister was born about the same time to my adoptive parents."

"That is a distressingly normal explanation," Jon said, "But I'll still refer to the fact that you have a mother-aunt now."

"I'm sorry," Ania said. "It must be hard to know you'll have to kill him."

"Wait, what?" I asked. That was when I noticed Alek was wearing one of the Marks of the Champion. Goddammit. That was what Veles had meant about corrupting my family.

Before I could explain to Ania I wasn't killing my cousin, incredibly poor decisions as he might have made, all the monitors on the security station started showing a test pattern before switching to an image of Valentin. He had his skull mask on and was framed in close-up.

"Hey Aaron!" Valentin said, his voice muffled by the helmet. "Don't bother responding. I can't hear you. I know you're in the dungeon, though, and I wanted to let you know I respect you managed to make it through most of Act I. You're never going to make it to Chernabog, though."

I stared at him. "I wonder if they've got a tech guy to take care of this or some wizard decided to put his image in the machines."

The image slid out and I saw Valentin was standing next to another dragon. This one was far more masculine seeming than Eva Poppy: bulky, muscular, and covered in armored plates up its back like a stegosaurus (or Godzilla). The dragon even had a kind of mustache with tendrils coming out of the sides of its face. Was it Boris Poppy? Maybe. But it seemed like I was meeting a lot of dragons lately.

Amazingly, though, that was not the most important part of the message being sent. No, that was the fact that Valentin was holding a German Luger to the side of a child's head. It was Georgie, my nephew. The fourteen-year-old with brown hair and green eyes, trembled in Valentin's grip with his lip quivering in terror.

"You've probably figured out your family has some special genes," Valentin said. "I'd like to say I hate doing this but, honestly, I'm pretty psyked about it. Children may not provide much EXP but they're easy kills."

Jon stared at the sight. "Crap."

"Come down to the heart branches where the sacred fire is kept," Valentin said. "Agata knows the way. We'll finish this. I promise you that no one will interfere with your passage because I want to rip your heart out and present it to Veles myself. You have ten minutes before I ventilate the kid and come in after you."

The image cut out.

"Damn," I muttered.

"I hate to be the one to bring this up but you can't turn yourself over to Valentin," Ania started to explain. "Not only would it not guarantee your nephew's safety but there's the needs of millions, possibly billions—"

"He doesn't have my nephew," I said, cutting her off.

"What?" Ania asked, blinking.

"My nephew, sitting still and serious with a gun to his head? In a giant tree by a guy dressed like General Kael? *Next to a dragon*?" I asked, shaking my head. "Only someone who had no experience with boys his age, let alone ones like Georgie, would assume he wouldn't be freaking out with joy over how cool all of this is."

"He wouldn't be scared?" Ania asked, obviously thinking back to her own horrifying experience with the Poppy Betrayal.

"Scared yes but impressed," I said. "He'd think it was awesome."

So would I at his age. Given I'd jumped in feet first to fighting a war on a (technically) alien planet, probably at my age as well.

"Scaresome," Jon said.

"Uh huh," Ania said, clearly not convinced.

"Your nephew sounds like we'd be friends," Sparky said, having assumed a human boy's form of about fourteen or fifteen years of age. He had milk chocolate brown skin and short hair with a red dyed shirt as well as lizard skin pants. They were something I suspected your typical peasant boy wouldn't be able to afford but he was a dragon, and it was probably made by his magic. I had to wonder if the clothes were conjured by the sorcery or part of his skin, though. Maybe dragons molted? Also, him appearing as a boy made me uncomfortable since he might be biologically not that much younger than Agata and Ania, but his mind was clearly in a very different place. I needed to sit down and have a conversation with the others about what to do with Sparky. However useful his dragon fire was, I wasn't about to employ a child soldier.

Okay, I needed to focus.

"Are you willing to bet his life on that?" Ania asked.

Given I was assuming Valentin had known we would go for the priestesses and probably planted the photo, I was risking a lot on the fact that I didn't believe in narrative contrivance.

Or destiny.

"Yes," I said, tapping the side of my head. "I have a plan."

CHAPTER FORTY-FOUR
MY PLAN SUCKS

Much to my surprise, Valentin did live up to his word that no one would interfere with our departure from the dungeon. Which was good because we ended up passing a veritable menagerie of horrific creatures and forces that would have made a damn impressive set of encounters to get through. Indeed, it was the biggest sign that the entire game was rigged that the best way to survive any of this was to simply bypass it. I had no doubt that Valentin intended to betray everyone, probably slaughter the witches once we left, but Agata seemed to have made her own plans with the Great Mother before we left. I had no idea what those plans were, apparently being blessed by their goddess wasn't exactly rare, but I hoped they pulled it off.

Because I was only about six percent sure of my plan.

"Does your plan involve pushing him off the top of the tree?" Jon asked as stood in another elevator, deeper in the tree branches. "Because I don't think he's going to fall for that one again."

"No," I said.

"Does it involve appealing to his humanity, so he sacrifices himself while throwing Chernabog down a reactor shaft?" Jon asked. "Because he's not your brother-cousin."

I sighed. "You're never going to let me live that one down, are you?"

"Nope!"

"I'm disappointed your family is involved with the incest too, Aaron," Bloodstorm said, holding Gaius' great sword up against his shoulder. "I thought you were one of the normal humans."

"Cousins aren't incest," Agata defended me in a way I absolutely didn't need. "I mean, when Garland turned out to be the son of Perun, it also turned out to be our father's cousin that he had a child with. That means we're third cousins and that's nothing."

"Third cousins who were raised together," Bloodstorm said. "Also, I'm going to say that any level of cousin is a major wood killer. Humans need to travel more."

Ania sighed.

I sighed and shook my head. "I know I'm going to regret saying this as it would be really nice to have any sort of distraction right now but I think we can skip the witty banter part of our journey. Silence would be good now."

The elevator arrived at the heart branches moments later and I took a moment to take in the fantastic sight I was led into. It was one of those moments that reminded me of why I'd been willing to accept this insanity as it was the rare moment to see true wonders.

The heart branches were basically the top of the tree where they had constructed the center of the Grand Temple. It was, of all things, a gigantic gazebo built around an enormous stone brazier. Since gigantic and enormous are words which don't provide specifics, allow me to state the gazebo was the size of a football stadium and the brazier was a sunken stone pool the size of a lake. Branches twisted around the interior of the gazebo but looked brown, almost dull, with the Eldritch Tree's shining light almost nonexistent within them.

Beside the brazier was a bell about the size of Valentine on a stand with a person-sized mace propped up against the side of it. The bell was metal and carved with horrific but beautiful images that reminded me of art from the Black Death. You know, skeletons chasing down fleeing peasants and robed figures overlooking the wailing damned. It was a bell of doom, an artifact of *Eldritch Ring*, that was used to summon the bosses of each dungeon. I was very glad to see it because otherwise my 'plan' would have been screwed.

Throughout the gazebo, hanging from the ceiling a hundred feet above our head, were twenty-foot-long spikes of blue crystal that shimmered with a silvery white mist. They were halfway between stalactites and icicles in their appearance. I tried to figure out what they were, and my downloaded magical knowledge kicked in: mana formations. By shutting off the sacred fire, the excess magic could be siphoned off to Veles but that still left a ton of crystalized energy to accumulate around the 'edges' so to speak.

My magically acquired knowledge warned me that mana crystals were extremely volatile when combined with necromantic magic like witchfire. Which was less a possible advantage than a way I might be able to take Valentin with me if I decided suicide was a preferable option to capture. That wasn't a particularly attractive option since it would kill people I called friends, wouldn't kill Valentin for long since he'd already come back from the dead once, and wouldn't meaningfully contribute to the salvation of the world since we were apparently the last resort. Unfortunately, the option of just spite blowing everything up looked potentially better and better given what was waiting for us.

Meeting us in the heart of the heart branches was, of course, Valentin's plan to simply overwhelm us with brute force. Which, honestly, wasn't a sign of his crudeness but practicality. After all, if you've got it, flaunt it. Valentin was sitting on his dragon in a saddle and holding the Fake Georgie hostage while looking bored. I also noticed that Valentin was strapped into his dragon's mount and took a bit of amusement from that sight. If nothing else, I'd gotten into Valentin's head, and I was living there rent free.

At the dragon's feet was a group of twelve armored goblins who looked less like the cowardly creatures of The Hobbit and more like Peter Jackson's Uruk-Hai, verging on full *World of Warcraft* bodybuilders. Each of them had a top knot that had been dyed red in blood and it gave them a sort of heavy metal samurai feel. It was a cool effect ruined by the fact all of them had a big skull and crossbones spray-painted on the front of their armor, as if we didn't know they were answering to the Skull King.

"Welcome to your end, last dying gasps of the light. The shadow spreads forth from Bald Mountain and consumes the world of men while you futilely rail against the inevitability of your deaths. Accept your doom and know...wait, are you dressed like George Clooney's Batman?" Valentin asked me, looking at me sideways. I wished I could read his expression, but it was still obscured by his skull mask. The juxtaposition of his nightmarish attire and frat boy posture was kind of funny, though. I'd also ruined his attempt at pseudo-Tolkien speech and that also gave me a bit of pleasure.

"No, I don't have the ears," I said, sighing. "This is the *Paladin of Mokosh Set.*"

"Why would Mokosh want you to dress like Batman?" Valentin said, sounding genuinely curious.

"I guess because she's into roleplay," Jon said. "Don't worry, Ania, I'm sure Aaron will make time for you."

Ania responded with a gesture that had clearly migrated between worlds.

Valentin stared down at Jon. "Ah, another ghost raven. You know, I got one despite the fact I was the first? I ended up killing him because he wouldn't shut up."

I wasn't sure if Valentin was the first of the champions, but I wouldn't have been surprised. "I see you've found a new dragon."

"Yeah, Eva has dropped off the grid," Valentin said. "Probably waiting for you to rebuild the dragon pit so she can join her sister at Dragon Keep. She's going to be waiting a long time or would if not for the fact the rest of her life will be measured in days."

"Uh huh," I said.

"Because I'm going to kill her," Valentin said, explaining his joke.

"Yeah, I got that," I said, looking up and down the dragon. "Can we get on with the prisoner release?"

"Sure," Valentin said, tossing the fake Georgie off of the dragon. Immediately, Georgie ran forward as if to embrace me before disintegrating into sparkles of illusions seconds earlier. "That was an homage to *Highlander 3*, starring Mario Van Peebles AKA 'We Apologize for *Highlander 2*, so we're just remaking *Highlander*'."

"I'm familiar," I said. "I prefer the series."

"If I wasn't going to kill you before, I'm definitely going to kill you now," Valentin said.

"How did you know about Georgie?" I asked, hoping to get some answers before we won or died.

"It was in your HR file," Valentin said, casually. "I had Babs send it over. I would have had them grab your actual nephew but they said he's off limits."

"Because of Alek," I muttered.

"Sure," Valentin said, displaying superhuman hearing. "Never liked the guy. He's too much like you. Sold himself to save your sister and her sprog. I suppose a deal is a deal in America, even if it's Ledziania."

I had a lot more questions now.

That was when the large, lumbering male dragon growled. "Valentin, I tolerate your presence for Veles' sake but even I have my limits. Let us slaughter them all and make them an offering to our shared master."

"Father?" Alexi said, standing beside me as he looked up to the dragon.

"Sorry, kid," I said, shaking my head. "I didn't mean to bring you into this."

"He's a bad guy, isn't he?" Alexi asked.

"Yep," Jon said.

Boris didn't do much to dissuade Jon's opinion. "Ah, it would appear that my insolent harlot of a wife has squired my useless simpleton of a son to the False Garland."

"That going to be a problem, Smokey?" Valentin asked.

Boris laughed with a deep and guttural tone. "House Poppy could have made its own claim to the throne of the Old King when Frederick became obsessed with prophecies and the End of the World following his sons' deaths. Instead, I was laughed at from the cloak rooms to the courts of power due to my heir being unable to do more than stare at walls for hours. If I'd had another child, even a bastard, I would have slit Alexi's throat."

Alexi stared, quivering. Despite his 'issues', the kid clearly was affected by his father's words. Plus, well, his father was a much bigger dragon than he was.

I put my hand on my shoulder to comfort him. "Neuroatypicals forever, man."

Alexi took my hand and squeezed it. He then looked at me, asking a question that I expected had been on his mind for a while. "So, are you like Garland's brother or what?"

I sighed.

"It's like the *Smokey and the Bandit* sequel where he's filling in for the Bandit," Jon explained. "Man, we could use Burt Reynolds right now."

"Damn, I thought I was dark," Valentin said. "Any last words? I'd offer a position for the rest of your party out of respect but, well, the only one I'd have for the ladies is on their knees and I wouldn't trust them down there."

"I'd bite it off," Ania said.

"What you say is blasphemy against Mokosh, Valentin Veles son," Agata said. "Also, I agree with Ania."

"I'm betting on Aaron here, Skull Face," Bloodstorm shouted back. He then leaned his head over. "You actually do have a plan, right?"

"Sort of," I admitted.

"Sort of?" Bloodstorm said, his eyes widening in horror.

Ania sighed. "If I die here, it will be as I lived, surrounded by idiots."

"Well, as fun as this has been, and it has been fun, broken necks aside, it's time to end it," Valentin said. "See you in Hell."

"You first," I said, squeezing my hands into fists. I was concentrating with my telekinesis on the mace beside the bell of doom. I barely managed to lift it up and bounce it against the side of the cursed metal object. A deafening noise filled the gazebo, far greater than a normal bell, would make and the air became ten degrees chillier.

BONG

BONG

BONG

Ania stared at me in horror. "This was your plan?"

Agata stared at the brazier in horror.

Valentin looked over his shoulder while Boris began gathering his fire before letting it go, looking where his rider was.

A large swirling black mist began to coalesce in the brazier. It was like someone made a waterspout of liquid shadow before it exploded outward. The results were a creature emerging into this world from a place that, if it wasn't Hell, was Hell adjacent. The creature, Chernabog, made its presence known first with its leathery bat wings then the rest of its demonic muscular body.

My bracelet began playing "Night on Bald Mountain" even as I saw the sight of the twenty-foot-tall creature with its wing-size raising its height to thirty. Greenish witchfire burned in both its eyes and from its mouth.

Chernabog's appearance was a combination of Disney's Fantasia with a Balrog or maybe both were based on the archetype of Big Horny Satan. Its face was a bear's with bull horns and on each of its hands was claws that I saw were tipped in icy mana. If Veles preferred to look like a popular Swedish actor, Chernabog simply preferred to look like a god.

"Well, that was stupid of you," Valentin said, unimpressed.

That was when I used my VENTRILOQUISM cantrip. "HAIL, CHERNABOG, ENEMY OF HUMANITY! IT IS I, VALENTIN, WHO DEFEATED YOU ONCE BEFORE! I COME TO CHALLENGE THEE IN THE NAME OF THE CAUSE I ABANDONED AND TO SEND THEE BACK TO HELL! COME, FACE ME, COWARD!"

Valentin stared at Chernabog for a second then back at me. "You son of—"

Chernabog let forth an animalistic roar before opening its mouth and releasing a blast of its inner flame on both Valentine as well as Boris the dragon. The blast was powerful enough that it poured past both man and dragon to strike some of the goblins. Valentin fell off the side of the dragon and landed on the ground, his saddle destroyed.

Boris responded by blasting Chernabog with his fire that had about as much effect as a water pistol against a man made of, well, water.

Seeing that effect, the red dragon showed his true colors by attempting to take flight. Chernabog didn't let that happen and summoned a whip made of thorns that he whirled around to grab the dragon by the throat, pulling him back to the ground.

"Let them fight," Jon said, doing a bad Ken Watanabe impression.

Valentin, much to my surprise, just got up off the ground and picked up his enormous maul. "We're going to have words after this, Aaron."

Valentin proceeded to run at Chernabog and used JUMP magic to fly at the demon gods' head, smacking him in the face with the maul like Thor fighting Surtur. For all of his humiliations, I was starting to see how Valentin had earned those twenty levels.

"Who are we rooting for?" Bloodstorm asked, stunned by the sudden turn around.

"Neither, both," Agata said.

"Jason!" Jon said. "Freddy sucks."

Ania shook her head then pointed. "Ourselves. Look!"

The goblin forces that were Valentin's praetorian guard had decided that fighting a god wasn't in their job description. Unfortunately, we were between them and the elevator. I also suspected they weren't about to run past us since they had their weapons drawn and were shouting obscenities in goblin tongue.

"Finally," Bloodstorm said, lifting his great sword and charging. "BARBARIAN RAGE!"

Sparky transformed into his dragon form and growled, glad to have something to burn.

Ania drew her blades.

Agata aimed her staff like a shotgun.

I sighed and summoned Stompy, pulling out my shield and sword. "This was a better plan in my head."

CHAPTER FORTY-FIVE
IT'S THE FINAL COUNTDOWN

The bracelet finished playing the Fantasia homage before switching to an orchestral version of "The Final Countdown" by Europe. I had no idea if it was Weis making these choices or the bracelet itself, but I had to admit it was both hilarious as well as distracting when I needed every bit of my attention to not die.

Valentin was battling Chernabog in a way that was difficult to describe but genuinely impressive. For all the fact he was a fat bastard, the man could move. He jumped around, smashing his maul against the side of the giant demon with blasts of lightning coming out each blow before speeding out of the way of the monster's attacks.

Boris the Dragon was faring much worse as he'd been choked, stabbed, and blasted with witchfire several times. The dragon could certainly deal it out but taking it seemed to be different story. Knowing his fire was useless, Boris had resorted to clawing and biting while striking with his tail. All the while he was pitifully saying they needed to stop and that he was willing to surrender.

I had no idea which of the monsters we'd end up facing after the battle between them was resolved but tended to bet on the one resembling a kaiju version of Satan. Valentin had supposedly beaten Chernabog before, but I was pretty sure he had to have had better backup. I was more focused on dealing with this group of goblins right now. Which told you everything you needed to know about how underleveled we were for this encounter, I think.

Still, goblins we could beat.

Bloodstorm finally got to release his barbarian rage, and it was a glorious sight to behold. I hadn't been thinking about it but he'd been denied multiple chances to rip into his enemies while traveling with me. Either I was trying to resolve things peacefully, which sometimes worked out, or I was using underhanded methods of dealing with my enemies like poisoning them. This was a rare occasion of brute force being the optimal solution.

Bloodstorm's eyes became mad with glee as he bisected goblin bodies with swinging blows like he was cutting through wheat. The goblins were elites of their kind and attempted to dogpile him or charge him with their own mad berserk fury, only to be overwhelmed by the sheer power of the bull-horned warrior. Even so, numbers had a quality all their several got past him to charge at us, firing black arrows from bone bows that glowed with demonic fire or attacking with serrated curved swords.

I caught three of the arrows with Lord Rose's shield as I charged on Stompy's back, blasting at the goblins before passing them and starting to do a circle around Chernabog. That took me out of the goblin fight, but I was pretty sure that was about to become irrelevant. Especially since Ania, Sparky, and Agata were handling the ones that Bloodstorm wasn't. Sparky was currently eating one and I decided I'd have to have a talk with the boy if we survived.

If.

"Okay, Stompy, I need you to fly," I said, sucking in my breath. I was doing some mathematical calculations in my head about how NOT to set off a chain reaction. It required me to believe that my brain really had been enhanced by magic and I knew a lot more about sorcery than I'd experienced over these past two weeks in-person. If it didn't work, I was dead. If it did work, there was still a good chance I'd be dead. I just hoped it didn't kill my friends.

I wasn't looking forward to once more riding on the back of my demon steed as he took to the air. I was barely managing to stay on as the horse was running but I was pretty sure the high ground would be necessary for Stage 2 of my plan, a plan that was undergoing a lot of rewrites as events rapidly overtook them.

"We're going to die here," Stompy said, under his breath.

"Probably," I admitted.

Stompy took to the air, using the momentum of his gallop to start ascending as if going up an invisible road.

That was when Chernabog conjured a sword the size of a bus, caused it to catch fire, and brought it down on Boris the Dragon's neck. The dragon screamed in terror before its head came off, ending House Poppy's patriarch. Sparky screamed out a battle cry and started flying toward Chernabog with smoke trailing from his mouth.

"UNHOLY SMITE!" Valentin shouted, jumping up in the air off Chernabog's shoulder to smash the demon in the face.

Chernabog managed to catch him in one hand and pierced him with his talons through his replacement armor, pulling on the traitorous champion with all his divine might. I'll avoid describing what happened next, lest I have to up the rating on this tale, but the Skull King met his end for a second time. Chernabog threw the two pieces of the fallen hero to the side like they were garbage.

That meant Chernabog was going to turn his attention to either me or Sparky. I wasn't nearly to where I needed to be for Stage 2 and serving as a distraction for Sparky would be suicidal. It would also be the right thing to do.

Curse my low WIS.

"Hey, ugly!" I shouted down at Chernabog, the weird acoustics of the gazebo making it sound like it came from a megaphone. "I am the actual champion of Perun (sort of)! You want to dance, then you should dance with me! I will score Perfect on Dance-Dance Revolution."

Okay, that was rolling a 1 on the d20 of fight banter. However, given Chernabog turned from Sparky to me, I consider it to have been a successful distraction. I mean, it was going to kill me and Sparky, but it was successful.

"I'll just regenerate in the Underworld but, well, it's been an honor," Stompy said. "I hope you enjoy the Hall of Heroes."

Chenabog opened his mouth and I saw the fire gathering down his throat to consume me. Given I was almost to the stalactites of mana above, that might have been enough, but it would still mean I was about to die. Much to my surprise, I saw Chernabog interrupted by a blast of flame to the side of the head like a pebble striking him. Following that pebble, he was struck by lightning, golden arrows of light, ice blasts, and beams of rainbow energy. There was even a silver falcon that slammed into his head before exploding into golden shards.

The Sisters of Mokosh had apparently decided to forego escape and join in the battle against Chernabog. They'd managed to get themselves to the upper heart branches and were now pelting the god's avatar with every spell in their possession. Most of them were low level but I swore I saw the Great Mother hurl a METEOR at the guy. Which, in a fair game, would have perhaps knocked the creature back to Hell.

He just looked pissed off.

"What now?" Stompy asked.

"Higher!" I said, looking at my witchblade sword. "By the way, if this doesn't work—"

"Yeah, yeah, anything you say will just be ripping me off!" Stompy said, coming within a few yards of a stalactite's bottom.

"JEDI THROW, MOTHERSUCKER!" I shouted, hurling my flaming sword and using telekinesis to throw it farther and faster than it would have gone normally before Stompy turned around. The weapon ended up hitting the top of the gigantic mana fragment and exploded where it struck. All the witchfire within it detonated and a massive crack spread through it, causing it to fall down.

Chernabog, who had his whip out to start wiping out the sisters, looked up. "Well shit."

The mana spike pierced the god's avatar through its chest. The spike went in one end and out the other as the mana interacted with his interior witchfire, causing an explosion that thankfully was just above the heads of everyone on the ground and below the branches holding the Sisters of Mokosh.

The shockwave from the first blast sent Stompy spiraling around like a helicopter gone out of control. Somehow, I managed to hold onto the reigns even as my body was flung into the air. Unfortunately, the next blast was even worse, and I saw Stompy disappear in the flames. He'd done his best to position himself between me and the blast. It had worked and I barely the flames licking my body. It left me in midair, though, with no mount and I fell toward the Earth. I managed to grab at one of the branches while descending but not being a movie, I couldn't hold my body weight and probably broke my arm before descending downward again.

A deep rumbling voice that I recognized as Perun's, speaking from beyond the veil oof the death, spoke two words:

"GOD SLAIN."

The deep dramatic effect of it all was somewhat ruined by the sickening crunch that accompanied my body hitting the ground from thirty feet in the air as I felt my body start to die. Worse, my bracelet started updating.

Which just felt ridiculous.

ACHIEVEMENT UNLOCKED: GODSLAYER
(A) - 50 - Kill one of the Old Gods

MAIN QUEST UPDATED

DEFEAT THE OLD GODS SERVING VELES (1/4)

Reward
+ 100,000 EXP (Chernabog)
+ 10,000 EXP (Boris the Red Dragon)
+ 6000 EXP (Elite Goblin Berserkers)
+ 10,000 GP

YOU HAVE REACHED LEVEL 8
Level 8 to 9
24,000 out of 135,000 EXPERIENCE

As my lungs filled with blood, never a good sign, I tried to use the last of my strength to tap away at the controls. Trying to just hit Y and accept the leveling up while everything went black.

I could hear Ania speaking over me. "Agata, get over here! He needs your help!"

I didn't respond as I felt her shaking my body. Instead, her voice sounded distant and echoing. As plans went, it had required a lot of improvising and use of the environment, but I think it had its merits. Mind you, any plan you didn't walk away from was probably a bad one. There was a reason that I'd only gone for this one when I thought I could avoid detonating the entire room.

And I hadn't!

Yay!

"I'm sorry!" Agata's voice spoke over me. "I prayed for combat magic instead of healing!"

"You idiot!" Ania shouted as I felt her hands rifling through my pockets.

"What are you looking for?" Agata asked.

"That damned coin of his," Ania said.

"You'd use it on…him?" Agata asked.

"Yes!" Ania shouted. "I would!"

I found myself genuinely touched even as I heard a shuffling noise around me before I felt a bracelet wrap around my other arm.

"What's that?" Ania asked, now almost inaudible.

It wouldn't be long now.

"A kind of magic," Jon said.

"A miracle hopefully," Bloodstorm said.

A set of words appeared in my mind, not on the bracelet's interface but behind my eyes.

WOULD YOU LIKE TO ABSORB DIVINE ESSENCE? Y/N

"Yes," I managed to say.

I found myself doing battle in the future location of the Death Mountains, my body a hundred feet tall as I did battle with an equally sized Veles. Veles was in his dragon form and each of our blows was tearing up the ground around us like it was dirt at an offroad dirt bike race. Lightning, fire, and earthquakes accompanied the divine display of power. Cities as far off as the Turqish Empire would be destroyed by the damage to the tectonic plates below.

"You don't have to do this, brother!" Perun shouted with my voice. "We fought the Twisted Gods together and they are bound!"

"By your power!" Veles shouted, raising his long draconic neck to the sky and shooting fire blasts upwards rivers of magma he'd conjured. "You will not win this battle between us! You've spent too much of yourself against them! And for what? The very humans who summoned them in the first place with their hatred, despair, and malice! They tried to destroy our people!"

"Humans are our people!" Perun said, shielding his face with his arm. "You have let the Twisted Gods get into you! Their ways bring madness and despair!"

"And power! I will use that power to bring order to this planet! To Earth! To every planet!" Veles shouted, turning back into a towering him and grabbing Perun by the throat. His magic began to drain the Sky God of his strength.

Perun smiled, bleeding from within. "Is this because Mat and Mokosh both prefer humans?"

Veles snapped his neck with all his Twisted God granted strength.

YOU HAVE GAINED DIVINITY SCORE 3

YOU HAVE RECEIVED THE FOLLOWING BENEFITS:

+ 1 to Attack Rolls
+ 1 to Saving Throws
+ 1 to Attribute
+ Attribute Maximum raised to 20
+ Your maximum level has increased
+ All damage and status effects are removed

+ You are now a Demigod

I opened my eyes. "Okay, I feel much better now."

Ania kissed me passionately then pulled back. A look of embarrassment was on her face. "I'm very happy you're alive."

"Oh, for Mokosh's sake," Agata said, shaking her head. "Just fuck him."

Ania glared at her sister.

Jon and Bloodstorm were visibly delighted at my recovery, both laughing with relief.

Sparky was back in human form with a despondent look on his face. His father was dead after all and partially due to my efforts.

I got up and gave him a hug.

Where Chernabog once stood, there was now a glowing and brilliant green balefire that seemed to be rejuvenating the branches around us. I didn't know if it would drive away the monsters around us or if they'd have to be cleaned out. At this point, I didn't care, though.

I looked around. "So, anyone want to play a game of Pwiffle?"

AARON'S ADVENTURES WILL CONTINUE IN
GUARDIANS OF DRAGON KEEP

ACKNOWLEDGMENTS

I want to thank George R.R. Martin, Andrzej Sapkowski, Margaret Weis, Tracy Hickman, Richard Knaak, R.A. Salvatore, Mark Lawrence, Glen Cook, and all the other authors that Larry C.C. Weis ripped off for the Dark Undermaster Saga. Haha. I also want to thank David Niall Wilson, Dawn Chapman, Matt Dinniman, MK Gibson, David Dodd, Steve Caldwell, Jan Clifford Godfrey, and several other people who helped me decide to make this book.

You see, I absolutely love *Dungeons & Dragons* and the many books written for its settings. I grew up reading Dragonlance, Forgotten Realms, and all the other stories that Jon read but Aaron didn't. Later, I switched to works like A Song of Ice and Fire as well as the Witcher. Plenty of other dark fantasy too. However, I never got into LitRPG. I'd heard of it when I'd become an indie author but only recently have become a fan.

LitRPG was something that intrigued me, but I found impenetrable. There were vast amounts of it published, especially as I was starting my career with works like the Supervillainy Saga (which I would have made LitRPG if I'd known about it), but I had no idea where to start. The many good people at Royal Road helped me find some true gems to help me acclimate to the genre as well as showed me how to do my own.

I've written high fantasy before and if you want to try something more serious from me, there's the Wraith Knight books. However, I consider the Dark Undermaster books to be a send up of all the grimdark and dark fantasy out there. It's what happens if you drop a capable player character into a world trying too hard to be edgy. Which is how I prefer these stories to go anyway. I may enjoy dark fantasy worlds, but I always end up playing the goodie-two shoes. Give me Jon Snow, non-crazy Daenerys, and Geralt over the Mountain.

I hope you all have enjoyed *Lords of Dragon Keep*. I hope it will have several sequels and your encouragements have been immensely helpful. I've rarely found a community as welcoming and supportive at the LitRPG/Progressive Fantasy one. Indie authors often act like they're rivals for a limited number of purchases by readers, but a rising tide lifts all boats.

I hope to pass on that to other authors.

LEXICON

A Court of Devils: The first Dark Undermaster book by Larry C.C. Weis, published in the late Eighties. It follows Garland growing up as part of the Rose family before their betrayal by the Poppys and the death of Lord Rose as well as the family's scattering.

Akoa: The former capital city of Ledziania and where the Old King used to hold his court. It is presently under the dominion of the Mad Queen.

Alchemist Stone: The most common form of alchemy aside from potions. You swallow a stone, and it provides magical effects for as long as it remains undigested.

Alignment: A sign of whether you are allied with White, Grey, or Black magical forces. Contrary to expectation, these don't precisely line to Good/Neutral/Evil. White is inherently lawful and self-righteous while Black is chaotic as well as vengeful. Grey is prone to empathy and balance.

Arcane Fire: A magical effect of where a wizard summons raw mystical force to use against enemies. It is almost useless against other wizards who tend to just absorb the energy but highly damaging to other beings.

Baba Yaga: The legendary crone and monster of Slavic mythology. She is the daughter of Veles and Mat Zemlya in the Dark Undermaster universe. She is the goddess of witchcraft and mother of the hag as well as ogre races. Her hideousness is possibly a curse from her father or mother or both. She alone is free of the Old Gods from Veles influence, ironically.

Bald Mountain: The headquarters of Veles and where his grand temple is located. It is the pilgrimage site of all evil witches once per year on the Fall Equinox. It is also where the Scholomance is located. It is in the Death Mountains and protected by a magical barrier that no one of good heart can pierce.

The Bastard Knight: Jorg von Piast-Jagiellon, the illegitimate son of the Old King and leader of the Mad Queen's forces. He has supposedly killed six dragons, a dozen Dark Undermasters, and a demigod.

Belobog: Chernabog's brother and the god of good fortune. He was corrupted by Veles and is now the guardian of the Elemental Temple of Fire.

Białowieża Forest: An immense forest bordering Poland and Belarus. Supposedly, the country of Ledziania exists somewhere within its borders. The forest is the only place on Earth where you can follow paths to Mokosh.

The Black Cat: Maelor's extremely opulent brothel, casino, and tavern. It is far too nice for Crossroad.

The Black Rose: The nickname of the legendary Dark Undermaster, Garland of Nowhere.

Chernabog: Belobog's brother, the god of ill fortune and "The Black God." He was corrupted by Veles and is now the guardian of the Elemental Temple of Earth.

Crossroad: The long-suffering village built around Dragon Keep. It is a farming community that is on the verge of becoming a small city if it can just avoid being invaded by the undead.

Cyber Dragons 2080: A non-fantasy game produced by Epic Dungoneering™. It was a bug ridden mess set in a post-apocalypse cyberpunk future.

Dark Undermasters: An organization of monster hunters and knights established by Triglav and Mokosh during the Great Darkness to battle the Chaos Gods in 900 AD. They have a writ from the Ledzianian king allowing them to use dark magic and whatever means necessary to protect humanity.

The Dark Undermaster Saga: The incredibly successful fantasy franchise by Larry C.C. Weiss. It has sold over a hundred million copies and been adapted across multiple mediums. It is generally viewed as painfully derivative of other popular franchises, even though it was technically written first.

The Dark Undermaster (Games): A series of three games that adapt the first three books of the Dark Undermaster Saga: *A Court of Devils, Dead Gods,* and *Princes of Sorrow.* The fourth book, Lords of Dragon Keep, has been delayed for almost ten years. This has infuriated the video game developers.

The Dark Undermaster (Series): A five season television series on the FANT channel that heavily involved nudity, sex, and adding more grimdark. It is wildly considered to have gone down in quality once they passed Weis' books.

Dead Gods: The second book of the Dark Undermaster Saga dealing with Garland's career as a monster-hunter, Ania learning to be an assassin, and Agata trying to survive in Akoa's courts. It also deals with the mythology of Perun's death at Veles' hands.

Death Lords: Totally not liches.

Death Mountains: A massive barrier between Ledziania and the Turqish Wastes brought about via a death battle between Perun and Velen in the late 1980s. It is populated by the undead, goblins, and cultists now.

Dragon Keep: An ancient castle established by the Rose family back when they were a legendary clan of dragon tamers. After their betrayal by the Mad Queen and Poppy Family, it was given to the Dark Undermasters to be their new headquarters.

Dragon Queen: The nickname of Celestyne von Piast-Jagiellon, who was cursed by her sister into becoming a dragon. She had that curse (mostly) broken by Garland of Nowhere and now seeks to reclaim her throne while promising populist reforms for the world's nonhumans.

Dwarves: One of the five great races of Mokosh. They are the children of Svavorg and live underground. Oddly, they're more stout than short. The ones who live on the surface primarily handle banking and financial jobs in addition to skilled labor.

Eldritch Ring: Another video game produced by Epic Dungoneeering™ that is a Soulslike. It incorporates some of the crazier elements of Weis' mythology played down by the books. The goal of the game is to kill Veles and ascend to become Perun's replacement.

The Eldritch Tree: A sacred tree to Mokosh and Perun both where they supposedly copulated for the first time. It is a mile tall and one of the greatest sources of magic in the world. It is also connected to the Earth and Poland. The Rus worship it as Yggdrasil.

Elves: One of the five great races. Elves have eternal youth until they reach 120 and promptly drop dead. They are the Children of Mokosh and live anarchic nature-loving lives with communal romances as well as hedonistic behavior. They are also all ruthless killers.

Elemental Temples: Four temples devoted to Mokosh that channel immense amounts of magical might into the natural world and keep it in balance. They also allow magical creatures to live and sorcery to function. They are all considered Grand Temples of Mokosh.

The Emperor: Constantine the Black is the revered demigod figure of the Empire who, in actuality, is a prisoner of the constant in-fighting of the Senate and Church of Mythras. He also struggles to avoid being a puppet of the Lord Centurions. His wars of conquest against the East are built around occupying his political enemies with foreign quarrels. Veles serves as his court astrologer but makes the infighting less severe.

The Empire: Also known as the Eastern Empire and Holy Mythran Empire, it was settled by the so-called "Lost Legion" of Rome in 120 AD. It has a Senate, Emperor, and established religion ruled by the Holy Father. The Empire has entered a conservative period with women's rights and religious freedoms being severely curtailed as it seeks to expand eastward. Its symbol is the bull, and its god is Mythras.

Epic Dungeoneering™: The world's largest video game manufacturer despite its relative lack of product due to buying up many smaller studios with their seemingly unlimited amounts of money. They also have a surprising number of deals with arms manufacturing, lumber, and other satellite companies.

Garland of Nowhere: AKA The Black Rose. The bastard son of Perun and Lilandra Rose, born shortly before the god's death. He was a legendary swordsman, womanizer, gambler, and sorcerer who achieved countless great deeds as a Dark Undermaster. Unfortunately, these caused him to suffer severe untreated PTSD and when he was betrayed by his fellow Undermasters, he opted against resurrection.

Five Great Races: Humans, Dwarves, Goblins, Ratkin, and Elves are the most common species encountered in Mokosh.

Goblins: A tribal race of green and olive-skinned humanoids. Contrary to their reputation as ruthless monsters, they are quite honorable, clannish, and serve Veles only because he is their creator.

Gods: A race of beings that came from the Primordial Chaos and brought order to the universe. Many of the ones worshiped on Earth are real, but not all, and a lot of what people know about them is nonsense. They can draw on faith and prayers for sustenance, but it is not the sole source of their power.

Grand Temple: The highest temple that any god has and the base of their religion. The Elemental Temples of Mokosh have been occupied by the Old Gods.

Great Darkness(es): The wars of against the Twisted. The last one was supernatural invasion of Mokosh in 1939 by a Waffen-SS battalion after the Twisted were freed by the Black Sun cult. (Lt) Colonel Helmuth Krieger recruited a rebellious Empire general and unleashed the Scarlet Death to aid his efforts. Perun and Veles put aside their animosity to fight it back. It and events on Earth caused Veles to believe all life had to be purged (so it could be ruled by him safely post-mortem).

Great Forest: The home nation of the elves. It's a forest with a lot of tree cities in it.

Hags: The female descendants of Baba Yaga. Ogres are the male ones.

High Grecian Empire: The once grand democratic state that has since fallen into disrepair, disunity, and casual corruption. The High Grecian Empire is a vassal state of the Empire but has mostly kept its autonomy. They worship the Olympians but combine the Ledzianian gods with their own.

Kalizov: The largest and richest city in Ledziania as well as the biggest supporter of the Dragon Queen.

Knights of Veles: Knights sworn to the God of Evil who are infused with the power of undeath without being undead themselves.

Ledziania: The former nation compromising all the Southern Kingdoms and "Fantasy Poland." It has been divided since the death of the Old King and is presently caught in the middle of a civil war, invasion by the Empire, and uprising of the dead.

Lesser Ledziania: The "heartland" of Ledziania that Crossroad is in and the most contested spot of the Southern Kingdoms. It is a breadbasket that has been fought over ruthlessly.

Lord Centurions: A not-so-secret society of high-ranking aristocrats and officers that wield vast authority in the Empire. They are trained in both magic as well as warfare. They are known for their ostentatious golden armor.

Lords of Dragon Keep: The fourth book of the Dark Undermaster Saga that fans have been waiting on for decades.

Mad Queen: Apollonia von Piast-Jagiellon, the twin sister of Celestyne. The most accomplished sorceress of her age, she is strongly disliked for allying with the Empire. Her son, Cesare, is believed to be the son of the Emperor, but possibly the son of Veles. Is not at all mad, just a bit testy.

Magyar: A now defunct kingdom formerly bordering Ledziania that were its historical rivals. The Hellmaster dynasty turned to black magic and Veles worship before being overthrown by the populace. The Empire proceeded to invade but the Magyar negotiated a surrender deal that kept most of their culture and autonomy.

Mal'bork: A land of rivers, fords, and trade between Ledzianians. It has tried, unsuccessfully, to remain neutral.

Mana: Raw magic stuff. The energy that powers sorcery.

Mark of the Champion: Magical bracelets made from river gold infused with the essence of Perun. The Wise Man was able to manufacture fifteen of them in total. For whatever bizarre reason, they primarily give a person abilities equivalent to *Dungeons & Dragons*-esque leveling. This includes rapid advancement in personal power and durability.

Mat Zemalya: Both the planet Earth and its mother goddess. She is the twin of Mokosh and the two are linked via Ledziania. Reckless abuse by her many children gods resulted in magic becoming scarce and most being either killed or forced into slumber. She appears as a seven-headed dragon and is the "mean Gaia" of Greek and Babylonian mythology.

Mokosh: The sister planet and goddess to Earth where magic remains abundant. It has so far only shown to have one continent. It is far less technologically advanced than Earth but more advanced in science (via magic) than it appears.

Mythras: The Sun God of the mostly monotheistic faith of the Empire. He is a warrior and protector of the innocent. In practice, his church has fallen into corruption with heavy elements of misogyny and racism against nonhumans. Mythras, himself, has largely abandoned the religion and only patronizes good-hearted warriors. He is a jealous god, though.

Old King: Frederick von Piast-Jagiellon, the grandfather of the Mad Queen and Dragon Queen. He outlived all his sons and left the kingdom divided due to his policy of playing noble houses against one another. He spent his final years obsessed with prophecies about the end of the world.

Old Gods: The name for the Ledzianian Gods before Mythras attempted to push his way in.

Perun: The sky god of the Ledzianian pantheon, creator of humanity, and god of good. He is the protector of mankind and very-very dead. Looks a great deal like Dolph Lundgren's He-Man and has the personality of Marvel's Thor except hornier. He expended most of his power destroying the Twisted summoned by Nazis from Earth and was defeated by his brother in a death fight decades later. Mythras, defying stereotype, answers quite a few of Perun's priests' prayers in honor of the sky god's sacrifice.

Poznan: One of the oldest settlements in Ledziania and presently occupied by the Empire. Its citizens are on the verge of open revolt as they refuse to convert to the New God or impose the Empire's social laws.

The Princes of Sorrow: The third Dark Undermaster novel following the romance between Garland and Celestyne, Ania losing her lover to the Bastard Knight, and Agata's torment as the bride of

Radu the Impaler. Apollonia invites the Empire to occupy Ledziania once she begins losing the war with her sister.

Pwiffle: A card game created by the Wise Man and the favorite of the gods after a board game from Earth involving dungeons.

Ratkin: A race created by Veles as cannon fodder and slaves for his goblins that was later given gifts by Svarog out of pity. They are still ill-treated by many other races.

Runes: Writing infused with magic. It is how magical items are created, generally.

Rus Kingdoms: Danish raiders had a history of getting transported to Mokosh due to their gods, the Aesir, hoping they'd conquer the place. Instead, they interbred with some of the Slavic folk to create the Rus kingdoms. They are a constantly feuding set of principalities and jarldoms that regularly try to invade Ledziania and Magyar. They occupy the North of the Southern Kingdoms, peculiar as that may be and still worship the Aesir but acknowledge the Ledzianian gods as real.

Sisters of Mokosh: A religious order of female sorceresses and priestesses who preach a philosophy of nature worship. Because of teaching sexual freedom and the equality of women, it is considered heresy by women.

Southern Kingdoms: The former state of Ledziania that has been broken up into smaller states after the death of the Old King. Confusingly, the Southern Kingdoms is also the name of the entire continent that once had another continent above it in ancient times. No one has any idea what happened to that.

Strigoi: The local name for vampires that come in greater and lesser varieties. The **greater** vampires, known as nobles, are intelligent conversational undead. The lesser vampires are feral zombie-like monsters.

Svarog: One of the three creator gods of Ledziania, he is the god of blacksmiths and creation. He has absolutely no time for any of his brothers' shit and is worshiped by dwarves as well as ratkin. He is the creator of both Mat Zemlya and Mokosh. Looks like John Rhys Davis with Arnold Schwarzenegger's body.

The Thirteen: Veles' death lord lieutenants and generals.

Triglav: The Divine Voltron. Triglav is a combination of Perun, Svarog, and Veles as well as an overgod AKA the most powerful beings even among the gods. The three can't combine without Perun and are now greatly weakened.

Turqish Wastes: Once known as the Turqish Empire, it was almost destroyed in a horrifying series of natural disasters following the battle of Perun with Veles. The remaining city states are still rebuilding but are more interested in trade than conquest. They are the only power that uses gunpowder, but this means less with magic. They worship Ahura Mazda and Mythras but reject the Empire as blasphemers.

The Twisted Gods: Beings that are even worse than Veles and defeated by the creator gods at the start of creation. They're a little Lovecraft, a little Clive Barker, and a little "Oh my god, what the hell is that thing?" Veles works to keep them in the Underworld's Pit. They are also known as the Ungods, the Neverwere, the Curseborn and several other epitaphs.

Underworld: Veles' domain and where all mortals go when they die. Strangely, he's quite fair and the only mortals who go unpunished for their crimes are his followers but even they don't go to the same place as heroes or the innocent.

Veles: The God of the Underworld, Death, Evil, and Wealth. Veles is a malevolent but congenial god that has decided that mortals must go. As a creator deity, he is one of the most powerful beings in the universe but limited by the fact he's stronger than almost all other gods individually but not all of them together. He looks like Peter Stormare from Bad Boys dressed as a Sith Lord.

Vukodlak: The local name for werewolves. They turn humans into huge hairy individuals even when not undead.

Westerlands: The lands beyond the Empire.

Zoryas: Twin goddesses who are the gods of Dawn and Night. They are lovers with both their brothers as well as each other. It is believed Mokosh can combine with to form her own entity capable of standing against Veles.

Zmei: The local name for dragons.

AUTHOR'S NOTE

I'd like to thank you for reading this book. The publishing industry is changing dramatically since the advent of eBooks. It is now very difficult to get any book noticed, regardless of quality. If you enjoyed this book, you could do some very simple things to help me attract attention.

Word of mouth is the number one source of success for novels, so simply telling family and friends about the book is a great start. Here are a few other ways of helping, if you are so inclined:

* Post a rating or review where you purchased the eBook
* Post a rating or review on Goodreads
* Talk about the book or write a review on Facebook
* Tell folks about the book in a blog post.

If you like any of my other books, please feel free to check them out. A lot of my series are interlinked, and you never know when you'll find someone familiar showing up.

You can also find the future chapters of this series as they are released on Royal Road:

https://www.royalroad.com/fiction/89337/lords-of-dragon-keep-an-isekai-litrpg

ABOUT THE AUTHOR

C. T. Phipps is a lifelong student of horror, science fiction, and fantasy. An avid tabletop gamer, he discovered this passion led him to write and turned him into a lifelong geek. He is a regular blogger and also a reviewer for The Bookie Monster.

Bibliography

Novels
The Rules of Supervillainy (Supervillainy Saga #1)
The Games of Supervillainy (Supervillainy Saga #2)
The Secrets of Supervillainy (Supervillainy Saga #3)
The Kingdom of Supervillainy (Supervillainy Saga #4)
The Tournament of Supervillainy (Supervillainy Saga #5)
The Future of Supervillainy (Supervillainy Saga #6)
The Horror of Supervillainy (Supervillainy Saga #7)
Tales of Supervillainy: Cindy's Seven (Supervillainy Saga #8)
The Fall of Supervillainy (Supervillainy Saga #9)

I Was a Teenage Weredeer (The Bright Falls Mysteries, Book 1)

An American Weredeer in Michigan (The Bright Falls Mysteries, Book 2)
A Nightmare on Elk Street (The Bright Falls Mysteries, Book 3)

Esoterrorism (Red Room, Vol. 1)
Eldritch Ops (Red Room, Vol. 2)
The Fall of the House (Red Room, Vol. 3)

Agent G: Infiltrator (Agent G, Vol. 1)
Agent G: Saboteur (Agent G, Vol. 2)
Agent G: Assassin (Agent G, Vol. 3)

Cthulhu Armageddon (Cthulhu Armageddon, Vol. 1)
The Tower of Zhaal (Cthulhu Armageddon, Vol. 2)
The Tree of Azathoth (Cthulhu Armageddon, Vol. 3)

Lucifer's Star (Lucifer's Star, Vol. 1)
Lucifer's Nebula (Lucifer's Star, Vol. 2)

Straight Outta Fangton (Straight Outta Fangton, Vol. 1)
100 Miles and Vampin' (Straight Outta Fangton, Vol. 2)
Vampiraz4Life (Straight Outta Fangton, Vol. 3)

Wraith Knight (Wraith Knight, Vol. 1)
Wraith Lord (Wraith Knight, Vol. 2)
Wraith King (Wraith Knight, Vol. 3)

Dark Destiny (Dark Destiny, Vol. 1)
Destiny's Paradox (Dark Destiny, Vol. 2)

Brightblade (The Morgan Detective Agency, Book 1)

Daughter of the Cyber Dragons (The Cyber Dragons Series, Book 1)
Revenge of the Cyber Dragons (The Cyber Dragons Series, Book 2)
End of the Cyber Dragons (The Cyber Dragons Series, Book 3)

Space Academy Dropouts (The Space Academy Series, Book 1)
Space Academy Rejects (The Space Academy Series, Book 2)
Space Academy Washouts (The Space Academy Series, Book 3)

Moon Cops on the Moon (Moon Cops, Book 1)
Moon City Vice (Moon Cops, Book 2)

Lords of Dragon Keep

Psycho Killers in Love

Tales of an Eldritch Wasteland

Anthologies (as editor)
Blackest Knights
Blackest Spells
Tales of Capes and Cowls
Tales of the Al-Azif
Tales of Yog-Sothoth

Curious about other Crossroad Press books? Stop by our website:
http://crossroadpress.com
We offer quality writing
in digital, audio, and print formats.

Subscribe to our newsletter on the website homepage and receive a
free eBook.

www.ingramcontent.com/pod-product-compliance
Lightning Source LLC
Chambersburg PA
CBHW030801260626
47169CB00001B/147